CURSE OF
THE AFFLICTED

Books by David Chill

CURSE OF
THE AFFLICTED

A Novel By

DAVID CHILL

For Paul Baron

Chapter 1

The Assassin entered the glass office tower at precisely four o'clock. He strode quickly through the lobby, absently flashing an I.D. badge at the sleepy security guards. They would not look twice at someone who knew where he was going. He did catch the attention of a pair of serious men in cheap suits, their earpieces identifying them as Secret Service. They directed him through a hastily set up metal detector, and then gave a quick once-over with the magnetometer wand before waving him through. He knew they would. The Assassin looked like any other office worker, nondescript and unremarkable. White shirt, bland tie, jacket slung over a shoulder. He pretended he was distracted, another sure-fire sign of an everyday Joe. The Assassin was pleased with his persona, and was convinced he embodied his role very well. But this was Los Angeles. Everyone was an actor.

He rode the elevator up to the thirty-fourth floor, stroking his black beard to make sure it remained in place. Removing his black-framed glasses, ones that had *clear lenses, he folded them and put them inside his jacket. Once the doors opened, he moved briskly off the elevator and past the gilded logo of a law firm with an elongated name listing half a dozen partners. Walking straight into the men's room, he checked the stalls to make sure he was alone before removing the ceiling tiles. He pulled down the nylon gym bag he had stored there last week and smiled. For the moment, everything was going exactly as planned.*

Replacing the tiles perfectly, the Assassin strode down the hallway and entered the quiet stairwell. The gym bag was heavier than he had remembered. Suddenly, an unsteady feeling came over him and he became light-headed. He knew he needed to slow down. So unlike him. He grabbed the banister to maintain his equilibrium, silently cursing to himself. It took a few seconds, but the wobbly feeling finally went away. He descended carefully down the single flight of stairs, taking extra measures to not make any noise. When he reached the next landing, he swiveled his body and used his hips to push against the horizontal security bar, opening the emergency exit door. He had arrived. This was where he would take care of business.

The renovation of the thirty-third floor was almost complete. The drywall was up, and the contractors only needed to install carpet and overhead lighting. The Assassin entered what would soon be someone's corner office and he closed the door. Placing a number of cement blocks against the door would prevent a nosy security guard from gaining access. If they even bothered to patrol here. Most likely, he would be alone for the next six hours. He wished he had the peace of mind that came with carrying that little handgun he normally kept in his pocket. The Ruger thirty-eight special was always a source of comfort to him. He regretted not packing it in the gym bag, but what was done was done.

Noticing the soft glow of a single naked light bulb hanging down from the ceiling, he reached into his pocket and put on a pair of latex gloves. Picking up a long iron rod that was amidst the debris strewn on the concrete floor, the Assassin gave a quick upward swing and smashed the bulb to pieces, then carefully placed the rod silently back down on the ground. No one should be able to see him here. The white-hot glare of the media would be shining on this spot soon enough. Darkness would be his friend tonight.

*   *   *

My back was killing me, and the pain was coming at just the wrong time.

Driving down the shady streets of Brentwood, I steered around potholes and fiddled with the lumbar support switch on my driver's seat. It wasn't helping. My doctor appointment would be at noon, a lunchtime accommodation from an old college friend. I'd just need to suffer through the agony of a painful client meeting. Next time I'd remember to bring along some Advil.

June gloom was in full swing. The morning air was cool and damp, and the marine layer trapped a canopy of gray clouds hanging over the region. But June also meant the Jacaranda trees were blooming, an annual emergence of gorgeous flowers falling gracefully from long branches, dusting the lawns with lavender petals. In Los Angeles, this is the closest we get to snow; the accumulation not of frosty white flakes, but of soft purple blossoms.

Blair had arrived early to the meeting, as good salespeople are taught to do. I sat down next to him, feeling small inside the soaring atrium of the Garter Vitamin Company's lobby. There was an odd plaque near the entrance, a sign boasting that Garter was now a wholly owned subsidiary of another wholly owned subsidiary. At the bottom of the plaque, it was noted their corporate headquarters were now in Ireland. What was not revealed was that Irish tax rates were far more attractive to wealthy companies.

The lobby walls featured colorful photos of capsules and drinks, popular Garter products from around the globe. Many had names I couldn't pronounce, much less understand. But that was why we were here. Garter had an exciting new supplement and they needed an outside research company to help them. They needed to formulate a better marketing plan to launch the product. We were hired because we had been successful as pollsters, and corporations often sought out consultants who were successful in other fields, hoping that whatever magic we created for politicians would somehow rub off on them. Promoting political candidates was not unlike promoting any other consumer product. We did this type of corporate work to generate revenue between political campaigns. But Blair was in the midst of crafting something far bigger for us, a venture that would be much more lucrative, and could propel us into the upper echelon of our narrow world.

"The vice president is supposed to call any day now," he said. "Sudeau needs a different approach if he's going to convince the public that he's presidential material. The Phelan crew is out; they just couldn't figure out how to do polling for a national campaign. I just know we're in line for this gig, and it's going to be a massive payday. This is the Super Bowl. If Sudeau picks us and we get him the nomination, we can retire. Become talking heads on CNN every other day. Work if we want, play golf if we don't."

"What are our odds?" I asked.

"Good," he responded. "Real good. After we unseated Governor Palmer last year, I thought we'd be in for sure. I can't believe Sudeau hasn't tapped us yet. Ned, I've been sucking up to the vice president's staff for months now. I swear if Randy Greece's ass ever snaps shut, it's going to break my nose."

I looked across the room at a small statue, a bronze work of art depicting an *asklepian*. This was the snake-hugging rod named after Asclepius, the Greek god associated with medicine and healing. It reminded me of our partnership, a study in contrasts. Blair was tall, olive-complexioned, and strikingly handsome, in a way that could make some women swoon. I actually heard one of our clients refer to Blair's good looks as knee-buckling. I was none of those things; rather, my appearance could best be summed up as short, stocky and mildly blemished. Fortunately, I didn't need to get by on looks. Blair liked to refer to himself as Mr. Outside, the rainmaker who was a magnet for clients and to me as Mr. Inside, the nerdy grunt who manufactured the actual work. But the reality is rarely that clear cut.

Blair Lipschitz was a master talker, a man who could ingratiate himself with complete strangers, allowing them to feel as if they were old friends within minutes. He was well spoken, but he also spoke very frequently. I used to view his act with no small amount of disdain, as phony and transparent as a huckster's money-back guarantee. But there was one fact, undeniable, which was simply that he attracted paying clients. And no matter how good my work was, and it was generally very good, without clients there would be no partnership, no money, no business. We were a matched pair, I thought, as I continued to gaze at the bronze statue across the room. The steady rod wrapped with an entwined serpent.

"Gentlemen," boomed a voice from across the lobby. It was John Quinn, a portly man wearing a dark gray suit, finely tailored to hide much of his girth. He ambled over to us, a big man with a big smile. "Sorry to have kept you waiting."

"Never a problem, Johnny-Boy," laughed Blair, as we followed him onto a silver elevator. "We're here to make your life easier."

What we were really here to do was earn a good living. Garter was about to unveil a supplement designed to enhance and extend female pleasure, a type of Viagra-for-women. They were certain it would be a boon to company earnings, and more importantly, to the executives' own personal wealth. I had nothing against people earning boatloads of money or getting more pleasure out of life. I did, however, hold serious qualms about how Garter would spread the word about their life-altering new product.

It was over ten years ago when my daughter, Angelina, just six years old and exceedingly precocious, wandered into our kitchen one bright Sunday morning to inquire as to the meaning of erectile dysfunction. My mouthful of Cuban roast coffee nearly spewed back into the mug. When my wife, Leslie, asked where she had come upon such an interesting malady, Angelina said it was while watching a cartoon on a heretofore safe kids' TV channel. She then asked us what bankruptcy meant. I deflected both topics by offering her a slice of cherry Danish, a ruse that temporarily focused her attention on something less disturbing. In addition to not wanting to educate a small child about subjects beyond her comprehension, I also didn't want her to know the ugly truth surrounding some of these kids' networks. That these channels, ostensibly aimed at providing wholesome entertainment for young children, had audiences comprised of a remarkably high percentage of under-educated, under-employed, middle-aged men. The ads, an eclectic mishmash of products, promoted toys and candy for children, in between more mature commercials geared toward a wildly different demographic.

John Quinn led us into a glass-enclosed conference room, a transparent bubble within a busy office. There were a half dozen executives already sitting around a large, black lacquer table, chatting amiably. They were all well-dressed and attractive, looking every bit the part of the successful corporate elite. A round of hellos and handshakes were exchanged, and we eased into our Monday morning meeting by floating tales of our weekends. Tennis matches, hikes in Ojai, box seats for an Angel game, and sailing trips to Catalina. The leisure activities of the well-to-do. I plugged my laptop's cable into the HDMI slot, waited for the small talk to subside, and hoped the pain in my back would ease up soon. When the eyes around the table began to settle on me, I invoked Blair's standard consultant posture, which was to tell the clients precisely what they wanted to hear, and gloss over the things they did not.

"Folks, I have some very good news. Exceptional, in fact. Reaction to your concept was great. We did eight focus groups, and virtually every woman loved the idea. Home run everywhere. Atlanta, Boston, Chicago, Dallas. The response was consistent. Their biggest question was simple. How soon could they get their hands on this product?"

Smiling faces and knowing glances spread around the room. "I told you so," crowed Gretchen, a smiling, middle-aged woman with shiny, golden blonde hair that drifted down past her shoulders. Gretchen Heller was the general manager and the interim CEO of Garter, which was a fancy way of saying she was the one in charge. Their previous CEO, Glenn Keane, had been dethroned last year, as quarterly earnings missed the target Wall Street had established. They missed it by four cents a share.

"You nailed it, Gretchen," said Victor, one of the young product managers, exhibiting not the least bit of shame in flattering the boss. "Got to give you all the credit. You fast-tracked this baby a few months ago."

"Good team effort," she corrected him. "We need something. Our numbers have to get back up quick. The board wants to see earnings turn around by end of year."

This reminded me of something, many decades ago, when I had registered for a finance course in college. On the first day of class, the professor harped repeatedly on his definition of money. There were three basic and unquestionable rules. More is better than less, sooner is better than later, and certain is better than uncertain. He told the class that if we recalled nothing more from him that semester, his job would be done. I took that as a sign, dropped the finance course, and enrolled in abnormal psychology.

"So, tell us," Victor said, turning to me. "How much can we charge for DX-101?"

"We can't really make that call with focus groups," I cautioned, thinking of the best way to lead them into the next paying project. "You need hard data. Price testing has to be quantitative. Discrete choice modeling would be a good method. We can handle that. If you're interested."

"Believe me, we're interested," Gretchen smiled, and a low level of chuckling could be heard around the table. "We also need a consumer-friendly name for it."

"Of course," said a round, balding man named Jack, whose face had a natural sneer to it, as if he had shoved a pair of peppermint lifesavers on the inside of his upper lip. "We'll need your full attention on our business. And we're assuming you guys aren't going to be distracted by doing political work in the near future."

"What?!" Blair interrupted, displaying mock outrage but making sure to keep a smile pasted onto his face. "Come on Jack, it's not an election year. Besides, one thing I can say and I guarantee this to be true, your business comes first. It always comes first. We love working with you guys. Garter takes precedence over everyone. Even the president. And I'm going to tell him that next time we speak."

More laughter around the room. The president wasn't running for anything now, and in fact, the last time he even spoke to Blair was twenty years ago when he was still a fledgling mayor in Phoenix, and Blair was managing the primary campaign of a woman who was trying in vain to unseat him. The gist of the president's comment to Blair was to angrily admonish him to stop lying about his record, or he'd be scattering Blair's ashes across the Arizona desert.

I led Garter's executive team through the remaining details of the focus groups, findings that should have come from our moderator, Haley Comey, who had conducted the groups last week. I omitted the gnarly details of our traipsing through airports choked with too many people, eating room-service sandwiches at midnight, and staying in supposedly smoke-free hotel rooms that still had the faint, lingering smell of stale cigarettes. I also didn't discuss Haley's flattering advances toward me, which of course, was my problem, not theirs. I regaled them with anecdotes about the women Haley interviewed, ones who described their marital relations in remarkably candid detail, women who were intrigued by Garter's fast-acting supplement. The new product could supposedly arouse them in mere minutes, evoking smiles from a few seniors whose eyes glimmered at the thought of jump-starting their sex lives again. The team listened rapturously to our results, as if I were relating how their young child swished a game-winning basket in a YMCA league.

"This is great stuff," said Luke, a sturdy-looking young man with the hint of a brown beard covering a square jaw. "But why isn't Haley here? You normally have the moderator present findings."

Taking a breath, I considered how best to respond to this. I also noticed my back starting to hurt whenever I breathed hard, and I tried to put the pain out of my mind. I normally moderated the focus groups, but in this instance, when the subject was of a sexual nature and the participants were all female, there was no way a man could lead this intimate conversation. Haley was one of our employees; the operative word being was, because I needed to dismiss her upon our return to L.A. Her work had been good, but her advances, both coquettish and churlish, had reached a breaking point on the trip. I had warned her about her behavior, but the warnings went unheeded, as they often do with people who maintain agendas.

After conferring with Blair when I returned to the office on Friday, I finally convinced him there was no other option. His argument for retaining her bordered on the personal. Blair and I were remarkably different in so many ways, but we managed to find common ground. Our company was the equalizer; we normally agreed to do what was best for the business. We had seemingly incongruous backgrounds, but they managed to come together to shore up the other's deficiencies. My South Carolina-low country sense of decency and morality, coupled with Blair's breezy L.A. sophistication. Our partnership had meshed, though at times it was jagged and uneven. We still moved in concert, but lately the dance had been strained. I was a little surprised at his resistance to dismissing Haley, but apparently there was more there than met the eye, mine being partially blind. That he had slept with her was a subject that went unspoken, but confirmed nevertheless.

I had taken Haley aside on Friday and delivered the bad news, told her that her services would no longer be needed at our Company, her personal belongings should be gathered and taken with her immediately. She demanded to speak with Blair, a request that would not be fulfilled, as he had conveniently departed the office for an exceedingly long lunch. After the initial wave of shock wore off, she angrily responded that a lawsuit would quickly be filed, and she also took the opportunity to relay her fervent wish that both Blair and I would rot in hell. Needless to say, it was not the type of professional parting one hopes for.

"We unfortunately needed to undertake ... " I started.

"Haley," Blair broke in, "had to tend to a family emergency. We told her to take all the time she needs. She'll be out a while. But Ned went to all the groups, he was in the back room, so he's totally up to speed on this. More so, in fact, since he was sitting behind the glass watching."

My partner came into our business knowing precious little about focus groups, but Blair did know how to spin a yarn. An improvisational actor with impeccable timing, the truth was like warm clay, stretched and molded to fit whatever purpose lay in front of him. It was a skill that came effortlessly to Blair, one which often left me befuddled. Blatant lying was a trait that was becoming tiresome to endure.

"I love this," Gretchen beamed and turned to Quinn. "Can you get the agency to start developing a creative brief, John? I'd like them to brainstorm and get some product names for Ned and Blair to test. PAA should also start looking at a media plan. This is going to be fantastic!"

John nodded enthusiastically and then looked up at me. "Say, Ned. Did you get any feedback from the groups as to how best to position this?"

"Thank you for providing a segue to my next chart," I said, the pain in my back growing more severe. I smiled broadly, not in reaction to John's question, but to avoid wincing. In some circumstances, a person exhibiting pain would evoke sympathy; this was not one of them. In the corporate world, appearing physically weak was akin to being weak in every other area. I tried taking a deep breath but the pain registered even more harshly. I thought longingly of the bottle of Advil sitting in my medicine cabinet at home as I soldiered on.

"Let me step back for a moment and explain what we did. We sometimes use what's called projective techniques in focus groups. This allows people to get creative and personify a product. It gives them permission to either praise it or trash it, but without losing the veneer of being polite. If the product were a person, we ask what they would be like, how would they look, how would they dress, where would they live, what would they eat. I once moderated a focus group and asked them to describe an internet site that was under-performing. Someone depicted it as a man who had been wealthy at one time and now ate most of his meals at Burger King."

"So what'd they think of DX-101?" asked Victor.

"In this case, we had them describe the kind of a car a person who used this new Garter product would drive. The answers we got ranged from Porsches to Lamborghinis. We then asked what kind of home they would live in and they said a swanky condo, maybe in Manhattan. Or Miami, right on the water."

"Wonderful!" someone said. "Sounds like we'll be able to charge a lot for it!"

"But a word of caution," I said, tightening my abdominal muscles as my back pain intensified. "The lifestyle this kind of person lives is not necessarily aspirational. We are still a sexually confused nation. On the one hand, people admire those who have an active, freewheeling lifestyle. But they don't necessarily see that in themselves. These people acknowledge they don't live in a Park Avenue penthouse, and were a little hesitant to do what it takes to get there. They admire the life, but they don't necessarily approve of it."

"Meaning?" John asked.

"Meaning," I said, grimacing now at the heightened degree of pain, and feeling less able to choose my words carefully, "this needs to be positioned in a classy way. Any sexually related product can be tricky to promote. This is one of those. Do it wrong, and it can kill you."

A pall of silence filled the conference room. Someone coughed. I took a deep breath and the pain in my back expanded sharply for a brief moment before starting to ease when I breathed out. Blair looked aghast for a moment, although he quickly morphed into good-old-boy mode. "But you guys'll never do it wrong," he told them. "You're Garter! You're the best!"

The tensioned subsided, Gretchen heartily agreed, and the conversation began to flow again. I sat down and pushed my back against the soft chair. I tried to listen, although I barely followed the discussion, focusing more on breathing slowly and rhythmically through my nose, keeping my teeth clenched. After a good twenty minutes of discussion, Gretchen concluded the meeting by thanking us and saying they would be in touch with next steps. John led us back down to the lobby.

"Great presentation, fellas," he said. "We definitely want you involved in the price testing. The discrete ... what was that?"

"Discrete choice," I said. "It's multi-variate research. We show consumers a product with different prices in different size jars featuring different brands. The consumers then get to select trade-offs. It works very well. You wind up with the optimal price point. The one where you make the most money."

"Well that's the one we want. And we trust you guys. We'll be in touch, this was great. Thanks."

We said our goodbyes and Blair and I walked silently across the lobby toward the parking garage. We passed a Starbucks, its long line snaking out all the way into the street, as caffeine-deprived office workers waited for their late morning fix. Had the queue been shorter, I might have stopped off for something. But I also sensed Blair's unusual reserve; Blair being quiet usually meant Blair wanted to talk. He just didn't want to do it in public. As we entered the garage area, he lit a cigarette and blew a plume of smoke toward the ceiling. We waited a long minute in silence before the garage elevator arrived. With timing worthy of a philharmonic maestro, Blair turned to me at the exact moment the elevator doors closed.

"Did you really need to ask that?" he snapped. "Do you want to blow everything?"

I stared at him. "Can you expand on that?"

"You bet your ass I can expand on that. Were you really going to tell them about canning Haley?"

"I don't think you need to worry about her."

"I'm more worried about you. And that other comment. That if Garter does it wrong, they'll kill their product? What was that about?"

"I don't know," I said, not wanting to talk about my back pain. "It just slipped out. Why is this a problem?"

"We're on the brink of landing the biggest client of our lives, the break we've been waiting for forever."

I felt my breathing grow rapid, and the pain in my back intensifying. "You're not talking about Garter. You're talking about the vice president."

"Of course I'm talking about the vice president," he said. "You've got to be very careful about what you say, and to whom you say it. Especially if we're going to start playing in the big leagues with Richard Sudeau."

"Don't you think your concerns are unfounded?"

"I have a funny feeling they're very well founded. There's something going on with you today. Don't you want to be successful?"

"Sure," I said, eyeing him warily.

"You're not becoming one of those guys who's scared of success, are you?" Blair asked, wrinkling his nose. "The ones that self-sabotage?"

"Of course not."

"Then you should feel very lucky I was there to step in."

"I'm beginning to wonder how lucky I am," I responded, the pain in my back weighing heavily. "I thought the meeting went well."

"It did. Because of me. What if I weren't there? Where would you be without me?" he demanded, pointing the lit end of the cigarette in my face.

"The same damn place you'd be without me," I replied, the restraint draining from me, but not enough to verbalize where he could stick his cigarette.

We stared at each other for a long second, our words resonating, becoming louder through the silence, as we had nothing else to fill the void. It was not the first tense conversation we had had, and I sensed it would not be the last. Our partnership often went down this rocky path. Argue, confront, reconcile, repeat. A cycle engaged.

The elevator door opened and we exited, Blair and I nodding silently, sullenly to each other as we walked off in different directions. Climbing inside my Honda Pilot, I shoved my back against the seat and grimaced at the pain. I wondered if this agony I was feeling was a harbinger of things to come. And I drove off, not realizing I was about to enter the wildest ride of my life, a hellacious journey that was beyond anything I could have ever possibly imagined. The pain in my back was merely the beginning.

Chapter 2

It only took a few minutes for me to reach the medical plaza, but I kept shifting my body around in the car, never quite getting comfortable. When I walked into the doctor's office, the waiting room was empty. I sat for a long twenty minutes before a nurse in dark blue scrubs ushered me into the exam room. Dr. Elijah Sterling had been my next-door-neighbor in the freshman-year dorm; we bonded over a love of basketball, spy novels, and Belgian ale. It had been over twenty-five years since we first hoisted those brown bottles of *Chimay*, a bit of contraband smuggled in by another kid in our dorm, a fast talking New Yorker who had acquired a reasonable facsimile of his older brother's drivers license. Eli had always dreamed of becoming a doctor, an internist just like his father. He aimed to be a caring, respected, distinguished member of the community.

My old pal had achieved his goal quickly, although being added to his father's burgeoning medical practice in his early thirties had smoothly paved his way. I had long been envious, not of his success, but of his single-minded passion. I was not blessed with his direction or vision; I did not have my path carved out. For many years I was unsettled, searching for what my calling was, dipping my big toe into various jobs, not staying long enough to spin them into a career. When I eventually settled into the profession that was right for me, it was only because survey research combined a dozen elements that I found intriguing. Eli loved to say that as a pollster, I had finally landed into the perfect situation, a career focused on asking questions rather than answering them.

"If it isn't the political wizard," Eli crowed as the door opened. He stepped inside, dressed in the customary white lab coat and with his staid professional demeanor, stethoscope hanging from his neck. His black hair was now flecked with gray, but Eli's face remained smooth, the confident physician whose worries never seemed to appear on his face. He placed a file folder carefully down on the counter and we shook hands warmly. "Last time I saw you, you were plotting to overthrow the governor of California."

"And we succeeded," I said, "although our candidate may have been in the right place at the right time. Governor Rex Palmer self-destructed. He didn't need much help."

"Modest. You helped change the course of California history."

"For a few people, I suppose."

"Well," he said lightly, "I can attest my life hasn't changed much."

I would not imagine it had. Elections rarely impact the lives of the affluent. They may pay a little more or a little less in taxes. They may see a surge in homelessness as they drive to their plush offices, or they might learn of a few more burglaries in their exclusive zip codes. The potholes in their tony neighborhoods might not get filled as quickly. It was always the ones down on the low end of the wealth totem pole whose lives were most affected. For people at the level of Elijah Sterling, politics was mainly theater.

"So I haven't seen you in awhile. How've you been, Eli?" I asked. "How's the family?"

"Oh, fine, all is well. Courtney won't be joining Angelina at the Brentwood School, she's headed to Harvard-Westlake this fall. I guess we jumped though all their hoops without tripping up."

"Doctors get special privilege," I observed. Harvard-Westlake was the premier prep school in Los Angeles, one of the most elite schools in the country. When two parents get together in L.A., the conversation almost inevitably drifts toward schools, who's applying where, and the odds of getting admitted. "I'm sure you're pleased she won't have to besmirch the family name and attend Beverly Hills High School."

"There's nothing wrong with public schools, Ned," he pointed out diplomatically, holding up a well-manicured palm. "We're products of them."

"True," I said. "Berkeley's a state school, but it's still pretty exclusive. Tougher to get in now than when we were applying. Angelina will find that out next year."

"Any chance of a scholarship for her?"

"No. My daughter's smart, but not driven. She doesn't think she has to be," I sighed. My own upbringing had been vastly different from Angelina's, in almost every way imaginable, culturally, financially, geographically. Coming out of South Carolina, my choices weren't robust. My family could afford junior college, and made subtle hints at my joining the army after high school. I lucked out by earning a National Merit Scholarship, which gave me a springboard out of the low country, and into a vast new world. It wasn't merely the other side of the country; Berkeley might just as well have been on the other side of the planet.

"Things have a way of working out," Eli said. "She might even get a free ride for softball. I hear she's quite the pitcher. Brentwood's having a great season."

"Long shot," I shrugged. "We'll figure out a way to pay for it. Business seems to be picking up. I've been doing some work for Garter Vitamins."

"I thought you were focused on political campaigns, not those supplements."

"Sometimes you have to turn a blind eye to things, especially when their business helps with the bills. You know, Garter's always looking for doctor endorsements. Would be an easy payday for you."

Eli gave a small guffaw. "Sorry. There's a fine line between medicine and snake oil. I've taken an oath. First do no harm."

"Good to know."

"So," he said, quickly changing the subject, "what brings you to my doorstep?"

"My aching back," I said. "It's been hurting like hell the past couple of days."

"When did this begin?"

I struggled to recall. It was probably over a month ago when I first noticed some irritation. Like many aches and pains that afflict the middle-aged, I just assumed it was the advent of a new phase of life, a distraction I would need to endure for a while. I imagined this ailment, like the many other annoyances that beset us, would eventually go through its progressions and then dissipate.

"Maybe a month," I said. "I told Leslie about it. She's been bugging me to come see you."

"Smart woman," the doctor smiled, instructing me to take off my shirt and engage in deep, methodical breathing. The pain ebbed and flowed as I took air into my lungs before sending it back out. Eli pressed the cold metal disk against various sections of my back and listened carefully through his stethoscope. He asked me where the pain was, and I stopped him at a spot six inches below where my neck and left shoulder connected. After a minute of poking and prodding, he stepped back and placed the stethoscope back around his neck.

"Thoughts?" I asked, feeling my researcher's deployment of open-ended questions starting to take shape.

"This is why married men live longer," he said, jotting a few notes down. "People think it's because of companionship, sharing experiences, regular sex. Nope. All wrong. It's very simple. It's because wives tell their husbands to go see the doctor when something doesn't feel right."

"And?"

"And then they nag their husbands until they listen."

"I'll remember that next time Leslie and I have a fight and I start conjuring up fond thoughts about one of the cute, young women I work with."

"Don't go beyond thoughts," he said, wagging a finger. "You've got a good deal there. Don't mess it up. All it takes is one dalliance and you're through. Wives never forget, even if they can forgive you. And you'll never hide it from them. They can practically smell the betrayal on you."

"You're quite the fountain of wisdom," I remarked, thinking back on my most recent business trip, and the dalliance that was offered up to me by Haley, who was simultaneously comely and predatory. The temptation was there, but so was the feeling that such a tryst would not end well.

"Second marriages can do that to a person. Socrates once said that when a man has a good wife, he becomes very happy. Want to know what he said about a man who has a not-so-good wife?"

"You're going to tell me regardless, aren't you?"

"He becomes a philosopher."

We both smiled. Leslie and I had married right after college. Neither of us dated much, we just blended together nicely, comfortable in the way a fuzzy, old sweater made you feel warm. Leslie was slender and pretty, she had those soft, delicate doe eyes that could tug on my heartstrings as well as light up my heart. We shared the same approach to politics, which is to say we enjoyed the strategy of a campaign more than getting into the nitty-gritty that came later, the wonky aspect of public policies, the actual act of governing.

"So, what's the diagnosis, Doc? Am I going to make it?"

Eli did not answer right away, instead he turned back again and wrote something in his folder. He looked down at it for a few seconds and then jotted down an address on a small slip of paper. Handing it to me, he gave me a long, concerned look.

"I think you need to go in for a chest x-ray," he said.

"Why?"

"I heard some wheezing. And the pain is in an unusual area. Might be something, might be nothing. But you should get it checked out. The imaging center is a block away. It'll only take a few minutes."

I nodded, a bit puzzled, but I didn't inquire further. Eli was telling me all he knew, and like a good doctor and a better friend, he was not going to speculate. I didn't want him to, either. I looked down at my phone and checked my afternoon schedule. Aside from returning a few phone calls, I was free.

"Sold," I said, putting on my shirt before Eli walked me to the exit. I was about to say goodbye and suggest we get together for a family barbecue soon, but one of the nurses came out from her station, phone in hand, a puzzled expression on her face as she addressed me.

"Mr. Baker?"

"Yes?" I said.

"I have this vice president calling you."

Eli looked at me curiously. "You're having your business calls forwarded to my office?"

I shook my head. "No. In fact, I didn't think anyone knew my schedule today. Except maybe Wanda, my project director. I just finished a meeting with Garter. Maybe it's their VP of marketing."

"Why would they be calling you here?" Eli asked.

"No clue. I suppose I could have left something behind at her office. But I can't imagine how she could have tracked me here."

"No, sir," the nurse said, a little more emphatically. "That's not it. Not at all."

"What do you mean?"

"I have the *vice president* on the phone," she said a little more emphatically.

"Which one?" I asked.

"The *vice president*," she repeated, her face showing signs of clear annoyance, "of the United States."

Chapter 3

When an important leader calls you on the phone, the first thing you do is wait. Vice President Richard Sudeau's assistant told me to please hold, and it was a long two minutes of silence. I lingered in the office hallway, with Eli and his nurse both sending sharp glances of disapproval. Finally, the audio shifted noticeably, as if a window to the outside world had just opened. The vice president presented himself on the other end of the line, the timbre of his voice familiar to the ear, a deep baritone, honed and smooth, as easy to drink in as a honeyed bourbon.

"Mr. Baker, good afternoon. How are you?" he began.

"Fine, sir," I answered, not bothering to detail the truth about my aching back or my doctor's worrisome thoughts. "And you?"

"Well, I'm fantastic. Listen, I won't take much of your time."

"Take all you need, sir."

"That's very gracious," he chuckled. "Look, Randy Greece asked me to give you a call and I'm happy to do so, start the process if you will. I'd like to meet with you and Blair. Tomorrow if you can swing it. I'm shaking up my campaign, changing strategists, changing pollsters and I might like to have you do some baseline work for us. You guys have a wonderful reputation. I'd like to get your thoughts. Would tomorrow work? I'll have Greece arrange for a flight. He'll let Blair know."

"Of course," I said. When the vice president calls, you simply acquiesce to whatever he wants. My mind raced frantically for something intelligent to pass along, but there was no need. The vice president, well versed in a leader's ability to vamp and make small talk, waxed on for another two minutes about how impressed he was at our ability to put Justin Woo in the California governor's mansion. He concluded by saying he looked forward to seeing us tomorrow, and his assistant would be in touch with logistics.

When the line went dead, I passed the phone back to the nurse, who provided a withering glare in return. I turned to say goodbye to Eli, but he was, of course, nowhere to be seen. Doctors, like politicians, are busy people too. Walking out of the building, I made a call to Blair and we discussed our itinerary, which is to say, our nightmarish red-eye flight leaving out of Santa Monica Airport at midnight. There was an era when private airports had an unwritten rule against late-night takeoffs and landings, but those rules, like many others, had been kicked to the curb a long time ago. People with means flew in and out when it suited them.

Since I had the time, I walked over to the imaging center, did my chest x-ray, and then headed home to change clothes, take a nap and get ready for my trip. Our house was in Brentwood, a neighborhood made infamous years ago by O.J. Simpson, and people still ask us if we lived near Rockingham. We were actually a few blocks away on Marlboro Street, and while our street rarely had a ton of activity, it felt even more quiet on this cloudy afternoon. Even the birds weren't chirping. The air was still and muted, to the point of being eerie.

I admit to being less than enthused when we moved here almost a decade ago, into a stately, extravagant home, one that was far more luxurious than I ever believed I'd own. But I also never imagined Leslie's parents would pass away early, victims of a horrific car accident. Her father was an attorney, and as the only child, Leslie inherited their house, albeit one that came with a spider's web of financial curiosities that included a number of unsettled slip-and-fall lawsuits. It was a beautiful home, but for the past nine years we had been struggling to pay the mortgage, the legal fees, and the back taxes, in addition to our own weighty expenses. I knew how important it was for Leslie to stay here, to maintain a legacy, the spurious connection with her parents, and we tried to make a go of it. But the nagging issue of having to clean up someone else's financial mess left me with an uneasy feeling. As did the ghoulish knowledge that even when you die, your debts do not die with you.

I parked in the driveway, walked up the flagstone path, past the pair of weeping willows out front. I hated these trees. They were fragile and brittle, the branches broke easily, and their roots had begun to worm their way into the sewer line. Mostly, they reminded me of the South, a world to which I no longer belonged. But I had finally stopped asking Leslie if we could uproot these and have them replaced with jacarandas, or even a pair of orange trees. The response was always the same. Let's keep things the same for a while. We'll see. Maybe in a couple of years.

But the couple of years came and went, getting pushed into that murky, vague image we call the future.

"You're home early," Leslie said as I walked inside our spacious home. "How did it go?"

"Fine, the client was happy. Should get more work. But the big news is we may have landed on Rich Sudeau's team. He wants to meet us tomorrow."

"Oh my! That's incredible news. But I was actually referring to your appointment with Eli."

I knew what she was referring to, but had hoped to avoid that topic. "He ordered a chest x-ray, pretty ordinary. I did it right after I saw Eli. Hey, listen. Sudeau's arranged for us to fly out to D.C. tonight. We're taking a red-eye."

"Oh," she said, processing this. "So, when will you be back?"

I shrugged. "I suppose when Sudeau's done with us. Tomorrow night, maybe?"

"You'll miss Angelina's play-in game."

"That's tomorrow?" I asked, reaching into the kitchen cabinet for a bottle of Advil.

"God, Ned. Do you remember anything I say?"

I normally do recall, but there are those instances when my brain just shuts down with Leslie. There are so many details and nuances and segues to irrelevant pieces of information that at times, I simply stop listening. My occasional grunt of affirmation keeps her talking and relatively happy. That is, until awkward moments like these present themselves. The happiness disappears and the fuming begins.

"Of course," I said. "I just have a lot on my mind. What time is the opening pitch?"

"It's at four o'clock tomorrow. Home game against Sierra Canyon. They win, they go into the CIF tournament. God, but you're lucky Angelina isn't here to listen to this. I don't think she knows how uninvolved you are in her life."

I bit my lower lip. Today was not a day for marital strife. To a point, Leslie was correct, I am not intimately involved with the daily details of my teenager's comings and goings. I attend her softball games when time permits. I don't wince in agony when the opposing team scores a run or two against Brentwood, or when Angelina whiffs on a surprisingly fast pitch. Generally, I just kibitz with the other dads at the top row of the bleachers, involved to the point of providing a decent role model and a more-than-decent lifestyle, but a step removed from the drama and petulance of teenage girl angst.

"I do the best I can," I sighed. "You know financially this has been a tough year so far."

While we had had a rush of business last November, the publicity from our election win mostly generated a lot of empty buzz. Helping to elect a governor put us on many corporate clients' radar. But the projects ended, clients drifted away, promises of future business did not always materialize. Only Garter stayed with us, feeding us enough ongoing projects to keep the cash flowing. The call from Vice President Sudeau could not have come soon enough.

"Well, it's not like we're starving," Leslie said. "And we can always tap into the home equity if we need to."

I shook my head and did not relish another fight about money. This is the subject couples are most likely to argue about, and we were not unique. "That's just digging a deeper hole. I hate living above our means. We still have a daughter to put through college and bills to pay. My income this year is barely even meeting our payroll. And I had to let someone go on Friday."

"Oh? Who?"

"Haley Comey. One of the junior moderators."

"That's no great loss," Leslie sniffed. "You should have gotten rid of that tart last year. My God, Ned. Why did you let a girl who behaves like that stick around?!"

"It wasn't my choice. I have a partner, and I can't control who he sleeps with. And you shouldn't give me advice on business," I said, walking into the den to remove myself from further bickering. This was an age-old pattern we kept on repeating, a ramification of two people living together for over twenty years. We knew how to press the other's buttons, bringing up stale arguments from long ago, the wounds still there, never fully healed, ready to spring back up at any moment.

Leslie and I had met toward the end of our sophomore year at Berkeley, and we dated exclusively for the rest of our time in college. I proposed a few nights before graduation, on one of those sultry, luminous, evenings where everything was right with the world. We had driven down to Santa Cruz for the day, lounged on the beach, sauntered along the boardwalk, rode the roller coaster. It was a warm night, a big moon, our casual ease fueled by a few margaritas. But it was our unease perhaps that led us to become engaged. The unease that came with graduating school, separating from friends, and being thrust out of the cocoon of college, into the tenuous independence that is the real world.

We held hands on the beach that night, as a soft humid breeze blew in off the Pacific, and we talked about the future. We could not see a future without each other, but that was mostly because we could not see what lay ahead. Draped in the comfort of an elite university, we dreamed our lives would be a fairy tale, when in fact, we barely even knew what had attracted us to each other. Over the years, I concluded it wasn't so much physical. Although Leslie was certainly pretty, there wasn't an emotional or psychic connection, it was simply that we were at the same level of maturity. It was how we could relate to one another, why we felt comfortable with one another. We were at the same parallel. Being with her was simply like looking into a mirror.

We moved down to L.A., Leslie's hometown; it was a place where we both felt comfortable. Clearly, she was not cut out for a life in the low country of South Carolina, and after Berkeley, I doubted I was either. Not any longer. My career stalled and then took off; Leslie's never really got in gear. I went back to school to get a master's degree, she worked at a non-profit charity in Santa Monica. Our lives melded together smoothly, the sense that we belonged together thickened over time. We started off moving in unison, the mirror images walking in tandem. At some point though, the images stopped moving together. But when Angelina entered our lives, a blossom of sweetness reemerged and we became one again. There was no going back, there was no growing apart. The only path led us to amble forward together as a unit, albeit not as smoothly as we had once thought, and certainly not as assured.

Angelina burst into the house just before six, her movements ramping up the energy level in our home. She was dressed in her white softball uniform, still sweaty, with her thick, blonde hair pulled back into a ponytail. She was the color of honey. Her long arms and legs were golden and smooth. Tanned, toned, shiny. She was a pretty girl, bright, a whirling dervish of energy. Her presence in our home changed everything, and certainly for the better. I counted my blessings every day, not certain why we had been gifted with such a child, whereas other parents we knew had kids who brought them more heartache than joy. I finally surmised that it was partly good luck, and partly the fact that we were only able to have one child. Leslie's pregnancy complications kept Angelina an only child, and we were able to shower her with attention. While some kids grow weary of their parents' doting, Angelina did not mind. She actually reveled in the spotlight we shined on her.

A few years ago we had next-door neighbors, both prominent attorneys within the entertainment industry, who used to boast of their parenting skills. We enviously watched their near-perfect son easily glide through adolescence; captain of his school's tennis team, dreamy girlfriend, valedictorian, and then on to Harvard. They were so sure of their abilities as parents that they had a second child, paying no mind to the fifteen-year gap between the kids. Perhaps it was because of the different constitution of child number two, or they were simply less involved, or maybe they were just marveling too much at their success with child number one. But the second child was an unmitigated monster, a kid who would think nothing of calling 9-1-1 as a prank, discharging a BB pistol at passing cars, or borrowing his father's hunting knife and bringing it into school to threaten other children. To the relief of the neighborhood, they eventually sent him to boarding school, where his malevolent behavior would, at the very least, be out of everyone's sight. Needless to say, our neighbors' boasts of writing a how-to book on good parenting never materialized.

Angelina threw her backpack and her softball glove at the foot of the stairs, announced her arrival, and darted upstairs for the sanctity of her bedroom. The door shut immediately and stayed that way for thirty minutes. What she did in there was a mystery, a teenage ritual, about which I was not eager to learn. Eventually, Leslie called us both in for dinner.

"I am just so looking forward to tomorrow!" Angelina said, bouncing into the dining room. She reached over and piled some grilled chicken and rice onto a flour tortilla, adding a dollop of salsa and a sprinkling of lettuce before wrapping it haphazardly and beginning to eat. Monday is often taco night in our household, the remnants of the weekend, be it barbecued chicken, grilled fish, or the occasional steak, chopped up into pieces and reconfigured with other leftovers which happened to be handy. This evening featured the rotisserie chicken we got from Costco last night, me being lucky enough to grab one of the last ones off the heating display before the supply ran out.

"Coach told us one of the Stanford scouts will be there. I think they're looking at Jordan, but I plan on making an impression."

I smiled to myself and did not respond. Angelina liked to goad us, knowing we had both gone to Berkeley, Stanford's arch-rival. Our daughter was a straight-A student, had high SAT scores, volunteered with Heal the Bay, and was a prefect at her high school. She was also a pretty fair athlete. And yet none of that would even remotely ensure her placement at an elite college today. Unlike some of her classmates, she wasn't legacy, meaning her parents had not attended Stanford, and we did not donate large sums to the school. And there were an awful lot of kids who were just like Angelina, smart, athletic, well-rounded. But most of them, nearly all in fact, who applied to Stanford would be turned down. There was just an abundance of qualified students, coupled with a dearth of spaces. America's population had been burgeoning over the past few decades, but slots at elite colleges had barely increased at all. This was unwittingly our saving grace. The thought of paying over sixty thousand dollars a year for college was staggering.

"Did Jordan ever re-take the SATs?" I asked.

"Yeah. But she got the same score."

Jordan was one of many ambitious schoolmates at Brentwood. An excellent student, she had wound up with a near-perfect score of 770 on her math SAT. But in the world of elite colleges, getting accepted meant going the extra mile, and taking the exam again in pursuit of a perfect 800 was certainly an acceptable, if not expected behavior. Even if she didn't improve her score, the college counselors whispered, it would look good that she had tried. We had suggested that to Angelina, but she had simply decided the school would look more approvingly upon her if she simply took it once, did well, and moved on. I didn't want to burst her bubble, so I simply let it be.

"Remember to ice your elbow after the game," I said. "Especially if you pitch more than five innings."

"Yeah, yeah, I know the drill already," she said absently and then stopped chewing. "Hey. Aren't you going to be at the game?"

"I'm a definite maybe. I've got quite an important meeting tomorrow. Want to guess with who?"

"Your big shot father," Leslie broke in, "is meeting with Vice President Sudeau. In Washington."

Angelina stopped in mid-bite. "Really? That's so cool. Oh, but he's supposed to be a total slime ball, isn't he? Still, you'll have to send me a picture of him while you're there."

"Sure," I smiled. "I'll take a selfie with the vice president. And why do you say he's a slime ball?"

"I dunno. Stuff on the internet. But it's still cool you're meeting with him. It gives you a get-out-of-jail free card."

Leslie and I looked apprehensively at each other. In my own, relatively tame South Carolina adolescence, I had heard this expression just once. The mother of one of my high school classmates had been involved in a brief yet torrid affair with a local handyman. Her husband walked in on them unexpectedly, and after chasing the soon to be ex-employee out of their house by waving a pistol and yelling vigorously, he allowed his hysterical wife to apologize profusely for her mistake. It was a topic that received an inordinate amount of neighborhood gossip, the story of a near-naked man, racing out of a house clutching his clothes to his chest was not one to be ignored. That the couple stayed together gave forth the humorous notion that the husband had earned the equivalent of Monopoly's cherished get-out-of-jail-free card. He could now engage in whatever sordid or elicit behavior he chose to, and his wife, having engaged in a similarly indecent act, would have little choice but to provide forgiveness.

"Just what do you mean, honey?" Leslie asked carefully, as we both leaned forward to hear her answer.

"Nothing," she shrugged in her breezy adolescent manner as she reached for another tortilla. "Only that if you don't make it to my game, Dad, you've got a good excuse. I have to forgive you."

Chapter 4

The Assassin took off his jacket, folded it carefully into a pillow, and lay down on the concrete floor. He rested for over four hours, fully aware he could not do anything yet. Once the late afternoon clouds evolved into a blackened canvas, when the final remnants of light had disappeared, that was when he could begin his work. This was Los Angeles, so he didn't have to worry about many stars twinkling in the evening sky. And even if the cloud cover had temporarily lifted, the lunar charts said that only a crescent moon would be out. All bases were covered, just the way the Assassin had planned it. This would be an exceptional night for hiding in the shadows. It would be very dark here indeed.

After rising from his nap, he walked near the window and opened his gym bag, unfolding the bi-pod and adjusting the height so it would be comfortable. He methodically put together the Barrett M107 sniper rifle, taking care to attach the night vision scope properly. The scope was everything. Placing the rifle near the window, he adjusted everything to his liking. He felt so comfortable with the M107, to him it was like an old friend. It had a range of almost two thousand yards, although he wouldn't need anywhere near that tonight. He just needed to be accurate, and the M107 was an unusual package that married accuracy with rapid fire. There was no margin for error. In his business, there was never a margin for error. But tonight was special.

He looked across at the Century Plaza Hotel, two blocks away. It had a distinctive, curved facade that unfurled across an entire city block. In a couple of years, this opportunity would no longer be available, as new construction was starting on a pair of residential towers that would block any line of sight from the office tower to the hotel. He thought back to a few years ago, when he actually used to stay at the Century Plaza, the days when he was with the Company. But since going freelance, his tastes had become more refined. These days he normally stayed at the Peninsula in Beverly Hills, but with the fundraiser, that was impossible. He decided to check into the Loews by the beach. The ocean air would be good for him.

The Assassin pulled a suction cup from the gym bag and fastened it against the window, a few inches up from floor level. Taking a grease pencil from his pocket, he drew a circle around the suction cup, with a six-inch diameter. Wide enough to focus on any room on the eighteenth floor, small enough so it was unlikely to be detected initially. No one would be looking for it from the hotel grounds, certainly not the B-level Secret Service detail that traveled with his target.

He took out the glass cutter, lubricated the blade with some sewing machine oil, and, using increasing pressure, repeatedly scored the area, roughly tracing the line created by the grease pencil. He would wait a few hours before yanking this section of glass away from the window, well aware that his target would not return from the fundraiser until after ten o'clock. By ten-fifteen, the glass would be out and he would have unfettered and direct access to the western-facing side of the hotel. The target would surely be staying in one of the rooms there, the man so loved looking out at the ocean. He would be staying near the top floor, but not on the very top. The agents always made sure the rooms above and below Peacock, their code name for his target, would go unoccupied. He also knew his target would come out onto the balcony before he went to bed. When the weather permitted, he enjoyed a breath of night air. It was part of his routine, a pattern that had remained very consistent. The Assassin liked people who didn't stray from their routines ...

*   *   *

I pulled into the darkened parking lot at Santa Monica airport at eleven-thirty and swallowed two Advil tablets before getting out of my car. That should get me through the flight. Blair had just arrived, lifting his briefcase from the trunk of his Jaguar. Last year, right before Justin Woo asked us to manage his campaign for governor, we took him and his brother to lunch. Blair, a forward thinker if there ever was one, decided that a Korean-American candidate would be duly impressed by a consultant who drove a Korean car. So Blair spent the morning hunting for a Hyundai Sonata to rent. The candidate was more amused than impressed, and informed Blair he hadn't driven a Hyundai in twenty years, and frankly didn't know anyone who did. As much as Blair trumpeted his act, we were ultimately hired in spite of, not because of, my partner's overt and shameless pandering.

"So, when are you going to get yourself a better ride?" he asked, looking down his nose at my Honda Pilot as we walked onto the tarmac. "I'm actually embarrassed to bring you around to meet my friends."

I didn't bother to tell Blair I had no interest in meeting his friends, if one were to even call them that. People like Blair had alliances, partnerships, relationships, and flirtations. Friends was a term loosely bandied about, a title bestowed and removed, without much earned equity. Blair drew people into his circle when it was beneficial, and he shed them when it was not. Even though our consulting firm had survived for ten years, I knew that it could end in the blink of an eye, when the value of our separating outweighed the price of our remaining together. Blair would always be able to find work for himself, people knew he could attract business, and anyone who could bring money in the door would have an honored seat at their table. My future was less certain, or at least it felt that way, and as such, my lifestyle was less extravagant.

We boarded the Gulfstream and a flight attendant told us to pick any seats we wanted. That was but one thing that differentiated flying on a private aircraft from flying commercial, for they were as similar as night and day. The cabin on the Gulfstream was more like a small living room, the seats were big, wide, cushy and inviting. Some faced forward, some backward, a few were lined against the windows. The seats were designed to maximize comfort, not maximize capacity. There were about a dozen people on our flight; they all looked important, smartly dressed, well-groomed, and yet all looked extremely weary.

The two of us settled into a pair of seats against a window, and Blair immediately pulled out a cigarette. He was about to light it when a pretty, stylishly dressed woman in her late thirties pointed out there was no smoking. She had deep green eyes that were alluring, yet hardened. Blair looked at her in disgust.

"For what we're paying?" he exclaimed. "We should be able to cook black tar heroin on one of these things."

"You've never been on a Gulfstream before?" she smiled, and then introduced herself as Iris Hatcher. She was slender, pretty, her soft brown hair laden with golden strands, but it was those green cat eyes that stood out. Eyes that seemed to have read your thoughts before you could even conjure them up.

Blair looked back at her carefully before sliding the cigarette back in the Old Gold pack. "I have," he said, choosing his words carefully, "just not on this particular Gulfstream."

"Well, then you know, the jet owner gets to decide. And you're not paying anything, so stop whining."

I laughed. "Is that little nugget in our itinerary, Iris?"

"No," she said. "I used to work for the vice president. I'm hitching a ride back to D.C. He was kind enough to arrange it. I always ask ahead of time who I'll be traveling with. Keeps me out of awkward conversations."

"Oh, really?" Blair asked, his facial expression suddenly more inviting. "What do you do?"

"I work in the speaker's office. Media relations. But since he represents the West Valley, I fly back and forth all the time. In fact, I'm only going back for a press conference tomorrow morning," she said, reaching out her hand. "You must be Rich's new hired guns."

"We are indeed," I said, jumping in. "What did you do when you worked for Sudeau?"

"Generally speaking, whatever he wanted," Iris laughed. "That's the best way to get along with him. And even then, it's a challenge."

"Not an easy boss?"

"No, but at that level, none of them are. It's the price of admission. And you fellows have your work cut out for you."

"How so?" I asked.

"The last campaign pollster didn't cut it. Or should I say the last three. With Sudeau, it's deliver results or you're gone."

"And deliver great results, even when he's the one calling the shots."

"You see the issue," she smiled. "But you're big boys. If you're good, you'll figure it out. Just do it quick. The first debate is in two months. If he's not at the center of the stage, you're toast."

I sighed to myself. There is no good way to handle a difficult client. Smart politicians are savvy to sycophants, but they also have little tolerance for contrarians. We were lucky in one respect. The vice president's campaign was not igniting, and the Phelan team had been fired last week, when polling results again showed Sudeau's numbers failing to take off. At the very least, we could go in and pitch him a message of course correction.

The president's second term would end next year, his popularity waning the way it does for most presidents. No matter how beloved they may have been, by the middle of their final term, voters have tired of them; not surprisingly, the presidents themselves have grown tired of the job. Endless wrangling with Congress, lofty promises unable to be fulfilled, a few staff members indicted over marginal accusations. Most presidents focus their energies on international affairs in their final years. Visiting foreign countries becomes a breath of fresh air, getting treated regally, as opposed to back home, where the countdown to their exit begins the day after they are reelected. A cagey vice president is able to navigate the path of embracing the president's successes while distancing himself from the failures. But even then, the presidency is still a very tough job to win.

"What do you know about Frank Phelan?" I asked, well aware his team had been outfoxed by Grady Sanderson's campaign pollsters recently. A *Des Moines Register* poll showed Sudeau slipping in Iowa, but that was a rigged survey. Sanderson's pollsters learned when the *Register* was conducting their poll, and they simply amped up the advertising in Iowa that week. Politics could be a crafty business.

Iris shrugged. "I've seen better, I've seen worse. Phelan's poll numbers were probably accurate. But every other candidate was doing push polling and they weren't. Sudeau looked bad by comparison. Sudeau hates that stuff with a passion, even if the polls are bogus he still wants to look good. Positive news makes him happy. But I guess in the end, the vice president is just too tied to the man in the oval. And even when the president's popular, it's unusual for his number two to follow him into the presidency. In the last hundred years, Bush forty-one was the only guy to do it."

I nodded. This was playing into the pitch that Blair and I planned to give tomorrow. Sudeau needed to break out from the shadow. The president was the alpha male, Sudeau was the beta, the little brother, the hanger-on, the second-string ballplayer warming the bench. It didn't matter that Sudeau had been a senator for almost two decades, a seemingly distinguished statesman. Once he signed on as the running mate almost seven years ago, his stature diminished. While he was a key advisor to the president, his main job was to make sure the president's pulse was still active.

Sudeau needed to do two things if he wanted to get elected. First, he needed to change his image. Second, he needed to reduce the number of candidates who had already plunged into the race. There were ten announced candidates, mostly sitting or former governors and senators, but none should have been serious challengers. Many were in the race to enhance their name recognition, fundraise prodigiously and live well off of the money they raked in. Following their unsuccessful run for the White House many would get a fat contract as a pundit with a cable news channel. Out of ten candidates in the primaries, nine would fail and one would advance to the general.

"We have plans," Blair said. "Once in a century? I'm going to change that."

Iris smiled a sexy smile. "Well, aren't you the confident one."

"That's what got me on this plane, babe," he said, and I looked away before I could roll my eyes. Confidence was fine, but Blair's was more bluster and bravado. I admitted it had punched our ticket onto this plane. But it had also gotten us, and especially Blair, into plenty of trouble over the years. I continued to look away, although I listened to Blair begin to go into his macho act, telling splashy, enhanced stories about his successes in life, not the least of which was his interest in a bright, beautiful partner to share it with.

Blair and I had met almost ten years ago, a partnership forged through a failed attempt by a Silicon Valley billionaire to win a senate seat. Cornelius Wetzel had brought Blair in as a strategist when he launched his campaign, and then brought me in as his pollster. We were a marriage of convenience, getting along well, mostly because I found Blair's act amusing and he found my work ethic valuable. Although the campaign itself failed miserably, it was mostly due to a blundering, incompetent and inexperienced candidate. But Blair and I learned we were a matched pair, our individual strengths shoring up the other's weaknesses. With better candidates, we might find success. So, for the next decade we worked as the Baker Lipschitz Team, running campaigns during election seasons, providing marketing research to corporations during the off years.

Our partnership flourished, sputtered, and flourished again. Last year's Justin Woo campaign was supposed to have been our big pay day, but it turned out all Woo needed from us was rote polling and some minor consulting. The big money, the avalanche of funds, came from producing a lavish advertising campaign, a task that was reserved for another consultant, who turned out to be Woo's cousin. We received a lot of notoriety, but not a lot of money. But good luck sometimes falls into your lap, and if the vice president bought our pitch to advertise heavily, we could create and place a media campaign, and the money would come flowing in.

"So, tell me," I said, interrupting Blair's discourse, and feeling the unspoken irritation shooting at me from behind his black eyes. "Iris. You worked as a staffer once. Is there anything about the vice president that the world doesn't know? Maybe something they *should* know?"

She turned toward me and gave me a thoughtful gaze. "Well, that's an interesting question."

"Thank you. Asking questions is my life."

"Most people inside the beltway know he was Double Ivy. Went to Yale undergrad and then Harvard Law. Rich likes to present an aura of being part of the local D.C. gentry. But he actually grew up in poverty."

"Wasn't he raised in Chevy Chase?" I asked, referring to

the upscale Washington suburb.

"He spent his last year of high school there, with an aunt and uncle who finally took him in. Growing up, his father was a drunk and his mother had a couple of nervous breakdowns. Making rent in Baltimore was touch and go. They moved a lot. The one constant he had was the church; he was an altar boy. When he talks of his childhood, he speaks reverently about the importance of his faith. And it probably did save him. That, and the priests recognized how bright he was. He got a scholarship to a great college and made the most of it."

"Why doesn't he talk about this?" I asked.

"I think he's tried to run as far away from his childhood as possible," she scoffed. "Would you want the world to know that?"

"Why not?" I asked. "It shows he's pulled himself up by his own bootstraps."

"Sometimes facing the truth about yourself is difficult," she said. "I doubt Rich wants anyone to know just how poor he was. How unsuitable his parents were. Probably a lot of shame there."

I shook my head. "It wasn't his fault, was it? He was born into it. And he found a way out. The only shame is in not letting the world in on the story, so they can appreciate who he really is."

Iris shrugged again. "It might work. You know, at this point I think his campaign is desperate enough to try anything."

Chapter 5

The flight to Washington took five hours, with most of us dozing off during the last three. The crew gently shook us awake a mere twenty minutes before we touched down. They generously provided us with mugs of freshly brewed coffee and freshly baked muffins. I reached into my bag and grabbed two more Advil tablets, washing them down with a long sip. I shook the bottle and saw I had just enough left to get me back home without doubling over in pain. I made a mental note to ask Eli for a referral about a chiropractor. And maybe a prescription for some pain meds.

We exchanged business cards with Iris, shook hands, Blair grasping her hand for just a moment too long. She seemed amused, I was not. Blair's behavior with women had long been a thorn on our company's side, a harsh reminder of the pitfalls of partnering with someone who brings different strengths to the table. The sun was already high in the sky by the time we descended the air stairs. We found a member of the vice president's staff patiently waiting for us, and he whisked us through the small private airport and into a gleaming black GMC Yukon.

While the vice president had an office in the west wing, he rarely used it these days. His campaign was now in full swing, which meant he either spent his time navigating the campaign trail or strategizing at his residence. The

Yukon sped onto the grounds of the Naval Observatory, where Sudeau lived with his wife and four dogs. After going through a security check at the black gate with a pair of Secret Service agents, appropriately decked out in their customary dark suits, sunglasses and serious demeanors, we entered the compound. Their home was gorgeous, not as impressive as the White House, but marvelous nonetheless. A large, three-story Victorian home, white with black shutters, situated high atop a tall hill of green grass. The front yard was wide enough to accommodate a football field. We climbed out of the vehicle, and another agent led us into the house, down a plush, softly carpeted hallway.

The room we entered was blindingly white. The walls were painted an optic white, with tall, narrow glass windows rising up near the ceiling. A hardwood floor was mostly covered by a fluffy white throw rug. The white chairs all looked plush, but oddly, none were the same style. A series of built-ins cradled more than three hundred books, their bindings smooth and distinguished, august tomes that did not appear to have ever been opened. The Secret Service agent told us the vice president would join us shortly. We sat down and waited thirty minutes in silence, neither of us bothering to speak a word.

"Welcome!" came the familiar deep baritone, and we turned toward the vice president, dressed in a red golf shirt and khakis. Even without his business suit, the vice president maintained a regal presence. Our conversation with Iris, shining a light on his modest background, gave an odd insight into what had to be a dichotomous, complex man.

"Mr. Vice President!" Blair crowed. "It's a pleasure to be here. I only wish I knew this was casual day."

"Ha," he said, smiling a big, white smile. "I've just gotten through nine holes with the majority whip. Would have showered but I didn't want to keep you fellows waiting. I imagine you're busy people, too."

"Kind of you," Blair said. "You know my partner, Ned Baker?"

"By reputation of course, and we spoke yesterday," he said, and shook my hand warmly, a politician's handshake, big, soft, warm and comfortable.

"Good to finally meet you, sir," I managed.

"Likewise. Sit, sit."

The vice president rambled on for a few minutes about his golf game, showing off his gift for filling time with words that sounded important but were really not. We were soon joined by two more people, the vice president's handsome chief of staff, and Amber, his fetching wife. The chief of staff was Randy Greece, nicknamed "Handy Randy" for his ability to grease the wheels and get things done. He was in his early forties, smooth skinned, glistening smile, curly blond hair, and movie-star looks. Greece looked like he could be a politician himself.

"I'm so glad you could stop by on such short notice," Randy said. "Maybe you can familiarize us with your backgrounds."

"No problem, we just happened to be in the neighborhood," Blair smiled, launching into the nickel tour of our company. Blair began with my background in polling and research and focus group moderating, moving on and giving more alacrity to his own background as a well-seasoned strategist, who was already acquainted with everyone in Washington. Blair didn't notice the condescending smiles around the room, but I did.

"I understand you have some history with the president," Amber said.

"You mean apart from the fact that he hates my guts?" Blair protested. "Yeah, I almost derailed his political career in Phoenix. He beat my guy fifty-one to forty-nine. I almost changed the course of American history. But it's water under the bridge. We're great pals now."

The vice president threw back his head in laughter, freeing everyone in the library to laugh as well. They knew what the president thought of Blair, and they knew how frivolous his comment was. In the business world, getting a forty-nine percent market share often meant you were wildly successful, often the dominant player, the market leader. But in the world of political campaigns, forty-nine percent was no different than zero. It just signified you failed to win, you came up short and you were out of the game. Forty-nine percent meant you were a loser and losing is not something to boast about.

"All right," Sudeau said, his smile fading. "The fact that the president hasn't been your biggest fan, well, that may work out okay. We're trying to distance ourselves from him. But I think you know why we asked you here. We've cut our ties with Frank Phelan as well as some other staff. I'm looking for something new. Not just someone to do polling, but to do strategy. Fresh start."

"Any problems with Phelan?" I asked.

"Yeah, his polls showed me losing. That's a big problem."

There was more laughter, but not on the part of the vice president. Sudeau looked at his chief of staff and motioned for him to talk.

"There were also some problems with the Phelan's methodology," Randy Greece said. "He was trying to build a model that included both telephone and online surveys, and no one could understand what he was doing. Plus, his voter turnout projections looked funny."

I nodded slowly. "Forecasting voter turnout is critical, especially among different age groups and ethnicities. And a simple thing like over-estimating turnout in Cleveland or Philadelphia can throw an entire poll off. Difference between winning and losing."

"Spot on," Sudeau said. "We don't want to get blindsided. Like what transpired with Trump."

"That was only partly turnout. The pollsters actually nailed the national numbers in that one, they had Hillary up by a couple of points, they got that part right. Things went haywire on a state level. Some events you can't forecast so easily."

"That can't happen here," he said definitively. "And I'm obviously not thrilled with how well this campaign is going, that's no secret. I never dreamed Grady Sanderson would ever be the frontrunner in this race. Guy's a governor from Montana, for goodness' sake. But his brand of liberal populism is catching fire. We need to douse it in a hurry."

"Hasn't Phelan done some oppo research on Sanderson?" Blair asked. "Everyone's got skeletons hidden someplace. I've heard rumors he's got a pair of illegitimate kids running around."

"You think there's anything to that?" Greece asked.

"Once it's out there, it doesn't really matter if it's true, does it?" Blair countered.

"I swear," the vice president shook his head. "That Phelan. He said the first goal was to do oppo research on me. I told him to forget about it."

I didn't follow up, although I noticed the vice president's wife begin to squirm at the discussion of opposition research. Phelan's suggestion of doing oppo research on his own candidate was right on the money. Before a politician unearths dirt on his adversaries, his first step is to go back and see if there's any nasty tidbits lingering around on him. Mud that someone else could throw, so the candidate would be prepared with a response. It's not something any candidate likes, but it's a step every candidate has to take. The last thing you ever want is to be caught unprepared. Especially if there's something in the candidate's shaky past that can emerge from the shadows. And in a presidential campaign, it almost always will.

"We'll uncover some stuff on Sanderson," Blair assured him and offered a wink.

"Good, good," Sudeau smiled approvingly. "Look, I've had my eye on you guys for a while. I was impressed with how you helped Justin Woo get a landslide win last year.

I'm just surprised you're still available, no one's snatched you up."

"We've been sitting and waiting for your call," Blair said, with the most innocent of expressions.

"Ha!" Sudeau laughed. "I'll bet. Randy, why don't you take them through where we are on the campaign."

Greece began to go over a litany of policy issues the vice president had voiced, everything from when to deploy troops to how best to divvy up the federal budget. It was policy wonk stuff, the vice president and then his wife chiming in with their need to better understand what it was the voters were looking for in a president. Greece said they wanted us to take the nation's pulse, and if the vice president wasn't in sync, then, well, the vice president needed to know what he'd need to change about his image. They wanted to start by doing some focus groups.

"That's a great idea," Blair said, suddenly deviating from our script. "We'd be happy to do that for you."

"Can I ask you a question, Mr. Vice President?" I broke in, noticing Blair give me a sideways glance, an unspoken admonishment to be careful about what I said.

"Shoot."

"Why do you want to be president?"

"Have you listened to the other ten guys who are running?" he asked.

"Of course."

"Then you know," he smiled.

I really didn't know. "Is that because you think they're unelectable?"

"No," he said. "It's because I think they're a pack of

idiots. And yes, I like to win. The first duty of any politician is simple. It's to get elected."

"All right," I said, trying to process all of this. "Let me run an idea past you. We think you need to differentiate yourself from the president. You're not him. You need to get out from under his shadow."

Sudeau gave me an odd look. "Go on. I'd like to hear what you have to say. And I respect you for asking me why I want to be president. Shows guts. And I didn't mean to be flip. But I really believe I'm far more qualified, and I can be far more effective than anyone else. I truly believe that."

I took a breath. "All right. But you can't be the candidate of inevitability. You can't be the one who becomes president just because you're next in line. You have to offer something different. And in this climate, you've got to be the agent of change. People get tired of presidents after two terms and they want something different. Sometimes they want the polar opposite. The president had a privileged background. You didn't. He grew up rich. You grew up poor. He was given everything. You had enormous obstacles to overcome. You're the candidate of the people because you're one of them. But the people don't know that. You need to tell them. You need to connect with them emotionally."

"Well, now you have my attention," he said. "How did you get all this?"

I smiled. "Research. You need to present yourself differently. People think you're part of the aristocracy here. That's gotten you to a high level. But that's not a good thing because the everyday Joe won't believe he can relate to you. They're not familiar with who the real Richard Sudeau is. And now is when it matters most. Every single thing you say and do going forward will be part of changing voter impressions."

The vice president nodded. "And how do we do that?"

"We test different personas. We can start by doing some focus groups. We present two candidates, the elite person you've tried to present yourself as, and the regular guy you really are. We don't identify you, just Candidates A and B. We start by seeing how they react to that. Once we get buy-in from voters, we can test this through a survey. Get some hard data. Forget the polling for now. We need to launch a campaign to show people the new you. Then we can get into the field and do polls. The real changes will show up there."

The vice president bobbed his head enthusiastically. "I like that. Yeah, I like that idea a lot."

"Wait a minute," his wife started. "This is a whole new direction. Why would people buy into this? They've known him for so long as this august figure in American politics. How can you just pivot and now present him as plain old Rich, the poor boy who made good? Who would believe that?"

I took a breath. This was a surprise. I had expected pushback from the vice president, not his wife. Convincing a candidate had its challenges; convincing the spouse was something else entirely. No one is closer to the candidate than their partner, no one else can have the intimate conversations, no one else would ever be accused of having ulterior motives or hidden agendas. This was the very delicate dance. And Amber Sudeau was as distinguished a political spouse as they came. She had been a congresswoman herself years ago, had even held a cabinet post under a previous administration. Secretary of the Interior. The Sudeaus were the ultimate power couple in Washington. And as uncomfortable as I was with Blair at times, he knew when to step in. Like siblings who would castigate each other mercilessly in private, they came together as a unified force in public.

"Mrs. Sudeau," he said.

"Call me Amber."

"Amber," Blair said. "We're here for a reason. What Rich's been doing isn't working. It's why you've been through numerous campaign consultants in the past year. Multiple pollsters. Frank Phelan is a good man. So were the others. But they've been using standard techniques. When something isn't working, you have to abandon it. In this case, we need to rebrand the vice president."

"Rebrand?" she scoffed. "You make Rich sound like he's nothing more than a pair of sneakers."

I looked at Blair. It was tough to tell someone, especially someone savvy in the shrewd tactics of political marketing, that their spouse was little more than a product, an image that was malleable in the eyes of consumers. But voters perceived them in much the same way, almost like a favorite football team, something to root for. And when they cast their vote, it was not unlike choosing what restaurant to eat at, or what cereal to buy at the supermarket.

"You know," Blair said casually, "people used to think of McDonald's as just cheap fast food, but when they introduced salads and *cappuccinos* to the menu, they changed consumer perceptions. And Mountain Dew was once a regional soda in rural America. Then they did a new ad campaign, promoted it as cool for kids, and sales took off. People looked at the brand differently. Yes, a candidate for president is much more than just a snack food. But the images a candidate projects can be molded and shaped in the same way."

"And we need to change his image," I added. "Fast."

"We really do," Blair said. "That's why we're here. People need to know the real Rich. They value authenticity. And it's like that old show biz saying. Once you can master authenticity, you've got it made."

There was an audible silence, a gathering of thoughts. I wondered how much of Blair's last statement was resonating. Faking authenticity. This was classic Blair, over-the-top rhetoric. But we were playing on a different stage now. My gnawing fear was that the vice president would thank and dismiss us. In fact, he did not.

"I think it might work," the vice president said absently, looking down at the carpet. "I should be leading in the polls, but instead I'm sliding into fourth place. Fortunately, no one else has broken out of the pack. Look, I've never come clean with the voters about my upbringing. Maybe I should. And I've got nothing to lose. If we don't nail the nomination this year, there won't be a next time. This is it."

"I think you're absolutely right. You need to mix things

up," Blair said, sensing an opening. "We can do it for you. It'll cost you some bucks, but it's worth it."

"Hold on," Greece frowned. "Money is an issue right now."

"Maybe so," said the vice president. "But the only times I've failed in politics is when I've gone cheap. Sometimes you just have to bite the bullet if you're going to win."

"I agree wholeheartedly," Blair crowed. "It's not easy and it's not inexpensive. But we can get the job done for you."

"What does not inexpensive translate to?" Amber asked. "Rich just started another fundraising push, in fact, he has a big one in L.A. in a few days. If he gets the nomination, we're looking at a billion-dollar campaign. We weren't counting on starting full-blown media spend just yet."

"With all due respect Mrs. ... I mean, Amber," Blair said. "If you don't start right now, you may not get another chance. And the beauty of starting an ad blitz now is it can scare others out of the race. Shock and awe. Keeps the field level. If you have ten people running, it's hard to get your message across. Too much clutter. Start now and you can shoot off to a big lead and get established as the frontrunner. Wait a while, and, well, you know ... "

Randy Greece spoke. "He has a point. No time like the present to take action."

Blair smiled, his enthusiasm growing. "Hit the airwaves hard. We believe in being aggressive."

I sat back and was reminded of something. When I was growing up, my mother had a saying, that if you worked hard, you should get a little something for yourself. It was a modest way of saying you earned something and you deserve something. But it also implied you shouldn't take too much. *A little something for yourself* meant just that. But I also knew that Blair's words spoke larger themes, the idea that a media campaign to change an image would be required for the vice president to ascend to the presidency. It would also mean a handsome commission for our firm, as Blair carefully omitted. But as he said it, the words of my father entered my mind as well, a signpost perhaps, a balancing of two visions of life. Whereas my mother's words were an encouragement that you could advance yourself, my father's were more of a warning. He only said this a few times, but the implications obviously stayed with me, and this tended to come into my thoughts when Blair was speaking. It was a backwoods saying, a vision to be heeded, a cautionary note that was fairly simple. Pigs get fed and hogs get slaughtered.

"I understand your concern, Amber. But I like what I'm hearing," Sudeau said. "We need a new direction. And a way to separate from the president. I think we need to explore this."

Amber Sudeau looked a little disgusted. "It's your campaign, Rich. You're the decider."

Sudeau nodded. "All right. Let's do this. I'd like to put your idea in front of some civilians. Can you arrange for some focus groups tonight?"

Blair looked over at me, his eyes casting the pleading look of a person who wants something badly, but can't use words to communicate. I knew Blair wanted me to say yes, we can do anything, including renting out a facility in a matter of hours, grabbing a group of twenty likely voters off the street indiscriminately, and whip up intelligent questions to ask them. With the stakes being the presidency of the United States, the leader of the free world, the most important elected position on the face of the earth.

"Tonight," I started, "wouldn't be a good idea at all. Too many things would have to come together perfectly, and you deserve better. We can move quickly, but we want to move intelligently. Give us a few days. A week would be better."

"Why?"

"We need to recruit the right people for a focus group. Registered Democrats, people who vote regularly in the primaries, consumers who are articulate, within a certain target age range. Men, women, certain income and education levels. All of that requires some thoughtful decisions."

"I'm not a patient man, Mr. Baker," the vice president said, the timbre of his voice deepening, as if to let everyone in the room know who was in charge. "I just want to hear from some regular folks on this."

"We want you to get accurate information, sir. You deserve it. The country deserves it."

"You know," Randy Greece said, looking up at the ceiling, "Thursday would actually work. In two days you'll be in L.A. for the fundraiser at the Peninsula. Timing's perfect."

I blinked a few times and felt my body stiffen. Another idea that needed tempering.

"The vice president should not be attending focus groups in person," I said, imagining an incredible scene of Secret Service agents tromping through a focus group lobby and participants getting exposed to a full-blown spectacle. "We'll set something up so that the groups are streamed and recorded. He can watch the groups live on a phone or iPad. Or the next night, or whenever. It's better for everyone. It's also better if you don't do the groups in L.A."

"No," Randy said definitively, and turned to the vice president. "L.A. is fine. The California primary is early next year, they moved it up to March. And L.A. is where the trends start. It's got everything. It's a deep blue state, and that's where a huge chunk of the delegates are. I think it's perfect."

I looked over at Blair, and his desperate eyes were now shooting darts. There were a million bad reasons to do political research in Los Angeles. It was an atypical market, a city loaded with people who had grown up elsewhere, in different states or different countries. It had a liberal tilt, and many people worked in one industry, entertainment. In short, L.A. was as big an anomaly as there was. But before I could utter another word of caution, my partner jumped in.

"If you think it's terrific, we think it's terrific," Blair declared. I tried not to roll my eyes, and instead felt my mouth and stomach tighten. Something felt very wrong here.

"All right, all right," Sudeau said, standing up and signaling our allotted time had ended. "I'm not personally crazy about L.A., but I see Randy's point. We have to win the nomination before we can do anything else. If this idea has legs there, maybe it can fly in the rest of the country. You guys work it out. But I want to find out right away if this rebranding makes sense. Let's see if it can do anything. What we've got now isn't going anywhere except sending me down the tubes. Work with Randy on this, fellas. Get an agreement signed, and let's move. But keep me in the loop."

We shook hands and the chief of staff led us toward the door. "Really appreciate you guys coming out," Greece said. "The vice president loves this kind of stuff. Really anxious to see what happens."

"Happy to help out, my friend," Blair said, patting Randy on the back as if the two had been pals for decades.

A different Yukon picked us up and took us back to the airport. I spent the time on the phone making arrangements with a focus group facility, pressing the owner to get the recruit right, and mostly not talking with Blair. I directed the facility owner to recruit a cross-section of ages, incomes, education levels, and ethnicities. All had to have voted in the last two elections. We'd have one group of men, one group of women. This was not how I liked to do research. In fact, it was how I hated to do research. Everything moving too fast, thrown together too quickly, garbage in, garbage out. The fact that the results might impact the fate of the free world was only starting to loom in the back of my mind.

We pulled into the airport, boarded a different Gulfstream, a slightly larger one, and a number of people joined us. A few looked familiar; one might have been a correspondent for a cable news network, another might have been a former congressman. As we settled in, I checked my messages and saw that I had one from Dr. Sterling. I placed a call as the jet slowly rolled toward the runway. The office receptionist put me on hold and I closed my eyes as I waited. Eli often had me wait fifteen or twenty minutes, his patients in the office taking precedence over most everything else. But less than thirty seconds later, his voice came on the line.

"Ned?"

"Yeah. What's up?"

"Listen, I wanted to get back to you right away. It's about your chest x-ray. There's something on it. We found a small mass on your left lung. It's possible this might be nothing, but we need to find out. I'd like for you to go in and do scans. As soon as possible."

It took a moment for the enormity of this to sink in. After a few seconds, Eli asked me if I was still on the line.

"I ... I am."

"Can I schedule something for later today or tomorrow?"

I lowered my voice. "How could this be possible?"

"Look, it's possible. Nothing can be ruled out. We need to do a CT scan. That'll tell us more."

I closed my eyes and listened to the engine noise begin to escalate. I managed to lower my voice even further, a whisper so low that I could barely hear myself speak. "So you're saying I might have ... I might have lung cancer? This is crazy. I've never smoked a day in my life. You know that."

"Not all lung cancer is contracted through smoking. But yes, there's a chance you might have it. If it's caught in the early stage, we could remove it through surgery. We just need to do more testing. We need to be sure. How soon can we get you in? Today or tomorrow would be ideal."

I took a breath. "Not today. I'm traveling today. Tomorrow."

"I'll schedule you first thing in the morning. The imaging center opens at six-thirty. I'll pull strings to get you in. I'm also going to schedule an appointment with a respiratory specialist, there seems to be fluid buildup in the lung. It's called pleural effusion, that's what probably is causing the back pain. We'll need to get that checked out, too, see if there are any malignancies."

"Okay," I managed, trying to get my head around this. "Hey, Eli. Is there a chance this thing could just be benign?"

He paused. "It's possible but we can't tell yet. We just don't know enough at this point. But it's worrisome. I have to be honest with you, Ned. It is very worrisome."

Chapter 6

My next five hours were spent staring aimlessly out the window of the Gulfstream. The blue sky, the small, distant land beneath us, the small dots that might be modest houses. The green fields which looked like pastures or farms, nestled between the vast spaces of dry, brown earth, terrain void of a single blade of grass. Long stretches of land where perfect circles sat within endless rows of perfect squares, the product of some elaborate irrigation process. A few wispy clouds hovered here and there. These were the long, rural canvases of America, artful landscapes which you could never see from the ground. Everything looked different from thirty thousand feet in the air.

I steered my mind toward the picturesque view but as much as I tried, I could not avoid my dark inner thoughts. I occasionally needed to nod emptily at Blair's jabber, fending off inquiries as to what was wrong with me. There are some subjects that needed processing before they could be discussed, and some subjects about which could not be discussed with Blair. At least not right away. The plane ride had blessed me with time to think, to ponder and to speculate, to sort out the good and the bad, all with the backdrop of evolving scenery below. None of this could provide any solid answers, but the lofty perspective provided a context to help me focus.

I had never been a smoker. I tried to lead a healthy

lifestyle. I was generally a good person. I went to church occasionally. My parents were both alive, well into their eighties. This glimpse into the abyss wasn't supposed to happen to me, not for decades, but here I was. I tried to avoid looking upward into what might be the heavens, as I gazed out the window. The five hours slipped by very fast.

The jet swooped, slowed, and eventually banged onto the runway, taxiing at what felt like a ferocious speed before slamming to a surprising and sudden stop. It was a jolt that brought me back to the here and now. As we walked down the tarmac, I told Blair I would see him tomorrow at the office, then I quickly sped off in my Pilot. I darted toward home initially, but then, looking at a black Audi in front of me, I saw it had license plate holders promoting the Brentwood School, and I was reminded of Angelina's game. I didn't need to go, and I had the perfect excuse not to go. But I also sensed that the more distractions placed in front of me, the less inclined I would be to drift into that dark place.

I waved my way past the school security guard, an affable sort, and drove down the small hill that led to the crowded parking lot. It was always congested, too many cars, not enough spaces. I drove around for ten minutes before an amiable-looking teacher pulled out of a space and I quickly slipped in. Walking to the softball diamond, I came across a few familiar faces, contented parents who nodded and smiled. I nodded as well, but I had trouble smiling back.

The game had begun, they were in the third inning, and there was no score. I climbed halfway up the wooden bleachers, careful to find a spot that was away from anyone I knew, or anyone who knew me. Leslie wasn't there, but I made eye contact and acknowledged a few of the moms nearby. My normal spot, sitting up in the top row, in the eagles' nest that was always lined with a cluster of other detached dads, was out of the question today. Small talk was not possible. I waved to the other dads when they noticed me, but made no other overture. Being alone in a crowd was what I sought, physically near others, yet spiritually untethered.

I watched Angelina pitch, her smooth motions, flexible and rubbery, whipping the ball furiously toward each batter. Her intensity, the perspiration shining from her golden face, her blue eyes focused and icy. She struck out half the batters she faced. The ones who managed to hit the ball did so with the dull clanging sound of an aluminum bat, but most were barely able to ground out to one of the infielders. One girl from Sierra Canyon, chunky and rotund with large hips, was finally able to sock a pitch up the alley between left and center field. She chugged into second base with a double, but she was stranded there, and the teams went into the bottom of the last inning with neither school having scored a run. Finally, one of Angelina's teammates reared back and slugged a pitch over the outfield fence for a home run, trotting slowly and vainly around the bases as her teammates screamed and jumped up and down, thrilled with their 1-0 playoff win.

It is an unusual feeling to witness joy in others and to not feel any of it resonate within you. To see your daughter exuberant, mobbed by friends shrieking with the glee of having achieved something for which they had worked hard. To watch the smiling parents clapping in the stands, proud to the point of being smug, high-fiving each other as though they had been performing on the field themselves, sweating and toiling for the victory. And yet I felt none of this, only the sense of being far removed from the jovial scene, as if I were seeing it through a distant and distorted lens. As if I was looking through the wrong end of a pair of binoculars, surveying a scene that appeared much farther away than it really was.

I waited outside the girls' locker room, standing a good twenty yards from the door, close enough to notice when Angelina exited, far enough away as to avoid any human contact. She emerged after about twenty minutes, saw me, and rushed over to kiss my cheek. In the next breath she told me that she was going over to Jordan's house with a few of the girls, and that she would see me later. I nodded and managed a weak smile; she didn't wait for an answer, instead she happily waved goodbye and raced back to her friends, gabbing excitedly as she scooted away from me. Her friends were nice and they were good for her. I had once told her many years ago, pick your friends, don't let them pick you. I'm not sure if my words sunk in, but the results were good. Either she had chosen well, or perhaps they had.

Our house was empty, Leslie was most likely still at work. I made a sandwich, ate it quickly, and then trudged upstairs to lie down and be alone with my thoughts. I heard the front door open after a while, no conversation, just the muted sound of a door slamming and grocery bags being slapped on the granite counter top. I made no effort to get up, in fact, I stayed there, lying supine on the bed, staring at whatever I could make out on the ceiling. Eventually the purple shadows began appearing in the bedroom, slowly growing darker and grayer. The small strands of light slipping through the cracks in the blinds faded until they finally disappeared. I tried to sleep, but all my mind would allow was to daydream amidst the twilight.

Leslie came up a few hours later, turned on the lights, and apologized immediately when she saw me on the bed. I kept my eyes closed, pretending to be asleep, any desire to talk tonight had vanished. I was not ready to discuss my situation, not ready to have that awful conversation with anyone. Not yet. I knew there was still hope, that the scans would reveal more than the x-rays, that Eli's worries could be unfounded. But his somber concern made me wary.

This was a process I thought I needed to initially go through alone. I didn't want to share my fears or upset my family without warrant, without being more certain, without greater knowledge. I would tell them when I knew more. Maybe the results would come back fine, and we could all have a collective sigh of relief, without putting them through the worry. So I'd wait. But as I eventually drifted off to a fitful and unsatisfying sleep, it vaguely occurred to me that I had not spoken more than a single sentence to a single soul since my conversation with Eli, over twelve hours earlier.

I slept for a long time, perhaps my body clock was

readjusting to the change in time zones, perhaps I was making up for the lack of sleep the night before, or maybe I was trying to slink away from a bleak fate that might be awaiting me. I rose a little before six o'clock the next morning, my mind keenly aware of my appointment. I slipped quietly out of bed, dressing in the bathroom so as not wake Leslie, and drove off as the gray light had started to form over the eastern sky. The streets were largely empty, a comforting reminder of what Los Angeles once was, many years ago: uncluttered, peaceful, and even beckoning.

The imaging center was housed in a gorgeous steel and glass structure just off of Wilshire Boulevard in Santa Monica. It had a palatial entranceway, a spiral staircase, and a gleaming blue marble floor. It was shiny and new and reassuring. I had once done a market research survey for a hospital chain, and patients were very clear in their opinions. If a medical center looked like an architectural masterpiece, it stood to reason, the care you received there would likely be first-rate as well. This was far from a truism, punctuated by the fact that the hospital chain who hired us later wound up being the defendant in a remarkably large number of patient lawsuits. But the initial image can sometimes qualm fears.

"May I help you?" smiled the pleasant receptionist.

"I have an appointment to do scans. CT and PET."

"And your name?"

"Ned Baker."

"Ned?" she asked, her soft gray eyes growing a little wide.

I nodded yes.

"What a nice name," she said.

"Thank you," I responded, a little puzzled.

"Don't see too many Neds around here."

She thumbed through her beige manila folders, smiled when she came upon mine, and handed me a clipboard holding a dozen pages of thin white forms to be filled out. The process took a little while, although I paused after I recorded my age. I looked at the number fifty that I had just scrawled, gazing at it for an extended period. I'd never considered where I might end up when I reached fifty, how I'd look, what my station would be in the world. My life's projection as a teenager mostly stopped at thirty, as if that were the ultimate age, and everything beyond that point fell haphazardly off a cliff. But I was fifty, there was no doubt about it, the five and the zero glaring back at me. I just had trouble accepting its meaning, contemplating it long enough to realize that I was indeed, and inarguably, aging.

After about fifteen minutes of idle wait, a young phlebotomist led me through a long white hallway, sterile, no pictures on the walls, only a sign or two pointing toward various labs and scanners. Once inside an exam room, she had me lie down on a cot and inserted an I.V. into my left arm, the quick jab of a needle creating a sting for a moment before melting away. After strapping it securely, she helped me up, and we continued our trek down the hallway. We passed through a pair of thick double doors that needed a good hard shove to swing open, and into a room with a cautionary yellow sign, complete with an ominous warning that nuclear medicine would be utilized past this point.

A warm, stocky technician smiled at me and stood up from her desk. The name on her badge was Janet, she had flaming red hair and was dressed in sea green scrubs. She was about my age, maybe a bit older, something that felt oddly comforting, a maternal feeling perhaps. She led me behind a curtain and instructed me to undress and put on a gown. Afterwards, I was directed to lie on a nearby cot and relax, which I took to mean check my email. Janet left the room but returned a few minutes later and gently admonished me for not following directions. Her tone also reminded me of my mother, gentle and understanding, yet firm and unyielding.

"Is this your first time doing scans?"

"Does it show?" I asked.

She smiled again. "You shouldn't answer a question with a question."

"Is there another way?"

Janet admonished me with a reproachful look, but I saw the hint of a smile as she walked out the door. After what had to be a good forty-five minutes, she returned, pretending to give me the once over with her eyes, as if to ascertain whether I was fully rested, and then she led me over to the scanner. Lying prone on my back atop a gurney, pillow under my head, cushions propping up my knees, she draped a heated blanket over me and instructed me to be very still. And for the next thirty minutes, the gurney slid into and out of the scanner, the occasional beeping and whirring letting me know that the scan was progressing. Toward the end, she released an iodine concoction into my arm, the warm feeling sweeping down through my body. It was pleasurable for a moment, but then I could practically taste the harsh mineral quality of the iodine, and my abdomen and pelvis suddenly grew hot. The warmth dissipated, although the metallic taste remained in my throat.

"That's it," Janet said, helping me off the gurney, her arms surprisingly strong. "We are done."

"So, what's the verdict?"

"Oh, I wouldn't know. The radiologist reviews the scans and then sends them to your doctor. You should talk to him later. Just drink plenty of fluids today. Water. Lots of water. Gets the radioactive chemicals from the scans out of your body quicker. And stay away from small children and pregnant women."

"Oh," I said, a little confused. "Am I radioactive?"

"Only for a brief period. But like most things, it will pass."

I shivered for a moment, then thanked her and left the Imaging Center for my next appointment. I walked the two blocks to the office of Eli's respiratory specialist. His name was Dr. Lynch, and he was a short, balding man with a serious expression.

"Dr. Sterling's taken me through your situation," he said, his face scrunched up in a dour expression. "And I've looked at the chest x-ray. There's definitely fluid buildup in the lung. I can do a thoracentesis now. That should help for a little while, anyway."

"A what?"

"Thoracentesis. We drain the fluid from your lung. It'll just take a few minutes. That should take care of the back pain. It's a first step."

"And then?"

"Well, it's only a temporary fix. Most likely, fluid will continue to build. You'll need to do a talc procedure if it continues. But the more important issue is we need to test the fluid for cancer."

The word unnerved me. *Cancer.* I shook my head. "I don't understand this. There's no history of any cancer in my family. I'm a non-smoker. I'm only fifty years old. How could this have happened?"

Dr. Lynch shrugged. "It could be any one of a multitude of factors. We may never know. Medicine is much better at addressing maladies on a go-forward basis than understanding what caused them."

"That's not reassuring," I said.

"I'm sorry. There are probably going to be a lot of unanswered questions. And we're making progress in treating it, but there is an epidemic of cancer in this world today. One in three people are likely to develop cancer at some point in their lives. It would be nice if we knew why. For now though, we're more focused on treating it."

The doctor left the room and returned a few minutes later, a nurse in tow. After I removed my shirt, Dr. Lynch inserted a needle into my back, a small sting, one that did not hurt much, perhaps because I didn't see it and didn't anticipate it. I remained as still as possible, and a few minutes later he told me they were done. As I put on my shirt, I glanced down at a plastic jar. It was nearly filled with what must have been over a liter of fluid, reddish-brown, the distinct color of apple cider. Or perhaps the color of watered-down blood.

"That came out of me?" I asked.

"Indeed it did," came the reply.

Chapter 7

The Vice President was ready for some recreation. Having flown in this afternoon from D.C., he was a little tired, but nothing that a good romp in the sack wouldn't cure. He grabbed a fresh tumbler from the small bar in his hotel suite, filled it with single malt Scotch, and added an ice cube. All you needed was one. A single cube of ice mollified the burn and opened the whiskey's bouquet, allowing the flavor to expand. But too much ice would be a killer. If single malt Scotch was served too cold, the taste would be muted. Not many people knew that.

He had just come from a Beverly Hills fundraiser, one of those grip-and-grin affairs Greece pushed him to do. He had been to plenty in his career, too many he thought, tiresome sessions where he had to ingratiate himself with a bunch of Hollywood phonies. Unavoidable, a job requirement which allowed him to tap into their multi-million-dollar veins and infuse his struggling presidential campaign with a new influx of cash. After loosening his tongue with a couple of watered-down drinks, he gave a rousing speech, making sure the studio moguls were left with the distinct impression that their interests were his interests. A great politician could make a progressive think he was progressive, and a conservative think he was conservative. And as he finished, he received an enthusiastic roar of applause, an encouraging bellwether that told him he would likely leave with a truckload of their money. In short, a worthwhile venture, but he was simply happy it was over.

When he arrived back at the hotel though, his debrief with the new pollster had given him pause. Ned Baker had struck him as different from that previous pollster, Frank Phelan, the dunderhead who kept coming back to him with bad news. But the response from tonight's focus groups was different. The voters just didn't know much about him. A two-term Senator, a vice president for almost seven years and yet he was still a blank slate. There were a few rays of hope, though. The groups thought he exuded the appearance of what a president should be. Strong, bold, distinguished. Kennedyesque. This was the sort of news he had been waiting for from Phelan. Baker had told him it was all preliminary, too soon to judge with certainty, but he tried to put a positive spin on this. He said the chances of the vice president ascending to the Presidency looked promising. He, Richard Sudeau, merely needed to show off that face and let America know who he really was. But what the voters really liked was Amber, his comely, mercurial spouse. She gave his candidacy a boost, the eye candy that also came with smarts. But she also came with an unsolvable problem.

Walking across the suite, he slipped in between the maroon drapes and the sliding glass door. Flipping the latch, he carefully opened the door and stepped gingerly onto the balcony. This would tick off the Secret Service boys if they found out. They always chastised him for *breaking the rules and for not paying enough attention to security. Fuck them. No one knew where he was staying. He lived life on his own terms. And he was starting on a path to become the most powerful man in the world in eighteen months. To emerge from his long years of solitude, of living in the cloistered shadow of his boss. He was finally exiting the cocoon. The Presidency was within his grasp. He could get there, but he had to play his cards right.*

He gazed out across the L.A. nightscape. The evening air was cool, or at least cooler than it was in D.C., where June had already brought a wave of sticky humidity. It was different out here, warm in the winter, cool in the summer. An odd place. Upside down. He had never really figured out Los Angeles, the city was a study in contrasts. Beautiful yet alien, straightforward yet vague. He didn't fit in here, but when he had to come, he liked staying in Century City. It was close to the beach, close to Beverly Hills, yet separate from them, a narrow enclave. This was a nice community, not really a neighborhood, more like a freakishly oversized business park. It was a high-end development, with some of the streets named for heavenly galaxies or clusters of stars. A classy area. So unlike where he grew up.

The vague hint of a crescent moon hung over the horizon and he could just barely make out the strands of light dancing off of the Pacific. The street lights flickered below him. Taking a deep gulp of scotch, he thought of the sexy package that was set to arrive in a few minutes, an old squeeze, and he relished the thought of her impending visit. But then he heard the sounds. A series of cracks, repetitive, unfamiliar, possibly the sharp noise of firecrackers going off nearby ...

*　　*　　*

The soft, cool, morning air hit me as soon as I walked outside, but it was fresh, sweet, and made me feel more alive. And the pain in my back was thankfully gone. I was suddenly very hungry and stopped at an iHOP, gorging on a stack of pancakes, thick, pillowy and sticky sweet with syrup. The bottomless cup of coffee was welcomed, although the vague mineral taste of the iodine concoction remained in the back of my throat, disappearing briefly as I ate, returning once I finished breakfast. I paid the bill and drove to my office, noticing that, having accomplished a few big items on my to-do list this morning, it was not yet ten o'clock.

The office of the Baker Lipschitz Team was active. I was barely at my desk for two minutes when Wanda, my project manager, burst in. She caught me gazing out the window, our view of the glistening Pacific being the one beautiful touch that came with our pedestrian office. The rest of our digs were mostly nondescript and modest.

Wanda had been with me through most of the ten years Blair and I had been together, and she was indispensable. I gave her as many raises as I could push past Blair, in a few cases, sacrificing some of my share of the profits to keep her happy and minimize the chance she'd leave us. Wanda periodically wondered what it would be like to work for a company like Garter, a client firm that had richer benefits and surroundings that were certainly more plush. I didn't want to burst her bubble, but she would not fit comfortably within a client company, if she could even land a job there. Corporations hired people who looked good and sounded good, amiable sorts who got along easily with colleagues. Wanda was none of those things. She was brash, plain spoken, and did not have the physical appeal that made prospective employers take notice. She simply worked hard and got the job done. In corporate America, that was insufficient. For us, she was perfect.

"Where have you been?" she asked in the mock-scolding manner, the one that a subordinate can temporarily use when she has a good relationship with her boss. "I've been trying to get a hold of you since yesterday morning. You simply have to start answering your cell."

"Sorry," I said, knowing about her calls, but not having felt capable of taking them. "Some things came up."

"Things more important than moderating focus groups for the vice president?" she exclaimed.

I shrugged and gave her the palms-up sign, the universal signal that certain events going on in the world were simply out of my hands. "What do you need?" I asked.

"Oh, let's see. I need to know how many people will be in the back room observing, should we get a camera operator for the video-conferencing, can the facility allow in people who participated in focus groups less than six months ago, should we cap the number of non-Caucasians who can attend. Should we pay to feed them sandwiches beforehand. Little things like that."

"And you can't handle this?" I asked her.

"Sure. But Haley screamed at me last time when I did. So I figured I'd ask first."

"Have I ever screamed at you?"

"Well ... no," she managed after considering this for a long moment.

"Good. Haley's gone, and so's the drama. No one will be screaming at you today."

For a moment I was relieved to think about work. To think about anything but the unthinkable. I gave Wanda the basic instructions. No one from the vice president's office was likely to come, but be sure to video-conference and record the groups. Get a camera operator, nothing in the world is worse than watching focus groups from a static angle that doesn't move. Only allow in past participants from other focus groups if we can't recruit anyone else. Yes, feed the participants dinner. Allow people from any nationality to participate, don't discriminate because of their ethnic background. Try and get a good mix. Make sure all the seats are filled, even if they have to pay people four hundred dollars each to come. Just kidding, but not really.

"Got it," she said, scribbling things onto a pad. "So, what happened to Haley? Heard she's not coming back."

"Just what exactly did you hear?"

"Well. That she departed under less-than-ideal

circumstances. Did that naughty behavior finally catch up with her?"

I let out a low whistle. We worked in a small office and gossip doesn't stay hidden. Haley's recent flirtation may have been the straw that broke the camel's back, but the camel's back is never broken by a single straw. The last straw just happened to be when she was traveling with me. Attempting to seduce the boss is not always a good career move.

"Well, look what the cat dragged in," interrupted a familiar voice. We both turned to see Blair strolling into my office. "Wanda, sweetie, can you give us a minute?"

"Sure," she said, rising and walking toward the door. "I'll catch up with you later."

Blair closed the door behind her and sat down. We had been in this office for almost ten years, Blair having insisted upon it, mostly because it was a short three-minute drive from his home in Santa Monica Canyon. My drive from Brentwood was a little longer and growing more so. As the blossoming of Silicon Beach added more and more office buildings to this seaside community, it also added more and more congestion. But the gorgeous view from my window was the constant, and I never passed up the chance to glance at the ocean when I could. And sometimes when I shouldn't.

"Nice day, isn't it?" Blair started.

I reluctantly turned my gaze away from the horizon and back toward him. "Sorry."

"Everything okay with you?" he asked casually, looking down as he examined his manicure.

"Why? Does something seem not okay?"

Blair kept examining his nails, and started running his thumb over them, moving it rhythmically back and forth. It looked like he admired his fingers so much that he had to touch them.

"Your back still messed up?" he asked.

"I think it's under control now. You noticed?"

"I notice everything. Things okay at home?"

"Is this twenty questions?"

"If it were, you'd use up all twenty," he said. "I'm starting to get ... concerned."

"About what? Me?"

"Yeah, you. We're about to reel in the biggest fish in the ocean. The largest whale we've ever come close to landing, and yeah, I'm concerned. I'm concerned you're going to fuck everything up."

I stared at him. "Have I ever?"

No," he shook his head. "You're the one who gets stuff done. I'm the one that gets stuff. And the stuff I just got could be the nicest payday we've ever had. Or might ever have. And it all rides on you tomorrow night. Those focus groups are critical. They have to go well. No, better than well. You have to hit a home run."

"A home run would be good."

"Make it a grand slam, then," he countered.

"You don't want to put any more pressure on me, do you?"

"I shouldn't have to. But I've been watching you the last couple of days. You're acting funny. Different. I just don't know what it is."

He was right, of course, things were different, very different. My world was suspended, balanced on the critical scans that could reveal my fate. If I would live or if I would die. But since I had yet to tell my wife and daughter about my medical condition, I surely wasn't going to confide in Blair. There was always a chance the scans could end up being negative, that this was just a big, needless scare, a mistake that any doctor could make, fearing the worst, steeling the patient for the unvarnished news that few people could bear to hear. That you might not live much longer.

This was the reality I was not able to ignore. There is no cure for cancer; no doctor needed to tell me that. But no doctor could give me a mental game plan either, a mission, a mode of thinking that could guide me. That had to come from within. I had no desire to take a trip around the world, I had seen enough of it. I did not need to go back and visit old friends, long lost acquaintances from Charleston or Berkeley.

"You don't have to worry," I managed, thinking in the back of my mind that I'd be doing enough worrying for everyone.

"I don't have to, but I do."

"Let me ask you something, Blair," I said, trying to change the subject. "What did you think of the vice president?"

"How do you mean?" he peered at me.

"I mean, when you looked at him yesterday, did you see a future president? Did you see someone you respect? Someone you wanted to lead this country?"

"You're really acting funny now."

"No, seriously," I said. "I'd like to know. What do you see?"

"What I see," he said evenly, "is a great big pile of cash. Starting with a big check that's supposed to arrive tomorrow with the FedEx guy. And listening to you, I'm also starting to see it vanish into thin air."

"Is that what drives you? Just money?"

"I want to be rich and famous. Just like Sudeau. That what you wanted to hear?"

I shook my head. When I looked at Richard Sudeau, I saw the same thing as when I looked at most politicians, a level of narcissism, but every politician was a narcissist to some extent. They had to be. It was what drove them, the tenaciousness to throw themselves into the bonfire of public scrutiny. Running for high office required a level of courage, as well as a neediness that bordered on the dysfunctional. The desire for others to exalt you. It was common in celebrities and political leaders and corporate executives. It was a trait of Rich Sudeau. And it was also a quality I saw in Blair Lipschitz.

"Look. I respect the vice president," Blair said, caustically. "As much as I respect any client."

"Which is to say not much."

"Hey. You know the drill. This is how it works. You don't have to love them. You just need to make them think you do."

And therein was another issue I was grappling with. Whether it was Garter's new product to enhance a woman's sexual experience or Rich Sudeau's new image designed to enhance the public's view of him. Something else was bothering me. With Garter, the product made me uneasy. There was nothing wrong with couples having more sex, but the idea of launching a supplement that wasn't FDA approved yet was a concern. There was nothing ostensibly wrong with electing Richard Sudeau as the leader of the free world, although he never answered my question as to why he wanted to be president. I looked at Blair and quickly realized my resolution on these issues would not come from him. And I reminded myself I still had a family to support.

"All right," I said, suddenly feeling the need to end this conversation quickly.

"All right what?"

"I'll nail it tomorrow."

"Atta boy. I sure don't want to have to go out and find a new partner."

I stared angrily at him. This wasn't the first time Blair had nibbled around the margins of that idea, but a joke often reveals the truth in a cagey disguise. When Blair and I argued, I sometimes sensed the invisible fraying of our bond, the snap of a cord that could propel us on our separate ways. Blair could replace me with someone who could roll up their sleeves and do the work, I could replace him with someone who could go out and scrounge up business. But the net effect would end up being the same. We had different roles, and our roles often chafed against each other. But like the person who angrily divorces their spouse and remarries, they often go find a new partner, different in some ways yet still having the same underlying and unsatisfying qualities, ones that brought out the exact same troubles that the previous spouse had managed to evoke.

"No need to test the waters," I sighed.

"Good," Blair smiled and stood up. "I've got the future mapped out. We're going places, you and me. Just watch what happens. This is going to be fantastic. For both of us. This is going to launch us into the stratosphere. My plans are coming to fruition!"

I stared at him and shook my head. No matter how keenly you planned things out, the world had an unfailing way of altering them.

Chapter 8

After Blair sauntered out of my office, I pushed myself back into work mode, preparing for the next day's focus groups. I crafted a discussion guide, an assemblage of questions and more questions to ask. I cooked up a scenario where I'd ask the groups to jot down their ideas of what an ideal president would be like. I'd then present descriptions of two nameless Brand X politicians, these would actually be the Rich Sudeau they most likely knew and then the Rich Sudeau we planned to unveil to the public. We'd reveal the vice president's name afterward so we could get reaction before and after. It was standard fare, elementary marketing research that could be applied to anything from soft drinks to shampoo.

My extensive breakfast, the heaping stack of pancakes and the endless cups coffee, kept me fueled well past lunch, but the inevitable three o'clock crash hit. I walked a few blocks to the Third Street Promenade, stepping into a Starbucks, which was doing a surprisingly robust business at that hour. I ordered an iced coffee, stopping at the sweetener bar to clarify the flavor and make it palatable. I looked down at the choice of blue, pink, yellow and green packets, randomly chose two blue ones and poured them carefully and evenly into the cup. I stirred vigorously, not realizing a very pretty, very familiar face, quietly came into view next to me.

"You must be Ned Baker," she started, interrupting my

thoughts.

"I must be," I said, turning toward her, scanning her face, trying to recollect why she looked familiar. She might have worked in my building, she might have been a parent of one of Angelina's classmates, she might have appeared on a reality TV show. In Los Angeles, any of these scenarios were possible, as well as all three combined being possible. A few years ago, I was walking along the Promenade and said hello to a good-looking man who I recognized from somewhere. I knew I had seen him before, and somewhat frequently as well. He gave me an odd look before quickly glancing in another direction. A few minutes later, blocks away, the embarrassing realization dawned on me that I had just interacted with Ryan Gosling.

"I'm Callie Saxon," she said in a perky voice and stuck out her hand. She was tall and pretty; her blonde hair, short and straight, stopped right at her shoulders. Her tawny eyes had that bright, intense gaze, the look of confidence, an aura of mischief. While her face was familiar, the name was a giveaway. She was an on-air correspondent for MSNBC. I grasped her hand briefly and gave her a puzzled look. People like her did not typically approach people like me.

"Pleasure," I said. "But how do you know me?"

"Oh," she said breezily, "I know *of* you. Through one of my contacts. I'm in town covering the vice president's campaign appearance tomorrow."

"I thought he was just coming in for a fundraiser," I said, adding, "Are you invited to that?"

"Nope," she laughed. "They would never let someone like me in. But he's in town, so he's giving a speech at UCLA tomorrow afternoon. Never passes up an opportunity to get his face out there."

I took a sip of coffee and decided it needed one more shot of artificial sweetener. I slit open a green packet this time, dumping the powder in less carefully before stirring quickly and sampling. Sweeter, better, more palatable. The green one did the trick. I snapped on the lid, jammed the straw into the too-small slit, and took a very long sip. I could practically feel the caffeine infusion, as I turned back to her.

"So, you must have some good contacts about Sudeau," I said.

"It's, um, through the vice president's campaign, actually. You'd be surprised how easy it is to get information in D.C., it's amazing. The maids and chauffeurs have remarkable access. They get paid so little, they appreciate the extra income. But this one came from a separate source. Sorry, can't reveal too much. I don't want to violate their privacy."

I laughed. "Feels like a lot of people's privacy is getting violated these days. Especially mine. What else do you know?"

"That you're on board with the vice president. That you've got focus groups tomorrow."

I stared at her and put my drink down on the counter so it didn't slip out my grasp. "Okay, that doesn't sound like the type of intel a butler would have access to, does it?"

"Nope," she smiled. "But I would appreciate it if you might confirm a few things."

"Such as?"

"Like the vice president's campaign is in deep trouble. That you're being brought in to try and salvage it. That the Baker Lipschitz Team has a plan to re-launch Sudeau as an outsider, to separate him from the president, give him some distance. Any truth to that?"

"You know full well I can't comment, right?"

"Why not? Everyone else in that town does."

While she was partly correct, I always felt there are certain confidences I needed to maintain. It is a delicate path to walk down, though. Revealing a candidate's strategies is not new in politics, and could enhance a consultant's public stature, but it does not make for good relations with the candidate. Being chatty with a reporter can help put a consultant on the map, provide the publicity that so many of us crave. But it is a double-edged sword, one that Frank Phelan, Sudeau's previous pollster, had recently experienced.

"I think your sources are impressive," I said. "But I'm honestly not sure I can add anything. It's not like the vice president's hiding something. Not that I know of anyway."

"Everyone in public life is hiding something," she said, her smile fading, a cold, harsh look of seriousness replacing it. "And the vice president is a big fish."

"You know my partner tends to be the public face of our company," I said. "He's the mouthpiece."

"Oh, I know Blair, believe me. Unfortunately he sounds just a little too, well, shady. Like the cool boyfriend a girl has to dump, even though he's tons of fun. He becomes more trouble than he's worth. You, on the other hand have an aura of, well, credibility. You come off as genuine. Viewers lap that up."

"I suppose I should take that as a compliment," I said.

She handed me her business card. "Let me know if you ever want to talk more. I help you, you help me. I might even be able to get you on air for a segment. Can't hurt to get your face in the public eye."

I slipped the card in my pocket and said I'd think about it. Never say never is a good motto to adhere to. And while I couldn't envision myself on television, there was something about Callie that I liked. Maybe it was her shrewd ability to see Blair unvarnished through the same lens in which I saw him. But her reference to me as something genuine was actually unnerving. I thought back to Blair's comment yesterday, in our meeting with Sudeau. *Once you can master authenticity, you've got it made.* But as I walked back to the office, I noticed I wasn't feeling so authentic today, and I didn't feel as if I had it made. In fact, I felt quite the opposite. I had tried to suppress the subject in my mind, but it inevitably came back to gnaw at me, the way unresolved problems always do. The chest x-ray that revealed a mass. The scans I had done this morning. The decision to keep my family out of the loop until I knew more. Things did not seem right.

Instead of going back to the office, I walked quickly into the subterranean garage and climbed into my Pilot and headed for home. Santa Monica was settling in to its normal afternoon gridlock, although for a change, I didn't mind. The traffic inching along San Vicente gave me time to think. I tried to decide whether to share my story with Leslie and Angelina. Whether I could release the burden I had carried with me for the past day. I thought of how I might disclose the tremulous news to the two most important people in my life. I tried to assess how best to move forward. What I ought to do. How I ought to do it.

But suddenly, the buzzing of my phone interrupted my thoughts. I punched the speaker button.

"This is Ned."

"Hi, Ned. It's Eli. Listen. Are you in Santa Monica? Can you come by the office?"

"Why?"

"I need to speak with you."

"Shit. No. Tell me now."

"I don't like to do this over the phone, Ned."

"Just tell me."

He cleared his throat. "Okay. Are you in a place where you can talk? It sounds like you're on the road. Maybe you should pull over."

"Sure," I said, as my stomach tightened. I swerved in front of a Mustang, just before Fourteenth Street. The Mustang's driver stopped long enough to offer me an angry stare and a reproachful middle finger before jamming his foot down on the accelerator and departing with a screech of tires. I slowed the Pilot to a stop in front of a huge Mediterranean-style home. The gated front yard was overgrown with roses of all colors. Some snaked their way up the wrought-iron gate that stood in front of the house.

"Is this what I think it is?" I asked.

Eli paused. "I'm sorry. Listen. I reviewed the radiology reports from the PET scan. A lot of things lit up. There are lesions in the pleural area. And in the nodes near the chest. It's spread to other organs."

"What does that mean?"

Once again, Eli waited a moment. "Look, there's no getting around it. I reviewed the cytology report. The lab tested the fluid they drained from your lung, and they found malignancies. And based on the scans, it looks like stage four."

"Yes, but again, what does that *mean*?" I repeated, this time with more than a hint of a tremor in my voice. "In English."

"It means," Eli said, his own voice now dark and gravelly. "You have cancer. it's spread beyond the lung, so it's inoperable. Metastatic. We can't simply remove this through surgery. It's just in too many places in your body."

I gulped, probably in an audible way. *You have cancer.* The words echoed through me. "What is my longevity?" I asked, refraining from adding the soldier's line of give-it-to-me-straight, Doc.

"Okay, let's not go there yet. There are advances being made. I'm going to set up an appointment for you with an oncologist, Gus Ashland. He's very good, he specializes in all types of cancer. He can provide you with some options. Bring Leslie. You're in shock right now, it helps to have your partner there. They hear things you'll miss. I'll try and get you in with Gus tomorrow morning. He's got a busy practice, but I'll ask him to make some time."

"Tomorrow?" I asked.

"Yes. The sooner the better. You shouldn't delay this. Lung cancer moves very fast."

Chapter 9

It was unclear just how long I sat parked in front of that magnificent home on San Vicente, staring endlessly at the roses crowding the front lawn. I replayed the conversation with Eli in my mind, before descending into worries, real and imagined. And then I returned to staring at the roses, their straggly vines and hooky thorns making the cluster of bushes in the front of the house look more like soldiers protecting a fortress.

My idle contemplation eventually came to an end, the sharp sound of a blaring horn jerking me back into the present. I looked over at an impatient woman driving a red Porsche Cayenne. She pointed at the house, annoyed and perturbed and gesticulating in a highly animated way. Apparently I was parked in front of her driveway. I silently apologized, slowly shifted gears, and gradually found my way home.

Our house was calm, empty and still. The silence offered me some time. Time to think, time to process, time to compartmentalize. Maybe time to mourn. Eli was probably right, I might well be in a state of shock. I knew this diagnosis might be coming, but nothing could have prepared me. And I was even less prepared to tell Leslie. And, oh dear God, Angelina. Before yesterday, I had never thought about my own death. My only thoughts of mortality lay in that conceptual framework, the knowledge that like every other living thing on the planet, I would one day succumb to the inevitable. Slide off the raft and into the dark abyss. Many decades from now.

My biggest concern was that I did not have many answers for my family. As always, I had more questions than answers. I liked to investigate, query, probe, and then probe some more. But now I was faced with the herculean task of informing my wife and child about an illness of which I had limited knowledge. There is no good handbook on how to tell your only child that you have a serious ailment, the likes of which might well prove fatal. I briefly toyed with the idea of not saying anything tonight, but that meant going to the oncologist tomorrow by myself. And it simply didn't feel right to *not* tell them. It was unfair and it was selfish. They deserved to know. The question was how much to impart.

There is a certain amount of information we withhold from others, no matter how close we are to them. Things that are kept unflinchingly private, hidden stories from our past, tales that we're either too uncomfortable discussing, or ones we simply never want anyone to know. But the advent of a terminal disease could not be classified as such, and given my impending appointment with Dr. Ashland, I needed to learn a lot in a short time. So, I began what I later discovered was frowned upon by the medical establishment, inadvisable for an enormity of reasons. I sat down at my computer and went on the internet.

There is no shortage of information on the Web, and certainly no dearth of opinions, be they amateur diagnoses or crackpot theories. I read articles of those who believed dogs were capable of assessing cancer through smelling a patient's breath. I sifted through the myriad of homegrown cures, from mixing cottage cheese and flaxseed oil to smoking a specific type of marijuana. I finally made it to what appeared like legitimate websites, ones imparting what might have been sound knowledge. But I also came upon a painful conundrum. Whereas the oddball sites, populated by random individuals of dubious stature, were at least encouraging, the more conventional websites were mortifying and dire.

Lung cancer is grouped into four stages. The first stage is where the tumor is just in the lung, and can be surgically removed. The second and third stages are where the tumor has grown and spread to various nearby lymph nodes. Stage four is where the cancer has metastasized, meaning it's expanded to other parts of the body. I heard Eli's words. *It looks like it's stage four.* I continued reading. There was no stage five.

There are times in our lives when we can physically sense we have entered a new phase. They can be times where we look fondly back upon the feeling of accomplishment. Be it piano recitals, scoring the winning goal in a ball game, graduation from school, first intimacy, first job, marriage, birth of a child. These are moments of lucidity, where we see ourselves propelled onto a different path, ones where we feel inexplicably changed and cannot change back. These are often the moments which mark our journey through life. The halcyon days that signify our time on earth. But the markers are not always good. And in this instance, I was forced to look at that sign post which pointed in another direction. Not the one from which I could springboard, but the one providing a glimpse of the time I might have left.

Stage four lung cancer. That was my diagnosis, that which would now define me. I combed through some articles, breezing past the technical discussions, the exegeses which tried to simplify reports in medical journals, but which only served to make them more cryptic. I moved quickly on to the statistics, the hard data from which I could distill something tangible, a lifeline to which I could cling, or at least in which I could immerse myself. I was briefly buoyed when I saw that almost one-quarter of lung cancer patients were non-smokers like me. But I also noted that some doctors drew the quick conclusion that lung cancer patients were smokers, hardheaded scoffers who had this fate coming to them. And as I sifted through the numbers, the lifeline quickly frayed. I trembled as I read the five-year survival rates detailing the life expectancy of stage four lung cancer patients. I had to look away from the glowing monitor, trying to blink away the percentages, the numbers that burned into my brain. The percentage of patients living five more years were in the single digits, unlikely and slim. And if less than ten percent would survive five years, the flip side of that sobering reality was that over ninety percent would not.

I felt the eerie stillness in the house and it made me jittery. Leslie and Angelina would be home soon, and I decided I needed to have a plan. Something to reassure them, a guide which would limit their fears, a pathway to provide them with some light in the grim darkness. It was not honest, but it was not unfair. I had been dealt a poor hand, a random grouping of cards that did not provide me with much confidence. But I felt the need to be strong, to maintain a steely resolve, to not allow my fate-scorched dilemma to infect my family. I would need to be something different than who I was, to evolve, to play a new role. I needed to avoid the most treacherous part, the risk of descending into that dark hole of self-pity. I thought back to something a high school teacher once said, an off-the-cuff remark that stuck with me. If you're not feeling brave, just fake it. No one will know the difference.

The faint hush of an engine became audible in the driveway, but was extinguished quickly. I heard excitement, Angelina's exuberance over something that happened in school, followed by the cautionary timbre of Leslie's voice, and then the tapping of footsteps on the flagstone path leading to the front door. The sliding of the key into the lock and the snapping sound that followed. The door opened and the molecules changed. Life entered our house, a vibrant energy, cheerful sounds bouncing off of the powder blue walls of the living room. My family was home, and a knot formed in my stomach as I prepared myself for the most difficult, most perplexing conversation of my life.

"We're home!" Leslie called, putting down a plastic bag.

"Daddy, I've got great news!" Angelina exclaimed.

"Okay," I managed.

"Aaron asked me to the prom!"

"Ah," I said, nowhere near as excited as my daughter.

"This is big news!" she insisted. "I've been working him for a month now. I even let his sister know that if he asked me, he'd get a definite yes!"

"Well," I said, not able to conjure up any further verbiage.

"Aren't you happy for me?" she asked, her expression more quizzical than deflated.

"Sure," I managed. "If you're happy, then, well ... "

"Is something wrong, Ned?" asked Leslie, looking carefully at me.

It is our partners that can often tell when we are hiding something. Whether it was the expression on my face, most likely grim, the lack of any lilt in my voice, or the overall dour essence exuding from me, Leslie had quickly sensed it. Most likely, it was my expression. I was not blessed with a poker face; rather, I had a face that was loaded with tells, those unconscious tics and habits that allow skilled observers to easily read thoughts.

"Yes," I said, maybe a little too forcefully, but for a brief moment I felt the strength that comes with releasing a true emotion. "Something is wrong."

"What is it, Daddy?"

"Yes, Ned. What is it?"

"Please sit down."

The two of them looked at each other and slowly eased onto the couch. I sat across from them in a rocking chair, an antique bentwood rocker we had purchased at a garage sale, one that Leslie loved and I did not. It looked more comfortable than it was. But the rocking provided me with a modicum of comfort, a back and forth swing that felt more reassuring than sitting motionless on a static chair.

"I need to tell you something."

Leslie frowned. "Does this have something to do with the vice president?"

"No," I said, my voice starting to crack. "It has to do with ... my visit to Eli. The chest x-ray. He saw something in it ... a small mass on my lung. He had me go in this morning and do scans. I also saw a respiratory specialist and they drained fluid from my lung. They believe it's ... cancer. Lung cancer."

"Oh, God, Ned." Leslie gasped.

"Daddy!" exclaimed Angelina. "How can that be? You're not a smoker!"

"It's not a requirement sweetheart. And I don't really know how I got it."

"Are you going to die?" she asked, the pool of tears forming in her blue eyes.

"No," I said and tried to smile, although I sensed I was failing. "I'm planning to live for a long time. We'll figure out a plan. There are treatments. There are options."

She attempted to process this. Leslie came across the room and kneeled down next to me, wrapping her arms around me in what might have started out as a hug, a comfort for me. But then she quickly buried her face into my chest and began to sob softly. I stroked her hair. Angelina moved to my other side and did the same thing. I opened my arms and drew them in, pulling them closer as they nestled their faces against me. I patted their shoulders and rubbed their arms.

It is often the stricken who are burdened with the need to dispense bad news. In so doing, we need to provide solace to loved ones, reassure them, qualm their fears, soothe them and bring them to a place of normalcy. A place of hope. Logic dictates that we, the affected, should be the ones to receive comfort, but the reverse is frequently the case. I had been afforded a small amount of time to process the news, my loved ones had not. My family needed an explanation, and perhaps a way to be shielded from the devastation, a task that was suddenly thrust upon me. It was ironic that the person who is diagnosed with the disease does not get this from their physician. Doctors, often experienced but unskilled in the sensitive art of providing bad news, mollify it as best they can, then let the patients sort out their emotions themselves. The patients are forced to shoulder that unfortunate responsibility, the staggering weight that comes with trying to remain calm in the face of an impending and frightening storm.

"What does Eli say?" Leslie sniffled.

"He's setting me up with an oncologist. I'm seeing him tomorrow. Can you go with me?"

"Of course."

"Daddy?" asked Angelina.

"Yes?"

"How can you be so sure you're going to live for a long time?"

I looked at her and didn't have a pat answer. Children inevitably discover their parents are fallible, not omniscient, and for bright kids that moment comes early. Angelina learned this years ago, most likely when I tried to give her advice on boys that didn't pan out. And not because I was necessarily wrong, it's simply that boys behave differently now than when I was their age. But the recognition sunk in, the sense that her father could be wrong, not knowing all there was to know. She had yet to grasp that there were just too many issues in the world, her father could not know everything. At some point she would be sympathetic. But when that point arrived, I suddenly realized, I might not be there to share it with her. I might be gone.

"The odds say that some patients will survive for a long period," I said, realizing my logic was not on firm ground, but also realizing I needed to say something. Anything. "There's no reason why I can't be one of those people."

The answer may or may not have satisfied Angelina, but she did not pursue it further. We huddled tightly for a while, separating long enough to order in a pizza, and spent the evening looking over old photos together, a hodgepodge of albums I had assembled over the years. They celebrated our life as a family, shots of us having fun, being silly, mugging and pouting for the camera, framing the years. But they were largely photos of Angelina, marking her growth and changes, freezing time accurately, in the way only still photos can do. I noticed that my face wasn't in a lot of these shots, the obvious reason being I was the one holding the camera. We smiled at the memories, but the warm glow didn't last long. They were fleeting moments of joy, a glimpse back at the past, but quickly punctured for me when my dark thoughts reemerged, the nagging fear of what the future might have in store for me.

I had not slept well the past few days, so Leslie gave me one of her sleeping pills, a drug called Dalmane. This was an old-school pharmaceutical that did a thorough job of knocking me out for eight hours, but it also left me groggy and in a daze when I awoke. A few cups of strong black coffee in the morning enabled me to slide back into the world. Together, we dropped Angelina off at school, her enclave in Brentwood, and headed off on our quest, to begin the next phase of our lives.

Chapter 10

The cancer business was booming. Dr. Gus Ashland had a thriving practice, with ten patients sitting nervously in the waiting room and another two dozen scattered about his clinic. Some sat in exam rooms, their doors only partially closed. Others reposed uneasily in thick chairs as they received chemotherapy infusions from tall, free-standing devices holding clear plastic drip bags. The machines would occasionally give off beeps, indicators that the process was working and the drugs were still seeping into veins.

I filled out reams of insurance forms, some asking about my condition, others requesting my Social Security number and driver's license, a tact to provide the clinic recourse in case I failed to pay my bill. After a short wait, a nurse escorted us into a sterile exam room and we sat quietly for another twenty-five minutes. A curious white poster was tacked to the wall. The poster instructed physicians on patient interaction, directed them to show empathy, ask questions about the patient's comfort and acknowledge the patient as an individual. The poster included a list of recommended questions to ask. There was also a reminder at the bottom that physicians would be evaluated by patient satisfaction surveys, and their bonus would be partially dependent upon achieving outstanding scores. It struck me as the type of survey Blair and I had conducted for corporations evaluating their customer service reps.

The door opened, and a serious-looking man entered, his salt-and-pepper beard making him look distinguished and important. He wore the physician's standard white lab coat, and carried both a folder and an iPad into the room. Placing them down on the counter, he opened the folder and scanned through a few documents, silently reading for a minute before looking up and introducing himself to us.

"I'm Gus Ashland," he said, holding out a hand. "I understand you're friends with Elijah Sterling."

"From college. Berkeley. Known him for over thirty years."

"Eli's a good man," he said.

I agreed and introduced Leslie. She shook his hand silently, her lips pressed tightly together. Leslie had hardly spoken this morning, unlike her in many ways, she was obviously still processing all of this. I sensed the shock of the diagnosis could be greater for her. In addition to feeling horribly for me, she no doubt felt badly for herself and Angelina, perhaps conjuring up a future far different from the one she had planned. I wanted to ask her about her feelings, but doing so might require me to share the depth of mine, something I was woefully unprepared to do.

"I've looked through your scans," he said, picking up the iPad and tapping it a few times. "And also your charts. But first, tell me about the pain in your back. Scale of one to ten, one being hardly any and ten being excruciating. What would you rate it?"

"Right now it's a zero," I said, moving into that comfort zone I had when dealing with data, a topic far easier than providing a qualitative assessment of my emotions. "Having the fluid drained from my lung worked for the back pain. Before that, I'd been taking Advil. About eight to ten tablets a day. Without it, I might have rated the pain a seven."

"That's a lot of Advil," he cautioned. "And draining the fluid is only a temporary stop gap measure. The fluid will probably gather again. Was it a constant pain?"

"Only when I breathed deeply."

Dr. Ashland typed something into his iPad. "We'll need to do a permanent procedure to stop the fluid from building up in the lung. It will require a hospital stay for a few days. The procedure's called a pleurodesis, we use talcum powder. It seals the pleural area so the fluid won't have a place to gather."

"Where will the fluid go then?"

Dr. Ashland smiled and kept tapping into his iPad. "The fluid will just go back into your body the way it normally should. We also need to do a biopsy of the tumor in the lung; we can do that at the same time. Kill two birds with one stone."

I choked in some air. "Poor choice of words," I managed.

He stopped and looked up. "Sorry."

"Can we figure out how Ned got this disease?" Leslie asked, her voice shaky.

Dr. Ashland shrugged. "Probably not. It says here he's a non-smoker. And you haven't lived in an area with high radon levels. Or any exposure to asbestos. It's possible air pollution was a factor. It might be genetic, even though it says here your parents are in their eighties, and they never had cancer. Possibly a recessive gene. There are just some things we don't know. Oncology is better at assessing how to move forward than analyzing what went wrong in the past."

"So just how *do* we move forward here?" I asked. "What are my options?"

"There have been a lot of advances in lung cancer treatments in the past few years. I've helped enroll some stage four patients into clinical trials. I do have a few who've been living for three years on these new drugs. It's been amazing."

Next to me I heard Leslie gasp. She beat me to the punch. *Three years.* For someone who had just turned fifty, whose parents and grandparents had all lived into their eighties, the mere possibility that my mortality could be short-circuited so fast and so abruptly was gut-wrenching. The doctor seemed to read this on my face.

"Okay. I know you're probably worried. But once we do a biopsy, we can test the tumor for genetic mutations. There are some targeted drugs that have been approved, and some more are in the pipeline. We're seeing cancer treatments evolve. It's no longer just a terminal illness. Medicine is aiming to make lung cancer a chronic condition. There are a lot of people living a long time with cancer, far more than you might suspect. It's becoming something that can be managed."

I tried to take this in. "What are genetic mutations?" I

asked. I looked over at Leslie and was glad she was with me. Between the two of us, maybe we could piece all this together.

"Well, to put it simply, those mutations are critical to understanding how to treat cancer these days. We can now identify many of the genetic mutations, and we have drugs that can treat certain types of tumors. We know if you have, say, the EGFR mutation, we can treat it with Tarceva. It's a pill you take twice a day."

"And a mutation is ... ?"

"Oh, I'm sorry," he said with a wave of the hand. "Genetic mutations are changes to your genes that can be linked to the type of cancer you have. These mutations are typically only found in cancer cells. If we can identify the mutation, we may have a drug that can inhibit the cancer from growing and spreading."

"And if you can't identify this ... mutation?" Leslie managed.

"We can treat it with chemotherapy, it can be very effective. It's an aggressive treatment, It does have side effects, but for some patients, it can add years to their lives."

I shuddered at the burgeoning sense that this nightmare was starting to feel real. That this wasn't a dream someone would gently end by nudging me out of a slumber. I knew very little about cancer, except that chemotherapy was a veiled poison, a shotgun blast of toxin that was injected into your body, a rolling barrel of chemicals that killed whatever was in its path. My recollection was it did not differentiate between healthy cells and cancer cells.

"Will any of this ... cure him?" asked Leslie.

Dr. Ashland paused. I didn't like pauses. They were often made for dramatic purposes, a signal that something untenable was in the offing. As if the doctor was trying to search for the right words, but in reality, he was allowing the emptiness of silence to provide a smoke signal for his thoughts, the ones he knew we did not want to hear.

"No," he finally said. "These drugs can control the cancer, reduce the size of the tumor, prevent it from spreading. It can put the brakes on the disease for a while. Sometimes for years. But the cancer cells are often able to adapt, they're difficult to eradicate completely. And like I said, there may be other options. If you can take a pill, that's better than taking chemo. And we're entering a new frontier in science, we're honestly not sure how long these pills will work on patients. Maybe a few months, maybe for many years. We don't know yet. But the pills have fewer side effects, and people can generally tolerate pills easier than chemo."

"But they won't rid my body of the tumors?" I asked.

He shook his head and began to frown. "Not necessarily. At least not permanently. We're making strides. But even these targeted treatments aren't guaranteed to last forever. At best they'll work for a few years. The trick is to keep you around for the next breakthrough drug to come along."

The comment hung in the air. *Keep you around.* The harsh clarity of his words formed a dark cloud that elongated the moment, stretching the awkwardness. My mind started to wander and I vaguely considered if I should direct him back to the list of humanizing doctor questions that were tastelessly fastened to the wall.

"You said something about three years," I said slowly, working to not stammer. "Is that typical?"

"Look, with cancer, there is nothing typical. Everyone responds differently to these treatments."

"I understand the five-year survival rate is low. Single digits."

He shook his head, almost vehemently. "Those survival curves are always out of date. You're referring to the Kaplan-Meier curves. I admit, they may look grim to an untrained eye. But next time you look at one of those, you'll see the tail of the curve extend for many years. There are always patients who outlive expectations. I even know one who outlived his oncologist."

I smiled, albeit very briefly, and asked the question that had been rolling around in my mind for the past day. "So you're saying there Is a chance, a possibility I might live into my eighties? I'm fifty now."

Dr. Ashland wiped his face with a broad hand and thought hard for a long moment. "I have one patient that's been with me for twelve years. We just don't know why. Not yet."

I sighed. The not knowing was the great difficulty, but also, at the same time, the greatest encouragement. It is the blind alley into which I was about to plunge, not aware of the direction in which I was going, only that it was better to be moving forward than remaining stationary. Because by doing something, anything, we can maintain a hope in the unseen, as fleeting and elusive as it might be.

"I have some more questions," I said. "I hope that's all right."

"Of course," he said. "In fact, Eli told me you ask questions for a living. Are you a journalist?"

"Not exactly. Market research. I conduct surveys and focus groups. But yes, that's what I do. I ask people things."

"All right. Go ahead."

"What if I do nothing?" I started, asking my Hail Mary question, the type of query one hopes and prays will be answered with a rejoinder that is cloaked with possibilities. "Is there any chance this could just fix itself and go away?"

"The ostrich strategy," he mused, as he began to swat this option down. "No, that's not a good plan here. Some cancers grow over a period of years. Lung cancer grows over a period of months. Doing nothing will simply bring the end about quicker."

I nodded cautiously and thought briefly about my client, the Garter Vitamin Company. "What about supplements? Do herbal or homeopathic cures work?"

Dr. Ashland smiled patiently. "You've been on the internet, I see. Not a great idea. Lots of scams, and lots of information that's outdated. There might be that one in a million patient who actually sees their cancer reversed by taking herbs, but I can assure you, Western medicine is light years ahead of these things. Taking herbal remedies is tantamount to doing nothing. It might make you feel good about yourself, but they're just not effective."

"Is immunotherapy an option?"

Dr. Ashland took a cautionary breath. "I wouldn't rule it out. But right now, immunotherapy works best on solid tumors. We release a small strain of a virus into your body, and your immune system gathers strength to attack it, and in so doing it will also attack the cancer. But two issues. One is that your cancer has spread to the nodes, meaning the cancer cells have become diffuse and it's harder to eradicate. But also, immunotherapy's a new treatment, and we're experimenting here. There have been cases where the immune system has overreacted to the virus strain, so much so that it can also overwhelm the body, to the point of possibly being fatal."

"Meaning the cure is worse than the disease?"

"In some ways, yes."

"Okay," I said, continuing my mental checklist, but sensing a growing discouragement taking shape inside me. "And how much good does a positive attitude do?"

"Actually, that means a lot," he said surprisingly, and getting my rapt attention for a moment. "In terms of quality of life. The way in which you view treatment is important. It can be the difference between tolerating side effects and being overwhelmed by them. But in the end, it all comes down to the efficacy of the drugs. Will they work on you. We've entered the era of personalized medicine. We just need to figure out which drug will work best on your tumors."

"But these drugs won't last forever?" Leslie managed. "The effectiveness stops after a while?"

"Yes. Unfortunately, few things last forever. The cancer

cells outsmart the treatment by rearranging themselves. It's been an extraordinarily difficult disease to attack. Eventually I think we'll find a cure. We have to. There are millions of cancer patients out there. More than you can imagine. The saddest part is some have it and they don't even know. You're a little further along because at least you're aware. We can take steps. Again, the goal is to keep you around long enough for the next new drug to become available."

"You mean like for a clinical trial you mentioned earlier?"

"Possibly, yes."

"How do I get into one of these clinical trials?"

The doctor's mouth tightened. "It depends. Some trials have strict requirements. We'll look into all of these. But bear in mind, a clinical trial is an experiment. There's no guarantee it will work. Or work for everyone. We're making advances. But we're not there yet."

My mood was descending from dark to darker. It wasn't the doctor's fault, he was just passing along his knowledge. He did not sugarcoat my situation, but neither did he provide me with sufficient encouragement. I had wanted to bounce out of his office, brimming with hope, but at this stage, I was more concerned I would slink out, reeling with dread, looking for the nearest roof from which to jump.

"If I'm this bad off," I said, "why do I feel okay?"

Dr. Ashland's grimaced. "Cancer often works silently. You don't know you have it, often until it's in the late stages. Especially with lung cancer. I wish we had caught it earlier. But the pain in your back was the only tell."

"I see."

"I'd like to schedule you for the pleurodesis as soon as possible," he said, closing down his iPad, signaling our meeting was drawing to a close. "Today's Thursday. We'll need to get insurance approval, but pending that, are you available next week?"

I said yes, albeit with a hint of trepidation.

"Don't worry, this is the easy part. I know an excellent thoracic surgeon. Once we do the biopsy we'll be better able to lay out the options. Let me get my assistant to check on scheduling this."

The doctor departed and I looked at Leslie. No words were spoken, but I saw the anxieties that sat pleadingly on her face. I saw a trickle of a tear slink down her cheek. I did not tell her everything would be all right. I wanted to, but I couldn't even tell myself that. The heavy pall we were immersed in was preventing us from speaking. The only sound in the room was our breathing, erratic, uneven, cloistered.

My own response to hearing the doctor was less anxiety, but more sadness, the maudlin feeling as I thought of Leslie, and especially Angelina. That my own mortality was staring me in the face bothered me less than the thought that my precious daughter could be entering adulthood without a father to guide her. That she was seventeen and needed little tending to was not the issue. She simply needed me to be there, even if it were in the shadows, close yet distant, available in the off chance she needed a father's touch, an encouraging word, a confident gesture. It is the same-sex parent who teaches a child the tangible things they need to become a functioning adult. It is the opposite-sex parent who validates, who provides the ethereal moments, the reassurance that can allow them to soar.

Dr. Ashland returned a few minutes later. "We can get you in next week for the biopsy," he said, jotting a few more notes on his iPad. "Just go back to your daily routine. In my experience, maintaining your normal life is the best medicine for now. What were you planning to do today?"

I took another deep breath. It felt good. No pain. "Helping Richard Sudeau become the next President of the United States."

He stopped what he was doing. "Really?"

"Yes. I'm planning to moderate focus groups among likely voters."

The doctor looked at me and said nothing. I imagined this was not how most of his patients planned to spend the rest of their day after having reviewed options for treating a terminal illness. *Three years.* The thought of my dwindling longevity raced through my mind, but so did the more horrifying thought of sitting at home, wasting away, idling through my time, waiting for the grim reaper to appear.

"Ned, is that a good idea?" Leslie asked. "With all of what you have going on?"

"I don't know," I said. "And I'm not sure how well I can concentrate, to be honest. But it beats dwelling on it. Anything beats thinking about this right now. Work isn't supposed to be a diversion, but in this case it might be my salvation. Talking to voters about an upcoming election. Wouldn't you agree, doctor?"

Leslie looked down at the floor. The nurse looked out the window. Dr. Gus Ashland closed down his iPad and smiled before answering. "If I were a Democrat, I suppose I might."

Chapter 11

Ignoring Leslie's protestations, I went straight back to the office and finished writing the discussion guide for the focus groups. I checked with Wanda about recruiting, fielded a phone call from a nervous Randy Greece, and endured a brief pep talk from Blair before finally deciding to get away from the office. I drove over to the focus group facility, which was tucked away in the twentieth floor of a high-rise building in Westwood, not far from UCLA. I had three hours before the groups began, which meant I would have two and a half hours of peace and quiet.

A focus group is a roundtable discussion. A group of ten strangers sitting awkwardly together, talking about anything from how they shop for a new car to why eating healthy is important in their lives. Or, as I discovered watching Haley moderate groups last week, what their sexual habits were like. It is amazing how open and forthcoming people will be with the most intimate and precious details of their personal lives. All it takes is someone asking them the right questions in the right sequence, using the right demeanor. And in the right setting. Push the buttons correctly and they'll reveal things they haven't told their own families or their best friends. I've had people begin crying as they discussed a painful experience, a situation where I needed to jump in quickly to lighten the mood. I've had other cases where people passionately disagreed to the point where they were ready to step outside and settle the discussion *mano a mano.*

Moderating focus groups is admittedly my stretch project. It forces me out of my bubble and makes me engage me with strangers. I have to interact with people, to be physically in the same room with them, yet also manage to hide in plain sight. I lead the discussion with pointed questions, but without having to provide any answers. I am the passive, impartial conduit in the middle of a fishbowl, keenly aware we are being watched by others. In the best of circumstances, the discussion takes on a life of its own, where I can sit back and listen and pretend to be part of the group, among them, yet apart. I probe and I prod, gauge feelings, and largely keep the conversation rolling. My job is to elicit as much information from these consumers as I can within a two-hour session. In return, the consumers receive about a hundred dollars for participating. In a good session, everyone leaves happy, content in the knowledge that their views might contribute to how a company shapes their strategy. Or perhaps they change their perceptions of the vice president of the United States.

When participants enter a focus group room they see two things right away. One is a large table that can seat about a dozen people, and the other is an elongated mirror which often extends across an entire wall. The mirror is called a one-way mirror, because inside the focus group room people can only see their reflections. In the viewing room, however, the mirror, coated with a thin layer of aluminum, resembles a tinted pane of glass, a convenient partition separating the focus group participants from the business executives who gather and observe. And unlike the cheap sandwiches and cans of soda for those partaking in the discussion, the executives, hidden away, dine on catered meals, bottles of wine, and mountains of M&Ms.

I've been fortunate to have been cast in all of the focus group roles, albeit at different times of my life. As a college student, I learned this was an easy way to land some extra spending money. As a moderator, I've sat inside the room, guiding the discussion and eliciting thoughts and feelings. And as a boss, I've watched my employees moderate, changing my role to managing executives' perceptions of the conversation. That role is usually more delicate, often forcing me to caution excitable businesspeople from drawing too-quick conclusions which can arise from one or two strongly voiced opinions.

The satisfaction for me normally emanates later, distilling all of the opinions into a cohesive summary, culling remarks and thoughts into a perspective, trying to marry conflicting points-of-view that can summarize a two hour group discussion. For some moderators, the fun part is to interact with people. For me, it is interacting with data, and transforming that into insights.

I sat alone in the viewing room, spending time studying my discussion guide, the list of pointed, sometimes provocative questions which would spur conversation and shine a light on certain topics. About thirty minutes before the first group started, Randy Greece called again from Washington to request I add a few questions about

Richard Sudeau's family, his wife, his two kids, his four dogs, or anything else which might yield a few nuggets into how voters viewed his personal life.

"We want to know how much appeal Amber has, how much do they really know about Rich's wife, are they aware she had a political career of her own once, that she was a congresswoman and held a cabinet position. Does it matter that Rich had two kids who served in the Marines? Does having four dogs humanize him? That sort of thing."

"Got it," I said, jotting a few notes onto the discussion guide. "So, is anyone from the campaign attending tonight in person?"

"I'm sending a couple of junior people, but no, the main campaign staff will watch it streaming. Good luck. We know you're going to do a great job."

About fifteen minutes later, in walked Blair, Wanda, and a pair of clean-cut young men wearing oxford cloth shirts, tan khakis and cordovan topsiders. They were attractive, had an air of entitlement about them, and looked as if they had just stepped out of a Land's End catalogue. Both carried expensive-looking briefcases. Their names were Sam and Jason.

"You guys been working for Rich Sudeau long?" I asked.

"Well ... not exactly. We're interns. Summer job and all. We just finished our junior year at Yale."

"These two fellas," crowed Blair, "are the future of the Democratic Party. They'll be running for office soon. Keep an eye on them, we'll be managing their campaigns one day. Terrific kids!"

One of them smiled shyly, the other flat-out blushed. "I don't know about that," one of them managed as they took seats, genteelly spooning out portions of peanut M&Ms into small bowls before nibbling. Blair put his arm around my shoulder and walked me out of the viewing room.

"Okay, this came straight from Greece," he said as we strolled down the hallway. "They're thinking of shifting the focus to Rich's personal qualities, and emphasize his background. See if his family man qualities shine through. Amber's a big part of that. By the way, her Secret Service code name is Pandora. Isn't that something? Sudeau's is Peacock. Boy, those Secret Service guys are something, aren't they?"

"Uh-huh," I mumbled."Look, I already heard about this from Greece. It's in the discussion guide."

"Yeah I know, he just wants to make sure. Sounded a little uptight about things. Running a campaign will do that to a person. Makes you do all sorts of crazy stuff. Lot of pressure and all."

"Right," I said, knowing it wasn't the first time we'd dealt with a high maintenance client, but it was never fun. "Whatever."

"Whatever is good. Hey, you feeling okay? You're still worrying me."

"I'm fine," I lied.

"That back of yours still hurting?"

"Actually, no. Got it cleared up."

"Chiropractor?" he winked.

"Something like that."

"Great. Nothing worse than back problem. The pain is

just killer. Glad you're ready. I don't mean to put pressure on you, but this is the most important thing you've ever done in your life, and probably ever will do. I spoke to Sudeau this morning, reassured him and all. I'm convinced that if the groups go well, we're in. This is what we've been waiting for. This is what we've been working toward. This is the Super Bowl we're headed into. If we get onto the Sudeau ship, we're sailing for life. Even if he loses, our names'll be in the national conversation for years. You gotta work your magic tonight."

"Glad you're not putting extra pressure on me," I said, but managed to smile.

"You know the score," he said. "I just gotta remind you."

"So what do you think is going on with these interns?"

"Beats me. I'll keep 'em in line. If they get too animated I'll sic Wanda on them."

We returned to the viewing room and waited for the first focus group to arrive and be seated. I sipped on some black coffee and felt good. My back pain had indeed vanished. I appeared to be in perfect health, although I clearly was not. I was struggling to keep the demons of depression at bay, centering my thoughts on the work, and not on the illness. I envied those people who could easily compartmentalize their issues, storing and retrieving them at will. That innate ability to patently choose and discard specific thoughts. My own thoughts required more effort to control, and the toxic ones oozed through all too often.

The hostess opened the door and asked if I was ready. I

told her she could bring in the first group. A minute later I watched them file into the room, unsteady at first, looking around, curious, a bit bewildered. They hesitatingly took seats around the table and set down their name tents, folded pieces of cardboard with their first names scrawled in bold marker. I had sat my name tent at the head of the table, the bright blue NED claiming my place as the leader. I found it interesting to watch this progression. The agreeable ones often positioned themselves directly to the moderator's right, as if it were their role to be the assistant. In biblical times, the aides seated to the leader's right were their trusted advisors. Eventually the term *right hand man* was coined as a result.

The group was indeed representative of California, although on the surface, it might not have reflected America. Of the ten, only four were Caucasian, the rest being an eclectic mix of African-American, Latino, Asian plus one woman who appeared to be Middle Eastern. It was a diverse group, a hodgepodge of the great experiment that was Los Angeles. An argument could be made that this collection of people represented what America was evolving toward. On short notice though, this was the type of group that got recruited in L.A., ten random people whose main commonality was that they were registered Democrats and that they voted. And had a pulse. Such is the spurious world of political research.

I left the darkened viewing room and walked briefly down the hallway. I tried to ignore Blair's words, his version of encouragement, something he thought would put me at the top of my game and not make me a nervous wreck. In all the years I'd known him, he still didn't understand what made me tick. Most likely because he thought everyone viewed the world through the same lens that he did.

Opening the nearest door down the corridor, I entered the brightly lit focus group room. The change in lighting was stark. I felt as if I were now on an illuminated stage, the hot white glare of the spotlight bearing down harshly. All eyes in the room turned toward me.

"Welcome," I boomed in my most authoritarian voice, taking care to paste a smile on my face. "Thank you all for coming tonight."

A brief and dim murmur of hellos was audible. I sat down and quickly ran through what we'd be doing. That we were here as a group, but I was interested in them as individuals. That everyone's opinion mattered, and to be respectful of others' views. To not interrupt or talk over each other. I told them we'd be discussing politics, and a few sighs could be heard around the table. This was hardly a shock to me, having conducted an abundance of research. Americans have come to view politics as distasteful, and there is no consensus on how to fix this, aside from having those who disagreed with them be moved far, far away.

"You all have one thing in common," I told them. "One thing we know of, anyway. You're all registered Democrats. Anyone here who isn't?"

I looked around the room. No one spoke. Finally, a man in his fifties with a graying goatee covering a pudgy reddened face gave the hint of a smug smile. The name Ed was scrawled on the name card in front of him.

"Good," he said. "No enemies in the midst."

There were chuckles, and the mood lightened. I started the discussion by asking everyone to write down the qualities they wanted in a president. By writing it on paper, they wouldn't be influenced by another person, and they would be asked to read aloud and commit to what they wrote. Groupthink in focus groups is a problem, and one or two dominators can be overpowering. The responses I heard when the group read their presidential requirements out loud was not surprising. Strength, fairness, intelligence and honesty were repeated over and over. But the last person, a Latino man named Rafael, said he wanted someone who could relate to the common man. Someone who understood how hard it is to get by. I asked if there were any politicians out there they thought had these qualities. A few were mentioned, but the name Rich Sudeau was not among them.

I then passed around a sheet of paper with a description on it, about a presidential candidate who came from humble origins, whose parents were troubled and had illness and addiction issues. A candidate who earned a scholarship at a top university, worked his way through law school, and managed to become a United States senator without having much money. I did not include anything about his political views, just his personal life. There were visual nods and approving comments. When I asked them to write down a one-to-ten rating on how interested they would be in learning more about this candidate, nearly everyone gave the candidate a ten.

Then I threw out some names of leading politicians, asking what they thought of them. The comments were middling, none were igniting much excitement.

"What about Richard Sudeau?" I finally suggested. "What do you think of him?"

The reaction was mostly one of silence, the whirring of the air conditioning the only sound in the room.

"He does look nice," an African-American woman named Tanya finally said. "Like a president ought to look. Like Kennedy. Right out of central casting."

"But," said Rafael finally. "I don't know much about him. I mean sure, he's the vice president and all. And I did vote for him, but mainly because he was on the ticket with the president. Can't split your vote on that one."

"Yes, I would agree," said the Middle-Eastern woman named Roo. "No one cares much about the vice president. You vote for the top of the ticket."

"Heck," replied Ed, the man with the gray goatee, "someone once said the Vice Presidency isn't worth a warm pitcher of spit. No wonder we don't know much about his background. Doesn't matter. Unless he becomes president, of course."

There were a few smiles, but the discussion reminded me of something I learned in an American History class in high school. Many years ago, there was a politician named Alben Barkley. In the middle of the last century, 1950 or so, a research company conducted a poll in President Harry Truman's home state of Missouri. They asked voters about Alben Barkley, if they knew who he was. The majority did not. The pollsters were surprised at this, but judging by the comments I was hearing now, perhaps they shouldn't have been. At the time, Alben Barkley was actually the sitting vice president of the United States.

"So, take a look at that description I handed out a few minutes ago," I continued. "About the man who came from modest circumstances. What if I told you that man was Richard Sudeau. That was his story. What do you think of him now?"

Heads began to nod, as the group re-read the description and re-thought their view of the current vice president. Lips were pursed impressively, chins were rubbed thoughtfully, and you could practically see the collective gears in their heads begin to turn.

"I had no idea."

"Sounds interesting to me. But I'd want to know more about him."

"His background is like my background. I didn't have it so easy growing up. I had to work for everything I got."

"Damn. How come he don't talk about this? Sounds like he's been hiding something."

"I thought he was just another rich, out-of-touch politician. Just like all the others. Now I wonder if he's a fraud. This makes a difference."

Indeed it did. And the more we talked about Richard Sudeau in this light, the odder he sounded to everyone. Inauthentic and confusing, at least to the people who knew a little about him. In some ways it helped that Sudeau's background had been a mystery to most people. In the marketing world, it is far easier to build a brand from nothing than to take a damaged brand and try to improve it. Painting on a fresh canvas is more effective. But it was nevertheless a concern when a candidate who had spent decades in politics had no image. When held up to the light, he didn't so much as throw a shadow.

Toward the end of the first focus group, one of the clean-cut young men from Yale walked into the room and handed me a note. This was not uncommon in focus group settings. Observers often have special questions they want the moderator to ask, things that might not have been in the plans. I just wasn't expecting this from an intern; I first thought Blair might have sent these in, but judging by the questions, that was unlikely.

"So," I said, unfolding the note and scanning it quickly. "Let me ask you something else. What do you know about Amber Sudeau?"

"Who's that again?" asked Rafael.

"The vice president's wife," I clarified. "Any thoughts about her? Any at all?"

"She used to be a politician herself, too, right?" said Lizzy, a white woman in her thirties.

"Oh, yeah," mused Rafael. "Now I remember her name. Amber. Kind of unusual."

"I like her," said Tanya. "She fits nicely with him. They make a good couple."

"Is that important?" I asked.

"Sure is," Ed broke in. "Best decision a man makes is who he marries."

"You've got that one wrong, Ed. The women are the deciders!" Tanya declared, and everyone around the room started to laugh. "Don't you know that?"

Ed got a little red in the face, but smiled anyway. "Yeah, I guess."

We continued to talk about the vice president. The more I probed, the more they liked the idea of Richard and Amber Sudeau in the White House. I passed around a photo of the two of them, dynamic and attractive, and heads began to nod approvingly. The group began to forget about the confusion surrounding Rich's background. They like having a pair of savvy, experienced leaders. Two for the price of one. A man who was born into a heinous situation, but managed to pulled himself out of it. He married wisely. And most importantly, Richard Sudeau reminded them not of themselves, but of what they might have liked to have become in similar circumstances. It almost felt like they could live vicariously through him. I finished by trotting out the projective exercise, asking the group to write down what Richard Sudeau would be if Sudeau were a car.

"A Cadillac," said Lizzy. "Something old school."

"I think a Mustang," Ed offered. "From like the sixties."

"Maybe a Nissan 350Z. Kind of like the old sports cars, but updated for today."

"That's great," I smiled.

I started to thank the group and prep them to leave, cautioning them not to say anything on the way out because there was a new group sitting in the waiting room, ready to come in. I didn't want the new group to overhear what we had been discussing over the past two hours. Then one of the interns walked into the room and handed me another note. It directed me to ask the same projective question of Amber.

"She's a Prius. Love the whole idea of that car. Good for the environment."

"A Tesla. New and exciting," Tanya gushed.

"She'd be something classy," Ken said. "Like an Audi."

"Maybe," Ed laughed and winked, "something with a nice, roomy back seat."

A burst of laughter erupted, albeit more from the men in the room. The women mostly rolled their eyes.

"And just what are you really saying, Ed?" asked Lizzy in a playful way.

"Oh, well judging from her picture," he responded. "For a gal her age, she's kinda hot."

I smiled paternally, quickly thanked the group, and got them out of the room before any more salacious and potentially degrading comments could be uttered. I again admonished them to be quiet until they reached the parking level, and I dismissed them with a reminder to stop by the front desk and pick up their check. Smiling at them as they departed, I gave silent thanks that for a few hours I was able to put aside my troubles and concentrate on something else. Work can sometimes be a blessing.

The second group dredged up more of the same attitudes, initial indifference to Richard Sudeau, the perception of him as a product of an indulged upbringing, a sycophant perhaps, but certainly an elitist. They exhibited the same surprise at his actual background, and gravitated toward the same solidarity, skeptical but open to considering him. And yet the best thing about Rich

Sudeau was again his wife, not well known, but oddly well liked. The vice president was surely going to be pleased with what these groups were saying, even though they were twenty responses culled from focus groups, far from a valid, quantitative sample. But focus groups offered something that raw numbers could not: a visceral response, a shift you could see, hear, feel, and practically taste. The reaction in the back room was jubilant when I walked in at the end of the second group.

"Bravo!" crowed Blair. "Great job!"

Wanda smiled. "That was amazing. I never thought I'd hear that the best thing about a candidate was his wife!"

"You never know," I smiled.

A cell phone jingled, an electronic version of one of those old-fashioned rings that sounded like it was emanating out of a phone from a half-century ago. One of the interns answered and held it outstretched.

"It's Randy Greece. He'd like to speak with you."

I took the phone and said hello.

"Ned, that was fascinating," he gushed. "Really happy at the results. Very encouraging. Loved it. Listen, I just got off the phone with Rich. He'd like to debrief with you."

"Sure, patch him through."

"No, no. He's in L.A. And not too far from Westwood, he's staying at the Century Plaza. He wants to meet in person. It's five minutes from you."

"He didn't watch the groups?"

"Nope, he's been at a fundraiser tonight. But he just got back to his suite. He's waiting for you."

"All right," I said, thinking we could just as easily have

talked on the phone, but when the vice president asks you for something, especially when he's about to become a high-paying client, you do what he wants.

"He's pretty tired, so don't spend too much time there. Just give him a quick recap."

"All right."

"Oh, and one other thing," Greece said.

"What's that?"

"He said he just wants to speak with you. No one else. Come alone."

Chapter 12

The vice president heard the series of cracks, the sudden, unseen danger, but he had no time to react. In a split second his body was jerked back against the sliding glass door. And then suddenly, he was on the ground gasping for air. The cracking noises stopped and it became eerily quiet. He rolled on the floor of the balcony, his legs banging against the metal railing as he thrashed desperately, gravely, trying to breathe. His lungs strained, and he worked with all his might to inhale.

This wasn't supposed to happen. He was meant to become president, it was his destiny, his reward for everything he had endured. This was not the way his final seconds were supposed to play out. He tried in vain to cry for help, but no sound emerged. He tasted the blood in his mouth. He saw the darkened sky, a murky gray path, devoid of stars. And then quietly, slowly, the L.A. night began to slip away from him ...

Two blocks away, the Assassin watched it all through the night vision scope mounted atop his M107. In most jobs, he normally took out his target with just one shot, but this assignment was different. There would only be one opportunity, and it would never present itself again. The moment could not be squandered, a clear kill was an absolute must. He had quickly squeezed out four rounds, connecting on all four. He had nailed a head shot, followed by three rounds which had torn through the upper torso. He allowed himself a long moment of self-congratulations, ogling his prey, knowing he had completed the job, and it was a job well done.

The Assassin stroked his fake black beard, taking pains to make sure it was still pressed tightly on his face. And with that, he left his rifle sitting on the bi-pod, but moved it a few feet away from the window. The FBI would be here soon enough. It would take them a few hours, maybe until the morning, when the sky would lighten again. There were, after all, only a few select spots where a sharpshooter could have nested. And once someone noticed the gaping hole in the window, the Feds would be all over this spot. He took one last look around the office.

The sniper rifle and the bi-pod would be left behind, souvenirs for the FBI. They would lead the agents down a primrose path to nowhere. There were no fingerprints on them, no DNA, and they were in no way traceable back to the Assassin. These models retailed for ten thousand dollars apiece, but they had cost him nothing. That was an advantage of having once worked for the Company, where he had discovered a small cache of weapons being stored by one of the Mexican drug cartels. These rifles never found their way onto the inventory sheet, in fact he still had one more sitting quietly in a safe house near Juarez. The cost of leaving evidence on the floor of the crime scene tonight was minimal. The bigger risk would be if he were caught carrying his equipment out of the office building. Leaving the evidence behind meant any connection that could be linked back to him was purely circumstantial. He just needed to exit the building posthaste, but without being perceived as hurrying.

The Assassin moved swiftly to the elevators and pushed the down button, but there was no response. Strange. He jogged back up the stairs to thirty-four and accessed the elevator there, riding it down to the plaza level, removing his latex gloves on the way. He placed them in his briefcase, snapped it closed, and put his black-framed glasses back on. He made sure to give a weary smile to the security guard, and mentioned to him it had been quite a long evening of work. A different Secret Service agent stood nearby, observing his movements, but stifling a yawn. Across the lobby, another agent was sitting on a chair, sipping coffee out of a Styrofoam cup.

Signing out rapidly with his own pen, he scribbled the name Richard Cheney. He smugly thought this was a nice touch. He also wrote the first three names of the law firm that had the gilded logo next to it, along with the exact time of his departure. Ten fifty-six. No one bothered to inspect what he wrote. Walking quickly out into the night air, he waited for the light to change on Constellation Boulevard. It was off to the parking garage in the mall now, where he had left his rented black Mercedes. He liked Los Angeles. The patchwork sprawl of the city was disorienting to some, but he found it comforting. He could rent a luxury car, and no one at the rental counter would remember him. No one would think he was special. Everyone seemed to live stylishly here, whether they could afford to or not. He blended in well.

Out of the corner of his eye, he saw two men, Secret Service agents for sure, racing from the hotel grounds toward the office tower. He smiled to himself as the light changed and he calmly entered the crosswalk. He'd be in the garage in a matter of seconds, and by then, he'd have disappeared into the wind. But as he crossed the street, he noticed a silver BMW stopped at the light. The woman behind the wheel was looking over at him, the hint of scrutiny on her face. Their eyes locked for a brief moment and he thought he saw her lips part in recognition. No, this couldn't be. No one could recall him with the beard. Or the eyeglasses. She couldn't possibly. Except maybe if she had known him from many years ago, back when he worked for the Company. When she worked for the Company as well. The woman looked at him hard, and she looked at him for a long second. The Assassin felt his gut tightening as he walked quickly into the parking garage. He no longer felt like congratulating himself. He really wished he had that little Ruger thirty-eight special in his pocket. He had a new problem now. A big one. A problem that needed an immediate fix.

*   *   *

The Century Plaza Hotel is a local landmark. It is a sweeping, curved building along a short stretch of parkway called Avenue of the Stars. In the grassy area in front of the hotel is a spectacular fountain, rhythmically shooting two dozen streams of water high into the air. The Century Plaza was once among the preeminent hotels in Los Angeles, and even though newer, more fashionable ones had sprung up, this remained the hotel of choice for many dignitaries.

I pulled into the driveway and handed over the keys to my Honda Pilot to the valet, perhaps a little more conscious now of my vehicle's lagging stature compared to the Porsches, Mercedes, and Audis sitting nearby. Maybe if the vice president took us on as full consultants, I'd upgrade to something more impressive. After I caught up with a few mortgage payments.

Walking into the lobby, I was approached by a pair of Secret Service agents, both wearing glasses, both stoic in their demeanor. They knew immediately who I was, and they stiffly addressed me as Mr. Baker, as they directed me through a metal detector and then swept me with a wand. They wore those standard dark suits and ties, earpieces in place, but one looked more professional. He wore trendy eyeglasses, had close-cropped black hair, and was lean and fit. The other had a sizable paunch, ginger hair that was unkempt, and a tie that was loose at the collar. The first agent seemed like he was straight out of central casting; the other appeared as if he was finishing an arduous day supervising a boiler room.

"Please follow us, sir," said the professional one, leading us to an elevator and nodding to a security guard, who opened the door right away. Both men got on with me and we rode quietly to the eighteenth floor. There were nineteen floors in the hotel.

"I'm surprised the vice president isn't staying in the penthouse," I mused.

"Never happens," said the rumpled agent. "We keep the room above him vacant."

"Chuck ... " the other agent said quietly.

"Oh. Yeah. Sorry about that, Dean. I figure with all those books out there being written by former agents, half of our secrets are out there as well. Feels like everyone knows our code name for him is Peacock."

"No sense in helping it along."

I raised my hand. "It's okay. I'll keep this to myself."

We got off at eighteen and walked down the wide, carpeted hallway. Not surprisingly, the corridor, like the building, was curved, and you couldn't see through to the end of the hall. Another agent was waiting partway down, and he led me past a few more doors before he stopped, rapped three times slowly on the door, and then followed it with two short taps. The door opened, and a smiling Richard Sudeau was waiting, his eyes dancing, his mood light. The vice president wore a blue dress shirt with no tie, the letters RBS embroidered near the cuff. He waved me in, thanked the agents, and told them, in a slightly slurred voice, that that would be all for now. There was an unsteadiness in his movements, he practically tilted as he walked, and it became very obvious, very quickly that our new super-client, the man who enlisted us to vault him into the highest office in the land, was unmistakably drunk.

"Come on in, my friend!" he smiled. "What can I get you? You like scotch? I've got a bottle of Lagavulin here.

Great single malt. Nice smoky finish."

"Thank you. But I'm more of a vodka guy," I said as I looked around the spacious suite. It was large and plush and befitting a dignitary.

"Sure, sure," he said, pawing over a few bottles at the small wet bar. "How's Grey Goose? Has a nice burn to it. Ice? All you need is one cube, that's the secret."

"Fine."

"We used to call this a See-Through," Sudeau said, putting my drink together. "Years ago. Ah, maybe that was made with gin, I don't know. Nowadays, everything's a martini. Gin, vodka, apple liqueur, doesn't matter. When someone offered me a chocolate martini I knew the world was changing and not in a good way."

I smiled. "Change can be positive sometimes."

"It can indeed," he said, handing me a tumbler that was filled close to the rim. "So, Randy called a little while ago. Said the focus groups were fantastic. Civilians loved the new me. He said I should hear it straight from the source. That your take? Come on, sit, sit."

Richard Sudeau navigated his way awkwardly to a maroon sofa and sat down. From a distance, he still looked every bit the part of the distinguished public servant; the rugged, handsome face, the square jaw, the confident smile, the perfect hair. There are people who gaze and others who are gazed upon, and the vice president was clearly the latter. I sat across from him and took a sip of vodka. The vice president took a long swig of scotch, gritted his big, perfect teeth and looked at me expectantly.

"So here's where we are," I said, choosing my words carefully. "Unaided, the voters don't have a strong opinion of you, one way or the other. Your name is well known but your background is not. They thought you looked presidential, strong and distinguished. A bit like Kennedy. But the people who thought they knew you were a little surprised. There are some challenges to altering an image, but yours is clearly not set in stone. It's something we can build on."

"How so? I've been in public life for over twenty-five years. The people should know who the fuck I am."

I stopped for a moment and tried to be delicate in my response, reminding myself that people with big titles almost invariably have big egos. "People focus on the president, not the vice president," I said slowly. "So, a lot of them don't know your back story, your history. That's the good part. We can shape their impressions."

"All right. Maybe you're onto something. But I have to tell you, my wife's been acting a little nervous about all this. Amber thinks the world should see us as the ultimate power couple. Almost like royalty. You know, the Kennedy family had that mystique, the Clintons tried it, but, well, the Arkansas thing mucked it up. Not to mention Hillary was an asshole. But Amber's not so keen on this. So tell me how the civilians reacted when they learned about my actual background."

"Good," I said. "Here's the thing. You're relatable. One of the people. They like that you've had challenges to overcome. That you were born into problems and climbed out of them. But those who know you a bit feel ... misled."

"How's that? That I've presented myself for so long as an Ivy Leaguer? There's some resentment?"

"I wouldn't call it resentment," I said, a little surprised at the path he was going down. "They like people who lift themselves up. Who've earned their positions. We'll need to change your image a bit, mostly just define it better. You're still an Ivy Leaguer, you just got in the hard way. You worked for it. No one handed you anything."

"All right," he said, sitting back in the sofa, taking this in. "But what about Amber? Randy said the group loved her. But you know, her background is a hundred-eighty degrees different. Everything was laid out for her. She was born with a fucking silver spoon in her mouth."

His statement was jarring, almost a recrimination of his spouse, and certainly not what I was expecting. It revealed something ugly, a disdain for his wife, a sneering sense that her upbringing was privileged, unearned. There was more going on here, a subtext I could not see. Then he took another long swig of Scotch.

"Whenever we mentioned Amber," I continued, "the reaction was extremely positive. But again, it's based to a very limited amount of data. Sure, she was a Congresswoman, a cabinet member, but most people don't pay attention to who the secretary of the Interior is. Unless they get indicted. People know far less about her than they know about you. But when I showed them a picture of you two together, something clicked. Maybe it was from a convention, an ad from years ago. It's interesting what sticks in people's minds. They loved it. She's not a concern. She's a big asset."

"She's a concern," he said.

"Oh?"

Richard Sudeau took another swallow from his glass. "My wife is a fucking bitch," he replied, and then rose to freshen up his drink. I sat in stony silence watching him, a powerful man who was harboring a distasteful secret. A hundred questions fluttered through my mind, none of which were appropriate to ask in this setting. But he opened the door to an issue, and I couldn't let it go untouched.

"No one has a perfect marriage," I offered softly, knowing that sometimes the best way to evoke more conversation is to not ask a question.

"But the people think I do," he snapped. "They think Amber's just perfect, but I can assure you, she's far from it. It took some doing to get the police records sealed, but there were incidents. Years ago. Before we came to an understanding."

"An understanding," I repeated numbly, trying hard to keep my jaw from dropping at the mention of police records.

"We were better together than apart. At least from the looks of things. Oh, we were *simpatico* politically, that part was all right. But personally, we've been leading separate lives for years."

"Never would have known," I said. "And surely no one else seems to, either."

"For now."

I took this in and began to frown. "So, there are police records."

"Yes. Amber has always been a concern. That's why we were interested in what people thought of her. If they sensed anything about us."

I considered this. Sealed records were supposed to be just that. No one could touch them. But if the police had been called to intervene in a domestic squabble, there were invariably a few parties who knew of the incident. The rank-and-file cops who were involved, the police brass who read the officers' reports, the prosecutors, defense attorneys, the judge who sealed the files. And while records might start out confidential, human nature is what it is. Especially when the party in question is running for president.

"You'd hardly be the first politician with some personal issues."

"None like this. Amber could help me get to the White House. But she could also be my undoing."

"Isn't it interesting how one of your biggest assets can also be one of your biggest liabilities."

Sudeau smiled unevenly. "Yeah, I suppose that's true."

"People love her," I said.

"People have always loved her. Look, it's best not to get too into the details. And I've probably said more than I should. Lord, when that Scotch kicks in, my tongue can get awful loose. I didn't mean to bring it up, but I guess I needed to talk about it with someone. At my level, there aren't a lot of sounding boards. Lonely at the top and all. A few old friends know about this, but they're not in politics. And Washington is just like they say. You want a friend there, get a dog."

"True. But why are you bringing this up now?"

"There have been rumors," he said, struggling to find the right words. "Talk that someone has had access to the sealed files. I'm concerned there may be leaks."

"All right. We'll need a plan to combat this if it gets out," I said. "But is Amber on board with all this? Is she going to keep quiet about what happened?"

"She better be. Amber has as much to lose as I do," he said as his phone buzzed. He glanced down at it, staring for a long moment at the message. He stood up, staggered slightly, and pointed to the door, an odd signal that our session was done. I only had so much time with the vice president, and I wondered if he was too drunk to adequately process what I had been saying.

"Randy will be calling you about next steps," he said. "But I want you involved in this campaign. Amber likes you, too. Can't have too many smart people around us."

"Quick question," I said as we walked to the door. "Why just me tonight? Why didn't you want Blair to come?"

The vice president considered this for a moment and then spoke. "The same reason why I got rid of Frank Phelan. He was on TV all the time, getting famous at my expense. He was hired to help me, not the other way around."

"And you think Blair might do the same thing."

"I like you, Ned," Sudeau offered, nodding slightly. "I want us to work together. But I have to tell you. Your partner has a big mouth."

Chapter 13

The same two Secret Service agents escorted me down the elevator and offered a brusque good night as we quickly parted company in the hotel lobby. My head was practically spinning. I thought about my day, starting with the oncologist meeting, soaring through two sets of focus groups and finishing with an audience with the vice president. I had barely taken a sip of my drink upstairs, so I figured I had earned one before heading home. I sauntered into the hotel lounge, found an open barstool inside the crowded pub and sat down.

A bartender slapped a cocktail napkin in front of me. "What'll it be, sir?" he asked.

"How about a see-through."

"A what?"

I smiled. "Vodka martini. Very dry. On the rocks. Lots of them."

He returned with my drink in under thirty seconds and slapped it down on the napkin. I tossed a bill on the bar, picked up the drink and sipped. Part of me wanted to go home and tell Leslie and Angelina about the rest of my day. Part of me needed to think about it. And part of me just wanted to sip a drink in a room full of strangers, unwind, let my mind drift, and think about nothing in particular for a few minutes. But that was not to be.

"Mister, you look like you need a weekend," came a strange voice with an accent I had trouble placing. A large, balding man about my age sat down next to me. "Or at least two more of those drinks."

I turned and looked at him. There was nothing familiar. He had the type of face I'd seen a thousand times in focus groups, and I wondered if he recognized me from one of those.

"Do I know you?" I asked.

"Doubt it," he said, and I identified a slight twang. He waved for the bartender to bring him a bottle of Blue Moon. "I'm just in from Denver. Here for a convention. Why they hold these things in Los Angeles in June is beyond me. This is the place to be in January."

"What kind of convention?"

"Cannabis," he said with a laugh. "Isn't that something? Bet you never thought the day would come when pot smokers would have their own trade show."

"Feels like everybody has one these days," I shrugged. Even political consultants had their own *soiree*, a gathering that included pollsters, strategists, advertising gurus, aspiring politicians, and staff members of public officials. For me, it was a way to learn interesting techniques, meet new clients, and go out for some nice dinners. Once in a while, someone, often Blair, would twist my arm and I'd join a few earthy guys for a night at a strip club. Personally, I preferred a good steak and a stiff drink.

"Got to make a living," he winked.

"I take it you're in the business."

"Oh, yeah. I own a retail shop outside Denver. Near Englewood. Best financial move I ever made."

"Probably not the type of career you wrote about in your college application," I said.

"Funny thing, you know," he smiled, removing an orange slice from his stein of beer and taking a healthy chug. "I never smoked it in college. I was one of those guys who was too busy with a job. Just putting myself through school."

"Try doing that today."

"Oh, man. Don't I know it. My kid's over at USC, I'm taking him to dinner tomorrow. Cost of his tuition is astronomical. Good thing for me my business is booming. You toke?"

"Not yet," I said cautiously, thinking again of my diagnosis.

The man frowned. "Something you're thinking about?"

"I was diagnosed with cancer recently," I said, surprising myself at the overt admission flowing out of my mouth. "Very recently."

It is odd how we sometimes feel comfortable sharing our most intimate secrets with strangers. The lessons of focus groups. It is remarkably easy to share your life's most intimate details with people you've never met before. Maybe we think we'll never see them again, and this allows our defenses to come down. I had just spent the day with my business partner and my closest assistant, and I never once thought of sharing news of my illness with them. If anything, I wanted to bury it, keeping them from seeing the vulnerability. With disease comes a level of shame, and even though I didn't cause my illness, its very existence weakened me, not necessarily in their eyes, but certainly in my own.

"Sorry to hear that, pal," he said in a way that was both sympathetic and breezy. "Join the club."

I looked at him. "You, too?"

"There's an epidemic of cancer in this country. An awful lot of people have it."

"When were you diagnosed?"

"Going on fifteen years. Started with colon cancer. Dealt with that okay, but then it hit the prostate. Then the thyroid. Mister, I've had more body parts removed than a sixty-five Mustang."

"Wow. And you're still here."

"Took a licking, and kept on ticking," he said, taking another swallow of his beer. "It's what got me interested in pot."

"I can imagine."

"Yeah, it don't look like it now," he said, giving his belly a smack, "but there were days on end where I had no appetite. Chemo can mess you up. My sister gave me a joint and said just try it. I figured I had nothing to lose. Damned if it didn't help. Helped the appetite and helped my attitude. Now it's helping me pay for my kid's tuition."

"That's amazing. Inspirational. Fifteen years."

"Sure. I don't think about it too much anymore. Don't even talk much about it unless someone brings it up. Say, what kind of cancer were you diagnosed with?"

"Lung cancer. Stage four. Non-smoker."

He nodded. "Don't need to explain. Even smokers don't deserve this. Rotten disease. You're lucky though. Back fifteen years ago, there wasn't much they could do."

"Lucky?" I said and almost felt myself laugh. "I don't feel so lucky."

"It's all relative," he pointed out. "When I got diagnosed fifteen years ago, they said some cancers simply had no cure. They told you to go home and put your affairs in order. The doc said lung and pancreatic cancers were the worst. Lung, they've made a ton of progress. Pancreatic, not so much."

"Fifteen years. So you're cured?" I asked.

He gave me a hard look. "You're never cured, my friend. Once it's in you, it's in you. Tough to fully get rid of. Oh, doctors can control it for years, I'm living proof. Cancer's not a death sentence, not any more. But once you're in the club, it's a lifetime membership."

I felt myself shudder as I took this in. It's one thing to talk to a doctor, a scientist, a clinician who is an impartial expert, a step removed from your affliction. There is an objectivity that allows professionals to talk with you in a way that mutes emotion, mostly their own. It is far different to speak with another patient, to look at them, to realize they have gone through what you're about to go through. There is a kinship, and there is a bond. But it is a bond built on trepidation, a connection that comes with a sense of the unknown, that our mortality is very present and very close. That we are in a special club, one that's just a little closer to death.

"Any advice?" I asked with a sigh.

"Sure. Be vigilant. Don't give up. And don't think about the end. One day I woke up and swore I saw the white light beckoning."

"White light?"

"You know. When you see the white light it's supposed to be a sign you're on your way to heaven. When I saw it, well, it turned out to be sunlight coming through the drapes."

"Okay. Anything else?"

"Yeah. Even if things look grim, keep asking what else they can try. Listen to the doctors but get second opinions. Or thirds. It's your body, not theirs. Docs are human beings too. Most mean well, but they make mistakes. Trust but verify, that's my motto."

I suddenly caught a glimpse of someone familiar approaching the bar. She was pretty in that L.A. way, slender, the nice hair, the nice smile. But it was Iris Hatcher's green cat eyes that stood out. Eyes that bore into yours. I watched her as she scanned the lounge. Rising from my barstool, I picked up my drink and turned to my new friend.

"Listen, it was nice chatting with you," I said. "But I need to go speak with someone."

He turned and caught a glimpse of Iris. "Don't blame you, buddy," he laughed and handed me his card. "I'm Tom. Tom Geary."

"Ned Baker," I said, slipping his card in my pocket.

"Ned?" he said and started to chuckle. "Love that name. Nice meeting you."

I moved away from the bar and toward Iris. She noticed me, blinked those green eyes a couple of times, and then motioned for me to follow her to a table at the back of the lounge. Her cat eyes were no longer playful; if anything they evoked fear.

"Funny meeting you here," I said. "Of all the gin joints in L.A."

"Funny," Iris replied, not cracking even the hint of a smile. She took a cigarette out of her purse and lit it. It was an Old Gold.

"You smoke the same brand as my partner," I noticed.

"Life is full of coincidences," she said. "So what brings you here?"

"Needed a drink," I said.

"Liar. You were meeting with the vice president, weren't you?"

"Perhaps," I said. While I had no trouble revealing my cancer diagnosis with a complete stranger, I suddenly felt disinclined to share an abundance of work information. I guess we categorize the things we confide and with whom. Iris worked for the speaker, and the politics played at that heady level were intense. What I said was unlikely to be kept confidential, and if anything might be bartered.

"How'd the focus groups go?" she asked, coolly.

I frowned. Apparently certain things might already have been bartered. How Iris knew about the groups was curious, to say the least. Maybe someone in Sudeau's circle had shared a tidbit with the speaker. Perhaps she picked it up from someone on a Gulfstream flight. But then something made me realize the source could well have been sitting in my own backyard.

"You've talked to Blair," I said, not entirely certain I was correct, but it didn't hurt to take a shot. Her eyes didn't give her away, but rather the next sentence exiting her mouth.

"Blair told you about us? Prick."

"Didn't have to," I said. "Hey, he's single. Good-looking. Some women would call him a catch. No reason you can't have some fun."

"I wish he didn't talk so much."

"Yeah, well. Me, too," I said.

She took a long drag on her cigarette, held the smoke deep inside her, and then blew it out slowly toward the ceiling. "Men suck. All of them."

"Thanks for letting me know."

"Sorry. I'm trying to sort some things out. How long have you been at the bar?" she asked.

"A little bit," I shrugged. "Maybe ten minutes. Could be fifteen. I really haven't been keeping track."

I took another sip of my drink and looked around. There was a commotion across the lobby, and soon there were at least twenty men in suits and ties darting about, barking into cell phones, giving terse orders to the hotel staff. There were some arms raised in exasperation, and voices raised in anger. Finally, two of the men in suits marched over to the glass door at the hotel entrance and stretched a piece of tape across it. An argument ensued with a couple of patrons wanting to get out, but the men in dark suits pointed to a couch on the lobby and snapped at them to sit down. They sheepishly followed the directive, the whirling confusion and nervous energy growing in force around them.

Two of the men in dark suits walked into the lounge and looked around. They walked through the place as if they owned it, sizing up the space, inspecting the faces, many of whom paid little attention to them. Finally, one of them cleared his voice and spoke loudly and authoritatively.

"Folks, this hotel is now on lockdown. You will not be able to leave the hotel or the lobby. We don't think it will take long, but no one will be allowed to leave, or even to go upstairs to your room until we're done."

"Who the hell are you?" demanded a middle-aged man with a graying beard and a receding hairline. "And just where do you think you get the authority?"

"We're the United States Secret Service. And we have absolute authority. And I would caution you to be calm and cooperate. This is not a joke. It's not up for discussion, either. So leave your moral indignation somewhere else, or you'll be handcuffed and taken into custody."

With that, the gray bearded man slinked away and faded into the background. I looked at Iris, whose face had tightened considerably. It was a look that went well beyond consternation and bordered on paranoia. She stabbed her cigarette out in an ashtray and immediately lit another one.

"Listen, Ned," she said quietly. "I think I'm in some danger here. All my jobs on Capitol Hill, those came in the last ten years. I started out with the Company. I think I know what's going on here."

"Maybe you can start by telling me who the Company is."

"CIA. I spent five years there. Right out of college.

Started out as an analyst. Moved on to field ops."

"Why are you telling me this?"

At that point, two more agents entered the lounge, Dean and Chuck, the ones who escorted me upstairs a little while ago. They strode quickly and purposefully to our table. They glanced oddly at Iris, and Dean shook his head slightly at her before turning to me.

"Mr. Baker," he started. "I'm glad you're still here. Please come with us."

"What's this about?"

"We'll get to that upstairs. Let's go. Now. And keep your hands where we can see them."

Chapter 14

I rose slowly, sneaking a glimpse of Iris, who was now staring down at the table, silent, detached and vacuous. I made no attempt whatsoever to get her attention, our conversation was over for now. The agents walked me briskly out of the lounge, and we moved across the lobby purposefully, Dean leading the way and Chuck directly behind me. We reached the bank of elevators amidst an absolute din of activity. There were numerous walkie-talkies squawking and blaring, and I managed to make out a few shrill comments that came barking out of their devices.

"We've cleared Little Santa Monica. It's open all through Burton Way."

"Total lockdown of the hotel until further notice. Commander's orders."

"Cedars is notified. They are on high alert."

"Peacock is in motion. Just cleared Wilshire."

"He's AB-positive. Get two units ready."

"The head of thoracic surgery has been notified. He's en route. ETA is four minutes."

A terse-looking agent stood holding the elevator for us. We got in and Chuck pushed eighteen. No words were spoken as we rode up. The elevator opened, and we walked down the corridor again, the same corridor I had just walked down a few minutes ago. It felt so different now. There was a flurry of activity around the vice president's suite, agents speaking in hushed whispers, and a number of agents openly carried long rifles.

Dean took off his glasses and directed me into a room across the hall. It was a suite as well, not as nicely appointed, but spacious. They told me to sit at a table and ordered me to hand over my cell phone. Chuck took it and passed it to an agent outside the room. Then Chuck closed the door slowly, carefully and tightly. There was no compelling need to add any more drama to the moment, but they went out of their way to do so. Slowly, and with great care, both men took seats across from me, stared incredulously and silently, not uttering a word for what was probably sixty seconds but felt like an eternity.

"Let me explain what's going to happen here," Dean finally said. "We need answers and we need them now. And you're going to provide them. You're not getting an attorney at this stage. You're not going to leave until we say you can leave. I urge you to cooperate fully. The vice president has been shot. You were the last person to be seen with him. I don't need to tell you that you are in very real trouble. This is deadly serious and I can only tell you that if you help us, you will be helping yourself. If you don't, you may be looking at spending the rest of your life in jail, and even at the possibility of a lethal injection."

I sat there dumbfounded. My mouth agape, I looked into their cold, hardened, stone faces. The sober, ominous tone in Dean's voice reinforced the gravity of the situation. His words didn't just feel threatening, they felt murderous. I had done nothing wrong, yet here I was, caught in the midst of a raging tsunami. If what they said was true, my livelihood, my freedom, and possibly even my life could come to a screeching halt. And yet I had only a pittance of information to barter, there was not much I could do to help them. Or to help myself. I knew very little, and that was not good.

"I wish I could offer something of value here," I said, my voice weak and almost cracking. "But the vice president was the one who asked me to come to the hotel."

"What did you talk about?" Dean asked.

"I debriefed him on some focus groups we did tonight. That's it. Nothing else."

"Did the vice president call you himself?"

"No," I said. "His aide. His chief of staff did. Randy Greece. He told me the vice president would be expecting me. But you knew that."

"Is that so?" Chuck asked.

"You were waiting downstairs for me," I frowned. "You knew what I looked like. You were the ones who noticed me. You led me up here. Of course you knew that."

"Let's focus on what you know, not on what we know," Chuck said. "Before we figure out what to charge you with. Murder or treason. That partly depends on whether the vice president makes it."

"Look," I said wearily. "You're way off base here."

"It's all right, Chuck," Dean said, holding up a hand. "If Mr. Baker cooperates fully, we might be able to let him go home tonight. Not charge him. He just needs to tell us what happened. Every single thing after we led him into the suite."

I had a vague sense that I should have stopped talking

at that moment. Demanded a lawyer. That any scenario of my being forthcoming might not be in my best interests. But these are the judgments made in the aftermath, the post-mortem analyses when you have the time and the clarity of thought to review events and reconstruct them in your mind. But in the ferocity of the moment, and in a less-than-ideal frame of mind, I did not even conceive of that as an option. And, clinging to the quaint notion I had done nothing wrong, it struck me that cooperation might benefit me in a way that being stoic would not.

I played back my conversation with the vice president as best I could. I felt numb. It could have been due to the fatigue, maybe the vodka, or perhaps the devastating meeting with the oncologist this morning, which felt like a lifetime ago. Or just the astoundingly catastrophic chain of circumstances that led me here. The agents asked me to repeat my conversation with the vice president, and I did, stumbling at times to recall the exact words. Their interest piqued when I mentioned the vice president's less-than-flattering description of his wife.

"What did he call her again?"

I licked my lips. "A bitch. No, a fucking bitch."

"Why would he say that?" Chuck asked.

"There had been incidents. He didn't get into specifics. He said there were police records."

"How long have you been acquainted with the vice president?"

"Not long. A few days. We were just hired in as pollsters. Campaign consultants."

"Why would he tell you this?

"I don't know," I said. "I think he might have been drunk."

The agents glanced at each other, knowing looks that communicated without words. It was clear that the vice president's lack of sobriety did not come as a surprise.

"You said 'we' a minute ago. Who's 'we'?" Dean asked.

"My partner. Blair Lipschitz. Vice President Sudeau hired us."

"Did your partner know you were coming here?"

"Yes," I said.

"How did he know?"

"I told him."

"Why didn't he come with you?"

"The vice president wanted me to come alone," I said.

"Any idea how someone could have smuggled a gun in there?"

I stared at them in disbelief. "No," I said, my voice starting to display some agitation. "My God. You had me go through a metal detector. You patted me down. How on earth could I ever get a weapon past you?"

"You ever been to this hotel before?"

"A few times."

"For what?"

"A few conferences. Met people for drinks. A Bar Mitzvah, maybe."

"Know anyone who works here?"

"No."

"Know anyone who works in Century City?"

"Sure."

"Who?"

"A few attorneys. My accountant has an office here. There's a market research firm I once did business with. I still know a few people there."

Chuck handed me a pen and a legal pad and instructed me to write the names of everyone I knew who worked in the area, and every instance when I had visited the hotel. Then he told me to write down my entire interaction with the vice president tonight, including my conversations with Blair, Randy Greece, and anyone else who might have known I was coming here. Exclude nothing. And write legibly.

It took me awhile, partly because I was tired, partly because I tend not to hold onto intricate details. Whenever I moderated focus groups, they were recorded and often transcribed. Writing a report was easy because I didn't need to remember every comment, and I could discern the nuances again when I listened to the recordings. But the real world rarely offers that luxury, to go back and review, and besides, my mind didn't operate that way. And the Secret Service agents did not look pleased with what they surely considered my attempt to obfuscate.

The door opened and another agent walked in and handed Dean a cell phone. "Pandora wants to speak to you," he said.

Dean took the phone, mostly listened, uttered an occasional "Yes, ma'am," and finally told her that he was talking to the "suspect" now. Yes, the head of the detail would keep her informed. Without a goodbye, he ended the call.

"I'm really a suspect?" I asked, eyes wide, the fatigue giving way to a burgeoning sense of outrage.

Chuck stood up and walked around the table. "You were the last person to be seen with him. You can understand our skepticism, surely?"

"No, I can't. And I don't see where you have a shred of proof. I'm not a lawyer, but I know what circumstantial evidence is."

"Were you on the balcony at all? Or near it?"

"No."

"Was the vice president on the balcony?"

"No."

Chuck shook his head. "There are security cameras everywhere. If you did something, we'll know. If anything about your story is the slightest bit inaccurate, we'll ruin you. Count on it."

"I feel like I'm in the middle of Kafka," I said, rubbing my eyes.

"Where's that?" Chuck asked.

I stared at him in disbelief. "Nowhere," I said.

"Look, Baker. Let me lay this out for you. We swept the area before the vice president arrived. No guns were in that suite. Maybe the gunshots came from outside. But we have agents on the ground. There was no one there at the time. There's an office building across the street, but we've had agents on the scene all day. And none of the windows open up there. The roof of that building is locked. So help me understand how anyone could have shot the vice president tonight without your help."

"I'm not a detective," I said. "I'm not a gunman. I don't

think in those terms. But I do think in terms of motivation. And I have none. My God. The vice president just hired us. He's a high-paying client. Why in the world would I ever want to shoot someone who's paying me good money?"

"What's your political affiliation?"

"Democrat. Of course I'm a Democrat, Sudeau isn't going to hire a Republican."

"Funny."

"How so?"

"When you were eighteen you registered as a Republican."

I stared at him, wondering how he could have gotten this so fast. "That was so I could vote for Reagan. I was in college. I switched my party affiliation a few years later. People change their stripes."

"Uh-huh."

"You don't believe me?" I asked.

"I don't believe anyone," Chuck said. "The world is full of liars. It's only a matter of time before they get caught. We'll find out the truth, believe me. Things will go much easier if you cooperate. Anything about your story you want to clarify yet? Anything you want to change?"

"No."

Dean's cell phone buzzed and he answered it. He didn't say much, just listened and said yes a few times. He ended the call, put the phone into his pocket, and took a long, deep breath.

"I'm sorry, Baker."

"What do you mean?"

"That was one of our agents. He rode in the ambulance with the vice president. They got him to Cedars but couldn't do much. Lost too much blood. He didn't make it. We are now dealing with a full-fledged assassination. And you, sir, are right in the eye of this shit storm. Right in the fucking middle of it."

Chapter 15

I spent the next six hours languishing at the suite in the Century Plaza, a few cups of coffee keeping me from sliding wearily off my chair. I repeated my story, then repeated it again for two new agents, then repeated it once more to an even more serious-looking man who identified himself as being with the FBI. When I asked Dean which agency was running the investigation, he and the FBI agent glanced disparagingly at one another, raising doubts that no one I was speaking with was entirely certain.

We were there all night and accomplished little. The moment that pushed things forward happened just as it was becoming light outside. Dean received a phone call and his posture straightened immediately. His answers were terse, but when he ended the call, he hung his head for a moment.

"There's been a development," he said. "A construction crew across the street found a weapon and a bi-pod. The weapon was fired very recently. And there's a window broken. It makes sense. We couldn't have seen the broken window in the dark. The shots had to have been fired from there."

The FBI agent immediately jerked out his phone and walked quickly out of the room. Chuck and Dean glanced nervously at one another. I refrained from asking for an apology. But I did inquire if it was all right with them if I went home.

"Not yet," Dean said. "We verified you did not leave the hotel grounds. Our guys have gone over the security camera footage. You're accounted for. What's not clear is whether you were working in concert with the shooter."

"Again," I sighed, "what motive could I possibly have?"

"We don't know. But I want the name and address of your partner, and that assistant of yours, that Wanda. We'll need to follow up with them. And the people you spoke with at the bar."

I shrugged and handed them Tom Geary's card. If I needed to buy medical marijuana, there were plenty of places in Los Angeles that could accommodate me.

"Don't have Iris's card on me," I said. "But you know her name is Iris Hatcher. She works in the speaker's office."

"Iris Hatcher," mused Chuck. "Where do I know her from?"

"Shut up," Dean told him, and he motioned for Chuck to follow him out of the room. An hour went by. Just as I started to doze off, they returned.

"All right," Dean said. "We're done for now. You can go home, but we'll be following up with you later. Don't leave town. Don't talk to anyone about this."

His tone grated on me, possibly because of my exhaustion, maybe because my righteous indignation hackles rose. After a night of interrogation, it grated on me to have someone tell me who I could or couldn't speak with, and where I could or couldn't go. I reminded myself I was in the midst of an extraordinary situation, the assassination of the second-highest ranking official in the country, an event which bordered on being a constitutional crisis. And since I had nothing to gain by making a smart remark, I kept quiet. In times of crisis, the people with the artillery get to rule. And at the moment, I was simply too weary to do anything more than acquiesce.

They returned my cell phone and rode with me down the elevator. When we walked out, Chuck motioned to a pair of agents that it was all right for me to depart. I glanced around the lobby. There were a few guests trying to check out, hotel employees working diligently to move things along, trying to maintain some semblance of normalcy, an impossible task. Dozens of federal agents were patrolling the lobby, some openly displaying handguns clipped to their belts. When I asked a valet for my car, he told me the garage was still on lockdown, and no vehicles could be retrieved yet. I walked down the street, and took an Uber home.

The sky was becoming lighter, the dark gray of the night giving way to the softer gray of an overcast morning. The long shadows still extended across the empty streets of West Los Angeles. When traffic eased up, this was a pleasurable city to cruise around in, but unfortunately these moments were fleeting. The congestion on the streets made drivers irritable and less inclined to be even marginally polite. But this morning was pleasant. And as we turned right onto San Vicente, a car turning left slowed to let us through, even giving us a good-morning wave. Others in the world were clearly in a more magnanimous frame of mind than I was.

As I unlocked the front door, Angelina gave a small

scream, the type of demonstrative yelp that was a mixture of joy and relief. She rose from the breakfast table, knocking over her box of Honey Nut Cheerios, and ran toward me in tears.

"Oh, my God! Daddy! Are you all right?!"

She threw herself into my arms and hugged me. Leslie came out from the kitchen and hugged me as well. I had received far more physical contact from my family in the past few days than I had in months. I appreciated it, albeit wishing it could have been evoked through less traumatic circumstances.

"My goodness, Ned!" Leslie cried. "We've been worried sick. I called the focus group facility, they said you left at ten, I tried Blair, but he wasn't answering his phone. At two o'clock I called the police, but they said a person needed to be missing twenty-four hours before they could do anything."

"Then we heard about the vice president being shot and taken to Cedars-Sinai, and well, Daddy, you could just imagine what we were thinking!"

I could indeed imagine the worry and grief they were enduring. I quickly took them through my endless day, a twenty-four hour whirlwind of absurdity, beginning with our appointment with the oncologist to discuss my terminal illness and ending with the Secret Service accusing me of being at least complicit, and potentially spearheading, a grand-scale assassination of a man who could have become the next president. I suddenly realized I hadn't given much thought to the death of Richard Sudeau, only insomuch as it affected my own personal freedom. A human being had been killed, shot to death, an act of sheer brutality. I hadn't even pondered the question of why anyone would want to commit such a crime. I was far too busy trying to extricate myself from being implicated and charged with his murder.

Leslie and Angelina listened rapturously, hanging on to my every word, their mouths open, displaying the shock one goes through when someone tells them a tale that is beyond any reality they have encountered this side of a horror film. I finished and they hugged me again, happy I was okay, comforted to know I was safe. Angelina told me she wanted to stay home with me. I smiled at her gambit, she was seventeen, but still displayed the childlike guile that was transparent. I told her she had to go school, adding that I needed to get some sleep and would be of no use to anyone for the next eight hours. Maybe ten. Before they left, Leslie remembered something.

"Dr. Ashland called yesterday, late afternoon. He scheduled you into Cedars on Monday morning. For the pleurodesis. And the biopsy. I told him okay, I hope that was the right thing to do."

"Yes," I said absently. "Of course."

"I should have called you, but with the focus groups, I didn't want to distract you."

"No, it's fine. Monday. I'll make it work," I said, unable to stifle a yawn. "I'll have to make it work."

Leslie left to take Angelina to school. The fatigue had caught up with me hours earlier and I stumbled through it. But I needed sleep, desperately, unquestionably. I climbed upstairs, hands gripping the banister unevenly. I reached the bedroom, tore off my clothes, and plunged on top of the covers, not even bothering to slip inside. I vaguely noticed I didn't have any pain in my back, a luxury in which I took no small amount of joy. I still needed almost a half-hour to finally drift off to sleep, the anxiety and atrocity of my ordeal having wired me up. I slept straight through to three-thirty, waking not refreshed, but not utterly exhausted either. I went downstairs and fixed a pot of coffee. I was on my third cup when the doorbell rang. I groaned at the thought it might be the Secret Service again. As I glanced through the peephole, I recognized it might be worse.

"Hello Blair," I said, opening the door and ushering him in.

"Hello yourself. And good afternoon. Or good morning, as the case may be."

We walked into the living room and Blair seated himself in the bentwood rocker and began to creak back and forth.

"Coffee?" I asked.

"Nah. The Feds poured about eight cups into me this morning. My head's about to explode."

I refilled my cup and sat down. "The Feds?" I asked.

"Yeah, once they got through grilling you, they must have figured I'd be jealous. Three FBI agents marched into the office and peppered me with questions for five hours. These guys act like they're the national police force. You know they even followed me into the men's room? They thought I was trying to ditch them."

It sounded as if the Secret Service already had a dossier

on Blair Lipschitz. It also sounded as if they were running low on leads. Questioning my partner was probably standard *de rigueur,* but keeping him for five hours was as poorly conceived as questioning me all night.

"What did they want to know?"

"Anything. Everything. Asked me where I went after the focus groups, as if it's their business, asked me why I didn't answer my phone all night. Christ, they even asked me who I was sleeping with. I told them I'd make them a list. Didn't even crack a smile. Those guys are just dorks."

I couldn't disagree, but I knew they had the unenviable task of trying to find a killer without a lot of information. Whoever shot Richard Sudeau was probably long gone by now. The Feds had to pick up the trail, and I sensed they were operating in the dark. They didn't quite know what they were looking for, so they'd interrogate anyone they could, in the slim hope someone dropped a morsel that could turn into a lead.

"Any news on the assassination?" I asked.

"Yeah, I can see you've been dead to the world today. They found the murder weapon across the street, an office building, they were doing construction on one of the top floors. Whoever did it used a high-powered rifle. Must've been a hell of a shooter, Sudeau had to have been three hundred yards away. My money says it's a Marine. The corps knows how to mold sharpshooters."

"But no leads on the killer?" I asked

"Nope. If we can get our candidate in, first order of business is to appoint a new FBI director."

I peered at him. "You understand that our guy isn't

going to be president, don't you?"

Blair nodded ever so slightly and I thought I saw the briefest glint of a smile. "Look, the Feds really messed up my day. They don't know what they're doing. But all the time they were grilling me, I was coming up with ideas."

"Ideas?"

"Yeah. To your point, our high-profile client is no longer running for president. We're up shit creek here, my friend. I have an idea but we need to do something fast."

"Such as ... ?" I asked, continuing to peer at him, trying to see if I could get a glimpse into the fertile yet twisted mind of my partner. Blair was an ideas guy, but his ideas were as likely to lead us up the highest mountain as they were to lead us off a treacherous cliff.

"You ever hear the saying never let a good crisis go to waste?" he smiled.

"I don't know as I like where this is going," I said.

"We have an opportunity, my friend. We need to capitalize on it."

I rubbed the bridge of my nose. After spending most of the night being interrogated by a series of sober, intense federal agents, I did not see any opportunity, rather, I thought we needed to do some serious damage control. Calling our current clients, reassuring them, and waiting for the dark storm to pass had been my first thought.

"Just what are you getting at?" I asked, starting to grow nervous.

"You and I are about to become famous my friend. You were the last person to see the vice president alive. That's big news. That's something the networks want a piece of."

"Oh, no."

"Oh, yes. You and I are going on *Hello America* tomorrow morning. I have a contact at NBC, Callie Saxon, she set it up. We'll be on the second half-hour, once they get past the update on the investigation. Merry Teale is interviewing us."

I shook my head. "I'm not flying to New York."

"Hey! Who said anything about New York? We'll do it out of their Burbank studios. Remote feed. It'll be early, I got to warn you. We're slated for seven forty-five but that's Eastern time. Four forty-five here. They want us at the studio an hour early. Not much traffic, I'll pick you up at three. Wear a nice tie. Nothing loud, nothing flashy. We need to make a good impression."

I lay down on the couch and continued to sigh. Maybe it was a moan. The last thing on earth I wanted was to be interviewed again, especially with a few million people watching this time. I was great at asking questions, awful at answering them, and feeling mildly nauseated at the notion of publicly analyzing the murder of a man who I'd been speaking with just a few minutes before he was gunned down.

"Hey, what's the matter?" Blair said. "I thought you'd love the idea. We could never ever get this publicity anywhere else. This is a golden opportunity and it just fell in our laps. We'd be crazy not to milk this. We absolutely have to get our faces out there. Most importantly, we need some business. We're in the big leagues now."

"Did it occur to you," I started, "that appearing to take advantage of someone else's tragedy and misfortune may not be a good thing?"

"And did it occur to you that sticking our heads in the sand and not having any future business is an even worse thing?"

"We have Garter. And a few other smaller clients."

"We don't have Garter. John Quinn called. The project's on hold. The whole Sudeau thing shook them up. So we need to get our faces out there. The check from the campaign didn't come in yet. Look. Don't worry. You'll be fine. I'm working another angle. Don't want to get your hopes up, so I'll hold off telling you. But I do need to let you know that a good showing tomorrow morning on national TV will help. A lot."

I didn't have an answer to that, and arguing with a crafty salesman is tantamount to arguing with a good lawyer. It's an endless cycle, and you rarely win. And I also sensed that Blair would likely go on TV without me, so being on air next to him might have some benefit, if only in limiting collateral damage. Oddly, I suddenly thought about my cancer diagnosis for the first time since I woke up. Nothing like being caught up in a national crisis to help me compartmentalize. I started to wonder what I had to lose. There were worse things than going on TV.

"Three o'clock in the morning, huh?" I said in a resigned voice.

"Yeah," he said, adding wryly, "maybe you should just stay up for it."

"We'll need to take your car. Mine's indisposed."

"Of course. We're not going to NBC in a jalopy."

I thought of something. "So where *were* you last

night?" I asked. "Why weren't you picking up your phone?"

"Had a date," Blair said. "Actually, I got stood up at the last minute so I called an old standby."

"Leslie said she'd been trying to call you all night."

"That was her? I saw the call coming in, but the number was listed as Unknown. I figured it was a telemarketer. They have no shame these days. Kept ringing so I had to turn it off."

"I'll bet you don't get stood up much," I muttered.

"Bet your ass I don't. But you know what? It was that honey we met on the plane back to D.C. The one with the green eyes, Iris."

"Iris stood you up?" I exclaimed.

"Yeah, why? You seeing her, too?"

"Good lord, no," I said, and my mind started to whirr. It was plainly apparent Iris was at the Century Plaza to see the vice president; obviously she was his next appointment after me. I tried to reconstruct our conversation, but things just didn't fit. Not yet.

"Hey," Blair continued. "You know Iris used to work for the CIA? Never would have thought, but stranger things happen. You know what they say about the best way a female spy serves her country."

I shook my head. "Look, she was at the hotel last night. I saw her in the bar. After I met with Sudeau. She was worried. She said something about being in some danger. Any idea what that would mean?"

Blair wrinkled his nose. "Danger? Nope. I don't worry about women's problems. I just like being with them. The way a fat kid loves cake. Don't always see the ramifications until later on."

"So, give me a hint. What's this idea is you're cooking up?"

"Well, look. It's not exactly my idea. But I think we have another presidential candidate waiting in the wings. Maybe even one that could get elected."

Chapter 16

The LAPD Detective got the call just after five in the morning, as he was pulling out of his garage in Palmdale. The chief's orders were clear and direct. Don't go in to the office, go straight to Century City, meet up with the FBI and Secret Service, get briefed. His staff would be fine without him for a day or two. His hands gripped the steering wheel. He knew what happened to the vice president, knew that the Feds would be all over this. The last thing they would appreciate was a local cop stepping on toes. But the chief had good reason to pick him. Two years ago he had thwarted an assassination attempt that had slipped through all of the agencies of Homeland Security. He thought of things that others did not. It earned him a promotion to captain.

Arriving on the scene wearing his blue LAPD windbreaker, badge hanging from his neck, the Detective handed his I.D. to the agent manning the elevator bank. He told him he was there by order of the chief of police. He told them his name was Karl Mooring and he was in charge of Robbery-Homicide within the LAPD. Everything was in order, but it still took fifteen minutes of discussion and phone calls before the Federal Bureau of Incompetence would let him go upstairs. He wandered around the thirty-third floor, talking to whomever would speak to him, picking up bits and pieces of what had transpired last night. The Feds did indeed seem a little annoyed at his presence, and while they were not overtly rude, neither were they very accommodating. The Detective overheard one of them make a comment about limiting access to too many jokers who might mess up their crime scene. He knew they were referring to him.

The Detective pieced together what he had learned. The Assassin knew where the vice president would be and when he'd be there. He knew there was remodeling being done on the thirty-third floor, in a structure directly facing the vice president's hotel. The Assassin was a pro, he had easily gained access to the building. The fact that he had left the murder weapon was curious, but the Detective knew it was a ploy. The FBI guys were excited about getting a lead, although it might have been the Secret Service; it was hard to tell who was in charge. The only thing he knew was that the FBI agents were the ones who were in far better shape. One Secret Service agent had a beer belly that would have been disgraceful even if he were just employed as an insurance agent. The Secret Service used to be a top-flight agency. Then they got absorbed into the DHS, suddenly had to compete for funds, and standards began to slip. They used to employ the best, now they were stuck with whatever. Something like this was bound to happen eventually. No one transferred into the Secret Service anymore. The good agents got fed up and left, the farts got fed up and stayed.

After a half-hour of milling about, the Detective went downstairs and talked to the security guard. Yes, he had been there all night, yes, the Feds had interviewed him and taken the sign-in sheet and all the pens already. The guard had seen a man with a beard leaving late, he assumed that had to have been the Assassin. Yes, the Feds were reviewing video surveillance video. The Detective asked the guard if the building kept records of which floors each elevator stopped at. The guard frowned and said no, he didn't think their elevators were that sophisticated. The Detective asked if there was anything the Feds hadn't asked him, anything at all that might be helpful. The guard thought for a moment and then pointed the Detective toward a construction crew huddled in a corner. Those guys might know something.

He approached a man who had an air of authority about him, as well as a lit cigar protruding out of the corner of his mouth. People weren't allowed to smoke indoors, but the Detective, a reformed smoker himself, was not about to enforce this law. He would settle for being envious. The man indeed turned out to be someone with authority, the foreman of the crew, and someone unhappy at having his day derailed. The Detective asked if the Feds had spoken to them, and surprisingly they had not. They simply ordered his crew to wait in the lobby. And not to leave.

The Detective asked if the foreman could provide any information about the thirty-third floor. The foreman shrugged and said he arrived at his usual four-thirty in the morning, heard street noise, and discovered the hole in the window and then the rifle on the floor. After calling it in, the FBI arrived and ordered his crew off the floor, telling them to stick around until they got around to interviewing them. The Detective asked if anything else *struck him as unusual, and the foreman thought about it for a moment, taking an extra long drag on his cigar. He mentioned that when his crew left for the day, they always turned off the elevator's ability to stop at the floors where they were doing work. Prevented looky-loos from snooping round and maybe getting hurt, but it also minimized petty theft. He assumed the FBI had ordered it turned it back on when they arrived on the scene.*

The Detective thought about this for a few minutes. It was now getting close to seven o'clock. A few office workers were starting to file in. By eight o'clock the building would be filled with people again, mostly employees waiting in the lobby until the FBI deigned to allow them back in. That might not be until tomorrow. He had an idea. Pulling out his cell phone, he called Ernesto Mendoza in Forensics. He picked up on the first ring. The Detective asked if Mendoza could come over to Century City right away. Yes, it was important. Crucial, perhaps.

In the twenty minutes the Detective waited, he pieced together a few ideas. He thought of sharing his thoughts with the Feds. But he remembered the last time he worked with them. He also thought of how they treated him up on thirty-three, like a local yokel who just got in their way. And he knew that while they might not dismiss his ideas, both the FBI and the Secret Service had a certain ugly history, not always publicized, of taking an investigation and royally fucking it up. The LAPD Detective decided he would keep his part of the investigation clandestine, at least initially. If nothing came of it, there was no one to laugh at him. If something did materialize, he'd be able to rub it in the Feds' faces. The idea was appealing. He saw Mendoza enter the lobby, his bag slung over a shoulder. Leading him to the elevator, they walked on and the Detective punched the round white button to take them up to the thirty-fourth floor, not the thirty-third. He doubted any Feds would be there. He assumed the floor would be devoid of law enforcement. He was right.

*   *   *

The Mercedes glided silently through the empty, darkened streets of Burbank. Blair kept up a steady chatter about what questions to expect from Merry Teale and how best to answer them. I mostly looked out the window and tried to ignore the running commentary.

We pulled onto the studio grounds, a lone security guard waving us through the gate and directing us to park in the reserved spaces near the newsroom entrance. I had passed the NBC lot numerous times, but this was my first opportunity to go inside. From the outside it looked like any other business park, although the familiar peacock logo was a reminder this was not just any business.

After checking in at the reception desk, a perky young assistant led us to the green room, where we would wait for forty-five minutes before entering the set. The green room is not green of course, and it isn't even very comfortable, it's just a holding pen where on-air guests wait until the network is ready to interview them. There was a countertop holding a large coffee urn, and a tray of bagels and pastries. I helped myself to black coffee, passing on any food. Blair loaded up with a raspberry Danish, and asked one of the staff to make him a pot of decaf. A makeup girl came in and insisted on dusting our faces with some powder, saying the bright lights would create too much glare on our faces, especially when we began to perspire.

"You all set?" Blair asked, between mouthfuls. "You ready to roll?"

"Ready as I'll ever be," I said. While I hadn't intended on following Blair's advice, I had indeed stayed up all night. My feeble attempt at napping produced nothing more than tossing and turning for a few hours. Every time I started to drift off, my mind nervously snapped me awake, racing at the thought of what questions might be asked. Leslie finally told me if I wasn't going to sleep, I might be so kind as to let her indulge.

At four-fifteen, we were led onto the brightly lit set, which was little more than two chairs placed in front of a green screen. We were told the background image would be an aerial photo of the San Fernando Valley at sunrise. The production assistant proudly showed us the pink and gold photo, with the purple mountains in the distance creating a gorgeous panoramic vista. It made for good viewing, but it was, of course, completely false, the image having been shot a few years ago and used repeatedly. We were not overlooking the Valley, the sun had not come up, and there were no windows on the set. And June gloom was still in full force, so even the traces of a colorful Valley sunrise this morning would be hidden behind a wall of gray clouds.

They put earpieces on us, and we had a brief run-through with Merry Teale in New York. She told us the first question she'd be asking, a general query into the vice president's final conversation, and that we would have seven minutes on air. She was upbeat, encouraging and, perhaps, sensing my nervousness, told us to relax and everything would be fine. Easier said than done.

We waited until after the news update at the half-hour, and a production assistant pointed to us and indicated we'd be on air in thirty seconds. There was a monitor facing us, so we could view the New York set live, and we could see Merry gathering her notes, and taking a last sip of coffee before checking her smile in a mirror. The assistant began counting down the numbers verbally while holding up the same number of fingers, going silent at two, then one. The show's soft theme music faded as we went live, and the distinctive voice of the morning anchor came through loud and clear in our ear sets. She sounded important.

"For our next segment, we'd like to welcome Ned Baker, the last man to speak with the vice president before he was so brutally gunned down in Los Angeles on Wednesday night. Mr. Baker is a pollster, and we also have Blair Lipschitz, his partner at the Baker Lipschitz Team. Gentlemen, thank you for being with us. I know it's early out there in California."

"Never too early for you, Merry," Blair said, smiling his dazzling smile. "Thank you having us."

"Our pleasure. So, Mr. Baker. You were the last person to see the vice president alive. Can you tell our viewers about your meeting with him."

"I'll tell you, Merry," Blair broke in. "The vice president had just hired us to do some work on his campaign, some important focus groups that Ned moderated. These were among likely voters, and it was just stunning to hear how much they loved the vice president. This country is going to miss Rich Sudeau, miss him terribly. I don't know how he can be replaced. We were totally convinced he was going to be our next president. This is so tragic."

"Ah ... yes. But let me get Mr. Baker's take on this, seeing as he was in the room with the vice president. What was his mood? Did he appear nervous about anything? Concerned?"

"No," I said quickly, not letting Blair jump in one more time. "The vice president was in a great mood. He was very happy. He wasn't nervous at all."

"Then there was no sense of premonition. That he might have known something was about to happen."

"If he did, I certainly didn't notice it."

"How do you react to the FBI referring to you as a person of interest?"

My body tensed for a moment, but there was no time to think, only to react. "I'm not aware of that, but I can only tell you it is absolutely ridiculous. I don't know how anyone who knows the facts could possibly say something so wrong. It is patently false."

"And let me also add, Merry," Blair said, "that the FBI has made more than its share of mistakes over the years. Same with the Secret Service. This is just one more in a long line of bungled pratfalls. Ned wouldn't hurt a fly."

"You know everyone is wondering how something like this could ever happen," she said. "The Secret Service is supposed to go to extraordinary lengths to protect the president and the vice president. This is really quite shocking, isn't it?"

"Merry," Blair said, "We're as shocked as you. Everyone in L.A. knows when the president or vice president is in town, because the entire city grinds to a halt. They completely stop all traffic. You would have thought they'd have secured the entire Century City area. But they failed. And now they're trying to hang my partner because of their own disgraceful performance."

"That's quite a statement, Mr. Lipschitz."

"And one more thing," Blair said, railing on. "The Secret Service agents who interviewed me looked incredibly out of shape. Don't they have a gym they can use? It's awful, Merry, really awful. The problem with the Secret Service is the whole agency is loaded down with nepotism. They really should just hand this investigation over to the CIA. Those guys know what they're doing. They're the real pros. I know a couple of these agents. They'll find the person who did this. They're the best!"

"All right, all right," she said, wanting to move on. "I hear you guys. We'll let the investigation take its course. But as your partner mentioned a minute ago ... Mr. Baker, you conducted some focus groups on Rich Sudeau's behalf the other night. Can you tell our viewers what was the purpose of those focus groups?"

"The vice president," I said, starting to wonder how much confidentiality still existed when the client who hired you was no longer alive, "wanted to get some insight as to how familiar the voters were with him. With his background. What was their impression of him. And how much more of his life story he needed to share with them. It was apparent not everyone knew the real Richard Sudeau."

"And let me also add," Blair interjected, "the vice president was keenly interested in the issues the average American has been concerned about. And even though this great man is no longer with us, we need to keep his spirit alive. We need to honor and cherish his memory. Even though he won't be here to lead us, the issues he cared so deeply about remain. And we only hope and pray that someone as capable as the vice president will come forward soon and throw their hat in the ring. And we look forward to working with them."

"That is fascinating," Merry said, intrigued, the hint of a smile forming. "Do you have any suggestions on a candidate?"

I looked over at Blair and wondered the same thing. And it was starting to become clear that Blair had an agenda, one that was seditiously covert, a codicil of sorts, a plan he hadn't bothered to share with me. Maybe he thought I'd object, maybe he thought I'd say the wrong thing. But Blair was simply good at ginning up an audience, generating curiosity, and allowing that twinkle in his eye to capture the viewers.

"Merry, there is no one who could replace Rich. He was a man of the people, someone who rose to become a giant in Washington. They didn't know the obstacles he was able to overcome in his life. And no one running right now has Rich Sudeau's breadth of experience. But at this point, all we can do is send our thoughts and prayers to his family as they try and get through this awful time."

And then it occurred to me what Blair was doing, the cunning hint, the subtle dropping of a reference, and the laying of the foundation for the next step of the presidential campaign, which was to say, the next step of our careers. I wondered how far Blair would go with this, two days after the death of Richard Sudeau, but it didn't take long to find out. And it struck me that Merry knew where Blair was going with this as well.

"Speaking of the vice president's family, can you comment on any plans that the family might want to do something, make a gesture perhaps, that might establish something in his honor?"

"I'd prefer not to speculate Merry," Blair continued. "The family needs this time to mourn and to grieve. But I was speaking with the vice president's staff, and there are indications that this may go beyond just building a monument to Rich's legacy. And we all know his wife Amber is a very formidable woman. She is one of the brightest lights in Washington. It would not surprise me one bit if she picked up the baton."

"What are you suggesting?" she asked.

"I think it would be a superb idea for Amber to

continue what Rich started in his campaign. Not only to honor Rich, but because Amber Sudeau would be a phenomenal leader in her own right."

"Well, now!" gushed Merry. "That is indeed a piece of news. How do you think the country would react to this?"

Blair began to respond. I wasn't entirely sure why I plunged in, maybe it was my feeling left out of the loop on this, feeling I needed to re-establish my own presence here. So I broke in. There's an old saying that if you want to be a leader, find a parade and jump in front of it.

"I have to tell you," I said, cutting off Blair, "that during the focus groups, Ms. Sudeau's name came up, and it was very clear how highly regarded she is. Voters are extremely impressed with her, and I sense they would be very open to hearing more about who Amber Sudeau is."

"Now before we go any further," Merry said, "I need to ask you, does this possibility we're discussing here, the potential candidacy of Amber Sudeau for the presidency. Could it in any way smack of political opportunism on her part? Of taking advantage of the public's sympathy toward a grieving widow?"

"I think the American people are too smart for that," Blair chimed in fast, grabbing back control of the conversation. "The American people know the real deal when they see it. Rich Sudeau was the real deal and so is Amber. No one is going to get conned here. And if anyone thinks Amber is going to run thinking she'll just be getting the sympathy vote, then they're going to be very surprised."

"Well, this is quite a remarkable turn of events," Merry

said. "I do hope you two will keep us posted and come back and talk again soon. Maybe we can even get you to fly out to New York next time."

"You know, we've got a very busy consulting practice, Merry, but we would be delighted to squeeze you in again," Blair smiled brightly. "We look forward to seeing you in person."

"Thank you for having us," I added, attempting to muster a smile, but knowing I could not match the thousand-watt dazzler that Blair displayed at every opportunity.

"Gentlemen, it's been a pleasure. And we'll be back after these messages."

And with that, the bright lights overhead were quickly turned off, and the studio became noticeably darker and cooler. One of the directors came over and congratulated us, reiterating Merry's invitation to return, and telling us this was a terrific segment. A different production assistant then led us out of the studio, down the hallway, and into the lobby.

"So, that was the angle you were working," I said as we walked toward Blair's black Mercedes.

"It was indeed. Sorry I couldn't give you a head's up. You know, some things are just better coming as surprises. Trust me, you're better that way. I know you. I can hit my mark, but you can't. You come off as more natural when you just react, rather than try and deliver your lines."

"I'll take that as a compliment," I said dryly. "But it sounds like we may have more work."

"We may indeed. But after this, Amber's going to let the interest in her rise organically for the next few weeks. She's a grieving widow and all. Like Merry said, she can't afford to look like she's taking advantage of the situation. We can't make her out to be Lady Macbeth."

"Certainly not," I said. "But that was quite a bombshell, nevertheless. How long have you known about this? Or did you instigate it?"

Blair stopped in his tracks and stared at me. "What are you implying?"

"What was your role?" I responded evenly.

"I was giving this some thought. And when I was talking with Randy Greece yesterday, I floated the idea. Greece didn't sound all that surprised, but you know how things are played in Washington. Those guys are figuring out all the angles, too. With Sudeau gone, his whole staff is going to be scrambling for work. Some can join other campaigns, but it's not like they'd be running the show. Not like here, with Amber. The transition would be seamless."

"And all you did was pass along an idea."

"What I did," he said with a smile and a wink, "was keep the money flowing."

Chapter 17

The first trickles of light were emerging in the eastern sky. We stopped for breakfast at a 24-hour coffee shop in Toluca Lake, a few minutes from Burbank. Even at five in the morning, there was no shortage of patrons, and the restaurant hummed with activity. In addition to NBC, the Disney and Warner Brothers studios were nearby, and production crews were readying themselves for an early shoot.

"Hey, listen Blair," I said, picking at my scrambled eggs. "I'm going to take a few days next week. I need some R&R."

"Oh? Going someplace?"

"Yeah, not sure where exactly," I said, still unable to discuss my medical condition. I had known Blair for over a dozen years, was keenly aware of his penchant for endless talking, and was reticent about sharing a confidence that could slip out in idle conversation. And I wasn't comfortable sharing my cancer diagnosis with anyone besides Leslie and Angelina yet. I had endured a number of life-altering events over the past few days. Incredible as it might appear on the surface, being diagnosed with a terminal illness actually got placed on the back burner. I needed time to think, time to talk more with Leslie and Angelina, time to absorb all of this. And I had an appointment at the hospital on Monday morning as well.

Blair drove me to Century City, where the hotel, still buzzing even as dawn was breaking, had removed the lockdown, and the valet was able to fetch my car. A number of news vans were still parked there, and I kept my head down to avoid being seen by anyone. I had had enough face time with the media for one day. But it turned out there was no cause for concern. Our *Hello America* segment would not air on the west coast for another hour.

I went home, kissed my family as they ate breakfast, avoided any in-depth conversation about my seven minutes of TV fame, and suggested programming the DVR to watch it later. I trudged upstairs, swallowed another one of Leslie's Dalmane capsules, and crawled into bed. The daylight was starting to creep in through the bedroom blinds, and I vaguely wondered how nocturnal animals like raccoons and opossums could snooze all day and prowl all night. My mind eventually eased, and I went to sleep, not stirring until late in the afternoon. Leslie told me the phone had been ringing off the hook all day, but I was blissfully unaware. I had silenced my cell phone and turned off the ringer on our bedroom landline. I had finally slipped into my own private world for nine hours and it felt good. I went downstairs and fixed another afternoon pot of coffee.

"Ned, I hope you don't mind," Leslie started.

"Mind what?" I frowned.

"I invited some company for dinner."

"Oh," I said, sensing that blissful feeling begin to disappear.

"It's Eli and Jill. And Courtney, too. They're concerned.

They want to get together. And I'd like someone to talk to as well."

"What do you mean?"

Leslie sat down. "Look, I know the diagnosis has been hard on you. And I respect that you want to keep it quiet for now. I personally wouldn't, although I think I understand. But I need to speak with someone about it. And I don't have anyone. Except Eli and Jill. Of all our friends, they're the only ones who know. And they're the only ones I can talk to. I've been keeping this bottled up the past few days and it's eating away at me."

I took a deep breath. It made sense. My initial annoyance that Eli had told his family about my situation quickly dissipated. They were our friends, they should know. I was compartmentalizing my diagnosis, but I also had so much going on, I could afford to. I had other things that diverted my attention, from the bizarre to the ridiculous, but this also meant I didn't have to focus on my illness. Leslie had no such outlets. And no matter what happened to me, the world would go on. A surviving spouse is the one who has to pick up the pieces and keep moving.

"All right."

"We'll order some pizza. Nothing fancy."

The pizzas arrived at seven, the Sterling family rang the front doorbell five minutes later. They gave us a round of hugs, Eli asking how I was holding up, Jill and Leslie fighting back tears. Angelina and Courtney, separated by three years, an immense gap at this age, were friendly, albeit distant. We ate out on the deck, where there was a cool, gentle breeze forming. It was close to the summer solstice, so the sky was still light out. But the marine layer continued to hover above us, obscuring the sun, continuing the gloom.

"You know, I'm really ready for summer," Angelina said, between bites of a slice of pizza dotted with mushrooms. "I am so done with this weather."

"All things will pass, honey," Jill said, and Leslie abruptly stopped eating.

"Do they?" Leslie said quickly. "Really?"

"Oh," Jill said with a start. "I'm so sorry. I didn't even think about that. I didn't mean anything by it. "

A moment of awkwardness ensued; it was a snipe that Leslie most likely did not intend for Jill. In moments of sadness, the anger turned within can sometimes misfire and spray whoever happens to be nearby. I stepped in, told Jill not to worry about it, and shot Leslie a glance. This was starting to play out as I had feared, the first signs of friends being forced to act differently, to walk on eggshells. To fall into the trap of making a seemingly harmless, off-the-cuff statement that previously would not raise an eyebrow, but now ran the clear risk of being misinterpreted.

"How are you holding up?" Eli asked me.

"It only hurts when I think about it," I mused. "So, I've been trying not to."

"There is something to be said for denial," he responded. "Dwelling on one illness can actually create another."

"How is that possible, Eli?" Courtney asked, addressing

her father by his first name. I knew the Sterlings liked to treat their precocious daughter as an equal, I had seen other families do this, yet I never bought into it. Angelina once addressed me as Ned, and I stopped her, saying she was the only person in the world who could call me Dad. I liked it that way. I didn't want certain things to change. I didn't want a lot of things to change.

"Well, you can worry about something so much, it can actually trigger another disorder," Eli said.

"Do you mean depression?" Angelina queried, putting her pizza down.

"Certainly a possibility. But I've actually seen the opposite, depression can actually cause a new illness. I've had patients who fell into a depression over something nasty, a divorce, a job loss, a foreclosure, all because they had trouble handling the stress. And a year or two later, they ended up being diagnosed with something more serious. In a few cases, cancer. I've come to believe the initial anxiety from that depression played a role in being diagnosed with a more serious disease. I've seen it numerous times. It's quite extraordinary."

"That is indeed extraordinary," Leslie said, adding, "I hope I'm not one of those. I've been feeling pretty terrible the last few days."

"I know it's a tough time," Eli said soothingly and put his hand over Leslie's. He rubbed it reassuringly.

We ate and chatted, although the mood became a little darker, a bit more grim. Eli nodded when I mentioned I was taking some of Leslie's sleep meds, and he offered to write me a prescription of my own. Rest was critical, he said. He also asked whether I thought I needed to speak to a psychiatrist, if I was feeling the need to talk to someone about my situation.

"What will that accomplish?" I asked.

"They can provide an outlet for you. Someone to confide in. I know you have a lovely wife and daughter to talk to. But psychiatrists are trained in this area. And there are some things that are so deeply personal, it's sometimes difficult to share, even with your own family. Having an outsider gives you the freedom to say what's on your mind. For some people, that's what clergy is for. I know you're not especially religious. Not yet anyway."

"Meaning?" I frowned.

"People often become more spiritual when things get tough. It's not uncommon. Or a bad thing, either. I know it's not for everyone. But everyone does need to talk. Just who you talk with, is the question. It needs to be someone you can feel comfortable with."

"I'll think about it," I said, wondering what other swirling winds were going to invade my heretofore cloistered and secure life.

"Well, no one's mentioned it yet," said Jill. "So I'll do it. Congratulations, Ned. You were wonderful on TV this morning."

"You saw it?" I asked.

"Of course I saw it. Leslie told me. How many friends do you know that get to joust with Merry Teale on television? You handled yourself well. Were you nervous?"

"I didn't really think about it," I admitted. "I just went in and treated it like we were having a one-on-one conversation. But Blair did most of the talking."

"He does that so well," Jill said. "How is he reacting to your diagnosis?"

I froze for a brief moment and then reached down inside a cooler and pulled out a bottle of beer. Twisting it open, I looked at the cap and then tossed it onto the table. "He doesn't know yet."

"You haven't told him?" Jill asked incredulously.

"Dear ... " Eli started.

"No, it's okay," I said. "I haven't told anyone else. Well, not exactly. I told a stranger. At the bar of the Century Plaza. After I met with Sudeau. That's all."

"Oh, for God's sake, Ned," Leslie railed. "You can only confide in a stranger?"

I shrugged. "It's complicated."

"But why?" she asked. "Why don't you want to talk to your friends? Your colleagues? They are your support system. They're the ones who'll be there for you."

I sat back and took a sip of beer. "I don't know exactly," I said. "I'm not sure how to tell people. How do you explain this to someone? How do you explain it at all? How do you get them to understand that it's not your fault? How do you avoid generating pity? How do you have that conversation and not move forward without feeling ... changed?"

"Ned," Eli began, "you're too worried about what other people will think. Give your friends some credit. Most people will be supportive. Not all, but you'd be surprised. I'm actually starting to get concerned about how *you* are dealing with this. You're too worried about other people's opinions."

I looked at Eli. "I spend my life asking people questions. What do they like, what do they dislike. Why do they think this way or that. I conduct opinion research. That's what I do. I study opinions."

"And yet," he said, "you're so focused on other people's opinions, what's happened to your own opinion? What do you care what other people think of you? You know it wasn't your fault you acquired this disease. It wasn't through smoking or an unhealthy lifestyle. It was through bad luck. Simple as that."

"Easy to say. But lung cancer has a stigma to it. I heard it doesn't get as much funding as a lot of other diseases. Don't some doctors even blame lung cancer patients for their situation?"

"Where did you hear that?" he asked, looking at me curiously.

"I read it on the internet," I said and managed to hold back a smile. "So, it has to be true."

Eli gave a small chuckle. "All right. Maybe there's a few kernels of truth in there. And I do happen to know a few doctors -- very few by the way -- that look down their noses at lung cancer patients. That the patients brought it on themselves, that they lied about not being smokers. They think some patients still sneak a cigarette occasionally. Look, there are crackpots in every field. Even medicine."

"Which is why," I said, "I am concerned about who knows what. And that some clients may not want me around. They may be fully aware that what I have isn't contagious. And they may sympathize. But that doesn't mean they still want to see me regularly, and watch me deteriorate."

"Let's not get ahead of ourselves. You don't know what the future holds."

"No," I said and took a final swallow of beer. "And I'm not so sure I want to."

Chapter 18

The Sterlings left at midnight, and I spent awhile combing through the internet again. I wasn't scouring the web for cancer stories this time, but rather, catching up on the news of the day, which is to say the assassination inquiry. There were no new leads, although a number of conspiracy theorists were claiming a certain Los Angeles pollster was surely the mastermind of this assault on American liberty. The last one to be with the vice president was naturally the first one to be suspected. After spending too much time reviewing other people's wildly incoherent postulations, I managed to push myself to bed at four o'clock, swallowing a Dalmane on the way, and slept to the almost respectable hour of twelve noon.

I checked my phone upon awakening, saw that I had twenty-three messages, and started listening to the most recent ones first. The first four were calls from old friends, expressing amazement and even congratulations at my newfound, though largely unwanted, fame. The fifth was a telemarketer wanting to sell me handyman services, but the sixth one grabbed my attention, perhaps to a greater degree than it should have. Iris Hatcher had left a message and asked if we could meet for lunch. Having slept through breakfast, feeling hungry and also feeling more than a little curious, I called back and agreed. The Baker Lipschitz Team was down a major client, and lunching with an aide to the speaker of the House had its appeal.

That she was a former CIA agent who just happened to be at the Century Plaza at the same time I was simply added to the intrigue.

"Should I make reservations somewhere?" I asked. "I know a few good bistros in Santa Monica."

"Oh, no," she said. "No place fancy. Let's go discreet. Someplace out of the way. I don't want to run into anyone right now."

"I suppose we could find a taco truck," I said.

"Fine. That's more my speed today."

"I was just kidding."

"I was not. Say, do you know where Kogi is?"

"Isn't that the crazy truck that serves Korean tacos?"

"It's not crazy," she said. "It's actually good. They have regular tacos, too. And they opened a storefront in Palms. Right at Overland. It's in a strip mall, kind of a dive. How's one o'clock?"

I got up and glanced into the mirror at my straggly hair, unshaven face, and droopy eyes.

"Two might be better."

"See you at two," she said and hung up.

Both Angelina and Leslie were out of the house; a note on the kitchen counter told me they had gone shopping. I fixed some coffee, got ready, pondered if I should let Blair know about this lunch, but finally concluded Iris might not want him to know. I wondered what she saw in Blair Lipschitz, and I wondered why she was at the Century Plaza the other night. Curiosity had led me into a full-fledged career. I wondered where it would lead me today.

Kogi was not really a dive, it was housed inside of a

busy strip mall, a two-story stucco building that was painted the color of spicy brown mustard. All the spaces in the lot were filled, and I needed to park a half block away and walk back. When I entered the small restaurant, only two patrons were inside, and one was waiting at the counter to order. Iris was sitting at a table by herself. She had a platter of half a dozen small tacos in front of her, untouched, as she sipped on a coke. I moved toward and she looked up. Those green cat eyes were always the first things that grabbed me.

"Hello there," I said, pointing to the spread on the table. "You must be hungry."

"Don't be silly," she said quickly, in her staccato voice. "I ordered for both of us, I got here early. It sometimes takes a while. Sit down. These are good, try the short rib taco. It's my favorite."

"They all look alike," I pointed out.

She gave me a brief tour of the taco plate, pointing out the short rib, the *carnitas* and the calamari tacos, and handed me an empty plastic cup to go get a soda. Then she told me she needed to go feed some quarters into the parking meter, but please start eating. This was a woman who was organized to the point of being robotic. I filled the cup with Coke, sat down, and pulled out a short rib taco. Taking a large bite, I chewed quickly, the sauce was spicy and tangy, becoming hotter as it made its way to the back of my throat. I swallowed and then took another bite, It was indeed very good. I was on my third taco when Iris sat back down.

"You're wondering why I wanted to meet," she said, not

bothering to even look at the food.

"Yes," I said between bites.

"It's not what you think," she said.

"It never is."

Iris swirled her drink around in the cup. It was clear plastic and looked like it held more crushed ice than cold soda. Frost lined the exterior. She stared at the beverage and struggled to put her thoughts into words. Finally she leaned in and spoke quietly.

"Listen to me, Ned. I need to pass something to you. It's an envelope and it contains information about who I think is responsible for Rich. I believe I know the triggerman."

I had picked up another taco but slowly put it down. "Go on," I said, my own voice lowered to a whisper.

"The other night I told you I used to work for the Company," she continued. "This man, he used to work for the Company, too. I recognized him when I was driving near the hotel. He was walking away from the crime scene. I did the time lapse. He was crossing the street four minutes after the shooting. We know the shots came from the building across from the hotel. It all adds up. He was wearing a disguise, but it was him. I never forget a face, even if it were disguised by a fake beard."

"Okay," I said, trying to make sense of this. "But why aren't you alerting the FBI? Or the Secret Service? They're the ones who can actually catch this guy. I'm not in law enforcement. In fact, I'm under a very large cloud of suspicion myself right now."

"What you must understand," she said, her voice scratchy and low, "is that I do not know who else was partnering with this man. He did not act alone, I can assure you. He is a paid assassin. He used to do work for the Company, but he's since gone off the grid. He has assets in other agencies, his tentacles reach far and wide. He knows some very important people. The last thing I want to do is alert someone who might be working with him."

"My God. You make it sound like anyone in the FBI could be in cahoots with this psychopath."

"I can assure you someone very high up in government -- maybe ours, maybe someone else's -- is in deep with him. I have no doubt about that. And while most federal agents are above-board, well, there are a few who aren't. I don't know who. And I can't risk it with such a high profile case like this."

I stared at her in utter disbelief. "And you don't know anyone, FBI, CIA, Secret Service, wherever, that you can trust to be above-board? After working in government for so long? I just don't believe that."

"Then believe this. The FBI has fucked up more than its share of investigations. You only know of the public ones. There are more. Even if I were sure which agents were straight arrows, there is so much opportunity for calamity here, I can't risk it. The agents may be all right, but their supervisors might not. And the Secret Service? Well, they grilled someone like you all night. Do you really think they have a clue about what they're doing?"

I could not disagree. But still, something didn't add up.

"Why not hand it to the media?" I asked.

"Are they any more trustworthy?" she countered.

"Think about it. What are their goals? They are a business. They are after ratings and readership. Advertising dollars. That's their life's blood. They would take this and milk it for all its worth. Their goal is to stretch this story out for as long as they can and squeeze as much capital out of it as they can."

"That's astoundingly cynical. In your eyes, everyone and everything is corrupt."

"Look at it this way. If I gave this to the media, the networks and newspapers would plaster his face all over the world. He'd burrow underground, and he would not be found."

"Maybe there's some truth to that. But here's what I really don't understand," I said, looking straight into those stunning green eyes. "Why me?"

"Why not you?" she countered. "Look, Ned, I hate to say this, but there aren't a whole lot of people in my life I can trust. Not my colleagues in the speaker's office, not a single politician in Washington. Not even law enforcement. And I know this man. I know who he is and what he is. It all adds up. My own life is at risk here. I'm in a bad place. He saw me the other night, just like I saw him. He knows me. He just doesn't know how to find me. At least I hope not."

"And you're going to entrust me with this knowledge? Of the man who assassinated the vice president?" I said, incredulous. "You don't know me. Yet you've ordained me to be the keeper of a monumental secret."

She nodded as if expecting this rejoinder, as if she were speaking with a small child who is unaware of the wily ways of a cold and unforgiving world. "I am highly skilled at a few things. Reading people is one of them. You're a good person, Ned. Deep down, you have goodness in you. And you're very smart. No, I don't know you very well, but I've checked you out thoroughly. You'll do the right thing, Ned. I know you will."

"And just what is that? What am I supposed to do with this great secret? If you, with all your years in government and law enforcement don't have anyone you can trust, how am I going to find that person?"

"At some point, that will become clear to you. If my life were not in such peril, I'd stay here and wait. I'm pretty sure someone tried to follow me here. Don't worry, I ditched them."

"Trust me, I'm worried."

"You're okay. I know you are. But I'm not. Look, if I'd seen the assassin but was sure he hadn't seen me, then I could stick around L.A. And yes, I'd have some time to figure out how to pass this along to the right person. There is a right person, Ned. I just don't know who they are yet. And I just don't have the time to find out."

"So, you're deputizing me," I sighed, trying to process all of this.

"I've been in hiding the past few days. I'm making plans to leave the country. I'll come back once all this has moved forward. Once things calm down."

"Where are you going?" I asked.

Her cat green eyes flashed for a moment and she smiled briefly, but it was a sad smile, nevertheless. She was pretty, she'd probably always been pretty. But she seemed very tired, and her face had the look of someone who had been burdened with far more than it could handle.

"Maybe Prague," she said a little dreamily. "Or Rio. Or Sydney. Capetown is nice. So is Alberta, this time of the year."

"All right. Better that I don't know."

"Yes. I wish I could do this myself. But I don't have the luxury of time. You do."

I took a deep breath. *I don't have the luxury of time.* Those words echoed harshly inside of me. If only she knew. If only she had some awareness that I might not have a lot of time myself. She was entrusting me but endangering me, too. And a thundering realization suddenly struck me, that it wasn't just me she was putting at risk. I had a wife and daughter. If this assassin ever found out about me, their lives could be placed in grave danger as well.

"No," I said, shaking my head. "I won't do it. I'm sorry. I have a family."

"They'll be okay. This man is a pro. He will not go after innocents. He doesn't believe in collateral damage."

"I can't take that risk," I said, standing up abruptly. "It's my wife and daughter. I'm sorry."

"It's too late for that, Ned," she said, standing up with me and moving closer, taking me by the elbow, squeezing it. The gesture did not feel invasive, but rather, disarmingly intimate.

I stared at her. "What do you mean?"

"Ned, I told you a small lie a few minutes ago," she whispered into my ear. "I didn't go out and feed the parking meter. You have the identity of the assassin. You have photos, background info, criminal history. You have a fairly complete dossier. I've spent the past two days putting it together. It's all in a brown manila envelope."

"I won't take it," I told her.

"You already have," she whispered softly, drawing her body against mine. "I put it in your car a few minutes ago. It's under the passenger seat."

"I locked my car," I said.

"I know," she responded. "I unlocked it."

Chapter 19

Iris darted from the restaurant before I could say anything else. It mattered not; the entire surreal episode had left me dumbfounded, as if I had entered a parallel universe. I sat back down and tried to piece our conversation together again, but little of it made sense. I stared at the now-cold plate of tacos. A few minutes ago they had looked very appetizing; now the very sight of them made me nauseous.

I finally got up and departed, walking down the street in a semi-coherent daze. I reached my Pilot, climbed in, and immediately bent over and glanced underneath the passenger seat. The manila envelope was there all right, looking both innocent and alien at the same time. Part of me wanted to open it and learn the identity of the closest living thing we had to a Lee Harvey Oswald. And part of me wanted to grab it, toss it in a nearby dumpster, and not get sucked into whatever insidious web Iris Hatcher wanted to ensnare me. Finally, I turned over the ignition, leaving the envelope where it was, unopened and untouched. I didn't have the foggiest idea what I'd do with this oversized nugget of what might well be a ticking time bomb. I didn't know where to begin or whom I could turn to. Best to let the envelope lie there for now, suspended in time, untouched by any more human hands.

Traffic was light as I cruised north on Overland, past

the Santa Monica Freeway entrance, past the various strip malls which all seemed anchored by various 7-Elevens. When I reached the gate at the Metro rail crossing, the arm was just starting to swing down, forcing traffic to a grinding halt. As I waited for the trains to glide through, I glanced into the rear view mirror and saw two men in ties and sunglasses behind me in a dark blue sedan. Had I not just met with Iris, I wouldn't have given these men a second thought. But fear is contagious, and even while recognizing how self-centered an emotion paranoia is, I couldn't help but let my curiosity get piqued. I briefly thought of doing an immediate U-turn just to see if they followed. Instead, I waited for the gate to go up and I drove slowly, turning west on Pico, then south on Sawtelle. The blue sedan, a Ford logo stuck on its grill, was still behind me, although it did allow one car to move in between us.

I slowed for a yellow light at National and then darted forward quickly, beating the light and momentarily losing the Ford. But as I drove further south, I had to stop at Venice Boulevard, and the Ford pulled up behind me once again. I turned right on Venice and did a full circuit around the block to get back onto Sawtelle, the Ford following slowly, but following me, nevertheless. There was no doubt now. I was being tailed.

Having someone follow you is an unnerving prospect to say the least. That I did not know who these men were, nor did I know what they wanted from me, made the situation even more precarious. That Iris Hatcher had just placed an explosive pile of documents underneath my passenger seat made the situation complete. I started to shake. These men might be law enforcement, or they might be the people behind the assassination itself. They might be both. I briefly considered flooring my Pilot and engaging in a car chase, a ludicrous thought considering I was driving an SUV, not a sports car. I quickly concluded the most likely outcome of such a ridiculous endeavor would be to either get pulled over by the police or propel myself into a car crash. I further imagined pleading my wildly preposterous conspiracy theory to a uniformed police officer, that a pair of men in ties and sunglasses were following me. I decided the men were most likely in law enforcement, for the simple reason assassins were not beholden to a rigid dress code. But after my lunch with Iris, the possibility of being tailed by the Feds did not make me feel very safe.

I headed a little further down Sawtelle when, thinking of the police, I hit upon an idea. Turning west onto Culver, I drove down the large street until reaching Centinela. I turned left, carefully allowing my tail to follow me. Moving into the center lane, I made another left into a parking lot, one with a large sign warning that this area was for authorized vehicles only. If I was going to have a problem today, I'd rather it be with someone at the Pacific division of the LAPD.

The Ford followed me into the area, which turned out to be a parking lot for police officers to leave their cars while on duty. I felt a small sense of relief that I was probably not being followed by a professional assassin. Whoever these men were, they didn't object to being in a police lot. I pulled into a space and waited. The Ford sat there in the middle of the lane, idling. After a few minutes, I noticed a pair of uniformed patrol officers walking by and I got out and signaled to them.

"Hi there," I said.

They gave me a quizzical look. "You're not supposed to park here," one said.

"I know," I replied, holding up my hands. "But I'm being followed and I figured this was the safest place to be."

"Who followed you?"

I pointed to the blue Ford. Its occupants were now rolling their eyes and already digging into their pockets for identification. The uniforms approached the vehicle, the occupants got out, and they spoke for a few minutes. They flashed badges at the officers, who pointed to me and smiled paternally. Finally, one officer walked back over to me.

"It's all right, they're FBI," he said, patting me on the shoulder and walking away.

His reassurance did not make things feel in any way all right, but it was probably the best I could hope for at this point. I thanked the officers and walked over to the Ford.

"Hello," I began. "I guess you know who I am."

"Most of the country knows who you are, Mr. Baker," said one agent, a tall, lanky man in his mid-thirties with black hair, slicked back.

I stared at him. "Look, I've already spent a lot of time with the Secret Service. And the FBI. I answered their questions for a good six hours the other night. What else can I tell you?"

"Well, maybe you can shed some light on your relationship with Iris Hatcher."

I shook my head. "I don't have a relationship with her. I've only met her a few times, usually by accident."

"But lunch today wasn't an accident, was it?"

I took a breath and thought how best to react to this. I didn't have a reason to lie, but I also had the uncomfortable feeling it might not be in my best interest to provide full cooperation. Again, thoughts of Iris Hatcher's trepidation about the people working for the United States government were weighing on my mind.

"She's scared," I said. "She doesn't feel like there's anyone she can trust. She thought she was followed to the restaurant. At first, I thought she was paranoid, but, well, here we are."

"Why would Iris need to trust anyone?"

"I don't know. She didn't tell me everything on her mind."

"But she did want something from you, didn't she?"

I shrugged, and then I had an idea. Put some space between us. "She's been seeing my partner. They're involved. She wanted to talk about him. Women. You know."

"Your partner. That's Blair Lipschitz?"

"Yes."

The agent gave a small chuckle. "All right. Blair Lipschitz. He's on our watch list, too. But it's funny how you all keep popping up together. Why were you meeting with Iris the other night at the Century Plaza?"

"I wasn't meeting with her. She just happened to be there."

"Oh, right. A coincidence."

"Didn't the Secret Service guys brief you?" I asked.

The agents looked at each other. "Um, communications between agencies aren't so great. Information doesn't always get shared."

I shook my head and refrained from inquiring about how efficiently our tax dollars were being used. "So, why follow me?"

"Your partner's been making some ugly comments about our investigation," he said. "And we keep coming up with you, your partner and Iris having meet-ups. We need to know more about what you're doing."

"We're doing nothing illegal," I said evenly. "At least I'm not."

"What does that mean?"

"I can only speak for myself. But why are you following Iris? What's her involvement in all this?"

"Why do you think?" he sneered. "Take three guesses."

And then things began to crystallize. Iris and Richard Sudeau. A former staffer when Sudeau was in the Senate. A late night rendezvous, a tryst at an out-of-town hotel. *What did you do when you worked for Sudeau? Whatever he wanted.*

"I think I see."

The agent shook his head and handed me a card. His name was Dirk Turner. "We're not getting anywhere here. Look, we won't hound you any more today. But if you think of anything concerning this investigation, anything at all, let us know. No detail is too small at this point. You can only help yourself by cooperating."

"All right," I said, thinking about the manila envelope in my car and briefly debating whether to hand it over. I didn't have a good reason not to, other than to follow the advice of a former CIA operative I had first met less than a week ago. I finally decided there was no great urgency. Sometimes standing still is the best way to move forward. *You'll do the right thing, Ned.*

"Oh, and Mr. Baker," the agent said, a knowing smile hovering about his lips.

"Yes?"

"Good luck with your procedure on Monday," he said, his smug smile telegraphing that he knew even more. There was no point in asking him how he had learned this or what else he had come across. The agent seemed to be taking no small measure of pride to conceal his smarmy attitude, and suddenly I was glad the manila envelope was still lying untouched in my car.

I watched him climb back into the Ford, share a laugh with his partner, and drive to the parking lot exit. I was still standing there, mouth slightly agape, alone in a cluster of police cars but not feeling very secure. I was suddenly feeling very unsteady, like the cartoon coyote who walks off the precipice of a cliff, not realizing the danger until he looks down and sees nothing beneath him.

The Ford swerved onto Centinela Avenue, I heard the engine being gunned and watched the sedan lurch forward, barreling quickly out of view.

Chapter 20

Detective Karl Mooring was getting frustrated. He had thought of almost everything, but now he was stymied. He wished he had a cigar to puff on. A stogie always relaxed him, but his doctor finally convinced him to give up the silent killers. It was also his final promise to Mary Lynn. She had relentlessly pushed him to quit smoking, but she had also pushed him to retire after twenty years. Things change. In ways he never could have conceived. He thought of her often.

Mendoza, his Forensics guy, had managed to pull both DNA and a thumbprint from the stairwell banister below the thirty-fourth floor. The two of them were cautiously optimistic, recognizing this DNA could have belonged to anyone. But they considered most people would not walk up or down thirty-four floors. And the law firm on thirty-four had no connection to any other office in the building. Thirty-three was under construction. There was no roof access. So most workers would simply be taking the elevator to and from the plaza level. There was little reason to do otherwise. The prints were fresh. There was a very good chance they belonged to the assassin.

Forensics ran the DNA through the CODIS database, a national archive that could identify over ten million felons. And yet there was no match. Nor did they get a match through their local records. They couldn't even get a match from the Department of Motor Vehicles.

Mendoza had a vague hunch the prints might simply belong to a janitor, perhaps undocumented, as was so common in Los Angeles. Illegal immigrants lived in the shadows, they rarely had legitimate drivers licenses, even if they owned a car. The Detective called the firm that subcontracted janitorial services for the building, and he tested every employee who might have had access to thirty-four that night. But nothing materialized. Zilch. Nada. Square one.

The Detective had hoped to solve this puzzle himself, to have something new to throw in the faces of the Feds. To keep showing them he wasn't just a local hick, but could outthink them. Outfox them. He considered handing over the DNA results to the FBI, but wondered if they'd botch this too. He knew he should cooperate with them, be a team player, especially in a matter this important. We were one country, he reminded himself, even if our law enforcement groups could barely stand one another.

He decided he'd try one last course of action. One last attempt. He called a former LAPD officer he knew, an old Acquaintance, a bright guy with whom he had started in the academy. The Acquaintance had quickly tired of mundane police work, and after two years on the force, was hired into the CIA. He owed the Detective a few favors, and should help him without asking too many questions. The CIA was good that way. When he got the Acquaintance on a secured line, the Detective asked if his old buddy could run the DNA samples through the Interpol database. The one that covered members of terrorist organizations, renegades, global operatives who worked off the grid.

The Acquaintance had asked him a few standard questions, but Detective Mooring was vague in his response. The Acquaintance did not like this and told him so. Matters of national security were not taken lightly, and no one was going to play cowboy on this. The Detective finally, grudgingly, told him his reasoning, his rationale, his theory. The Acquaintance agreed to help. He called the Detective a few days later with his findings. They had a match, but there was a problem. The man they had identified had indeed been a former CIA employee, a clandestine type who moved in the shadows. Or had at one time. But the agent was now dead, having been killed five years ago in a covert operation gone bad on the outskirts of Karachi. At least that was what his file stated. The body had never been found.

So the CIA would provide him with no name, no picture, nothing. The CIA would investigate this matter internally. The old Acquaintance did thank the Detective for cooperating, and complimented him on his patriotism. The Detective felt his mouth tighten and his rage grow. He had been played, just the way a local yokel would always get played by the Feds. It was time to look for a new tack. Do some old fashioned police work. He ended the call with his old Acquaintance silently, hanging up, without bothering to thank him. Without bothering to say goodbye.

*   *   *

Following my lunch with Iris and my latest unsettling encounter with the FBI, the rest of the weekend was spent in a quiet, idyllic cocoon. I wanted some peace before my procedure on Monday. Angelina and I watched a Dodgers game on TV, their pitcher tossed a one-hit shutout against the Mets. Leslie and I cuddled and held hands as we quietly listened to music, an eclectic mix ranging from Bruno Mars to Jerry Garcia, from Miles Davis to Gustav Mahler. I read a book on the healing power of the human psyche, wondering if it extended to healing metastatic lung cancer. We ate Chinese takeout. In short, we did what we might have done on any normal weekend. But our lives were no longer normal. I might not have too many more weekends like this. And whenever one of the ladies in my home started to bring up a maudlin subject, I bobbed and weaved, deflecting any deep conversation. My thoughts were dark enough; I didn't want them spoken. I wanted a weekend apart from the madness of the world. Monday morning would come soon enough, there was no doubt about that. It arrived quicker than I wanted.

Saint John's Hospital in Santa Monica was an architectural masterpiece. The exterior shined with patterns of blue glass and brushed steel, the interior framed by soothing, blond oak paneling. A soaring atrium that rose a good six stories high made for an extraordinary lobby. Near the ceiling was a window made of stained glass, undoubtedly the sign of a chapel. The stairway looked like it could have been lifted out of a Disney movie.

On one wall was a statement of the hospital's mission, a row of framed pictures meant to show off the associated physicians, but coming closer to displaying something akin to their employees of the month. I moved through the lobby in a daze, Leslie guiding me upstairs to the correct room. I had not fallen asleep until three last night, and my mood, already impinged from getting too little sleep and absorbing too much drama over the past week, was quite hazy.

We checked in, and after a brief wait, Leslie and I were led over to the prep room, where I changed clothes and was handed a hospital gown. The nurses installed an I.V. into my arm, checked my heart rate, and prepped me for the procedure. About forty-five minutes later, the thoracic surgeon, Dr. Silverstein, came in and briefly explained the procedure, walking out before I could ask any questions or inject any lighthearted remarks. The only comment I was about to make was the nervous observation that being treated by a Jewish doctor in a Catholic hospital would surely bring me double the good luck. In hindsight, I was glad I didn't verbalize my quirky, sleep-deprived thought. My anesthesiologist then came over to speak with us, his easy, reassuring tone meant to calm the frayed nerves of anxious patients. His name was Dr. Erman. I asked him where he went to medical school, and he smiled as he told me it was UCLA. I acknowledged this was a good school, and then reminded him that all of his training and education had led him to this crucial moment in time, and nothing he had ever done to this point, or would ever do in the future, could be as important as his work today.

Leslie gently took my hand and told me to shut up.

I was eventually wheeled into the operating room, and after more testing, the anesthesiologist placed a breathing device on me and asked me to count backward from ten. I got to seven and then suddenly found myself being wheeled back out of the operating room. For a moment I thought I saw the white light, but there was far too much commotion for this to be anything but a busy hospital hallway, and the bright lights were simply shining down from overhead fixtures. A nurse was asking me how I felt now that the procedure was over. I told her I felt like shit, and she stopped and admonished me not to swear around her or she'd be unable to help me. After providing her with a colorful opinion of her intractable moral requirements, a long void ensued. I stared up at the ceiling and waited a while until someone else, with a different voice and more amenable attitude toward honest answers from a semi-coherent patient, however blunt, took over and wheeled me into the recovery room.

Dr. Silverstein swung by again to tell me everything had gone well with the pleurodesis. There should be no more fluid buildup. He said it would take a week to test the biopsy for mutations, and he would check back on me again the next day. I nodded hazily, my mind not fully processing much more than that all was well. After another long wait, I was taken to a room on the eighth floor, and Leslie came in shortly after with some pastrami sandwiches from a local deli.

"I remember hospital food from when I had Angelina," she said, laying out lunch in front of me. I glanced up at the clock and saw it was already close to noon.

"Thank you for getting this," I said, suddenly realizing how hungry I was.

"Husbands in hospital rooms get special perks," she smiled. "How are you doing?"

"I think I'm starting to feel okay," I said, smearing some mustard on my sandwich and taking a large bite.

Leslie looked at me. "We haven't talked much the past few days. So much going on. I feel like I heard more from you when you were on TV. Or when we had Eli and Jill over."

"I know," I said, continuing to chew. "I'm sorry. I'm still sorting through a lot of what's happened."

"But can't you talk about these things with me? I know you prefer asking questions to answering them. But I'm feeling shut out."

I put down my sandwich. "I didn't mean for that. Do you understand what I'm going through?"

"I understand. But you have to let me in."

"I know. Look, I've been on a ridiculous roller coaster ride. Unlike anything I could ever have imagined. Think about it. One week ago, I was summoned to Washington to work on a presidential campaign, hired to conduct focus groups. A few days later I sat for a one-on-one meeting with the vice president, five minutes after which he gets assassinated on the balcony of the hotel room I had just been in. Then I ran into a political operative at the hotel bar, she apparently was having an affair with the vice president. The Secret Service dragged me back upstairs and grilled me for the next six hours, took my phone and wouldn't let me call an attorney. Can you imagine what's going through my mind?"

"I'm sure it was horrible."

"Then the next day my big-mouthed partner arranged a TV appearance for us, in which he took the liberty to attack our entire federal law enforcement as grossly incompetent. Then I got a call from that same political operative who wanted to meet, so she could hand me a dossier on some psychopath she's convinced committed the assassination. But she wouldn't tell the authorities who it was, because she was too scared. So she enlisted me, even though I didn't want anything to do with it. And oh, by the way, in between all this shit, I get diagnosed with terminal lung cancer."

Leslie put her sandwich down as well, and she blinked away a few tears. "Ned. I am so sorry."

"Yeah. I don't know how I could possibly get caught up in a criminal investigation of this magnitude, can you?"

"I meant the cancer. I'm so sorry."

"And I'm sorry for you and Angelina. The more I think about it, the worse I feel. The thing that grinds me the most is that Angelina may have to enter adulthood without a father. It just tears me up."

"We're not certain that's going to happen, Ned."

"I know, I know. And I'd like to stay positive, but can you see what a struggle this is?"

"You're going to a bad place way too soon."

I did not disagree. I was fifty years old, and I'd lived a life. I didn't regret much, but the most painful part of this process was thinking about the lost future, not mine, but

Leslie's, and especially Angelina's. The embraces, the conversations, the laughter. I think of Angelina and wonder what she'll do after college, where she'll be living. Whether she'll get married, have kids. What kind of life she'll have, how I could have helped her. The things you sign up for when you become a father. The perfunctory assumptions I had taken for granted, the myopic belief that I'd always be there for her, to be a part of her life. That vision had begun to fall into the shadows. I feared her memory of me was going to be placed in a box, tied with a bow and slipped deep within a drawer. Like an old photo album you dust off periodically, dredging up remembrances of the past, ones that become more distant and more faded and indistinct over time.

"I'll try not to," I said. "But it's hard. Staying busy and not thinking about it helps. At least it's kept me from falling into a depression."

"You know," Leslie said. "Millions of people are living with cancer. Some are stage four. It's no longer a miracle. I've been doing some reading on this, too. There are drugs in development. The doctors may not have a cure for cancer yet, but they are keeping people alive."

"Yeah," I agreed cautiously. "That guy I met the other night at the hotel bar. Said he's been living with cancer for fifteen years. Looked in reasonably good health."

"Well, that's reassuring. Is he still working?"

"Yeah, he owns a pot shop outside of Denver."

Leslie threw her head back and laughed. It was nice to see and nice to hear. I hadn't seen Leslie smile in a week, the ever-present frown on her forehead concerning me. I felt responsible for her despair, even though none of this was my fault. My illness went beyond my own suffering, it had launched misery in those closest to me. I wanted to ease their pain. It is a curse to be forced to witness the suffering of loved ones. Seeing the hurt in their eyes is harsh and torturous, an anguish that ends up being greater than your own.

"Well, owning a marijuana shop actually sounds safer than politics," she said.

"Never would have thought that a week ago."

"But what's this about a political operative?" she asked. "And an affair with the vice president?"

I told her about Iris Hatcher and my three-taco lunch, a meeting that ended with the identity of a renegade CIA agent secured in an envelope under the seat of my car. An envelope that was now starting to feel radioactive. And that despite my pleas to the contrary, Iris had arrived at the absurd conclusion that I was better suited than anyone else in the world to hold onto this precarious information. Simply because she thought I was a decent guy.

"My God," she said, her hand covered her mouth.

"And right now I'm in possession of what may be critical knowledge that involves national security. And by not turning it over to the authorities, I may be complicit in a federal crime. The Secret Service goons hinted if I actually knew anything, I might be tried for treason. Back then I didn't know anything. Now I do."

"Did you open the envelope?"

"No. I didn't want to get my fingerprints on it."

"Then it sounds like you still don't know anything."

"That's a lawyer's game. The type they invoke when you're on trial, the type where lethal injection becomes secondary to going down in history as having betrayed your country."

"I think you need to talk to someone," Leslie said, picking up her sandwich again but not biting into it.

I shrugged. "I'd been wondering about speaking with a lawyer ever since the Secret Service began to grill me."

"No," she said definitively. "That wasn't what I was thinking. Not at all."

"Then what were you thinking?"

"What Eli brought up the other night. About a psychiatrist. I think it would be a good idea right about now."

I let out a breath and told her I'd consider it. We spent the rest of the afternoon talking and playing Scrabble, and then Angelina came by. Still dressed in her dark blue softball uniform, she told us she had pitched Brentwood into the next round of the playoffs, beating Campbell Hall 3-2. They would now advance to play Viewpoint on Saturday morning. We also learned she had decided not to attend the prom; her mood was not festive, and she thought it would be boring. While I liked to believe it was due to my condition, she did let it slip that Aaron was no longer perceived as cool, having not gone out of his way to talk with her in the past week. She did, however, achieve her goal, which was simply to be asked to the prom, and even though she wouldn't be going, she would still have that proverbial notch on her belt. I tried to remember my own high school prom experience and mostly drew a blank. I vaguely recalled it was heavy on alcohol and light on drama.

On my first night in the hospital, I discovered I had forgotten to bring any Dalmane with me, but I decided not to call and make Leslie drive all the way back over with it. After tossing and turning for an hour, I finally reached for the remote, and without bothering to turn on a light, flipped on ESPN. After an hour of watching baseball highlights, a nurse in light blue scrubs walked in and asked if I needed anything. She was African-American, about my age, and looked remarkably alert for one-thirty in the morning.

"A sleeping pill would be great," I said.

"Lots of things would be great. But you only get one if the doctor ordered it," she said and looked on my chart. "Hmmm. Dr. Silverstein didn't order it. You don't get one."

"My tough luck."

"I tried sleeping pills for a while," she said. "I work a lot of night shifts. But you know what? They made me too groggy when I woke up. Plus, I read somewhere they can cause lung cancer."

"Not my problem anymore," I said.

"Say what?" she frowned.

"I already have cancer," I explained. "Stage four. Diagnosed last week."

"Oh?" she said, and began straightening a few things up near my bed. "You a smoker? Or just one of the unlucky ones?"

"Unlucky. Never smoked."

She took a long breath and let it out, in much the way a smoker might. "Not fair, is it?"

I chuckled. "That's life."

"I know. Believe me. I know what's not fair. I used to work the ER. I'd see car accident victims, usually in the middle of the night. Young kids sometimes. Nothing sadder than seeing someone be taken before their time."

"Very true," I said cautiously.

"I'm curious," she said, looking at my chart again. "Your name's Ned. Tell me something, Ned."

"What's that?" I asked.

She looked up at me and paused for a moment. "Have you made your peace with God, yet?" she asked.

I sat up and squinted at her. "That's a rather strange question to ask, isn't it?"

"Not really. I ask that a lot. We're in a Catholic hospital. Being in touch with God is allowable."

Now it was my turn to take a long breath. I looked up, the light from the TV dancing merrily about on the ceiling, drawing random patterns which quickly appeared and then disappeared just as fast. I had not made peace with God because I had not made peace with myself. I had not come to grips with my illness, my fate, the random nature of my malady. In fairness, I had not had much time to think about it, but I also knew I had not made any effort to do so yet.

My life had been filled with things other than religion, which was strange, perhaps, coming from a place like South Carolina, where religion is frequently woven into the culture. I was a casual believer, more of an observer, a witness. I had never come face to face with the question of my mortality, never needed to address the subject of how long I might live. I had taken some things as givens, such as a life well lived is a life lived long. I had no reason to think otherwise, no reason to think of this subject with any depth. I was, in a way, like the adolescent who assumed he would live forever, never taking the time to reflect or appreciate that life is indeed not forever, that the path we are on has an end point. The wakeup call of my diagnosis changed that. But I had not addressed the inner meaning of that wakeup call.

"No," I finally said. "I don't believe I've done that."

"Well," she said, "I'm not one to tell people what they ought to do."

"But you're doing so anyway, aren't you?"

She gave a sly smile. "Uh-huh."

I pondered this. "So, you think this works? Making peace with God?"

"Look, honey," she said as she removed a couple of plastic water glasses from my tray. "If you have an illness, you go see a doctor. And he starts the process to try and heal you. It doesn't mean the treatment is always going to work. But starting treatment is better than not starting it. The illness won't go away by itself. Same with making peace. You have to start somewhere. You can't ignore it."

I considered this, but I was unable to come up with anything that made sense. "And if I make peace with God, it's going to help me?"

"Ain't going to hurt. But it basically means you don't blame God for what's happened to you."

And then the crux of her point began to sink in. Whether I blamed anyone for my predicament. Clearly, I was not about to blame myself, but I was at a loss for just who was at fault here. It would be easy to simply shrug my predicament off as an inchoate case of bad luck, a randomness for which no one need bear any responsibility. The inherent unfairness of life that comes attached to certain diseases. But in the end, I mostly tried to avoid thinking about it. I didn't ponder the question, because I had no answers.

"It's hard not to blame someone," I admitted. "Although the doctors really don't know how I got cancer. It could have been air pollution, bad genes, anything is possible. Where do you start?"

"That's why you need to make your peace. Gets rid of the doubt."

Chapter 21

I dozed off at some point and when I awoke it was light out, and a different nurse was puttering around my room. This one showed no interest in engaging in any discussion of peace or spirituality, but rather wanted to take my vital signs, update my chart, and get on with her day. After she left, I picked up my phone and began listening to music. I had no interest in thinking about anything that required introspection right now. I wanted to allow my mind to drift, to give my psyche a rest. To heal. I listened to a Jimmy Buffet tune about life on a tropical island. And then just as the song was ending, the door opened.

"Well, this is some vacation you're taking," came a familiar voice. I looked up and watched Blair Lipschitz walk in, carrying a box of See's chocolates underneath a pair of spy novels.

"Oh, wow," I said, bereft of anything more intelligent to utter.

"Oh, wow, is right," Blair said, looking around and sniffing. "What kind of a villa is this?"

"The kind we normally keep secret."

"Yeah, and you did a poor job of it," he said, placing the candy and books on my night table. "Had me fooled there for a minute. You should tell me the truth."

"You should tell me how you found out."

"Your lovely wife," he said, sitting down next to me. "She spilled the beans."

I frowned. "That's not like her."

"Maybe yes, maybe no. She did look pretty stressed out when I saw her. Ah, don't blame Leslie. I'm good at charming women into doing things they didn't plan on."

"I'm not sure I want to hear much more of that."

"Relax, will you? I just stopped by your house to drop something off. A present I got. Figured I'd share the pain."

"Pain?"

"I'll tell you about it in a minute. But imagine my surprise to see Leslie there. You said you were going on vacation, but people like you always bring your wives along on a getaway. For a minute there, I thought you might be having a romp with some skank."

"You thought that, huh?" I asked dryly.

"No, I didn't. That's not you. I told her about this urgent business matter, needed to speak with you right away, asked where you were. I have to tell you, Ned, your wife is not a very good liar."

I closed my eyes. No, she was not. It is interesting to hear one of your spouse's virtues being sullied as a vice in need of fixing. Leslie was like me in that regard, neither of us had a poker face, our thoughts were practically scribbled on our foreheads. Being poor at lying was a liability in some people's orbits though, the world of Blair Lipschitz being one of them.

"So, what did she tell you?" I finally asked.

"Everything. Look, don't blame her. Leslie needed to talk. They get like that. It's hormonal. When women feel they can't discuss things, they get very unhappy."

"And you made her happy."

"I know what buttons to press, my friend. Yeah, she told me. Tough one, lung cancer. My uncle died of that, but he had it coming to him."

"Bullshit. No one has cancer coming to them," I retorted.

"Yeah, I disagree. Uncle Fritz was a two-pack-a-day man. Newport, that was his brand. He knew what it would do to him and he kept right on doing it. Smoked in front of my Aunt Jenny for years. Lord only knows why that second hand smoke didn't make its way to her."

"Well, regardless. I never smoked."

"Yeah, I know. Tough break. Kind of like getting herpes from a hot tub. You miss out on the fun and just get the disease."

"Charming."

"I just want to know one thing," Blair said, eyeing me caustically.

"And what's that?"

"Why you didn't say anything. I'm your partner. You have a fiduciary responsibility to share this sort of thing."

"Nonsense. I don't have to share my personal life with you."

"If it affects our business you do. And I have to tell you. Not confiding in me about this? It means you don't trust me. I feel wounded."

I rubbed my face. It is bad enough to have to comfort people you love when you reveal bad news about yourself. It was unfathomable that I might need to apologize to Blair for making him feel unhappy that I was diagnosed with a terminal illness, and didn't have the courtesy to share it with him. But the feeling of owing Blair a debt quickly passed.

"I would have told you soon enough," I said. "On my terms, when I was ready."

"Well, the business world doesn't always follow your timetable."

"How do you mean?"

"How do I mean? I mean we get the green light from Garter to do the research project. That's a six-figure study, the discrete choice thing. Figure out the pricing of that sex pill."

"I thought it was on hold. That it might not happen."

"I made it happen. That's what I do. Bring in business."

"Go on."

Blair gave a sample of his dazzling smile. "I told them I had my ear to the ground. Kept in touch with my industry contacts. Told them my pal over at Opinions and Surveys was doing a project for Nature's Light. Said they had something similar in the works. A sex supplement for women. They were in the middle of developing a marketing plan for this. Planning to launch later this year. Boy did that get the folks at Garter scurrying! They forgot about everything else, and now they want to move on this!"

"So, you made it up."

"Of course I made it up. We need some business. And we need you back in the office, Leslie told me your procedure went well. Glad to hear it. Would have liked to have heard it from you, but good news is good news any way you get it."

"Look," I said. "This is part of a process. You don't just rid yourself of lung cancer."

"You don't just lie around in bed either. Not good for the spirit."

"Thanks for the pep talk."

"Well, what's your next step? When do they discharge you? Or do I need to bust you out of here?"

I shrugged. "I'm supposed to be released tomorrow. I can be back in the office when I feel okay. If I feel okay."

"How do you feel right now?"

"Good Lord," I sighed. "I just had a procedure yesterday. There's something called healing."

"Sure. But I know you. And I know you don't like hanging around the house. You like working. You like being productive."

"And you like making money."

"I do. And I can make more of it when you're pitching in. Look, I'll start Wanda on the Garter project. But it needs your magic. We'll email you a first draft of the questionnaire and you can review. Shouldn't be too stressful. If you like, you can telecommute for a few days."

"Big of you. But you're not my boss. I'll do this on my timetable," I said, still feeling a little sore from the procedure.

"We need you, buddy," Blair said, his dark eyes looking big and pleading all of a sudden.

"I'll do my best," I responded, shaking my head.

"Atta boy. And I got some good news on our aspiring presidential candidate. Spoke with Greece yesterday, got an Amber alert. She's still the grieving widow, but the buzz around Washington is getting intense. Some people are generating petitions urging her to run. For Rich's sake. For his legacy. It's becoming a movement and it's taken on a life of its own. It's incredible!"

"What's our role here?" I asked, not feeling entirely comfortable about having gone on national television last week, helping to promulgate rumors of her impending candidacy, but not feeling entirely bad about it, either. My knowledge about presidential campaigns is that most will fail. But as Blair hastened to remind me, they also generate plenty of publicity and billable hours for the campaign consultants. With my longevity uncertain, and with a daughter to put through college, the idea of some serious money coming in was getting my attention. I also knew I was sick; I just didn't feel sick. I thought back to my first meeting with Dr. Ashland. *Cancer often works silently.*

"If Amber's in, we're in. Greece likes us, and that's what counts. Used to be that politicians made a lot of the decisions, both for public policy and their campaigns. Now all they do is fundraise and get their faces on TV. Their staffs run the show, and their donors tell them how to run it. And I think Amber is good with Greece. And Greece loved the work you did on those focus groups last week. Terrific insights on Amber. I think that helped push the needle with her."

"All right." I said and reached for the box of See's. I opened it, took out a piece, and bit into a dark chocolate chunk, clustered with peanuts. Not my favorite, but that's what happens with a box of chocolates. You get what you get.

"Is it good?" Blair asked.

"Chocolate's always good," I mumbled, chewing slowly.

"Leslie said you liked See's. Personally, I would have preferred a bottle of Tanqueray, but that's just me."

"Chocolate works better for my system. And, oh yeah ... you said you stopped by my house for a reason. How come?"

"You weren't picking up your phone. Guess the Wi-Fi isn't so great in a hospital. Unbelievable how Starbucks can master what modern medicine can't."

"What were you calling me about?" I asked.

"Good news and bad. The check from the Sudeau campaign arrived. That'll keep us going for a while."

"Good," I nodded with more than a little relief. "And?"

Blair reached into his pocket and pulled out a sheaf of papers. "And Haley. She said she'd get even with us for firing her. Guess she was right. Lawsuit time."

"Oh, crap."

"Oh, yeah. Sexual harassment. Can you believe that?"

I shook my head. "Why did you hook up with her?"

"With a body like hers? No reason not to. Half of the Westside was doing Haley Comey. Funny thing is, I didn't have to work at it. The whole thing was her idea. All I did was say yes."

"Funny," I said wearily, "And all I did was say no."

Chapter 22

I spent another day at Saint John's before getting discharged by Dr. Silverstein. A resident had come in early that morning, a nice, baby faced young man who seemed a little unsure of himself. He examined my charts at length, said something unintelligible about white blood cell counts, and recommended I stay another night in the hospital. Then Dr. Silverstein came in, scoffed at the idea, and told me I was better off at home. Hospitals, he continued, were among the worst places to stay if you want to remain healthy; certain viruses were rampant and patients commonly acquired new infections. He also shook his head and muttered something disparaging about white blood cell counts, saying young residents needed to be seen and not heard.

Leslie drove me home, and I stared absently at the gray cloud cover, the continued manifestation of June gloom. The rest of the day was spent resting, watching TV, and avoiding anything stressful. I checked email and saw that Wanda had already put together a questionnaire draft for Garter, but I decided to let it wait until tomorrow. Maybe until the day after. I was feeling especially calm. Then Leslie sat down next to me, watching silently, waiting for a timely moment to summon my attention.

"What's wrong?" I finally asked.

"Nothing," she said quickly.

"Feels like something."

"Promise you won't be mad?" she asked cautiously.

"Sure," I said, sensing the impending storm.

"I did something I probably shouldn't have."

"We've all done that," I said, waiting for her to tell me she had let Blair know about my illness.

"Um, yes. Listen, Ned. I called that doctor. You remember. The one Eli told us about."

I took a breath. Yes, I did remember, all too well. The psychiatrist. An unknown scribbler of notes, someone with whom I would share my deepest darkest secrets, my most paranoid fears. I didn't like that idea much. My experience with therapists was limited to the one session Leslie dragged me to before we were married. It was during a crazy period before our wedding, when arrangements were being cancelled, and madness ensued. When the caterer who committed to us had a change of plans, when the minister discovered he was double-booked and chose the other couple, when the band we hired broke up because of a spat over a girl. Anything and everything had gone wrong, it was as if the stars had aligned in precisely the most inopportune way for us to exchange our vows. And instead of doing the sensible thing, clinging to one another and working together, we instead began to bicker, an ugly tendency that previously gone undetected in our relationship. Before long, we were arguing every day and the partnership itself began to teeter.

Leslie was given the name of one of the super doctors, a laughable term assigned to a small group of local physicians not because they were necessarily good at what they did, but because they were well-known amongst the right circles. Our psychoanalyst presented himself as a couples counselor, and I regretted the session from the moment we walked inside his incense-infused office. The blinds had been drawn, and the darkness did not make me feel at ease. The good doctor wore a forest green cardigan sweater, and while I would never recall his face again, the green cardigan for some reason remained fresh and present in my mind.

The bulk of our session consisted of Leslie and I talking about what was bothering us, but neither of us were allowed to respond to each other, except to play back what the other had said. It was a maddening thirty-five minutes, drawn to a close by my raising my voice at the therapist and telling him the whole session was a bunch of utter nonsense. He held up his hand and said the gist of our issue was money, pulling out a calculator and reviewing the price of our wedding. He recommended where we could cut some corners, suggesting the cost of the reception might even be tax-deductible. He then announced our fifty-minute hour was up and asked if we could write him a check on the spot, apparently his office rent was due. As we waited for the elevator, Leslie and I looked at each other, burst into laughter, and hugged. In a convoluted sense, the therapy session worked. Neither of us felt the need to return, and our wedding turned out to be a fun day. We hired another caterer, picked a different minister, and used a DJ instead of a band. And we reduced the stress because we simply chose not to worry about the small problems.

"So," I said, "you do recall our one and only episode with a shrink."

"Of course. That was the turning point in our relationship."

We both laughed for a moment, and then, as if on cue, we both got serious. We looked down at the carpet for a while. "I'm not mad at you for calling the doctor," I said and looked into her eyes. "But do you really think I need to do this?"

"Yes," she said. "You're going through a horrendous period. And you feel you can't talk to me. I'm sorry for that. But I love you and I think you need to speak with someone. And I didn't think you'd do this on your own. That's why I made you an appointment."

"For when?"

"Tomorrow. Eleven-thirty. I hope you're not angry with me."

"No," I said quietly. "Not with you."

So the next day at eleven-fifteen, I pulled up in front of an office building along San Vicente Boulevard in Brentwood, inserted a credit card to pay for an hour of time on the meter, and walked inside. Dr. Heck's office was on the fourth floor, and as I walked down the thickly carpeted hallway, it occurred to me how eerily quiet it was. Unlike my office, there was no whirr of activity, no loud conversations, no one poking their head into a doorway, no dull tapping of keyboards. There was just an emptiness, many closed doors, and a gnawing sense that I might be the only person alive in here.

I walked into Dr. Heck's waiting room, sat down, and

thumbed absently through a magazine, not reading, not focusing, barely even looking at the pictures. After a few minutes I tossed it back onto the table and looked around the room. A couple of paintings lined the walls, landscapes of sunsets or sunrises, it was hard to tell which was which.

After sitting for ten minutes, the office door finally opened and a short, seventy-ish man with graying, rumpled hair, gold-framed glasses, and a stooped posture, motioned me inside. He introduced himself as Dr. Heck and pointed to a black leather chair for me. He eased down into an identical one, facing me, about six feet away. I sat down, got comfortable and waited. And waited. I looked at Dr. Heck and he looked back. I didn't say anything and neither did he. The silence grew awkward, and after about ninety seconds, I finally spoke.

"Well, I guess you win, don't you?"

"How do you mean?" he asked.

"I spoke first."

"Did you think this was a game?"

"In my line of work, it sometimes is."

"Oh. What do you do?"

"I ask people questions," I said, giving my standard line, which normally was followed by further probing. In this case, Dr. Heck said nothing. Rather than endure another long gap of silence, which at two hundred and fifty dollars an hour was wasteful, I spoke again.

"I work in research. Political polling," I added. "I conduct surveys and focus groups for politicians. And for corporations, to help bring in money for us when the political well runs dry."

Dr. Heck looked at me. "And what brings you here today?"

I took a deep breath and let it out. "Last week," I said, "I was formally diagnosed with stage four lung cancer. My physician, Eli Sterling, he's been a friend for a long time. He thought it might benefit me to talk with someone. So did my wife."

"I see," he said. "What do *you* think?"

I did not answer right away. It was interesting to see his dispassion here, the same reaction that doctors and nurses had when learning of my illness, a subject they took at face value, an ongoing part of their job. The revelation that a person had a life-threatening disease did not faze them. I suppose they've seen this many times before, medicine is a field devoted to treating sick people, so this is what they encounter. It is reassuring in one sense, unsettling in another, that a person can take another's impending mortality in such easy stride. I could only conclude this is how they remained sane, that if they got emotional over every patient, they would be rendered unable to do their jobs properly.

"I admit I'm probably in a state of shock. I never planned on anything like this happening."

"How could you possibly?"

"My parents are both in their eighties. I had no reason to think I wouldn't make it as long as they have. I've lived a healthy lifestyle, never smoked. Nothing in my family history ever indicated cancer. I'm stunned by all of this. I'm still trying to figure it out."

"What are you feeling?" he asked.

"Not much," I admitted. "That's maybe what scares me the most. Maybe this hasn't fully sunk in yet."

"Why hasn't it sunk in?"

"I don't know. I suppose ... I haven't allowed it to. I've had too many other things going on in my life. I've been crazy busy, and not in a good way."

"How so?"

I took the doctor through my ordeal, the living nightmare that wouldn't go away. I explained my interaction with the vice president, that I was the last person to meet with him before he was assassinated. I related my episodes with a variety of federal law enforcement agencies. I omitted the part about Iris and the envelope; there were some things I felt were best left unsaid to a stranger, even one with whom I was supposed to be fully candid. A part of me regretted sharing that with Leslie. The doctor listened carefully, then got up and walked over to his desk. He turned on his computer and began combing through some websites. I stared at him, bewildered. Finally, he came back over to me, sat down and took of his glasses.

"I'm sorry," he said as he wiped his glasses with a piece of cloth, and then put them back on again. "I don't normally do this in a session. But I have some patients who are delusional, they believe they play an active role in current events. That world leaders know who they are, and that secret agents are out to get them."

"And you thought I was one of those."

"I understand that you're not delusional. You are actually living through a scenario many patients only envision in their mind's eye. And as odd as it might sound, those patients are easier to treat."

"Because they can be coaxed out of their delusions?"

"Sometimes, yes. Your situation is apparently very real. I can help you deal with certain aspects, especially with coming to grips with the cancer. It's called psychosocial oncology. Regarding those other events, well, perhaps I can help you try and cope."

"All right."

"I'm curious about something. How have your friends and family reacted to your illness?" Dr. Heck asked, bringing me back to my own situation.

"I ... I haven't told anyone outside my wife and daughter. And Eli of course. And ... well, Leslie told my partner as well. Business partner."

Dr. Heck raised an eyebrow. "Why haven't you told people?"

I thought about this. "Fear, I guess. I haven't even told my parents. They're frail. I don't want to worry them. But there's another concern. How people will look at me now. How it might hurt my business, maybe clients thinking they can't trust that I'll be there for them."

"Why would you think that?"

I sat back for a moment and thought. "I guess early on in my career, someone I worked with had a heart attack. He recovered, but people were uneasy around him. No one wanted to be responsible for that happening to him again. We were nice to him ... but ... I don't think we trusted that he'd be the same."

"Maybe you just didn't trust yourselves."

"Maybe. I don't know. But when I told my wife and daughter about my diagnosis, it was ... awkward. I was the one who had to comfort them, not vice versa. I needed to reassure them I'd be okay."

"Do you believe that?" he asked. "Do you believe you'll be okay?"

The weight of that question bore down on me. I realized I did not. Despite the encouragement from Eli, from Leslie and Angelina, from the confident doctors who treated me, I could not run from the feeling that I simply would not be okay. Eli told me not to pay attention to the chatter on the internet, but I could not deny the statistics. The majority of stage four lung cancer patients die within two years of diagnosis. Even if the numbers were a little dated. Even if advancements were being made. Even if those patients were older than me. Stage four was stage four. *There is no stage five.*

"No," I said weakly. "I guess I don't think I'll be okay."

"Do you want to be okay?"

I looked at him sharply. "What kind of a question is that? Of course I want to be okay. I have a wife, a seventeen-year-old daughter, a family to take care of. Yes. How could you think to question me on that?"

He held up a hand. "I'm just asking. But tell me something. You say you're stage four. Just how far has the cancer spread?"

I stopped. "I'm not sure, really. I ... I just was told it had spread to other parts of the body."

"You don't know?"

I shook my head. "I've had so much on my mind the

past week. So many things to process. I'm not a scientist, these things never ... occurred to me before."

"It's important to find out," he said.

"Why?" I asked.

He leaned forward. "Because you need to own your cancer. You need to know what you have so you can be part of the decision process," he said and took off his glasses once more. "This is actually very important. More so than you might think."

"Isn't that the doctors' responsibility? To guide treatment?"

"It is. But doctors are human. It's your body and your life. And it helps if you have a plan."

I tried to take this in. "I'm not sure I follow," I admitted wearily.

"You have to have an approach. It's different for everyone, but you have to have yours. Are you going to try and live every day to the fullest? Are you going to try and do some things you always wanted to do? Write a novel? Travel the world? Climb the highest mountain? It's all right if you don't want to do any of those things. It's all right if you want to just take it easy and not flood your body with chemo. You get to choose. But it's important to have an approach. Everything you do from here on out will flow from that."

I thought for a minute. It made some sense. And I hadn't given myself much time to think through all of this, so many ancillary things had been coming at me fast.

"I believe," I said, "I have an idea what mine might be."

"Oh?"

"I want to live a normal life for as long as I can live it. That's all. No interest in climbing Mount Everest. Just doing what I've always been doing. Until I can't do it anymore."

The doctor smiled for the first time. "Now I think we're finally getting somewhere."

We finished the session shortly thereafter and I returned home. Leslie was at work, Angelina was still at school, and I had an empty house in which I could ponder my new approach. But as I was thinking through what Dr. Heck had said, my thoughts were interrupted by an unexpected visitor.

Any doubt that I was still under law enforcement scrutiny was removed during last week's run-in with the smarmy FBI agents inside the LAPD parking lot. But on a lazy afternoon, with me just one day out of the hospital, the front doorbell rang, and I found myself staring out at the latest federal agent assigned to my case. The man was middle-aged and was mostly nondescript, except for a well trimmed brown goatee that he rubbed a few times.

"Hello, Mr. Baker," the man said and quickly flashed an important-looking gold badge. "Rob Lamb. I'm with the DHS. I don't mean to disturb you. But I'd like a moment of your time, please."

"The DHS?" I asked.

"Oh, I'm so sorry," he said apologetically, "Department of Homeland Security. I just have a few questions for you. May I come in?"

I stared at him for a long moment before finally opening the door. "I guess I don't need to ask what this is about."

"No, I suppose not," he said and as he entered the living room and sat down on the couch. "It won't take long. This is mostly background information."

"All right," I said. "But I don't know what else I can help you guys with."

"I'm sure you've had a rough time of it," he said, with all the fake sympathy of someone who could likely care less. "And if it will make you feel any better, I'm really looking into your business partner."

"Blair? Why?"

"Mr. Baker, your partner has been making some nasty public insinuations about the federal government. He's hardly unique, but we believe he's become a bit of a loose cannon."

"Fair observation," I said dryly. "But I can assure you, other than his mouth, he's harmless."

"That's not so harmless," Lamb responded, eyeing me curiously. "We'd like him to stop."

"Me, too. Hope you get farther than I have."

"You've spoken with him?" he asked curiously.

"What I've told him is that his big mouth will get him into a lot of trouble one day. But it's his stock-in-trade," I said. "It brings in business and it brings in women. That's mostly what he cares about."

"Ah, yes. The women. I was going to raise that subject. His relationship with Iris Hatcher. You're familiar with her?"

"Yes," I said. Now it was my turn to be curious. "And how do you guys know about his relationship with Iris?"

"You *guys*?" he repeated.

"Yes. I was stopped the other day by a pair of FBI agents. They wanted to know the same thing. They were tailing me."

"Oh," he said, frowning. "I see. What did you tell them?"

"Not a lot. I don't know a lot about Blair and Iris."

"Ah, fine. But how much do you think your partner knows? Blair. He and Iris were having a fling, weren't they?"

"I guess. Brief. They just met recently."

"Do you know if Iris had told him anything?"

I shrugged. "I wouldn't know. What's this all about?"

The man rubbed his goatee again. He struck me as unusual, but I didn't have much of a yardstick with which to compare. My reference points were FBI and Secret Service agents who came off as haughty and demanding, insular personalities who pledged allegiance to a particular team, with interlopers unwelcome. Rob Lamb looked more like an outsider, a person who was seemingly uncomfortable in his skin.

"We at the DHS have reason to believe Iris Hatcher was actively involved in the assassination. She was acquainted with the killer. She may have been helped facilitate it. We're still investigating, although there's only so much we can do at this point. But anything you know, Mr. Baker, anything at all, would be helpful."

I sighed. "I keep saying the same thing to everyone. I'm a pollster. I was hired to conduct some focus groups for the vice president. I met with him at his hotel. That's all I know."

"And with regard to Blair ... ?"

"Blair," I said, "I don't imagine he was involved in any of this. Why would he be? Sudeau was our client, we had every reason to want him to get the nomination. But did Blair learn anything after the fact? Did Iris tell him things? I have no idea. But why aren't you approaching Blair about this? Or Iris?"

"We're trying to be thorough at the DHS. Methodical. We obviously can't speak with Iris, but yes, we've spoken to Blair, and he is of interest. And I agree with you. His only involvement in this is probably what he learned after the fact. And what he's not saying."

"And why can't you speak with Iris?" I asked. "Has she disappeared?"

The man's eyes narrowed. "Mr. Baker. You haven't heard."

"Heard what?"

"It appears you have not turned on the news today."

"No, I haven't," I responded, starting to get a little testy. "Why should I?"

"Because," he said, a stern look crossing his face, "Iris Hatcher was found this morning in a parking lot near the airport. Or, I should say, her body was found. Next to her car. Cause of death was suffocation. They're doing an autopsy, but apparently someone strangled her."

I took a breath. "Oh, my God."

"I understand you didn't know Iris well. But is there anything about her you could share with us?"

I looked down and thought about the dossier in my car.

You'll do the right thing, Ned. The voice of Iris Hatcher was etched into my psyche. She thought she was in danger, and she was correct. I briefly considered handing the manila envelope over to the DHS agent. But there was something off-kilter about this man, something that did not feel right. I couldn't quite pinpoint what it was. A few weeks ago, I might have reacted differently. Cooperate to the fullest. Capitulate and hand over everything. But my conversation with Dr. Heck was looming in my mind. I needed an approach, not just to the cancer, but to these unwanted intrusions that were floating in and out of my life. I also thought about what Iris had said. *You'll do the right thing, Ned.*

I turned back to the DHS agent. "No. I'm sorry. I don't know anyone who would harm her," I said. "No one at all."

Chapter 23

The Assassin lounged near the big pool, sipping on a virgin piña colada. A few small children ran by, screaming and splashing the puddles of excess water that had sloshed onto the deck. A few drops landed in his drink and he put it down disgustedly. The operation was not going well at all. This was not how he liked to work. His modus operandi was to spend some up-front time in a city, scouting his assignment, executing the plan flawlessly, and then departing in a hurry. Sticking around could bring him no good.

He had already finished some solo clean-up work, deftly removing the pretty operative who had recognized him in Century City. With all of his excruciating attention to detail, who would have thought someone from his past would be driving down the street, a former agent who could actually recognize him in his disguise? He liked his habit of wearing the nondescript suit and tie, the fake beard and clear eyeglasses, during an operation. There was a comfort level to his regimen that made him feel secure. This was his workaday outfit, the uniform he put on when he was going to fulfill a contract. It allowed him to separate, to conduct his business anonymously, to play a part, to assume a role. To even pretend he was dressed as a character in a movie.

The Assassin terminated lives for money, actions that were surely barbaric, but no, he did not consider himself a barbarian. He simply earned a living, plying his trade, applying the tricks he was taught, the skills for which he had a profound level of expertise. And if he chose to decline a contract, it would certainly not change the victim's fate. If he said no, there would be others who would say yes. If a person needed to be removed, it was only a question of how best to engage. At least he was efficient and didn't take pleasure in anyone's demise. He tried to end things quickly for them. A compassionate killer. At least that's what he told himself.

His pattern was inconveniently altered this time. His identity had been compromised. Naturally, he used a different disguise when he choked the former operative, yanking hard until he was certain she had taken her final breath. The sultry woman with the bright green eyes, the kitten who had left the Company many years before, securing a cushy job on Capitol Hill. She had gone on to work for the vice president when he was a mere Congressman, and had apparently continued to service him. Smart woman, foolish choices. If only she had stayed home that night instead of driving to have a hotel tryst with a man who could surely care less about her. Those green eyes. He knew those eyes had recognized him as he crossed Constellation Boulevard that night, and they recognized him again, albeit too late, as he wrapped the twine around her neck and tugged until her body went limp. But a more crucial concern lay in front of him, the very real possibility she had alerted someone, revealing his identity to an operative cunning enough to thwart him.

This particular job was special, the opportunity of a lifetime. It was the Super Bowl for people in his line of work. The payday was huge, a gigantic windfall, but one that came coupled with enormous risk. Everyone would be looking for him, and there was no clandestine place to hide, other than in plain sight. He had received a phone call the day after he removed the vice president; he was ordered to stick around Los Angeles. He wasn't told why, he was never told why. Just that there would be another assignment. At first, he thought the next step was Iris, a task he had taken upon himself to fix. Finding her wasn't difficult, a few calls to the speaker's office allowed him to con an unsuspecting staffer into revealing the name of her latest boyfriend. Staking out the man's home in Santa Monica Canyon made it remarkably easy to find her. And after following her to the airport, he was able to act fast.

But even after he had taken Iris out, he was told to await further instructions, his client had other plans. And so he waited. The compensation was robust, so he was outwardly agreeable. He was always agreeable. He never made waves. But he also knew that he needed to leave L.A. soon, to distance himself from the growing risk that his identity could be compromised. The longer he stayed, the greater the chance of his being apprehended, and that was just something he could not allow to happen. Not again. And yet, there was nothing he could do. He had to remain in a holding pattern and wait for further directives. Disobedience could keep him from continuing to do what he was doing. Earning what he was earning. Defining himself in a world where most people lived undefined lives. And it was a sober fact that in his line of work, an unhappy client would likely result in a death sentence for him. That was just how this business operated.

He would receive more details when the time was right, but he was told the final step here should be very rote. That it would have to be routine. The Assassin had a hunch who this might involve, and he had already begun baseline work on his new target. The man was a civilian and had no background in espionage. He was told to prepare for an everyday killing, as simple as a drive-by shooting, one of those random freeway murders that happen in L.A. Road rage, a disagreement, perhaps on who should be in which lane, there could be a dozen plausible explanations for this one. The beginning of the Santa Monica Freeway would be perfect if it could be arranged. It just needed to be done, and executed without leaving any footprints. And he could no longer wear the facial hair and glasses. Maybe this time he would mix it up and wear a light blue UCLA baseball cap. Or one of those silly football jerseys that grown men wore, emulating their gridiron heroes. He smiled as he thought of it, a momentary pleasure that was quickly erased by the screaming children running by him again, in the opposite direction this time, but loud, shrill, and still managing to splash him once more. He glowered at the children and silently thought of ways he could voice his displeasure.

*   *   *

Dr. Ashland's assistant wanted me to come into the office the next day, and I did not take that as a good sign. Eli once told me that when doctors have good news, they often call you themselves, they relish the moment when they can hear that sigh of relief, the heartfelt gratitude and to enjoy the brief moment of serenity. Physicians, especially oncologists, encounter too much heartbreak, too many people they cannot cure, lives they can only extend for a short period of time. It was an unfortunate conundrum of working in medicine, he told me, that many treatment options are available, but there were some illnesses doctors just could not fix.

Leslie and I arrived at the clinic, but we did not wait long. We were quickly whisked into an exam room and told the doctor would be right with us. Dr. Gus Ashland came in two minutes later, a dour look on his face, his eyes cast downward, ostensibly reading my radiology reports, but to my mind, simply averting his gaze. No one wants to look at the condemned.

"Hello, Ned," he said softly, finally turning to us, nodding formally to Leslie and then shaking my hand. "How are you feeling?"

"All right," I said apprehensively.

"Well, the good news is that the pleurodesis procedure went well. I spoke with Dr. Silverstein and you won't have any more back pain. At least not because of the fluid buildup in the lungs. The talc procedure took care of that."

"Okay," I said and swallowed.

"But I do have to tell you about the genetic testing. We could not determine a driver mutation. That's not to say there isn't one there, we just can't identify it at this time. I have an idea for further testing, but it may take a little while. I've heard of a new clinical trial. I just don't want to delay treatment for you. Time is not on our side."

"What does that mean?" Leslie asked, as if reading my mind.

"It means we can't put Ned onto a targeted drug right now. At least not one we think will work."

"So," I said, my mind racing, "what are the options?"

"I would recommend starting chemotherapy. And bear in mind, there are some fairly new chemo drugs that have been developed specifically to treat lung cancer. The one I have in mind is Alimta. I'd like to start you off with a triplet, three drugs: Alimta, Avastin, and a platinum agent called Carboplatin. They're all effective, but taken together they have a synergistic effect. You'll also need some B-12 and folic acid beforehand."

"I have some questions."

He smiled paternally. "I remember. You work as a researcher."

"Yes. Good memory. So. Is this what you might call an aggressive treatment?" I asked, remembering some gem I pulled down off the internet last week.

Dr. Ashland nodded. "Yes, very much so. Three chemo drugs at once is aggressive. We'll see how you handle it. But I think it gives us the best chance."

"How soon will you know if this works?" I asked.

"We can do scans after the second infusion. We try to do six infusions, that's about the max most people can stand. The Carboplatin can be difficult to tolerate for an extended period. I like to do the infusions three weeks apart. Attack the cancer cells quickly."

"How will this affect the quality of my life?"

"Hmmm. Interesting question. The first few infusions shouldn't be impactful. But it's cumulative. The more chemo you do, the harder it gets on the body. But we also give you Decadron at the same time. It's a steroid. It'll help keep some of the nastier side effects at bay when the chemo's being administered. In fact, it actually gives you a bit of a lift. It's when you stop taking Decadron that you crash two days later, and fatigue sets in."

"Okay. Is it important to start chemo right away?" I asked.

"There's no reason to wait," he responded, hastening to add, "but if you feel the need, you should explore options."

I took a deep breath. "I'm not an expert here," I said, my mind thinking back to my session with Dr. Heck. "But shouldn't we get a second opinion? No disrespect. I just want to make sure this is the best thing for me."

"Ned," Leslie said. "Don't you think we should trust our doctor?"

"No, no, he's right," Dr. Ashland said. "If you like, I can give you a few names of lung cancer specialists. One is local. Or I can call a few myself, I know a number of them around the country. Whatever you like. It's your decision. You have to be comfortable with it."

For a brief moment, I felt reassured. Not about the disease but about the control. That the doctor was willing to cede authority here felt important to me. I needed to be the one in charge, even though my level of knowledge was extraordinarily pedestrian. I just had to get smart in a hurry.

"I'd like to speak with someone," I said, "but you can call a colleague as well. Can't have too many opinions, right?"

Dr. Ashland frowned and didn't say anything for a minute. "I suppose. Bear in mind, different doctors have different ways of doing things. There is no one right answer here. But go ahead and get another opinion or two. What I would like to do is schedule you in next week to start treatment. Monday's already booked solid, but I can squeeze you in on Tuesday. We can always change the schedule. What we shouldn't do is wait too long. Your tumor measured six centimeters. And as I told you last week, lung cancer moves fast. There are a number of options. The only option we should avoid is waiting. Time is not your friend."

I shuddered at his last sentence but kept an outwardly calm demeanor. As we prepared to leave, the doctor's assistant gave us the name of a lung cancer specialist in Beverly Hills and offered to set up an appointment. We waited at her desk as she made the phone call, spoke for a minute and then looked up.

"Dr. Knott has an opening this afternoon. Can you make that?"

"Of course."

She spoke for another minute on the phone, hung up, and wrote out an appointment card with the address and a two o'clock arrival time listed. She also handed us a disk and a stapled report.

"You'll need to give this to Dr. Knott. So he can review your scans."

I thanked her and we departed. After leaving Dr. Ashland, I sent a text to Eli with a number of pertinent questions, and he got back to me an hour later. Yes, Dr. Knott was a legitimate oncologist, no, he had not been sued for malpractice. He also graduated from Harvard Medical School and was considered one of the leading lung cancer experts on the West Coast. Eli hoped my concerns were assuaged. I did not provide him with an answer.

We arrived at my next doctor's plush Beverly Hills office, which was located just a few blocks from Rodeo Drive, and the decor was quite fitting for an elite physician. Marble floors, a glass-and-slate coffee table, and real artwork hanging in the reception area. Not surprisingly, it was over forty-five minutes before we were invited into an exam room, where we waited another fifteen before the door swung open and Dr. Jacob Knott strode in.

He was a big man, barrel-chested, and had a white beard that was neatly trimmed. He looked as if he were in his late sixties. The doctor nodded at me and then let his eyes wander over Leslie for a moment longer than was acceptable. He picked up the disk, and without a word, slipped it into his computer and began to jones the mouse, shimmying it back and forth. He brought up body images of a figure lying prostrate, the initial screen shots resembling a highly detailed chalk outline. The doctor clicked through a variety of images until he settled on one and stopped.

"Here we go," he said. "This is the one."

"What do you see?" I asked.

"The nodule in your left lung. There's also activity in the pleural area," he said and kept clicking. "And the kidney. Yes. And the liver."

"What are my options?"

He said nothing, lifting up the radiology report with both hands. He flipped quickly through the pages, speed reading them, as if picking off the necessary data and ignoring the noise in between.

"Unfortunately, chemo is what we're looking at right now," he finally declared. "There are some clinical trials, but without an identifiable mutation, I don't hold out much hope. At this point, chemo is your best option. And it's not a bad option, mind you. It's just more of a shotgun blast than a targeted approach."

I swallowed. "I thought that chemo was the last option."

"No, not necessarily. We just need to find a treatment that works for you. If it's successful, we put you onto chemo maintenance."

I frowned. "What's involved here?"

"You start with a regular chemo regimen for five or six cycles. Usually a triplet, three types of chemo at once. I'm sure Gus took you through that. The first few cycles are normally pretty easy. By the fifth or sixth, your tolerance will wane. But if the tumors shrink, we reduce the chemo levels to something manageable. Then, once a month, you come in for an infusion. It's called maintenance."

"How long does that go on for?"

Dr. Knott looked back down at the papers. "For as long as it works. When it stops, we put you on something else. And I have a couple of patients who have been on chemo maintenance for five years."

"Oh?" I said, my spirits piqued momentarily.

"Look, the goal here is to keep you around long enough for the next clinical trial. For medicine to come up with something better. There's a lot in the pipeline. We're making progress."

"All right. So, what do you recommend? Dr. Ashland said something about a drug called Alimta."

Dr. Knott continued to comb through the report. "Here it is. No, no, I don't think Alimta will work on you. Your T.S. levels are too high."

I frowned again. "What does that mean?"

"T.S. is an enzyme. If the levels are too high, it can interfere with the medicine and inhibit it from working to attack the cancer cells. The Alimta might not work. I would recommend Taxol, not Alimta. They're both chemotherapies."

"What's the difference between the two?"

"Alimta was developed specifically for lung cancer, it's more easily tolerated. Taxol is more of an all-purpose chemo, it's used to treat many different types of cancers. But it has harsher side effects."

"And harsher means ... ?"

"Neuropathy, hair loss, nausea. We know more about what to expect from Taxol."

"That doesn't sound good. What is neuropathy?"

"Pain in the extremities. Fingers, toes. Sharp pain, increased sensitivity, sometimes numbness."

"Does that mean Taxol is more effective?" I asked somewhat cautiously.

Dr. Knott thought for a moment. "Not necessarily. And it depends on the patient. Different patients have different reactions. Alimta can be a blessing or something entirely different. And my theory on T.S. levels is based on only a few cases. It's something I read about in a medical journal this year. It's not something that's been clinically proven, but, well, it hasn't been disproven either. I'm just basing this on my experience. Thirty-five years of treating lung cancer patients. It's a hunch, but my hunches are normally borne out."

Leslie spoke. "If we go onto one chemo and it doesn't work, can we switch to the other?"

"Yes, you can always go on to something else. We do whatever we can to find a treatment that's effective."

I rolled this around in my mind. "I wonder why Dr. Ashland didn't mention this about Alimta."

Dr. Knott shrugged. "I know Gus. He's a good man, a good doctor. His judgment is not wrong. We can't be fully sure. This is why you get second opinions. Not everyone has perfect knowledge."

It was the last line that stayed with me through the remainder of the day. No one, not even the best doctors, could be certain what was optimal for a patient. They looked at the lab results and made their best guesses. Two bright people, looking at the same data through the same prism, and yet they arrive at different conclusions. And when two doctors recommend two different treatments, it is up to the patient to sort it out. I thought back to my session with Dr. Heck. *You need to own your cancer*. The statement didn't make much sense at the time. Now it did. Two doctors offering two different recommendations. I had to make the decision on treatment. Or did I?

I thought back to something. Maybe I learned about it in a philosophy class at Berkeley. Maybe I read it in a fortune cookie. But the wisdom stayed with me. There is an old proverb that says when torn between two choices, pick the third. I didn't have a third choice. But I did have a third doctor.

Chapter 24

I had initially suggested to Eli that we meet at a coffee house on Saturday morning, but when he learned Angelina would be pitching in the playoffs, my friend the doctor insisted we go watch the game together. We found an isolated spot in the bleachers, close enough to see and be seen, but not so close as to have our conversation overheard. I carried two cups of black coffee from Peet's, but Eli declined his. He had already had his one cup of the day. Too much caffeine made him jittery; I got jittery from not having enough.

"Some guidance would be greatly appreciated," I began, but waited until Eli motioned for me to continue. "It's about the decision on treatment."

"Let me guess," he smiled. "Gus and Jacob have differing views."

"Um, yes. Does this happen often with your posse?"

"All the time," he said, shaking his head. "Ask ten doctors a medical question and you'll get ten different protocols. It's an occupational hazard with us. We wrestle with these decisions all the time. Honestly, medicine is as much an art as a science."

My view of things was confirmed, but my qualms remained. The discrepancy in opinion was not unique, but it was still a problem. There was no doubt that the doctors Gus Ashland and Jacob Knott were brilliant and knowledgeable. But there was also no question that when it came down to recommending the best treatment, one of them was going to be wrong. I didn't know which one, and neither would Eli. But a decision needed to be made.

"All right," I sighed. "There are two ways for me to go on chemo. Dr. Ashland recommended Alimta. It's specifically for lung cancer and it's easier to tolerate. Dr. Knott has a theory that Alimta wouldn't work on me because of something called high T.S. levels. He recommends Taxol. Harsher, more side effects. No guarantee either will work, no guarantee they won't. What do you think?"

Eli looked out at the softball diamond for a long moment and processed this. "I'm not an oncologist, so it's difficult for me to weigh in. Professionally speaking."

"But you're my close friend. Believe me, I'm not suing anyone if they're wrong."

"I know, I know," he waved. "I want you to have the right treatment. Just like the others. I can call another lung cancer specialist. He's not local, otherwise I'd have you see him, too."

"Is he far away?"

"Nevada. He moved his practice a couple of years ago."

"Nevada?" I blinked. "As in Las Vegas? The gambling Mecca of the world?"

"Um, yes. He told me he left L.A. because of taxes. And Vegas has a lot of smokers. Sometimes you go where the market is. But, well, he has a math mind. He likes blackjack."

"Wonderful," I said and looked over at the softball diamond. Angelina had taken the mound and was warming up. The first batter for the Viewpoint School stepped to the plate, swung at Angelina's first pitch and hit a weak grounder to first base for an easy out. The crowd applauded lightly. A couple of dads sitting up in the top row waved at me and signaled for me to come join them. I waved back and turned again to Eli.

"I suppose it couldn't hurt to get a third opinion," I said, and then I began channeling Dr. Heck. *You need to have an approach.* "But I sense I'm going to be the one to decide this in the end. It's my body, it's my cancer. I think I'm going to have to own this. And if I'm in the game, I should be the one dealing the cards."

Eli turned and stared at me. "Is this the new Ned? You're the guy who only has questions. This is a bit of a transformation."

"Dr. Heck helped. Thanks for the referral, he's good. One session and he's got me thinking in a new way."

Eli chuckled. "That wasn't quite what I had in mind. I was thinking you needed an outlet, a safe place where you could let your emotions loose. They're bottled up inside you. I can practically see it on your face. So can Leslie."

"And you think they're still bottled up?"

"Sure. Let me ask you something. Have you actually let yourself go yet? Emotionally?"

I shook my head. I had not. I was not able to. Not at this point. There were decisions to be made, plans to map out, paths to explore. Couple all that with being tangentially involved in a capital crime, running a business, and suddenly having a high profile role in the media world, and there were just too many elements coming at me. Letting myself go was not on the table yet.

"I don't have time to cry."

"Okay, understood, but recognize you'll need some outlet for your emotions, otherwise they will eat you up from the inside."

"Duly noted," I said dryly.

"All right. Let's get back to your treatment options. You do own the cancer. What are *your* feelings toward the two treatments?"

"I keep thinking there's got to be another way."

Eli shrugged. "There are other types of chemo that can be explored. But Alimta is supposed to be the best choice for lung cancer. I'll call my pal in Nevada and ask about Jacob's theory on high T.S. levels. I'm sorry they didn't identify a genetic mutation. That might have made it easier to decide."

"Dr. Ashland says he's trying to explore more options there. More tests. Possible clinical trials. But, yeah. That was a blow."

"And you want to be the decider here," Eli chuckled. "That's not such a bad thing. You're smart, you're analytical. And if two very good doctors have two different recommendations, your selecting one of those is hardly the worst idea."

"That's what I'm thinking," I said.

"So, Doctor Ned. What's your decision process going to be?"

"My goal here is to live a normal life. For as long as I can live it. That means avoiding things that are disruptive. If I need to do something harsh and painful, well, sure, I'll do what I have to do to survive. But if I have a choice? Why wouldn't I take a chance on the treatment that offers the least amount of problems."

"Even if might not work?"

I took a breath. "No one knows for sure. Might is the key word. When you talk to your pal up in Sin City, could you please ask him about that? Dr. Knott might be right, he might be wrong. I'd like someone who knows about this to weigh in."

"Okay."

"Maybe have him give me some odds, too. The overs and unders and all that."

Eli chuckled. "No need to get snippy about it. But I'll ask him what he thinks. How's everything with Leslie? How is she holding up?"

I turned my palms up. "She's worried. Angelina, too."

"Important to stick together through all this. Lots of stress. Hard as it is to believe, I've seen marriages crumble under this kind of weight. Everyone has so much on their minds, so many worries. It doesn't take much to set someone off. That's why I passed along Dr. Heck's name. Maybe Leslie should see him also."

"I'll suggest that," I said absently, "but if I do, I'm going to duck. And then pin the blame on you."

He smiled and we turned back to the diamond. The next batter had worked her way to a three-two count and fouled off three straight pitches before taking a big swing and a miss. Angelina gave a small fist pump of exhilaration before quickly composing herself. The next batter popped out on the first pitch and the side was retired. The Brentwood parents gave a nice round of applause.

"You've got a terrific kid there," Eli said.

"Yes. Sometimes you get lucky."

"It's not luck. You worked at it. Kids from good families don't always turn out so great. I just saw one who's dealing with a meth problem. Dad's a partner in an accounting firm, mom runs a tech company. Means nothing if they're not around for their kids."

I doubt Eli knew what he was saying nor how I would interpret it. *Means nothing if they're not around for their kids.* I knew he didn't intend it that way, and I knew I shouldn't respond badly to it, but I did. That I might not be there for Angelina. *I might be gone.* Not of my own doing, but gone, regardless. There is a guilt that comes with a deadly diagnosis, that even if the malady is not your fault, you somehow absorb the blame. And just because a child is bright, it doesn't mean they're able to forgive and move on. I didn't want her to think of herself as the girl whose father died too soon. But I didn't get to tell Angelina what to think. She was old enough to decide for herself.

Eli departed, telling me he needed to make rounds this morning at Saint John's. I debated about climbing up into the eagle's nest with the other dads, finally succumbing to the siren call. When someone has had a high public profile, everyone wants to talk to them. I had little interest in sharing, but with Angelina being a junior, I did have one more year with this crew. Maintaining good relations sometimes meant doing things you don't want to do. A metaphor for other things in life. I climbed to the top of the bleachers.

"Hey, Baker," called one of the dads, a portly man with a shaved head that glistened even though there was no sun out today. "What's cooking?"

I smiled graciously. "Looks like we're off to a good start."

"Angelina's got her groove going," said Dan Collins, one of the head eagles. Dan was in charge of fundraising for the school, the annual giving campaign that supplemented the school's coffers on top of the already hefty tuition revenue. "I also see there's a reporter from the *Times* over there. I'm wondering if they're here covering her or you."

A few chuckles broke out among the men. I waved it off. "I'm yesterday's news," I told them.

"It's a long news cycle," said Phil McManus. "You've become quite the celebrity. Feels like there's something about you in the news every day. I'll bet you never thought you'd be this famous."

Truer words were never spoken, and I desperately wished that whatever fame or infamy hovering about me would quickly dissipate. Angelina had told me my appearance on TV had spread like wildfire around the school, albeit more among parents than the kids.

"It's not the type of fame I ever wanted," I told him, and then paraphrased Andy Warhol. "But everyone gets their fifteen minutes. Mine will be up soon."

"Nah," Dan said. "Someone posted that *Hello America* segment of yours on YouTube. It'll be there until the end of time."

"Hey, should we even be talking to a person of interest?" joked Eddie Andrews. "Next thing you know the LAPD is going to be knocking on *my* door."

I turned to Eddie. "The LAPD? What makes you say that?"

"There was a detective being interviewed on TV last night. He was investigating that woman who was killed. You know. The vice president's girlfriend."

"Oh?" I asked.

"Yeah, that woman. Iris something-or-other. Worked for the speaker but was supposedly at the Century Plaza that night. The reporter said she had some ties to you."

"I met her a couple of times, hardly a conspiracy," I said and then thought of something. "Do you happen to recall that detective's name?"

Eddie furrowed his brow in thought. "Weird name. A phrase or something you might hear at a yacht club. Like an anchor. Buoy, maybe? No, it was Mooring. Karl Mooring."

At that point my cell phone rang. I answered and it was Blair. He was loud and animated, more enthusiastic than usual. I rose and walked a few feet away.

"Hey, get your big boy pants on, my friend. We've got a meeting this afternoon. Five o'clock."

"With who?" I asked.

"With the next President of the United States, that's who. Amber Sudeau."

I took a breath. I marveled again at the lack of pain. But I couldn't stomach another whirlwind day. "Where?"

"No worries, we don't have to get on a Gulfstream this

time. Pandora's coming here. Keep quiet about it, this is super-top-secret stuff, can't have the media getting wind of this. Amber's still a grieving widow."

"I'm not the one we need to worry about keeping secrets. Why is she in town?" I asked.

"To meet with her new strategists," he laughed.

I took another breath. This one did not come as easily. "I take it that's us."

"You take it correctly, *señor*. We're back in the picture."

"Which hotel are we meeting her at?" I asked.

"No hotel, it's at a friend's house," he said. "Obviously, she's steering clear of the Century Plaza. Doesn't want any part of that place. You shouldn't, either."

Blair swung by my house later that afternoon and picked me up. The address we were given was in Beverly Glen, one of the many canyons that slither through Los Angeles. For most people, the Glen is just a commuter artery connecting the San Fernando Valley with Beverly Hills and Century City. For the ones living there, it's a rustic enclave, a scenic hideaway that more resembles a lowbrow, backwater community than a ritzy area adjacent to Beverly Hills. We drove up the winding, two-lane road, with its humble-looking general stores, but the shiny new BMWs and Mercedes out front gave the facade away. Beverly Glen was not unique in that regard; some of the priciest real estate in Los Angeles is tucked away inside of secluded areas nestled in the Santa Monica mountains, multimillion dollar homes sitting on the edge of a long, steep gulch.

As we snaked our way through the canyon, Blair finally

came upon the address we were looking for, and we turned into a carport. I looked around and shook my head. There were no homes nearby.

"Does someone live around here?" I asked.

Blair pointed to a funicular, which was a tram-like rail with a cart attached, a device with two green plastic benches that might have once been in use at Disneyland.

"Hop in," he said. "This is the only way you can get to the main house."

We climbed inside the contraption, pressed a metal button, and slowly the cart began to escalate up a fairly steep hill. It was a rickety ride that took about ninety seconds. We finally settled in front of a marvelous home perched upon the edge of a cliff, a series of wooden stilts holding it up. We were met by a pair of Secret Service agents, ones with whom I was thankfully unacquainted, who quietly and efficiently ran us through a metal detector and did the wand swipe before signaling to another pair of agents that we were okay. The door opened and we stepped inside.

The home was a shrine to glass. It had polished, white oak floors, high beamed ceilings, and a wall of windows facing the mountains. On a sunny afternoon, this house most certainly would provide a sensational view. But not today. Murky clouds, silent and levitating against the cliffs, projected a darkened gloom.

"Welcome!" came a voice. We turned to see a tall, slender man with shiny silver hair approach.

"Jimbo!" said Blair, and he gave the man a brief hug. "Thanks for arranging this."

"My pleasure," the man said and turned to me. "I'm James Zeppa."

"Nice to meet you," I said, shaking hands. "Gorgeous home. A bit inaccessible."

"Part of the charm. I like living away from the crowd."

"Jimbo's one of Amber's Angels," Blair cracked. "The first of the big donors. King maker. Or Queen maker, in this case."

"Well, let's hope so. Come on in, they're waiting for you," James said, leading us into a den area that was lined with windows as well. They were shiny, clear, and spotless. I wondered who climbed the ladders to clean them.

Amber Sudeau was standing in a corner with Randy Greece, looking out at the distant hills, their conversation quiet and muted. Greece noticed us first and turned and smiled. Amber's face was welcoming but subdued, a serious expression befitting a grieving widow. Greece was formal, in a white shirt and navy tie; Amber's attire was more relaxed, a gold knit top and black slacks.

"Gentlemen," she said, shaking hands coolly. "Thank you so much for coming on short notice. I hope I didn't interrupt your Saturday."

"Our time is your time," Blair crowed.

I made eye contact with Amber and spoke. "Not a problem. My daughter had a softball game, they're in the playoffs, but that was earlier."

"Did she win?"

"As a matter of fact, they did. She pitched a shutout. They advance to the state quarterfinals next week. High school. It's exciting."

"I can imagine," Amber said. "I played basketball in prep school. One of the best things I ever did was participate in sports. Builds confidence, especially for a girl. It's important."

"We're very proud of her," I said.

Amber Sudeau nodded and motioned for us to sit. The meeting could not have felt more awkward for me. We had last met two weeks ago to discuss propping up her husband's fledgling campaign. Now he was dead, Blair and I were the subject of an ongoing and seemingly endless federal assassination inquiry, with the killer still at large. And we were invited here to discuss how best to position Amber to pick up the mantle and claim the party's nomination as President of the United States. If anyone else in the room felt the surreal circumstances, they did a good job of hiding it.

Taking a cigarette out of her purse, Amber suddenly looked at Zeppa. "James, do you mind?"

"Of course not," he said, reaching over and placing a green onyx ashtray next to her. She lit the cigarette, and Blair, taking it as tacit permission, quickly lit one up as well.

"I didn't realize you were one of the bad kids," Blair said, blowing some smoke in the air.

"Nervous habit," she said. "I keep quitting. Then something overwhelming happens, and I just go right back to them. It's like building a sand castle. You put in a lot of hard work. And then one wave washes it all away."

I tried not to cringe. *One wave washes it all away.* I

tried to focus on Amber, but those words, a metaphor for life, my life, were bound to stay with me.

"We wanted to thank you, first of all. For the focus groups. Great job, Ned. Fascinating info. I streamed them. It was a nice testament to Rich."

"No problem," I said. "I'm just sorry things turned out the way they did."

Greece spoke. "Yes. We're all terribly saddened. But through adversity, well, opportunity sometimes arises."

"It does indeed!" Blair broke in. "And let me just say, she would make an excellent president. We're in her corner."

"Um, yes," Greece said, his jaw jutting out and his lower teeth showed over his upper lip. They looked a little crooked. "We're interested in pursuing this a little further. Just exploratory, mind you. We'd like you to do polling this week. Evaluate Amber as a candidate. Let's field it in Iowa and New Hampshire to start. If we see traction there, we can launch a national poll."

"Sure thing," Blair said. "We can be in the field tomorrow if you like. Whatever you want, we'll handle it."

"Right. Listen," Greece said, picking up Amber's cigarette and taking a puff before handing it back to her. "It's important there are no footprints here. Put Amber's name in along with a bunch of other celebrities. No one can know that Amber has a poll out. It's critical this be kept quiet. We can't have her appear opportunistic. Looking to take advantage of all this."

I nodded solemnly. Blair prattled on about our discretion, but I couldn't help but think opportunistic was exactly what some people would think. Whether she jumped in the race now or in six months. Whether or not there was a movement afoot to "persuade" her to run. There was the sticky stigma of gratuitous exploitation lurking in the shadows. And no matter whether it was her idea or she was propelled by others, there would always be that whiff of cunning and greed surrounding her candidacy. Part of me had severe reservations, but the other part could not ignore the financial windfall. Every time my conscience rose up and shined a light on what felt remarkably wrong here, I came straight back to my illness, my mortality, my desire to take care of my family. That, coupled with the realization that no one else here seemed to give a whit about morals or ethics or anything besides fame, power and the hefty payday that would follow.

At that point, Amber took a final drag on the cigarette, blew the smoke toward the ceiling, and quickly stabbed it out in the golden ashtray. She looked directly at me, her big brown eyes settling on mine for a second too long. She was a handsome woman, finely polished, nicely coiffed. Just like her late husband, Amber looked every bit the part of the distinguished public figure; she even had Rich Sudeau's big white smile.

"Tell me something, Ned," she finally asked.

"What's that?"

"How are you doing?"

"I'm fine," I said, looking back at her for a long moment, too. The words were unspoken but her silent gaze was crystal clear. She knew. Somehow she knew about the cancer. Either someone had uncovered it or someone had told her. I probably should not have been surprised, but I was, and it was evident she was reading it across my face.

"It's all right," she said, trying to reassure me. "Certain things have a way of getting around. I just need to know you'll be okay."

I wracked my brains trying to think of how she could have found out. How the FBI agent I spoke with last week found out. Was I being paranoid, were my movements being watched, did someone have a way of observing my every step, hearing my every word, reading my every thought? I wanted to ask, but certain questions could not be asked of certain people. And even if I did ask, the truth would not be forthcoming.

"I guess privacy is a thing of the past," I sighed.

"Perhaps. But how are you *really* doing?"

"Fine, I feel great. I've had treatment and the issue is resolving itself. Nothing to worry about, the doctors are very optimistic. And I'm feeling one-hundred percent now," I said, not bothering to put that figure into a context. When you sense no one is telling the truth about things, a bizarre sense of legitimacy emerges. Dishonesty suddenly becomes an acceptable norm. One becomes easily complicit.

"That's wonderful news, Ned. I feel much better."

"Me, too. Say, do you mind if I ask *you* a question. It's the same question I asked Rich. Why do you want to be president?"

"Why is that important to you?" Greece asked.

"It's not so much me. But someone on the campaign

trail is going to ask Amber. She has to have a good answer. Being better than the other guys won't cut it with voters. Running on behalf of Rich's legacy won't cut it, either."

"I see your point and it's a good one," Amber said and turned to Greece. "Randy, could we have one of the speechwriters start working on that? I agree with Ned. It's important to have an answer."

"Absolutely," said Greece. "And Ned, I'm glad you're feeling good. We've already fired one pollster this month. We'd like to keep you around for a while."

"I'd like to stick around as well, " I said, privately disappointed that Amber, like her late husband, didn't have a well-thought-out answer for why she wanted to be president. At least not one she was willing to verbalize to me. I decided to change the subject. "I have another question. Could you tell me about Frank Phelan. What happened there? Why did he fail?"

Amber and Greece glanced at each other. "It's not something we think will affect you," Greece finally said.

"I'm not going to sugarcoat things," I said. "If the polling shows weak support, you need to know about it. I'm going to tell you. And you'll need to have a plan to combat it."

"Look," Greece replied. "I know Rich was unhappy with his standing in the polls. But despite what he said, he didn't blame Phelan for that. Yeah, Phelan got outsmarted by the opposition. I'm sure you heard that story, that Sanderson's people got wind the *Des Moines Register* was in the field with a poll, and they upped their ad spend so their poll numbers would spike. But that wasn't the reason."

"Okay. Then what was it?"

"Ned," Amber started. "We've been following you two since last year. The job you did for Justin Woo in California. You do great work. And you're quiet about it. You go about your business and you don't look to get your faces in TV."

"Except for last week," I muttered.

"We understand that," Amber said. "And we did want to float the idea of my possible candidacy. But Rich was upset with Frank for going on TV and simply using the vice president to self-promote. Frank Phelan's face was on the air as much as Rich's. Maybe more. We can't have a pollster or a consultant on our payroll going rogue. It's about the candidate and the movement we're leading. You have to buy into it. We didn't feel Frank Phelan bought into it."

I considered this. When Blair and I consulted for Justin Woo, the whole Woo family was intimately involved with running the campaign, and Justin's brother Arthur was the campaign manager. Everything went through the family first, and they decided Justin would be the face of the campaign, with Arthur appearing on news outlets occasionally as his surrogate. No one else was allowed to talk to the media, and Blair and I respected their wishes. We knew that inside the political community, people were keenly aware of our contributions, even though we were not public figures. And ultimately that led us to Rich Sudeau. And now Amber.

"We're in!" Blair said. "No worries about that."

"And we'll respect your wishes," I interjected. "If you don't want us in front of the camera, we won't be."

"Fine," said Greece. "This campaign has to be about Amber. It's incredibly sensitive, especially when it comes to Rich's legacy. People need to be assured Amber isn't perceived as being calculating. There has to be a consistent message and it needs to be cautious. We're in unchartered waters here. Either we're going to pull off a coup or we'll wind up on the ash heap of history."

"Understood," I said. "None of us want to see that happen."

Chapter 25

I was a little surprised when Frank Phelan agreed to meet me for a cup of coffee, and he even suggested we do it right away. He had answered his phone on the first ring, expressed no resentment about the pernicious reality that we'd been hired to replace him. In fact, he even offered some congratulations, sounding envious that we had deftly threaded two needles: getting handpicked by Rich Sudeau, and then being kept on by his widow.

Frank was sitting at a small table inside of Stan's, a landmark donut house in Westwood Village, just down the street from UCLA. Stan's was legendary among donut aficionados. The bakery had been around for many decades, and had a few unique treats. I waved at Frank, who was already digging into a large frosted donut. I turned back to the counter and hesitated momentarily before ordering a coffee and a Reese's Pocket, which was a thick, chocolate-enrobed gut bomb, stuffed with peanut butter. I walked over to his table and set them both down.

"Good choice," he said, pointing at my breakfast, "but murder on the waistline."

"I have a new motto. Life is short, eat dessert first," I said, taking a bite and breaking through the chocolate glaze, digging into a deep vein of peanut butter.

Frank chuckled as he took a sip of coffee. He had a short, chunky build, and he maintained a nice personality baked into average appearance. I had run into him over the years at various research conferences and focus group facilities. We had engaged in small talk, gossiped about which pollster had landed which client, but never sat down and had a long conversation. We were colleagues, which meant we could share each other's pain when it came to clients, their picayune requirements and sometimes unreasonable requests.

"Well now, how are you holding up?" he asked as he finished eating a donut with flakes of coconut sticking out of thick white frosting.

I looked at him and didn't answer right away, chewing methodically and enjoying my breakfast. I vaguely wondered if he also was privy to my cancer diagnosis; it was beginning to feel as if nearly everyone did.

"I'm doing okay."

"Secret service finished grilling you?" he asked, indicating he was talking about a different type of misfortune.

"I guess. You know, the investigators I've spoken with are all from a hodgepodge of agencies. FBI, DHS, Secret Service. We even had an LAPD detective swing by the office. I don't think these guys ever talk to one another. They mostly just ask the same questions."

"Dysfunctional government. Sometimes makes me want to vote Republican," he said and then held up a hand. "Just kidding, of course. I know where my money comes from."

"You ever vote for the other side?"

"I'll never tell," he smiled. "But upon occasion I've voted against my own client in a few primaries.

Sometimes after you get to know a politician, you realize they're a walking dumpster fire. I call it patriotism."

"That's noble of you."

"Ah, in those cases I probably would have been fired before the general anyways," he laughed. "Well, how did you enjoy your brief tenure with Smilin' Rich?"

"He did have a nice smile," I admitted. "Cosmetic dentistry?"

"Ha! To say the least. I knew Rich Sudeau was a phony from day one, but you take what you can get at that level."

"So what happened with you and Sudeau?" I asked. "Campaigns move consultants in and out all the time. But a pollster like you? You've been in this game for decades. We just show them the landscape, how they're doing at any given moment, and advise them on next steps to get their poll numbers up. I doubt your survey skills have eroded."

"Nope. It was complicated. Look, I'm a little annoyed they dumped me. But Sudeau already had another pollster who was feeding him different numbers."

"Oh?" I said, getting a little nervous. "Anyone can do a survey these days and make the numbers say what they want them to say."

"Yup. Polling's gotten trickier, you know that. Lots of people just have cell phones, caller I.D., they don't answer their phones if they don't know you. And you can't reach everyone with online surveys, either, so you have to do modeling. Believe me, I cut the data a hundred ways, and Sudeau was still coming out a loser, no one's getting elected when they're polling in single digits. Rich had some name awareness and not much else. Nice smile, but nothing behind it. People thought he was in it for himself. No one knew much about him. Twenty years in national politics, and he was a blank slate."

"You're preaching to the choir here," I said. "But Amber told me you were getting your face on TV too much. More than the candidate."

"Believe what you want," Phelan said.

"Uh-huh. And I also heard Sudeau was a bit of a wayward husband."

Phelan smiled an ugly smile. "You heard about that too, huh?"

"I met one of his paramours. Iris Hatcher. You know her?"

"Sure, the one they found near the airport. Funny how they haven't released any details on what happened. Just a middle-aged woman discovered dead near LAX."

"Funny isn't a word I'd use."

"Right, sorry. Look, Iris was one of many. Rich walked around D.C. with his fly open. Not too particular about who he hooked up with. If they weren't so public a couple, Amber would have divorced him ages ago. Their marriage was a political partnership. Rich got the limelight, Greece got to pull the strings off stage, and Amber got her own behind-the-scenes power. It was all working out, and then it wasn't. Everyone liked good old Rich, but no one in America wanted him to be president."

"This is fascinating. Thank you for being candid."

Phelan smiled again and waved his hand. "No problem. And I have my reasons. They'll become clear soon enough, pal. But again, how are you holding up with all of this? An assassination is nothing you ever, ever want to get close to, much less be implicated in."

"I didn't do anything."

"I don't doubt that. But there are forces at work that may not have your best interests at heart. And you're a good guy. I don't want to see you get hurt."

"So kind of you."

"Look, you're a person of interest, and you always will be. Until the real killer is apprehended. And it's been almost two weeks and the Feds have nothing. If they can't find the culprit, they'll look for a fall guy, they always do. That's how the Feds operate. Each agency wants to claim credit for catching this guy. Makes them look like heroes, and the others look like chumps. They're going crazy right now, and no one's cooperating with each other."

"Interesting. And what do you suggest I do about this? Go conduct my own investigation?"

"I wouldn't go that far," he warned. "But I'd be careful, Ned. Very careful. When the Feds want to put the screws to someone, they do it. They don't care if it's above board or not. And these guys can get away with it, they've done it before. Sometimes the person gets vindicated, but there's nowhere to go and reclaim their reputation."

"And you think they're targeting me?" I queried.

"They need someone. I heard you had an alibi for where you were when Rich got shot. Downstairs in the hotel lounge. That's good. Witnesses. But they can still try and hang conspiracy on you. Say you were part of the plan."

"Tough to do without any evidence," I shrugged and

took another bite of my donut. This time I didn't hit a peanut butter vein and was a little disappointed.

"Just be careful who you trust," he said, his voice growing quieter. "You're not part of their inner circle. Plus, you were the last person seen with Rich before the shooting. Maybe they're keeping you on because Greece just wants to find out what you know."

"What I know won't take long to find out," I said dryly. "So, what are you going to do now? Sign up with another client?"

Phelan smiled again, this time it was a little sly. "I've already got a new client," he said. "It'll be released soon, but I figured I'd give you a heads up. Cal Barkin."

"I was half-joking," I stared at him. "Barkin? The old governor of Iowa?"

"Oh, yeah. He'll start off as a favorite son, but that'll take the Iowa caucuses off the board. Every other candidate will just pass on Iowa now and go straight to New Hampshire."

"Interesting."

"You might want to give Amber a heads up on that," he chuckled. "Save her some money. She's going to need it."

"She's a grieving widow," I said. "Not a candidate."

Phelan smiled and held up his hand. "No microphones here, Ned. No one can hear you."

"Feels like there are microphones everywhere," I said. "And video cameras. You can't hold many secrets these days."

"True. I think Smilin' Rich was tapping my phone. He seemed to know a lot about me, more than he should have."

"Oh, really?" I asked, my eyes widening.

"Yeah, that's what I concluded. It didn't bother me that much, I don't have a lot to hide. And personally I think privacy is overrated. In the end, this actually makes for a more honest society too, don't you think?"

"More like an Orwellian nightmare," I said. "Pretty soon they'll be reading my thoughts."

"That's how dictators stay in power. They sense when a supporter is going to become disloyal. Some of those tyrants say they know it before their supporters even do. That's how Saddam Hussein stayed in power so long. No palace coups when you kill off most of your lieutenants."

"Glad America's not there yet."

"Getting close. Oh, by the way," Phelan said, his voice getting even lower as he leaned forward, "I did want to mention something else to you about Amber. Since we were on the subject."

"Oh?"

"There's rumors of a sealed file that the Bethesda police have. Relates to the Sudeaus. Spousal battery. Thought you might appreciate a heads up."

"I actually heard something about that," I said, thinking back to my last meeting with the vice president at the hotel. "Rich was worried it'd get out."

"Yeah, not surprised he had it sealed. But nothing stays secret in Washington forever. Especially not when a presidential campaign gets going."

"Rich is gone. Why would anyone care at this point if he beat his wife?"

"Rich?" he laughed. "You've got it all wrong, my friend. Rich was the victim."

"The victim?"

"Oh, yeah. Juicy story. It'll get out eventually, you'll see. I guess Amber finally got sick of Rich's cheating. He was starting to get blatant, practically flaunting his infidelity. She was the one who took care of business."

"I don't believe it."

"You will, my friend. Apparently, that lady has quite a temper. And quite a right hook, too. Knocked Rich's front teeth right out."

"Wow."

"Oh, yeah. Ever wonder why the vice president had such a gleaming smile? It isn't the genes. He had a very good orthodontic surgeon. Put Humpty Dumpty's teeth back together again. Good as new. In fact, maybe better."

Chapter 26

Iris Hatcher. The more the Detective researched her background, the more he sensed a connection to the Assassin. She was at the Century Plaza that night for a reason. She was connected to the vice president. She was connected to Blair Lipschitz. And all paths led to Ned Baker. If the Assassin was still in town, he might very well approach Baker. Even just to take his temperature. Find out what Baker knew. Would the Assassin kill him? If he needed to, yes.

The Detective found the office address for the Baker Lipschitz Team and drove there. It was like any other office, but it was on Ocean Avenue and had windows facing the Pacific. They probably kept it because the view would impress clients. Nothing about their operation struck the Detective as compromised. So how was it possible they got caught up in the assassination of the man who was a heartbeat away from the presidency?

He first spoke with Baker and then with Lipschitz. He liked Baker, despised Lipschitz. Baker was the upstanding citizen, the family guy, the man in the gray nondescript suit. Lipschitz was the flashy one, the L.A. sharpie, the pretty man with a quip and a smile and a deflection for every question. The Detective hated phonies like Lipschitz, but men like him were everywhere in this town. They were mostly harmless, gnats that just got in the way. Could this one be wrapped up in the biggest murder case L.A. had seen in decades? Unlikely. But there had to be a connection, a link, some unseen tie to the Assassin. He knew it, he felt it in his bones. Iris Hatcher. Lipschitz had a brief fling with her, and she was Rich Sudeau's long-term mistress. The Detective interrogated Lipschitz relentlessly, pushing all the right buttons. Lipschitz cracked, the way weak men do, finally yelling his answers back. The way a cornered animal would react. But there was little to learn from Lipschitz, he was a dry hole. His involvement in the assassination was, at best, incidental.

In contrast, when he talked to Baker, he knew intuitively something was different. The Detective could read Baker's face like a book when he brought up Iris Hatcher. There was an involvement, perhaps not sexual, but some kind of visceral connection. He read it in the brief movement of his face, the momentary twitch, the odd look in his eyes. The man was not a poker player, but it wouldn't have mattered. The Detective had been doing this job for a long time. There was something about Iris that had touched Ned Baker, an untold story that lay slowed beneath the surface. The Detective knew something was bothering the man. Mary Lynn had once told him he had the gift of reading minds. He missed Mary Lynn. It had been three years since she had passed.

The Detective asked Baker if he had driven to the Century Plaza that night, and of course he said yes. He asked him to recant the events of that night, and couldn't help but notice the sigh, the exhaustion at having to go through this ordeal yet again. The chance meeting with

Iris Hatcher surprised him. Baker seemed to be telling the truth, that he had simply run into Iris inadvertently that night. The Detective knew about her affair with the vice president, he just didn't know why Sudeau had risked allowing the paths of Baker and Iris to cross. Maybe Sudeau was just sloppy, the clumsy scheduling of an inept politician. The Detective had met many of these so-called leaders over the past few decades. They were no different than the average Joe. Some were bright, some were stupid, most were in-between. He didn't know much about Sudeau, but he sensed the vice president was not one of the sharpest knives in the drawer.

But then Baker said something jarring, an off-hand comment that sometimes emerges from witnesses, unwittingly providing an errant piece to the puzzle. Baker shook his head at what happened to Iris, how awful it must have been, the woman being strangled near the airport. The Detective paused for a moment. This was a delicate slice of evidence, a finding that had not been disseminated to the public. The media were told that an unidentified woman was found dead in an airport parking lot, a tidbit designed to avert public intrigue. A brief mention on the ten o'clock news was not going to evoke much interest. Not in L.A. The details of Iris's death were left intentionally vague, per a request from the CIA. The truth would remain a secret. Yet Baker somehow knew she died and how she died. He was involved.

The Detective finished up the interview by asking Baker for a copy of his driver's license and car registration. The man frowned, but the Detective assured him it was strictly routine. He loved saying that, it meant nothing, but it allowed him the leeway to ask for things he had no business asking for. Baker went out for a minute, returning with copies and handing them to the Detective. He asked if there was anything more he could do to help the LAPD. The Detective told him not at the moment. But they would be in touch.

The Detective took the elevator down to the garage, found the unflashy Honda Pilot, and matched the license plate with the registration form. He then applied a GPS device inside the Pilot's fender. It was illegal as hell, but the Detective had stopped playing by the rules years ago. The rules hindered, the rules did not help. But when the Detective affixed the device, he felt his hand brush against something. He bent down further and checked under the fender. Strange, he thought, as he pulled out a small flashlight to look closer. Well, well. It was another GPS device. Apparently someone had the same idea as the Detective. He thought of removing it, but there were limits to how much you could mess with federal law enforcement ...

* * *

My first chemo infusion was administered on a dark gray Tuesday morning, and per Dr. Ashland's directions, I had started taking Decadron the day before. He told me the drug would offset the nastier side effects of chemotherapy, but it also provided me with a remarkable jolt of energy. For the first time in weeks, I felt revitalized, alive enough to even drive down to the office. I quickly wrote the questionnaire for the Amber Sudeau poll and passed it to Wanda with instructions to proof and send it back to me the next day. I sorted through file drawers, an exercise I had delayed for years, always finding a reason to put it off. Suddenly it was easy. I read industry journals that normally piled up on a corner of my desk. I even welcomed in an uninvited LAPD Detective, Karl Mooring, who was doing an investigation into Iris. I calmly answered the same old questions, although I probably exhibited a slight trace of annoyance. I couldn't say the same for Blair, however. His loud voice, outraged and aggrieved, could be heard throughout the office, and probably on the next floor as well.

As I moved swimmingly through the day and into the evening, I discovered that one of Isaac Newton's theories was absolutely correct. For every action there is a reaction. And the problem with taking a steroid like Decadron was that the surge it generated could not be switched off so easily. I arrived home at five o'clock and grilled some chicken using my Carolina gold barbecue recipe, a concoction that included *Dijon* mustard, something I loved and which Leslie and Angelina tolerated with mild exasperation. I watched a movie, read the better part of an old Raymond Chandler mystery, and yet by midnight I was still alert and beaming and ready for more. Sleep finally came, but it came very late, I dozed off at about two-thirty in the morning, a slumber that was neither long nor deep.

Six o'clock arrived quickly, and I woke to the sound of my cell phone buzzing and twinkling. It turned out to be Eli, calling to tell me he had been in touch with his oncologist friend in Las Vegas, who said that Dr. Knott's theory on T.S. levels was not widely shared. Eli hastened to add that Dr. Knott might, in fact, be correct in the end, but an unproven theory is just that. A theory. The smart money said Alimta was likely to work for me, and with the thought of fewer side effects dancing around in my head, I thanked Eli for taking the time to make the call, and for his guidance.

Leslie and I arrived at Dr. Ashland's infusion center at seven-thirty. After a brief huddle with the nursing staff, they led us to a lounge area that had easy chairs, hassocks, and long poles holding up clear bags of fluid. A number of patients were already set up with an I.V. tube and a drip mechanism, the chemicals flowing directly into their veins. A few were reading, others were making light conversation, one was fast asleep. Two patients were completely bald; both were women, both about my age. I began to recognize that at some point, concern about vanity slips away.

One of the nurses came over and told me her name was Helena and she'd be taking care of me today. It was not unlike the friendly greeting typical of a perky waitress in a restaurant. She asked how I was doing and if I needed anything right away. I did not, so she told me she'd be back to hook me up once the doctor approved my protocol. After about twenty minutes, Dr. Ashland approached.

"Good morning. Are you all set?" he asked.

"Ready for lift-off."

"All right. Listen, I spoke with Eli this morning. I gather there was some concern about which chemo to use. I'm okay if you want to go with Dr. Knott's suggestion. I won't be offended, believe me. I just wanted to confirm you're good with Alimta."

I nodded. "I'm good with it."

"All right," he said and waved Helena back over. She drew some blood for testing and set up an I.V. in my left arm. She told me that with three chemo treatments lined up for me today, putting in the I.V. meant she only needed to stick me once. When one chemo was finished, they would be able to seamlessly transition to the next treatment. I had no idea what she was talking about, but acted as if I did.

"Let me set you up with a pump," she said, wheeling over one of those long poles with a clear bag of fluid attached. "This is the Avastin. Should take about an hour to drain into you. Then we'll move on to the Alimta next."

She smiled and asked if I was comfortable. It was a well-meaning question, but one that fostered all the soft-edged charm of asking a condemned man how he was enjoying the unsteady walk to the gallows. There is no good way to remove the thick cloud of the untenable fate I was feeling. We all know our time is coming, but we don't typically dwell on it until the moment is thrust upon us. And as deftly as I had been avoiding these ominous thoughts for weeks, the simple act of jabbing my arm with a needle and connecting it to a tube of poison, motivated me to stare face-to-face into my own dark reality.

Leslie stroked my arm reassuringly, and I managed a weak smile in return. I watched the clear fluid drip into me, medicine designed to kill off the cancer in a shotgun approach that would not discriminate between cancer cells and healthy ones. Everything suddenly came full circle. I tried to recall all of the optimism and the encouraging words people had voiced, ones that pointed to cancer evolving from a fatal disease into a chronic condition which can be successfully treated for many years. I thought of my parents, octogenarians with whom I still had not summoned the bravery to call and discuss my disease. I thought of the pain they would feel when they learned of my situation. I thought of Leslie and Angelina. I thought of the colleagues I worked with. I also thought about myself. I was grabbing the maudlin baton for others, the ones who would survive me, who would feel pain at my passing, miss me for a period of time, and then adjust to my absence.

I thought back to my moment in the hospital with the nurse who was working the night shift. The one who thought nothing of asking the most deeply personal and intrusive questions, the ones I had not considered, the ones I did not want to consider. *Have you made your peace with God yet?* I had not and I did not know if I could. My resentment at acquiring this disease was still raw, partly because I had not had the time to think it through. My life had become a whirlwind of controversy and opportunity.

The past few weeks had spun me along the shifting sands of having, losing, and magically re-gaining access to clients wielding enormous power. Of becoming embroiled in an assassination plot that would have historical implications. Of seeing enormous business opportunities appear and disappear; the ability to take good care of my family thrust into my lap before evaporating into thin air and then materializing once more. Even though I now had time to think, that brief opportunity also came entwined with a triplet of toxins, a chemotherapy session designed to help me, but which also dragged along the nagging fear that the cure could be as crushing as the disease. As much as I tried, I could not escape my reality, the periodic beeping of the pump machine next to me making it impossible to close my eyes and forget where I was for even a few minutes.

I did try to consider what that nurse had asked me in our middle-of-the-night encounter. I had not yet made my peace with God. I struggled with how to even approach that. Religion had been ancillary to my life, always nearby but never fully embraced. My life had been good, but I never considered why that was. Or why others' lives were not. I had tried to live a decent life and do noble things, succeeding at times, failing occasionally. I had fallen victim to the temptation of vanity and expediency, doing what needed to be done, whether that meant partnering with a Blair Lipschitz or promoting a political candidate or corporation whose views and products I did not like and did not respect. The easy decision was to go with the flow, take what life offered. I did not consider what life might have in store for me. It did not seem reasonable, logical, or fair that I would be stricken with a terminal illness at age fifty. Cancer was not something I had bothered to prepare for because it was not something I could have possibly anticipated. And yet here I was, and as a person of reason, I was forced to confront the unreasonable.

My thoughts were interrupted as I heard a nearby conversation. Helena was leading a pleasant-faced man about my age to the chair next to us. He had the look of peace about him, a placid expression, one that did not reveal any inner turmoil. Maybe he was just good at hiding things, but his glow piqued my curiosity. She sat him down, ran through the exact same spiel she had taken me through, not surprising, but perhaps disarming. We were all the same, patients to be processed in, treated, and sent on our way, with instructions to return in a few weeks to do it again. Lather, rinse, repeat. I waited until Helena left to retrieve the doctor's directions, and was able to begin a conversation with him.

"Good morning," I started.

He looked at me and smiled. "Yes, lovely morning, isn't it?"

I looked out the window at the gray clouds and frowned. "I was hoping for a sunny day today. We haven't had one in a while."

"Every day is beautiful," he said. "Every day is a gift."

"That's a healthy attitude. Do you mind if I ask how you got to that place? Or are you simply a glass half-full person?"

"I'm more half-empty. Or at least I was. People can change. I was diagnosed four years ago. Thought that was it. But it turns out I won the lottery. Tested positive for EGFR, got placed on Tarceva. I guess I had the right genetic mutation. Was on it for three and a half years before it finally stopped working for me. But it was a gift."

"What was Tarceva like?" I asked.

"Not bad, some side effects, mostly minor. Had a few rashes and some gum issues. In the grand scheme of things, having to deal with that stuff is better than not being around to deal with them. Minor cost to get a new lease on life."

Leslie spoke. "I hope Ned can do as well as you."

"First time?" he asked

"Just diagnosed," I said. "Couple of weeks ago. I'm trying to get my arms around all this."

"It's tough at first. I joined a support group, but it was a mistake. For me, anyways. There's a lot of sadness there. People you become close to, well, not all of them make it. You just need to remember everyone's different. No one has an expiration date stamped on them."

Sage advice, I thought, and true, not just for those stricken with a calamitous disease. We do not know when the end will come, but for the lucky ones it comes at a time when they feel they have fulfilled their destiny, but before sedentary helplessness sets in. My grandmother once told me that the drawback to a long life is that you outlive your friends. It is the type of realism that comes from someone who has lived long enough to feel both blessed and burdened with longevity, knowing that living a long full life does not guarantee you will have a long, good life.

"What you said a moment ago was interesting," I told him. "You used to be a glass half-empty person. I'm sure I am, too. I still don't know how you transitioned."

The man looked past me and thought about how best to answer this. "It isn't just about outlasting cancer. The medicine will or won't take care of that. You only have so much control. Oh, I used to think praying helped, and well, maybe it does. I'd like to think so, Lord knows I've done a lot of it these past few years. But in the end, I just can't be sure. Once you hit rock bottom, you either change or your soul withers away."

"I guess cancer can do that," I said. "But I don't know that I've hit bottom yet."

"Well, for me it was a little different," he said. "I used to be an executive with a large company. Head of international sales. Was doing great, had the big house, the boat docked in the Marina, traveled abroad a lot, drove the Mercedes. I had a good deal. Then the lung cancer hit and, well, I like to joke, it all went up in smoke."

I gave a small chuckle. "Ironic humor."

"Yeah. Gallows humor is more like it. I was a smoker for twenty years, started with cigarettes in high school. Got up to a pack a day. I used to laugh when people told me about the dangers. I said they'd surely come up with a cure by the time I got old. I finally did quit smoking when I turned forty. But wouldn't you know it? Fifteen years later, I get diagnosed with lung cancer. I like to say I probably shouldn't have quit. But in reality, I just shouldn't have started."

"But what happened with your job?" Leslie asked. "Did your company stand by you?"

"Nope," he said, shaking his head sadly. "In fact, a month after I told them I had cancer they laid me off. Didn't get so much as a thank you for everything I did for them, and I did a lot. I helped build their business. But I was fifty-five, and I guess they thought I was near the end. Maybe they didn't want to watch me go downhill. Maybe they didn't have faith I'd get through it. Maybe they thought the medical bills would be too steep. That was a really tough road to go down. The betrayal and all. You know, we often hear about companies who stand by their employees when they get sick. And some sure do. But a lot don't. You just won't hear those stories."

"That's terrible," Leslie cringed. "I imagine you had grounds for quite a lawsuit."

"Funny thing about that. I did have grounds, but you know what? My lifespan became an issue. The company offered me a package, it was decent but nothing special. But what if I sued and passed away before the suit came to trial? They knew my longevity was in question, their lawyers are pros at this stuff. They learned from the tobacco companies, just keep delaying until the guy isn't around anymore. I could have rolled the dice and tried, but I needed to take care of my family. So I took the package. I had made a lot of money in my career, but you know, we lived well, too. Spent most of it. I just never thought I'd be out on the street so fast. Or so harshly. You don't plan for this."

"And so how did that lead you to being a glass half-full

person?" I asked.

"One word," he said and looked me dead in the eye. "Forgiveness. It's the key to life. It's the only thing that'll get you through. At least it's the only thing that got me through. Gave me peace. I don't know where I'd be without it. Frankly, I think the anger would have just eaten me up."

Chapter 27

The chemo infusion process was finished at eleven-thirty. And even though I had less than four hours sleep, the Decadron had me soaring with energy. Leslie parked her car in the driveway, and as we were getting out, I told her I was going into the office.

"Ned, are you serious?" she asked.

"I feel great," I told her as I kissed her cheek and moved toward my Pilot. "Hard to believe I'd feel like being productive after three doses of chemotherapy, but I'm flying. The doctor said there'd be a crash afterward, so I might as well take advantage of this energy while I have it."

Leslie sighed and gave me a wave. It took about twenty-five minutes to battle lunchtime traffic and reach my office. I was at my desk for no more than five minutes when in walked Wanda.

"Welcome back!" she exclaimed. "We've been worried about you!"

"I know, sorry. I haven't been myself lately."

"You're sorry?" she said, practically shouting. "We're the ones who are sorry. Oh, Ned, I was so shocked to hear."

I look at her. "Um, Wanda."

"Yes?"

"What have you heard?"

"About the cancer. Blair told us. How is the treatment

going?"

I shook my head at my partner's indiscretion. "So far so good. I did my first cycle of chemo today."

"My word. And you're back in the office? How do you feel?"

I shrugged. "Right now I feel surprisingly good. Wired, in fact. But I'm on a steroid for a few days, so it won't last. I'm not sure what to expect when I go off it."

Wanda moved around my desk and gave me an awkward hug, the type of hug one gives when they're unsure of how it will be received. I briefly thought of Haley Comey, a far less caring employee, who undoubtedly would have had no such reserve when it came to providing a full embrace. I patted Wanda on the back, awkwardly as well, feeling the need to give her some reassurance, even when I couldn't reassure myself. I told her the doctors were optimistic, the treatment I was getting was the best they had available. None of that was untrue, but neither did it feel good to me. Interestingly, it did seem to satisfy Wanda, as the concern in her face began to abate. As she left my office, she told me how happy she was that things were looking good.

"Oh!" she said, stopping suddenly and poking her head back into the doorway. "The Amber poll went out this morning. We're in the field. Should get results back in a day or two."

I smiled and thanked her. After a few minutes of combing through emails, another visitor darkened my doorway.

"I knew we couldn't keep you away," crowed Blair.

"Can't keep a good man down!"

"I'm feeling energetic," I said, eyeing him carefully. "They tell me it's the steroids. I stop taking them tomorrow, so my energy's likely to ebb. Might as well make the most of it while I can."

"Steroids, huh? I guess you'll be bench-pressing your weight soon."

"Not that kind of steroids."

"Whatever. Hey listen, I'm glad you're here, I want to talk to you about something. Maybe we can grab some lunch. I'm buying."

"Generous of you."

"Yeah, listen maybe you can also drop me off at my mechanic on the way back. The Jaguar's in the shop. It's just over in Westwood."

"I figured you had an ulterior motive," I said.

"Ah, relax. I just need a favor."

We went down to the garage and climbed into my Pilot. I ignored Blair's continued admonitions that I needed to get a new car, that the owner of a successful and prominent business needed to maintain an image, an aura that shouted success. He barked the words ceaselessly, but I had been hearing this for years and largely tuned it out. I pulled out of the garage and turned right onto Wilshire, heading east. As we drove, I looked over at the various buildings and stores, the coffee shops, bakeries, small ethnic markets. Few of these had been here when I had first moved to L.A. over twenty-five years ago. In another twenty-five years most of these would be gone. Life was fluid. Things didn't stay the same.

"Damn, you're pretty quiet," Blair finally remarked. "Feels like I'm holding up both ends of this conversation."

I shook my head and noticed out of the corner of my eye that Blair was pulling a cigarette out of his pack of Old Golds and lighting it. My mouth opened but no words came out at first. Part of me wanted to smack the cigarette out of his mouth, part of me was stunned at the utter gall of it. There are instances when you can feel a fine line being crossed, the point at which a new, more distinct line needs to be drawn.

"And how'd the chemo go today?" he asked casually.

"Do you really give a shit or are you just making conversation again?"

"Hey, that's not fair," he protested.

"Don't you dare talk to me about what's fair. And if you don't put that cigarette out right now I'm going to shove the lit end down your fucking throat."

"All right, all right," he said, straightening up and looking around for a place to dash out the cigarette. "They don't have ash trays in cars nowadays. I don't know what to do with this."

"You want some ideas? I have lung cancer, for Christ's sake. You think I should worry about an ash tray? Where the hell do you get your nerve?"

Blair finally opened his window and tossed the cigarette out and it disappeared. He didn't bother to roll the window back up, but the breeze actually felt good.

"Look, I'm sorry, all right?" he said, his eyes suddenly getting that pleading look. "I know you've been under a lot of pressure."

I had indeed been under a lot of pressure and had thought I had been doing a good job of controlling it, under the circumstances. But maybe I needed to stop trying to control things, to let the emotions just boil over and spurt out. Maybe that was needed for me to keep my sanity. Maybe playing the role of the good soldier who absorbs what life hands me should come to a merciful end. If nothing else, I was starting to feel good about this, and wiping the cocksure expression from my partner's face gave me no shortage of satisfaction.

"Tell me something, Blair. Who else did you tell about my cancer?"

"What do you mean?"

"I mean Wanda knew. I sure as hell didn't tell her."

Blair squinted. "She was suspecting something. She had a feeling something was wrong."

"That didn't give you the right to tell her. That should have come from me."

"And just when were you going to tell her?" he snapped.

"When I got damn good and ready."

"Okay, look, you're right," he said, holding his hands up. "When you're right, you're right."

A thought suddenly entered my mind. "And Amber Sudeau? You tell her, too?"

"No," he said shaking his head before stopping suddenly. "Well, not exactly."

"Not exactly?!" I yelled. "What the fuck?! Either you did or you didn't!"

"Look, it was a way to secure the campaign for our business. Our business. Yours and mine."

"Go on," I said rolling my eyes. "This I have to hear."

"Okay. Someone told me Randy Greece was a cancer survivor, colon maybe, I don't know. One of those internal things. Got diagnosed a few years ago, when he was working for Senator McAllister. He got forced out. McAllister didn't want to deal with looking at someone losing their hair from chemo and all that. The whole experience left a mark on him. I figured by mentioning your situation, we could play the sympathy card. Pull on the heartstrings and all that. Believe me, I was doing this for your benefit. For our benefit, I mean."

I stared straight ahead as we crossed the invisible boundary that separated Santa Monica from Los Angeles. I really couldn't look at Blair at that moment. I glanced to my left and saw we were driving past Douglas Park, a grassy patch that took up most of a city block. This was where I used to take Angelina to play when she was young, an urban pasture where we'd bring our mitts and I'd throw grounders and high fly balls, and she would shriek with delight when she'd catch one. It was a blissful time for me, a time to bond with my daughter, but a time that was now relegated to the distant memory bank. Angelina still played catch but it was with her teammates now, she had moved on. I was beginning to think the business relationship I had with Blair might need to be moved on as well. Nothing lasts forever, whether it is good or it is bad.

"I am a private person," I finally said, "and this cancer is mine. Not yours. You don't get to decide who you want to tell. I don't care what it does for the business. This is my life. It's not a damn marketing tool."

"All right, look I know you're probably going through hell right now," he said.

"You don't know what I'm going through," I snarled. "No one does. No one can. Don't pretend you do. And stop saying you're doing all this for me. Or for us. You're doing it for you. At least have the decency to admit it."

"Hey, Ned. I'm not a bad guy," he protested. "I'm just selling a product. And the product is us. You. Me. It's the business. It's not personal. Does it matter if I stretch the truth a little to get ahead?"

"It didn't used to matter," I admitted as we waited for a light to change at San Vicente. "But it does now. Things are different. I'm struggling to understand it all. But things are different. I can't simply look at life through the same prism anymore."

The light turned green and I eased the Pilot forward. We were in the center lane of a three-lane parkway, a stretch of road that curved back and forth, twisting around the Veteran's Center complex. There was an office park to the right and a medical building to the left. I was about to ask Blair what lane I should be in when the blast happened, and it happened oh-so-fast, and oh-so-suddenly. It was jarringly quick, an explosive, deafening, earth-shattering attack that shook me to my very core.

Out of the corner of my eye, I saw the car behind us whip into the right lane and speed up. This was not unusual for Los Angeles. Impatient drivers, irate at the speed of traffic, would frequently dart in and out of lanes, whizzing by other cars, occasionally blaring a horn in annoyance. But this car stayed even with us. It was black, and that was all I could remember. The driver was unremarkable, he might have had sunglasses on, perhaps a baseball cap. There was nothing odd about him.

The first gunshot hit Blair in the right side of his head, the blood spattering mostly along the front panel, with traces flying throughout the car. His body jerked sideways, banging into me, and I struggled to maintain control of the Pilot. The second shot caught him in the neck and emitted another fuselage of blood, spraying it onto the windshield. By now I was in full panic mode, jamming on the brakes, only to have my vehicle spin sideways out of control and slam into the car to the left of me. I pulled back to the right after sideswiping them, yanking the steering wheel back and forth to prevent the Pilot from turning over on its side. My vehicle finally swerved to a merciful stop just after the San Diego freeway overpass, ending up positioned diagonally, spilling across multiple lanes. To the right was the Federal Building. To the left was a cemetery.

I looked around wildly. The car I had collided with was behind me. Traffic had stopped in both directions. But the black car, the car from where the gunfire had emanated, was gone. It had disappeared. It had not gone past me, the villainous black car was simply nowhere to be seen, as if, in some peculiar way, it had simply vanished into thin air.

Chapter 28

The time had finally arrived and the Assassin had moved quickly. He had been tracking the target for a number of days now, wondering when he would show up at work. He was almost ready to move to Plan B, but then he observed on his monitor that the two cars were now in the same parking structure. He drove to the Ocean Avenue building and waited outside, his rented black Mercedes purring softly as he sat in a red zone. Finally he watched the Honda Pilot emerge from the garage. Everything was in place.

The Assassin followed them along Ocean Avenue, hoping they would turn down the California Incline and onto Pacific Coast Highway. A freeway would have made it so easy, almost too good to be true. Instead, they turned eastbound onto Wilshire and drove across Santa Monica and into West L.A. Traffic was moderate, but he knew the terrain well. This would work. He knew where to engage them. And as they crossed over San Vicente and accelerated toward the V.A. Center, the Assassin readied himself. No one was behind them, no one was beside them. The scenario was about to play out well. Even their passenger-side window was wide open.

Pulling quickly into the right lane, he drew even with the Pilot and glanced over to his left at the pair of men. There they were, the sitting ducks placed just where he wanted them to be. Baker was driving and Lipschitz was riding next to him. The time was perfect, but he needed to act, and act now. The Assassin lowered the driver's side window, letting in a stiff breeze. He kept one hand on the steering wheel as he maintained the speed of the Mercedes to match the Pilot. He grabbed the pistol grip of his forty-four Magnum and pointed it at the passenger, aiming quickly, just like they had taught him at Langley. He squeezed the trigger, and then squeezed it again. The two loud pops were muted by the breeze, but he was satisfied when saw the head of Blair Lipschitz jerk forward, and the red blood spattering throughout the vehicle.

The Pilot careened to the left, just like the Assassin knew it would. A driver always steers away from the danger. There was another car in the far left lane that Baker crashed into, in his frenzy to try and maintain control of a situation where no control was available to him. The Assassin had seen to that. His client had suggested eliminating both men, just to remove any complication, to obstruct any pathway for the shooting to be traced back. But the Assassin cautioned against it, at least for the time being. Baker knew nothing, he had no direct connection to any of this, and the Assassin did not like removing people when removal was not needed. The Assassin killed for money, he killed to solve problems, he killed to define himself. But he did not kill recklessly. Baker posed no imminent danger to his client, nor to the Assassin. He was an everyday Joe, and the world needed everyday Joes. The world did not need Blair Lipschitz.

His job completed, the Assassin stomped the accelerator, swerved quickly to the right, and zoomed onto the entrance ramp of the San Diego Freeway. He merged into the connecting lane that would take him back to Santa Monica. He could see a few patches of blue in the cloudy sky, and it looked like it might actually turn into a nice afternoon. That was what he envisioned summer in Los Angeles to be. Maybe he'd go for a swim. Maybe the unsupervised children, the ones who had been racing noisily by the side of the pool, would have already checked out. He hoped so. The Assassin liked his off-hours to be filled with quiet solitude. It allowed him to be alone with his thoughts. It allowed him peace.

*   *   *

The first wave of law enforcement to reach the scene was a black and white LAPD cruiser just minutes after my damaged Pilot had skidded and stopped in the far left lane. The other driver was unhurt, but she did a double take after seeing Blair slumped and bloodied in my front seat. There were worse things in life than some dented sheet metal, she said as she crossed herself and averted her gaze. The paramedics rushed up a minute after the first officers arrived, racing over to Blair to assess him, but their faces drooped with the realization that he was beyond saving. The police officers placed orange cones around both vehicles and waved traffic along, many of the drivers slowing to gawk and rubberneck at the nasty scene. One man shouted a few choices invectives at me, furious and obscene, for my having the temerity to make him late for an important meeting.

The first officers were young, most likely anticipating a routine traffic accident but instead finding themselves in the midst of a homicide. A few minutes after the paramedics arrived, an unmarked police unit pulled up and parked in front of my vehicle. Detective Karl Mooring, the very same detective who visited our office and questioned us yesterday, walked quickly over to me, unruffled, as if he were fully expecting me to be at this very spot. After confirming I hadn't been injured, he instructed me to go wait inside his vehicle. I climbed into the front seat and noticed he didn't get in right away. Instead, he made a careful inspection of my Pilot, to the point of bending down near the undamaged right fender, poking and prodding at a space just above the front tire. Finally, he walked back over and got in next to me, in the driver's seat.

We sat in silence for a long moment. Detective Mooring was a stern-looking man, serious, his blue eyes guarded and suspicious. A cop's eyes. The eyes that knew quite a bit, but revealed very little.

"All right," he finally said. "Please start from the beginning. What happened?"

I took a deep and uneven breath. I was not hurt physically, but I was badly shaken, nevertheless. I had seen death in my life, but never murder, and certainly never at such close proximity. The sheer horror of it was just sinking in, that a pair of bullets had brutally ripped through someone I knew, a man seated precariously beside me. I was inches away from death. I looked down and noticed that my clothes were dotted with dark red bloodstains, the remnants of a human life, one that was no longer being lived.

"I ... I'm honestly not sure."

"Mr. Baker, I know you're in shock, I've seen this many times before. I won't sugarcoat it for you. It's going to get worse before it gets better. This is hugely traumatic. It would be traumatic for anyone, even people who've lived through wars. You just don't get used to it."

"How could someone ever get used to it?" I asked, suddenly feeling myself trembling slightly.

"Listen. I've worked homicide for fifteen years. I've seen a lot. Someone you may have known for a long time. One minute they're there, the next they're gone. It's not easy. It's not fair. It doesn't make sense. Over time, you'll come to grips with it. Doesn't make it any easier, but I thought I'd tell you anyway. You strike me as a decent guy."

I nodded and said nothing.

"But I also need to ask you some questions. And it's vitally important that you tell me everything you know right now. If we're going to catch who did this, time is critical. The more we know, the quicker we can act. Every moment is crucial here. So tell me what happened. Where were you going?"

"I was ... taking Blair to pick up his car at the shop. And lunch. We ... we were going to stop somewhere."

"Who else knew you were going?" he asked.

"No one. Wanda maybe, I think he told her. I don't know. She works in our office."

"Did you notice if anyone was following you?"

"I can't recall. I wasn't looking. This car just pulled up alongside ... I don't get it. I wasn't driving too slow or too fast. I ... I didn't make any gestures. There was nothing, nothing hostile. I don't think Blair did anything either."

The Detective shook his head. "I don't believe this was road rage. I think this was a hit, Mr. Baker. A planned execution. It wasn't a random act. Whoever did this knew what they were doing."

"That's incredibly frightening," I said, the trembling starting to increase.

"I want to tell you something," the Detective said, his voice lowering and becoming more intense. "My experience here is extensive. I've worked cases like this before. Whoever did this was a consummate pro. And what that means is, you're alive because they want you alive. It may mean lots of things. But it also means they have no reason to want you dead right now. If they wanted to kill you, they would have killed you."

I took a shaky breath, and began to recall something. It was a prescient warning, the knowing words of a person who knew about the danger that was lurking in the shadows. The danger nearby. The voice of Iris Hatcher entered my thoughts. Her voice was soft but firm. Definitive. *He will not go after innocents. He doesn't believe in collateral damage.*

"Okay," I managed.

"What do you recall? Tell me everything you can remember."

"It isn't much. A dark car pulled alongside us. Almost immediately I heard two gunshots. Bangs, not pops. I saw Blair's body move twice. It jerked harshly before it suddenly moved again. Then there was blood spattering, and I lost control of my vehicle. Sideswiped someone to my left. We collided."

"And the dark car? What happened to it?"

I shook my head. "I don't know. It just seemed to vanish. I know that can't happen, but I didn't see where it went. I honestly don't have any idea what happened to it."

"Any possibility of the make or model?" he asked.

"No. It was too quick. It all happened too quick."

"Where did he engage you?"

"I don't know. Maybe fifty yards back. Maybe more."

"All right," the Detective said, processing this. "I want to talk about something with you. The thing I brought up yesterday. In your office. That woman you met a few times, Iris. Is there anything more you can tell me about her? This seems to be the connection. I can't prove it, I'm not positive, but my gut says there's an involvement here."

I stared at him as if he were reading my thoughts. "I was never involved with Iris. Never."

"How did you come to know Iris had been strangled?" the Detective asked, looking me dead in the eye. "Was it from watching something on TV? Something on the news?"

I shook my head. "No. An agent from the DHS came by my house. An investigator. He was following up on the assassination. But he told me Iris had been strangled."

The Detective's eyebrows arched. "Do you recall who that investigator was? Did he leave a card?"

"No, I didn't get a card. He just flashed a badge quickly," I said as I thought back to the agent who kept patting his goatee. "I think his name was Lamb. Rob Lamb."

The Detective jotted this down. "What was he asking you about? Specifically."

"It was odd. He started off by asking about Blair. Something about Blair making charges against the federal government."

"Did that sound like your partner?" Mooring asked.

"It did. Blair was outspoken. Too much so. He got people's attention, albeit for the wrong reasons. But Blair didn't deserve this. It's sickening."

"What else did this Rob Lamb ask about?"

I rolled the thought around in my mind as I tried to recall our conversation. Then something struck me. "Iris," I said. "The agent was asking about Iris and her relationship with Blair. How he knew that, I'm not certain. But he insinuated Iris might be part of the assassination attempt. The whole thing sounded a little ridiculous to me. I don't pretend to know Iris well, I only met her a few times. I don't like to think she -- or Blair -- could have been involved in any plot to kill the vice president. But it was horrifying to hear about what happened to her."

Yes," the Detective mused. "Horrifying. I have to tell you something, Mr. Baker. The cause of death for Iris Hatcher has not been publicly released. And the idea that a DHS agent would be sharing that type of information with a private citizen is disturbing. I don't have the greatest respect for the feds, but they're not likely to let something like that slip. Tell me more about this Rob Lamb. What did he look like?"

"Nothing special. He wore glasses and he had a goatee. Thick one. Funny thing. He kept rubbing it. Patting it."

"You mean like it was irritating him in some way?" asked the Detective.

"Maybe," I thought. "But he kept pressing it. It looked real, but the more I think about it, the less sure I am. I suppose it could have been fake."

The Detective pondered this. "Mr. Baker, I'd like you to come over to the station house and look at some photos. I think we might be on to something here. I can't prove it yet, but something tells me this Rob Lamb, which is probably not his real name, is somehow connected with Iris, with Blair, and maybe with the vice president. It feels as if this is a messy puzzle that's about to fall into place. There are just a lot of moving pieces, and we don't have a lot of time."

I looked at the Detective and began to consider something. *I don't have the greatest respect for the feds.* Was this the person Iris had in mind for me to trust? There was no way to tell for certain, no litmus test I could apply. I did not have a gauge for who was and who was not trustworthy, other than a vague sense of intuition. For someone who mostly asked questions, settling on an answer that carried with it enormous magnitude would be a giant leap of faith. A horn sounded behind us and we both turned to look. I saw my Pilot, with Blair still inside, his body bloodied and lifeless, tended to by a coroner's unit that had just arrived. I turned away quickly. Not every life is lived in a noble way, and not every death is judiciously meted out. I thought of the final words Iris said to me. *You'll do the right thing, Ned.*

I looked over at the traffic inching past, and then I looked back at the Detective. "There's something else," I told him. "I don't know if this will help, I honestly don't know what's inside. But there's a manila envelope under the passenger seat that I think you should look at. I didn't put it there, I didn't so much as touch it. But I think you're the one who should take a look. Iris left it there."

Detective Mooring's eyes bored into mine. "Under the passenger seat, you say?"

"Yes," I replied, sighing as deeply as I ever have. He climbed out of the car, put on some gloves, and walked over to the Pilot's passenger door. He said something to one of the technicians and they stepped aside. Ignoring Blair's body, and seemingly acting like it did not even exist, Detective Mooring reached down into the vehicle and pulled out the envelope. He unsealed it, guiding a pencil underneath the flap, and then lifted out some documents. He walked back to the car, climbing into the driver's seat again, but this time inserting a key into the ignition and turning the engine over.

"Let's take a ride," he said in a commanding voice. "I want to look at something. And I want you to look at it, too."

I didn't raise any objections, I sensed none would be

permissible, or even acknowledged. The drive to the West L.A. Division, below Santa Monica Boulevard, took less than five minutes, and we did it in silence. The police station was housed in an ordinary white stucco building, situated next to a courthouse. We walked inside together, neither of us speaking a word, Detective Mooring nodding to a few officers along the way. Reaching his office, he began to rummage through a desk drawer. Eventually he located a file, opened it, and removed a blurry black and white photo. It looked as if it were taken by a security camera.

"Does this guy look familiar?" he asked.

It was a photo of a man walking through a lobby. He wore a dark suit and a white shirt, and his face was covered by a beard and glasses. He could have been any office worker. Except he wasn't. This was the DHS agent who identified himself as Rob Lamb. The beard was a diversion. This was Rob Lamb.

"That's him. The man who came to my home last week."

The Detective pulled out a photo from the manila envelope that was in my Pilot. "How about this guy?"

It was the same man, only there was no beard, no goatee, no glasses. It was a mug shot of a middle-aged man, unsmiling, with dark hair neatly combed. There was a height chart behind him, and he looked like he was about five-foot-ten. About as average as you could get.

"Same guy, no facial hair," I said. "Are you thinking ... this is the ... the one who just did this?"

"Good possibility," he said.

"And maybe ... the one who hunted down Iris?"

"That's what I'm thinking."

"And ... the vice president?" I whispered hoarsely.

The Detective nodded slightly, almost indeterminately. "Yes."

"What happens now?" I asked.

"I have a few ideas," he said. "But there is a very real chance this man will soon disappear. He's very clever and he's very dangerous. If he senses he's at risk, he'll go into the wind. And we won't find him. People like this can travel undetected for years. They're like chameleons. They change their identities on a dime."

The enormity of the situation was starting to dawn on me. "How much am I at risk here? I have a wife. A daughter. What do I do?"

"Like I said earlier, I don't think you're in any danger. But I can't guarantee it. Short-term, I'm going to assign a couple of officers to you and your family. It's only for a few days, but I want someone nearby on the slim chance that he does try something. After that, this man will have either been apprehended or he'll leave town. I don't think he has any more reason to stick around. In fact, I'm surprised he's stayed this long."

Chapter 29

I finished giving my statement to Detective Mooring, and he quickly arranged for a pair of plainclothes officers to watch over my family for the next day or two. The officers drove me home, a necessity given the fact that my Pilot would be impounded by LAPD Ballistics for review. And even after I'd be allowed to retrieve it, there was the unfortunate chore of replacing the left panel, where I sideswiped the other vehicle. Not to mention all the blood. Blair's blood, which would soon be dried, caked and difficult to remove. And even if I were able to rid the fabric of the stains, I could not rid myself of the memories. The haunting image would still be lurking. I began to think about a new car. Maybe I'd try a Toyota 4Runner this time.

Both Leslie and Angelina were in the house when I arrived. I gathered them in the living room and sat them down, taking noticing of the nervous glances they were silently sending to each other. I reassured them I was physically fine, that the chemo infusion had gone smoothly, and they should put that particular fear out of their minds. Then I told them about Blair, the gunplay, the subsequent accident, the horror of the entire incident, and most disturbing perhaps, the mystical disappearance of the shooter. I did not tell them about the manila envelope, or about my interview with Detective Mooring at the West L.A. station house. Mooring had instructed me to maintain an unequivocal silence about that subject. He said that if he could detain me overnight, he would. But that wasn't possible, the law did not permit it, so he needed to trust me to not utter a word. It was in everyone's interest, especially my own. Then I told them about the plainclothes officers downstairs in the unmarked police car. I had no good answer for what followed.

"The police? Daddy? Are we in some kind of danger?" exclaimed Angelina. I could sense her reaction was mostly driven by fear, but a small part was likely fueled by a warped sense of excitement. It was the type of outsized sensation for which only a teenager could envision lively possibilities.

"No," I said, reassuring them in a way I could not reassure myself. "Not at all. The Detective was very clear on that. I was not targeted. They wanted me to walk away from this. And if I'm not in any danger, you're certainly not in any danger."

"Then why are the police outside?" she pushed.

I struggled to come up with a reassuring answer. Having a gifted child meant becoming a parent who needed to stay on his toes. "They say it's strictly precautionary," I answered. "Routine. It should only be for a day or two. And frankly I don't think they're needed at all. But the Detective offered, so I thought, why not?"

Leslie spoke. "How are you holding up, Ned? Just when I think you can't have a worse day, things manage to become more horrible than I could ever imagine."

I took a deep breath. "I'm doing the best I can, Leslie. There's no opportunity to slow down here. But I really think I need to talk to someone right now."

"What do you mean?"

"I think I need to pay Dr. Heck another visit. I don't know if he can take me on short notice, we'll see."

"You can't talk to your family?" Angelina asked, wide-eyed.

"Of course I can, sweetheart," I said slowly. "But neither of you are trained in dealing with this."

"I think," Leslie said, "all things considered, that's not a bad idea. Do you want a sandwich? I don't think you've eaten much today."

"Not hungry," I said. "And after what I've been through, I'm not sure I could keep any food down."

I gave both of them hugs, the physical embrace that communicated more than I could speak. They both clung to me for a very long period, ten to fifteen seconds each, the tears spilling out onto my shirt, the raw emotions they could allow to float to the surface in a way that I could not. I went into another room and left a message for Dr. Heck. He called back in twenty minutes and told me he could see me later in the day. I made arrangements for one of the plainclothes officers to remain outside our house, the other would ride with me in Leslie's Prius.

It was nearly six-thirty when we arrived at Dr. Heck's office, and this being June, with the summer solstice approaching, there was still plenty of daylight. The clouds were fading, and large swatches of blue was visible overhead. The sunset would still be blocked by a myriad of gray and white clouds on the horizon, but the sun looked like it was starting to burn its way through the mire.

We sat in Dr. Heck's waiting room for a few minutes, the plainclothes officer picking up a copy of *Sports Illustrated*, while I stared aimlessly at a wall. The doctor opened the door a little after six-thirty, and invited me in. Noticing the plainclothes officer, the doctor asked if he could help him. The officer did not look up from his magazine as he said no and flashed a badge. I motioned to the doctor that he was with me.

"This is highly unusual," he said.

"Let me tell you about unusual, doctor," I said as he closed the door. "I can redefine that word today."

"You sounded very stressed out over the phone. What is going on?"

"Have you seen Wilshire Boulevard this afternoon?"

"Yes, coming back from lunch. I was headed in the opposite direction. Terrible accident. Do you know what happened?"

"It wasn't just a car accident. My partner was murdered, sitting in the front seat of my SUV. Someone in another vehicle shot him. He was targeted."

Dr. Heck said nothing, looking at me expectantly, the tactic that is employed to get others to speak. Questions do not need to be asked when silence serves as the open invitation to talk. I blurted out an overview of Blair's many indiscretions, mostly verbal, some sexual. One of those inappropriate actions apparently led to someone deciding his life was expendable. And in a brief and violent moment, he was extinguished. He was forty-five years old and he would always be forty-five years old. Death not only ends life, but it freezes and frames their persona as well.

"Blair and I had unfinished business," I said. "And now we'll always have unfinished business."

"How so?"

"Lots of things, although the least of which is going to be our company, but that's something the lawyers will work out. There were betrayals. I am a private person. I'm not interested in the world knowing about my cancer. I know that must seem strange to people, we hear about the patients who share their whole regimen with the world."

"And the world provides support, doesn't it?" Dr. Heck asked.

"Sure. Maybe more than you want or more than you can handle. I've seen others go through it. People call them brave, but I'm not sure that describes it. When you're on the other end of the battle, It feels more like having become a victim. People ask how they're doing but they really don't want to know. They just want to hear you're doing well. If you're having a bad day, you don't know how to tell people, and they don't know how to process it. People are used to success stories. They want success stories. They want to feel insulated from whatever pain surrounds them."

"Maybe they're just rooting for you."

"Sure they are. And they may get disappointed. They may have known someone who died of cancer. And that colors how they approach you. Blair went and told one of our employees about my affliction. I saw that maudlin look in her eye, the sadness, the pity. That was my concern. It wasn't what I wanted."

"No one wants that. But do you think maybe you're not giving people enough credit?"

"I don't know. I'm new to this. My story hasn't been fully written yet. But on my first day of getting a chemo needle inserted into my arm, I get to witness the instant death of a man I knew well. I can't say as I liked him or respected him, and frankly I was pretty ticked off at him. But he's gone and I won't have any opportunity for resolution, or to tell him what I fully think. Or even to forgive him, not that I'm in a forgiving mood right now. And that really sucks."

Dr. Heck thought about this and his lower lip protruded for a moment. "What did you want to tell him?"

I took a breath. "I wanted to end our partnership. Dissolve it. Move forward down a different path. I had grown weary of Blair and his antics, they brought in money but they also brought in complications. And I don't need any more complications in my life. I have plenty that are deep inside of me."

"Well, if you don't mind my saying so, it appears the world has ended your partnership for you. Brutally, perhaps, but the world has a funny way of working. It's not always what you expect. That's the challenge, but also the opportunity."

"Opportunity?" I frowned.

"I know you can't see it now. But you have an opportunity to do something else with your life. In this case, it unfortunately comes cloaked in tragedy. But the opportunity for you is still there."

"If I get through this," I agreed. "But what if I don't?"

"What if you do?"

I put my face in my hands. "Some days I'm confident I'll beat this thing. That I'll be one of those single digits that live for five years and then some. Those are real people, and I think, Why can't I be one of them? I wonder what their secret is, if they even have one, if they even know what it is. On other days, I'm not so full of bluster. I think about the odds. They're not good."

"But some people survive, don't they?"

"Yes," I said and thought of something. "Last time you talked of my needing an approach. And my approach has become I want to live as normal a life as I can for as long as I can."

"I remember."

"But the world isn't letting me do that. What I'm going through now is anything but normal. I am literally surrounded by death."

"Maybe the world has other plans for you. Remember what I just said about opportunity."

I considered this. "Yes, I suppose. Opportunity to do something else, whatever that might happen to be. I don't know what that is. But I keep thinking back to my wife, and especially my daughter. I'm the provider. I have a responsibility to my family. When you bring a child into the world, I've always felt it's on you. They rely on you. And I don't know that I can be relied upon going forward."

"Maybe that's okay. Family has a way of adjusting. I'm more concerned about you adjusting. You've been putting on a brave face and that's admirable. But maybe it's okay to let them take care of you for a change."

I slumped and thought back to when I first told Leslie and Angelina about my diagnosis. How I tried to be strong for them, to absorb their burden. But what I really absorbed was a curse, the curse of the afflicted, the perceived need to be the exclusive owner of my illness, to lock everyone else out. To suffer so their suffering would be minimal. And yet I still couldn't control their torment, and my attempts to sugarcoat it came up flat and empty. Neither were fooled; even Angelina, teenager though she was, saw straight through my performance. It wasn't fair to her, and it was most likely selfish. I could not stop her from feeling pain, nor should I have tried. Even children have the right to feel sad at a sad event, the right to mourn, the right to cry. I wondered why I hadn't afforded her that license. I wondered why I hadn't afforded myself that, either.

The first sting of regret hit my eyes, the wall of tears that I had managed to corral and control was starting to crack. The dam was bursting. I felt the sudden sting of deep sadness, a physical twitch that jerked my body forward for a moment and forced my eyes to snap shut. I felt the raging stream of self-pity begin to emerge, the raw, shameful emotion to which I never wanted myself to succumb. And yet there it was, flowing out of me suddenly, effortlessly, easily.

I reached across the coffee table and grabbed a handful of tissues, swiping them one after another until I had a bundle, a wad large enough so that my face could be buried in it for an interminable period. And I stayed that way for a long while, my body hunched over, heaving at times, moving the wad slightly away for a moment so I could take a breath and then return, the tissues pushed hard against my face, not to block the tears or hide the tears, but rather to absorb the tears. I thought of Rich Sudeau and Iris Hatcher and Blair Lipschitz, lives cut short through the whim of a dark evil force, someone who managed to inflict horror and mayhem, and then disappear untouched. But those thoughts formed a trail that soon led back to me. The life I might no longer be able to live. And the loved ones I might soon leave behind.

There are times in life when you have a right to be selfish, and this was one of them. It was a selfishness borne of a desire to wallow in emotional pain for a long moment. To try and cleanse myself of the horror of my prognosis and the horror of today. To try and heal myself. I had once heard that sadness was simply anger turned within. I was indeed angry, and I had no worthwhile outlet for it. It was an anger at unfairness, at injustice, and at the tragedy that life displays at times. And oddly, the jagged emotions flowing out of me started to feel good, after having blocked them so desperately. And the more agony that bubbled to the surface, the better I felt. For quite a while, I did not want this to stop. And I made no motion to do so. I figured I'd let my body tell me when I was done.

I wasn't entirely certain how long I stayed that way, my body curled forward in a state that probably resembled a fetal position more than anything else. I finally moved the wad of tissues from my face long enough to reach over and grab another pile of them. This time it was merely to clean up, not to descend back into another outpouring of emotional agony. I wiped my face, sniffled a little, swallowed, and cleared my throat. I composed myself, tried to make my appearance presentable again. My vision, blurred from the tightly clenched eyes and watery fountain of tears, struggled to focus. I managed to look down long enough to allow my eyes to hone in on my watch. It was five minutes to eight, well beyond my fifty-minute hour. To his credit, Dr. Heck never interrupted me, did not, in fact, say a single word. He understood what I needed, the place I had to descend to, the rock bottom I need to hit in order rebound, in order and pull myself back up.

"I'm sorry," I finally managed.

"For what?" he asked.

"It looks like I've blown well past my time."

He waved a dismissive hand. "You were my last patient of the day. I normally leave at six-thirty but from the sound of your voice, I figured your session couldn't wait until tomorrow."

"Thank you. I hope you didn't have dinner plans."

"I did, but it's all right. This is why I became a doctor. It's not a nine-to-five job."

"I appreciate that," I said, standing up. "I should go."

"Are you okay now?"

"Yes," I said, taking an unsteady step. "This has been more than helpful."

"You know, I can wait a few more minutes if you want. Take your time."

I reached over and shook his hand. "I'll be fine. But thank you. Again."

I walked out of the office, the exit door leading straight into the hallway. I walked halfway down the hall before realizing the officer escorting me was still in the waiting room. I went back and got him. By this time he had finished with the *Sports Illustrated* and was quietly napping. I cleared my throat and got his attention. Interestingly, he snapped awake immediately and was on his feet in an instant.

"You all set?" he asked.

"Yes," I answered, and we took the elevator back down to the ground floor. We walked across the lobby, the gray marble floor shiny and gleaming. It was getting a little dark outside, and when we pulled open the glass doors, I immediately began to feel lightheaded.

It was a feeling I had never experienced before. I initially attributed this to the searing emotional experience I had just undergone. But I was suddenly feeling faint. I stopped for a moment to try and steady myself. It was as if sparkling water had washed over my brain. My face felt slightly flushed. I tried taking another step, but I felt myself stagger, as if I had lost the ability to control my body. I felt the ground beneath me begin to sway. I tried to steady myself, to regain my balance, to regain my bearings. I reached out to grab onto something, but there was nothing to grab onto. I saw myself lurching forward, hurtling toward something, although I couldn't be fully certain if I was actually moving, or if it was the world swirling around me. And then suddenly, and quite harshly, the pavement seemingly floated, and the ground rose up to meet me. I sensed my face striking the cement sidewalk, but I didn't feel any pain; my body had grown numb. And then everything began to fade, the world became blurry, and reality slowly, quietly, began to leave me.

Chapter 30

It was almost time to leave L.A. The Assassin had just received his payment from the two young men, the clean-cut preppies who said they were from Yale. They had no idea how much cash was sitting in the locked briefcase they handed him. The text from Greece gave him the key code. He opened it and counted his payment. It was all there, tight piles of hundred-dollar bills. The fee for services rendered. There was still the unresolved matter of his compensation for taking out Iris Hatcher. Greece had gone cheap on him, insisting that this was not part of their agreement. The Assassin knew otherwise, that the presence of Iris in Century City that night was no accident. Even if she hadn't seen him, Iris was there because Greece wanted her there. The same reason he wanted Ned Baker there. Removing her was a necessity. Removing him was an option. The Assassin made a mental note to deal with Greece at a later date. In his own way. He had a long memory, and he always evened the score.

He removed five bills from the briefcase and placed them in his wallet. Dinner money. He usually concluded his final night in town with a celebratory dinner, a toast to his success. In L.A., he liked to go to Capo. It was a short walk, a block from the ocean, just down the street from the hotel. It had an Italian theme, the pastas were nice, and he always ordered a bottle of champagne. But what he really looked forward to was the dessert. He so loved the candied bread pudding, the mere thought of it made him salivate. The reward for a job well done.

The Assassin put on a suit and tie and took the elevator downstairs. The lobby was buzzing with activity, guests checking in, couples talking with the concierge, mingling. But there was something wrong, something amiss, unsettling. Something officious was going on. He could feel the danger in his bones. He noticed a man waiting at the lobby entrance, a tough looking man, unshaven, tie open at the throat, the type of man who did not look at home here at Loews. He was not a guest.

The Assassin needed a diversion. He ignored the gruff man at the entrance and turned to walk over to a desk clerk. Handing her a hundred dollar bill, he smiled and politely asked if she could make change. For tips. The clerk smiled in return, counted out some bills and passed them back. He stuffed them in the pocket of his pants and glanced over at the rough-hewn man who had begun to approach him. The Assassin glanced around nervously for possible exits. None were reachable. He thanked the desk clerk, straightened his tie and moved directly toward his approaching adversary.

"Mr. Kyle Wolfowitz?" the man asked, flashing a gold LAPD badge.

The Assassin smiled bravely. "I'm so sorry. The name's Lamb. Robert Lamb. You must have the wrong person."

"I don't think so," the Detective answered. "I need to ask you some questions."

"I'm sorry," the Assassin repeated, continuing to smile as he moved his left hand inside the breast pocket of his suit jacket. "I have an appointment I'm late for."

"You're appointment is with the LAPD," he said. "Let's not make a scene here, pal."

Oddly, it was the Detective's tone that irked him the most. Uncouth and unrefined. He'd wait and let the tough-looking cop try and accost him, and then turn and shoot him in the belly. In the commotion, he'd find a way to flee. But as the Assassin began to turn away, he stopped abruptly. Two uniformed police officers were approaching from the other direction, their hands resting on holstered pistols. It was over, it was all over. Everything. The moment had arrived. The Assassin suddenly knew he had only one option. He closed his eyes and let everything go. He let his legs become rubbery and his spine turn to jelly. He allowed his body to swing in a spastic motion. His head swiveled slightly as his body dropped quickly to the carpeted floor. His left hand found the little Ruger thirty-eight special, he grasped the rubbery handle and jerked it out of his pocket. But he did not aim the gun at the Detective. He did not aim it at the uniforms. There was no point. He could take out one man, but not three. Taking three officers of the law out in a highly public area would be difficult. And he knew it would not allow for a clean departure.

He always sensed this day would come. The end of the road. But it had to end with a bang, not a whimper. Go out in a blaze of glory. He did not plan on spending any more time in prison. The six months in Karachi was more than enough. He knew what it was like, and it was a fate worse than death. Especially in his case, because he would never be paroled, never be pardoned. The rest of his life would be spent wasting away in isolation, watching the hours and the minutes slowly tick pass. No, that was not going to be his fate. He made his move to invoke the final solution.

Opening his mouth, he pushed the gun past his lips. He could feel the cold taste of steel on his tongue. His index finger reached for the trigger. But then his wrist was suddenly snapped back. His left hand was immobilized. He reached for the gun with his other hand, but the gun was not there. Instead he felt a sharp blow to his temple. He cried out in pain. No, no, no. Things could not possibly end this way.

"Please," he whimpered. "Let me do this. I'll take care of it This is the best way. For everyone."

"Sorry, pal," the Detective said, the Ruger now securely in his hand. "That's not how it works. You don't get out of this so easy. You don't get to die quickly like your victims. You're going to live for a while. I don't really care about you. I care about what you know."

*   *   *

The white light poured in. I tried to open my eyes, but I quickly shut them again, tightly, the light being just too harsh. Finally, I sensed the cool shadow on my face, a good sign the light was being turned off or aimed in another direction. I slowly blinked my eyes open and focused. A number of figures were looking down upon me, observing me in much the same way people observe animals in a zoo, with a modicum of interest, the mild curiosity which could be turned on and off at will.

"He's back with us," I heard a male voice say.

"Took him long enough," added another.

I stirred enough to begin to realize I was lying on my back. "Where am I?" I asked. "Heaven?"

"Not even close," said a soft, familiar voice. "You're at Saint John's."

"Is that Leslie?" I asked, raising my head and trying to focus, the simple act telling me I was in the throes of a nasty headache.

"Yes it is," she said. "They checked you in last night. You gave everyone quite a scare."

"What happened?"

"The officer said you just collapsed. Hit your head on the sidewalk. Lucky he was there, he got paramedics to the scene right away."

"What time is it?"

"Five-fifteen."

"Morning or afternoon?" I asked, still in a bit of a daze.

"The morning, sweetheart. Try and get some rest. You're going to be okay."

And with that, I faded back to the same unconscious state, into a dreamy world where the sky was blue, and the sun was softly distant. There was no danger lurking, inside of me or out. I was back in the low country of South

Carolina, hiking with friends, making a campfire, toasting marshmallows on long, smooth oak branches. It was warm and it was safe, but it did not last. It stopped eventually, the steady beeping noise of a nearby machine injecting reality into my escape and slowly dragging me back into the present. I heard someone call out, perhaps announcing my stirring to the world once again. And as I opened my eyes, a cluster of people in green scrubs came into view, chatting, motioning, and handling equipment.

"Ned?" came a voice that was clearly not Leslie's, but was faintly familiar.

"Uh-huh," I managed. "I'm in here somewhere."

"How are you doing?"

"All things considered?" I asked.

"Yes," came the reply.

"I've had better days."

A few chuckles were heard, and when my eyes finally focused, the sight of Dr. Eli Sterling came into view, along with what looked like a couple of young physicians, and an even younger nurse.

"I'm sure we've all had better days," Eli said. "Your wife included. I sent Leslie home to get some sleep. She was here all night."

"I remember waking up earlier."

"We've been waking you every three hours. You just don't remember."

"What time is it?"

"Almost noon. You going somewhere?"

"Probably not," I sighed.

"Nope, we'll keep you here for another day.

Observation. You have a concussion, but you should be fine. It could have been worse. Much worse."

"My head hurts," I said. "But it doesn't feel as bad as when I first woke up."

"All good signs," Eli said.

"What do you think happened? I guess I passed out."

"I'm not certain. I spoke with Gus, it's unlikely to have been the chemo, but It might have been the Decadron. Might also have been the ridiculous amount of stress you've been under. And it also might have been something much simpler, like not eating all day."

"How do you know that?"

"Your wife told me."

I nodded dreamily, and then slowly drifted back off to sleep again, only to be woken up three hours later by a male nurse in dark blue scrubs who apologized and told me he was just following protocol.

"When will your protocol allow me to get some rest?"

"Probably tomorrow," he laughed, ready to walk of the room. "But you seem more chipper now."

I looked around the room, thinking about nothing in particular, other than it felt good to be alive, my headache notwithstanding. I noticed some sun streaking in through the windows. This time I didn't go back to sleep. About a half-hour later, the nurse returned.

"Well, how are you feeling right now?" he asked.

"Wonderful. I guess that means I'm probably delirious."

"No, I doubt that. By the way, are you up for a visitor? A woman's been waiting to see you for the past hour. I didn't want to mention it when you woke up. Figured I'd give you a little time to get acclimated to the world again."

"My wife?" I frowned, wondering why they didn't just let her in.

"No. Says she knows you, though. The famous Mr. Baker."

I shrugged. "Sure. Why not. Send her in."

The pretty woman who walked into the room a minute later was familiar, but I couldn't quite place her. She was tall and blonde, and her tawny eyes were bright and inquisitive. She carried an arrangement of colorful flowers. I had seen her recently, but I just could not figure out when or where.

"Mr. Baker. It's so good to see you."

"It's good to see you, too, but I can't quite recall who you are."

"Callie Saxon," she said, looking around the room. "Hmmm. No vase. I'll put these in water later."

"Name rings a bell. I hope I don't have amnesia."

"If you did, you probably wouldn't remember the word amnesia. I'm with MSNBC. I ran into you a few weeks ago at a coffee house. I heard you were here, and believe me, I had to do some digging for that. I thought I'd come by. You're quite the man-about-town right now. Lately you've developed a knack for being in a, oh, how should I put this? A newsworthy place?"

"Really?" I asked, wondering just what had been transpiring while I was asleep. "What's been happening?"

"Yes, I know you've been out for a while. The police caught the man who assassinated Vice President Sudeau. Oh, it's not public yet, the LAPD won't release details, but my sources tell me they have a suspect in custody. Grilling him right now, I believe."

"Who?"

"Some renegade. A killer for hire."

"CIA?"

Callie Saxon gave me a long look. "Yes. Did you know that or were you just taking a shot?"

"I knew."

"Interesting. I'd love to hear what else you know. Especially given your candidate was planning to announce today."

"Oh?" I asked, a little bewildered. "I didn't know I had a candidate anymore."

"Well, my sources said Amber Sudeau was going public with her announcement. Throwing her hat in the ring to run for president. That's what they said, anyway. I guess when Amber heard a suspect was in custody, they figured now might not be an opportune time. I did hear her polling numbers were looking quite good."

I stared at her. "That's not possible. We're just going into the field with our survey."

Callie scrunched up her mouth. "Well, Randy Greece likes to employ the Noah's Ark approach when it comes to political pollsters."

"Meaning?"

"Two of everything."

My head sank onto the pillow. It didn't hurt as much as it did earlier, but learning this tidbit of news didn't help. My mind was full of cobwebs, and I tried to think back to our meeting with Amber and Greece up in Beverly Glen.

Nothing snapped together cleanly. They seemed motivated to hire us. They were interested in my health. They were tolerating Blair. They were sharing a cigarette. The same cigarette. I thought about this some more. Sharing the same cigarette. The type of gesture only intimates do.

"Let me ask you. How did you know the suspect was CIA?" she asked.

I thought of an idea. "If I tell you, will you do me a favor?"

"Maybe."

I smiled. "It's in your best interests. And mine. And maybe even the country's."

"Go on," she said, her voice tinged with the timbre of mischief as she pulled out a notebook and a pen.

"You'll need to find a contact in the Bethesda police department," I told her. "There's a file on Amber Sudeau. It's sealed, but maybe you can work whatever magic you have. People have a way of talking. Amber has a police record. A record of violence. That alone won't disqualify her from being president. But you'll be surprised at what you find. And I'll bet the voters will, too. At the very least her donors will back away from her like scared rabbits. It's not like she can fund a presidential campaign on her own. I have a strong hunch that Amber's pseudo-candidacy is very likely going to implode."

Callie Saxon scribbled quickly into her book. "This is ... fascinating. Why are you telling me this about your candidate?"

"Because she's not my candidate," I said. "I just fired

her."

"That doesn't normally happen," she observed cannily. "Anything else?"

"Isn't that enough?" I asked.

"I like to be thorough."

"Check your sources inside the Secret Service. Amber and Greece."

"I'd love to," she said and looked up at me. "But their detail doesn't talk about those things."

"You know what they say. Where there's smoke, there's fire."

She nodded, the mischievous grin returning. "They do say that, don't they? A golden oldie."

"Oh, yeah," I responded, and thought of something. Maybe now was the time to take care of lots of unfinished business. "There is one other thing you might have some interest in. Have you ever heard of company called Garter Vitamins?"

Chapter 31

The Peet's Coffee on San Vicente had once been my Sunday morning ritual, a refuge I found back in the halcyon days before Angelina was born. I would get up early and tiptoe out of the house so as not to wake Leslie, grab the Sunday *L.A. Times* from the doorstep, and make the three minute drive. I would spend a couple of hours drinking dark coffee and reading every section of the newspaper. Then Angelina was born, and she took after her daddy in waking early. When she was young I would take her with me, slipping her Madeleine cookies while I went through cup after cup of coffee. But as she got older and was less inclined to sit through what was really my tradition, I simply made coffee at home, and played cards and games with her. Giving up my custom was just a minor part of accepting the changes parenthood brings. And as the Sunday *Times* had shrunk over the years, I was now able to read it cover to cover in about forty-five minutes. Things change.

I was seated near a window. The sky outside was bright blue. It was July now, and the ugly, overcast sullen cloud cover had lifted, the days of uninterrupted sunshine a welcomed return. I felt good, the type of good you get when you feel energy surging through your body, your mind and your soul. My next chemo infusion was set for tomorrow, but the Decadron I took early this morning was already kicking in. Dr. Ashland said he couldn't be certain what caused my blackout. It would have been highly unusual for me to have a reaction to the drugs. He ultimately concurred with Eli and Leslie. I had gone most of the day without eating. Lack of food and loads of stress can send anyone spiraling into the ground. So we'd do the same regimen again this time, only I was under strict doctor's orders to avoid arguments, car accidents and targeted killings. And to make sure I ate lunch.

I was halfway finished with my second cup of coffee when I saw Haley Comey open the glass door. A few men turned to look at her, she had that affect, a sexual magnetism that draws men in and it wasn't just the tank top and tight jeans. Haley was tall and statuesque, with large breasts, a slender waist, and flaring hips. Her thick brown hair tumbled past her shoulders. She had a distinctive look, one that featured big brown eyes and a protruding nose, a face I always considered more tough than pretty. But it was the type of look that a lot of men liked. She radiated sexuality more than beauty. And she knew it.

I did not stand up when Haley approached, instead pointing to a seat and asking if she'd like something to drink. She shook her head no, but did have the courtesy to thank me for offering.

"I appreciate your coming this morning," I started.

She looked at me coolly as she sat down. "I figured I owed you that, Ned. You've been through a lot. And with Blair ... well, I never in a million years could have imagined that string of events."

"Me, neither."

"So, how are you doing?" she asked.

"Getting by. I go in for my next cycle of chemo tomorrow. I'm on a three-week rotation. We'll do scans next week and see if my body's responded. I've been told I have options, some genetic testing came back looking promising. That's a good thing. I'm lucky."

"I'm sorry about your cancer. You don't deserve it. Neither does your family. It isn't fair."

"The world is unconcerned about what's fair. Last week, my daughter's softball team lost in the regional finals. Windward beat them by one run, and the ump blew a call at the plate on the last play. Would have tied the game. Instead, they left the go-ahead run stranded at third base. It ended and they lost. It wasn't fair. But life goes on."

"There are worse things than losing a softball game."

"I agree. But I had to spend a lot of time consoling my daughter. Everyone's got a different perspective on what's important."

"I guess," she said.

"So, how are you doing, Haley?"

She gave me a hard look. "Do you really care?"

I considered this. "Probably not. To be honest."

"My lawyer didn't want me to see you."

"But here you are," I observed.

"Like I said. I owed you this. A meeting. Listen to whatever it is you want to tell me. We worked together for two years. I liked you. I just didn't like what you did to me."

"Because we fired you."

"Yes."

"All right," I said, feeling my face grow stern, the Decadron providing me a jolt of needed energy and bluster. "Look, first off, I do want to apologize for how sudden our actions were. We didn't give you notice, we didn't give you warning. That probably wasn't right."

"It wasn't. A lot of what transpired wasn't right."

"Well, I couldn't control what Blair was doing. And if the two of you were engaged in an affair, that was your business. Until it spilled over onto me. When you tried to seduce me."

Haley shrugged. "Blair and I had split up by then. I'm not as horrible as you think."

"Why did you come on to me?" I asked. "I don't look like Blair or act like Blair. I'm married and never made any overtures toward you. Haley, what made you think I'd be receptive?"

Her expression grew icy. "Do I really need a reason? I liked you, I felt close to you. You were a mentor. Maybe all that sex talk in the focus groups got me going. I don't know. We were in a hotel, traveling together. Hotels are like an escape from the world you're in. It felt romantic. You said no. I could accept that. I couldn't accept getting fired over it."

"I understand all that," I said, and tried to keep from growing too testy. "But I want to explain a few things to you, and I hope you'll consider them. I've gotten legal counsel. They've told me I should expect to spend, at minimum, twenty thousand dollars as a retainer, and probably more as this moves through into depositions and arbitration. You know you can't get a jury trial. Part of your employment agreement."

"I can win at arbitration."

"No, you can't," I told her. "Or, you won't in the end. That's what multiple attorneys have told me, and you should look at all of this very carefully. There's a reason employers push for arbitration. The arbitrators are retired judges, they do this as a sideline. They're hired by employers and most of the time they side with employers. They want to get hired again. If you had a solid case, with solid proof of any harassment, you might prevail. But you don't, and it will cost you a lot."

"You don't know that I'll lose," she said defiantly.

"Not for certain. Of course not. But the odds say you will, ninety percent of these cases are decided in favor of people like us not in favor of people like you. I'm not saying this to be cruel. This is just how things work. But think about something else. Going forward you won't have a career in this field. What employer would ever hire someone who filed a lawsuit like this? You think word won't get around? It sounds unfair, and it's probably illegal. But most companies are low-risk these days. Anyone who brings with them even the hint of trouble is not going to be hired. That's just the business world today."

"And just what are you suggesting? That I drop the suit? Just like that? Just because *you* think I'll lose? You sure are sounding definitive. You're usually the guy who has all the questions, not all the answers. Is this the new Ned?"

I took a breath and then a long sip of coffee. "I'll let you in on my plans, Haley. I'm sure you know Amber Sudeau's political career is dead in the water. Garter is pulling their sex drug. One of the networks did a hit piece on it, Garter's being referred to as a company selling snake oil. I won't be getting any more work from them and I don't really care. And with Blair's passing, our company is being shuttered. There is no Baker Lipschitz Team going forward. No BLT. I've told the staff. It's finished."

"Well, you'll just re-open under another name. Big deal."

"I'll probably do some work as a consultant. Maybe Wanda might work with me if I get some focus groups to moderate. Maybe I'll do something else. Once our daughter's in college, we'll be selling our home. Nothing lasts forever. To be truly honest, I really don't know what the hell I'm going to do because short-term, my future is, to say the least, cloudy."

"Then what do you want from me? I'm not dropping the suit."

"Here's what I'm proposing. You filed a multimillion dollar lawsuit. You won't win, but even if you do, I don't have anywhere near that kind of money. You'll never collect it. But I do have some assets, and I want this lawsuit to go away. So your attorney is probably working on contingency. He collects one-third of whatever you get, right?"

"Something like that."

"I'll pay you thirty thousand dollars. You'll get twenty, your attorney will get ten. He'll go for it because it's an easy ten grand for him. These types of attorneys are more like financial negotiators. All he had to do was file some paperwork. Ask him. And ask yourself if it's worth the risk of getting nothing, ruining your career, all for a little revenge. And remember. I never had sex with you and never instigated anything with you. And whatever your relationship was with Blair, I'm sure it was consensual."

Haley looked down at the table and processed this. "I don't know. I'm very upset about all this. I wasn't treated right. Someone should pay."

"I know all about not being treated right," I said softly. "I know all about the unfairness of things. More than most people will ever know."

She looked up at me, and I sensed a softening in her eyes. The toughness in her face no longer looked tough. In fact, it looked a little fragile.

"I want to ask you something," she said. "And please be honest. I need to know. Why did you turn me down? It would have been easy, it would have been fun. No one had to know."

I sighed. "Look. You're attractive, you're desirable. I'm married, but it isn't just that. I had a life I liked. An existence that made sense. One that I wanted to continue. Unabated. Having a fling might have been fun. But it would have upended the apple cart I spent so long trying to build."

"And then the apple cart got upended anyway."

"Apparently it did."

"Then in the end it might not have mattered."

"It would have mattered to me. I still have to live with myself. For however long. And I need to do it with a clear conscience. If I have to be looking back on my life, I want to do so without a lot of regrets. Sleeping with you would have been a regret. Sometimes you just have to look beyond what's right in front of you."

Haley turned away, her gaze toward the window and the traffic flowing along the twisty path of San Vicente. Spanish for Saint Vincent. I recalled a Sunday school teacher once telling us the backgrounds of some of the saints, and Vincent was one them. There were a number of Saint Vincents, the most famous of which passed away in a drowning accident. He died because he could no longer breathe.

"I guess this is my history," she said wistfully. "It keeps playing out."

"Why do you say that?"

"Growing up. My parents got divorced. My dad cheated on my mom. With his secretary. Then he married her. And then, surprise, surprise, he went and cheated on her, too. It all came full circle. He's on his fourth wife now."

"You thought that's what people do in the business world. Because that's what your father did."

"I guess. All it took was five years in therapy to figure that out."

"And then you repeated the pattern," I said. "Except you played a different role. Have you forgiven your father?"

She thought for a moment. "No, I suppose I haven't."

"I know it's hard. I know that all too well. It takes time."

"Apparently," she said sadly, an empty look on her face. "You know, I'll need to speak with my attorney about all this."

"Of course."

"I'm not promising you," she said, a bit of bravado coating her words. "But I'll consider it."

"That's fine. And if you agree, I'll even write you a letter of recommendation. I want to be fair with you, Haley. You did a good job. There's no need to part as enemies. This can be worked out."

She took this in and I thought I saw the hint of a smile, however fleeting. Finally she got up to leave, moving her shoulders back to accentuate the protrusion of her breasts, a movement that was no doubt intentional, a display to let me know what I had missed out on. I had the briefest thought of asking if more therapy might still be in order, but some questions, as well meaning as they might be on the surface, should clearly never be asked.

Chapter 32

The Detective sat back in his chair and put his feet up on the desk. He wished he could have lit up a cigar. That's what he used to do when he had a good day, and today was a very good day. The phone call this morning put a smile on his face. Chief of Detectives. Reporting to the Deputy Chief of Police. The big promotion that would now lift him up out of Robbery-Homicide. At one time he would have reached into his drawer and pulled out a big, fat Robusto to smoke. But that was years ago, before his doctor advised him that the human body was equipped to keep him alive for a long time. If he played by the rules.

In his career, the Detective had worked scores of murder and manslaughter cases. He had seen firsthand the senselessness of killing. The husband whose limits had been stretched to the point where stabbing his wife had crossed into the boundaries of acceptability. The commuter whose outrage at having someone raise their middle finger and shout obscenities at him was suddenly too much to endure. The gangbanger whose neighborhood had been disrespected by a rival, to the extent that he scoured enemy territory every night for a week before finding and destroying his prey. If indeed he found the right culprit.

But these were crimes of passion. Eruptions where stress and anger and pride had boiled over. Even the cholo who prowled his rival's turf night after night was consumed with a red hot fury, the misguided notion that he was protecting his neighborhood. They were just the human element overreacting, failing to set reasonable limits, unable to control animal instincts. It was sad, it was mindless, it was a stain on humanity, but the Detective was able to see it from the antagonist's point-of-view, whether he agreed with them or not.

This case was different. A demented killer who did not have any passion, nor did he claim allegiance to any particular side. The Assassin was the consummate professional, cool and detached, the one who did not kill indiscriminately. He plied his craft for a well-thought-out purpose, but a purpose which emanated from a place the Detective could not understand. The Assassin was paid handsomely, and he was well regarded in the circles in which he moved. But he was different from all the other killers the Detective had faced. The man killed because it gave a sense of meaning to his life. He was smart and he could get away with it. He even floated the insane idea that he was compassionate. But only the irrational mind could ever go down this path, the twisted idea that his actions came from a place of kindness. Taking lives in order to establish and define who he was. But in this instance, the Assassin was not alone. It didn't take much for him to give up the vice president's chief of staff, whose reasons for involvement were far more obvious.

Amber Sudeau and Randy Greece. The Detective was now playing in a more sophisticated league. He was initially stunned at the plan Greece had hatched, to get Amber to the White House by first using her husband and *then removing her husband. He made sure Ned Baker and Iris Hatcher were around the Century Plaza when the Assassin took out the vice president. Nice smokescreen. Gave the Secret Service boys something to chew on for awhile and it allowed Wolfowitz to leave the scene unscathed. But something always goes wrong in these capers. And after the word spread that the Assassin was in custody, Randy Greece had disappeared, finally being spotted a few weeks later in the Ukraine, where the Russians grabbed him before Interpol could. The vice president's chief of staff laughingly pleaded for asylum, but it was clear Greece would be extradited eventually. After the Russians got what they needed from him. As for Amber, there was nothing that could be traced back to her, other than some flinty accusations that would not stick. It was the age-old story. Underlings take a bullet for the boss. It does not work the other way.*

The Detective had never worked a case with an ending that was this gratifying. The Chief of Police had concurred, and when they went public with their findings, the attention of the world became focused on the deft and canny work of the LAPD. How they cracked a conspiracy that had baffled every federal law enforcement agency. How they did it the old-fashioned way, simply sending the photos Ned Baker provided to local hotels, asking if the Assassin had stayed there recently. Fortunately, Loews responded quickly and informed them he was still a guest. After the collar, the data boys combed through his laptop and saw he had purchased a plane ticket for Bali, scheduled to depart the very next day. They linked the GPS device the Detective found on Ned Baker's Honda Pilot back to the Assassin. The Detective still relished the reaction of the Feds, the humiliation that some local yokel had bested them at their own game. He didn't need to hack into Baker's emails or monitor his phone calls, he solved the case without resorting to being a peeping Tom. If only the Feds understood what good detective work really involved. And their final response was even more laughable. The FBI blamed the Secret Service, who in turn blamed the DHS. And they all blamed the CIA.

The CIA. The Assassin had been with the Company for years, and he had kept a lot of things bottled up inside. The Detective knew about men like that. Deep down they wanted to talk, they needed to talk. These operatives had few outlets. They had seen all sorts of atrocities, but they could rarely speak of them. Some agents would talk quietly amongst themselves, but the Assassin had left the Company years ago. He had no confidantes.

In the end, the Detective knew it would be a relief for the Assassin to talk with someone. He was a tough hombre, but the Detective wasn't about to serve him up to the Feds so they could get credit. He made it easy for the Assassin. No threats, he just laid out his options. The man revealed the intricate details to the Detective, because he did not want to reveal them to the Feds. Their mutual distaste for Federal law enforcement became their bond. The murder of Blair Lipschitz was an airtight case, and that was what caused his dam to break. The knowledge that there was no way out. The realization that the

Assassin had no cards to play, only the desire for a lethal injection that would never come. Not in California. Not anymore. But he told the Assassin he could arrange for him to die quickly. Prison yards did not have many rules.

The CIA had abandoned the Assassin years ago, burned him, left him to die in Pakistan. That was a risk these agents took when they signed up for covert operations, the government will hang you out to dry if a situation deteriorates. But even when that happens, most agents don't go rogue. It wasn't just the money and it wasn't just vengeance that led Wolfowitz down this murderous path. The man's case was highly complicated in a psychological sense, but the Detective was able to simplify it. The Assassin needed to validate his self-worth. This is how he chose to do so.

The more the Detective mulled over things, the more he realized he had gotten lucky on this case. But he also knew that an investigator could make his own good luck. That by simply being nearby, being accessible, the Ned Bakers of the world could find their way to his door. Baker had done the wrong thing for the right reason. He never should have withheld this evidence from the Feds. But had he gone and relinquished Iris Hatcher's gift indiscriminately, the paperwork Ned Baker had sitting on the floor of his Honda Pilot might indeed have fallen into the wrong hands. Maybe into a bureaucrat's hands, the hands of those who held a badge but did not comprehend the meaning of the badge. Maybe into an incompetent's hands, those kind were found everywhere, nestled silently within the body of the bureaucracy, the type that would slowly kill an organization. But the net result would be the same, a psychotic murderer roaming free, another death looming, an active cancer preying silently on the global community. And the Detective would still be searching, in this instance, for a long, long time. The Assassin was very smart. And he was able to adapt. Just like cancer.

He thought of Ned Baker. The man had been calling this week to speak with the Detective, to ask questions, to get closure. The Detective would meet with Baker eventually, he owed him as much. A month had gone by since that vehicular homicide, the seemingly ordinary car accident, the one the Detective had insisted on handling himself, rather than passing it down to a subordinate. The murder that had brought the case full circle, the one mistake the Assassin had made. Had the Assassin left town quickly, he could have indeed disappeared into the wind, and the critical manila folder in Ned Baker's car would not have been worth anything.

Baker surely wanted to know more about the Assassin, why Blair Lipschitz was targeted and why he was not. Why the Assassin came to his house after Iris Hatcher was strangled. The Detective could provide some answers now, and more when Wolfowitz was convicted and sent up to Pelican Bay. The answers might or might not provide Baker with the closure he was looking for. That Lipschitz knew too much and Baker knew too little. That Lipschitz casually provided intimate answers while Baker was more likely to just ask questions. That the crucial element sparing him from death hung on the judgment of people who judged life to have marginal value. For once, curiosity did not kill the cat, and in fact, it might well have been Baker's salvation. He'd let Baker know this. Just not today.

The Detective had been on the job for twenty-two years. He could retire, but he wouldn't. There were too many victims he needed to help, too many bad people he needed to put away. Mary Lynn had all the plans laid out for their retirement, the world travel, the visits to see the grandkids, the ideas to start a home-based business. That was before she got sick, before she was taken from him. Her death was one of those random horrors of life, the type of shattered dream he had previously only seen in other families. The irony that he was a smoker but she was the one who contracted cancer was not lost on him. Life did what it did. The Detective thought of Mary Lynn and sighed. He wished he could talk to her right now, celebrate with her. He reached into his drawer, not certain of what he was looking for, but he did find a Milky Way bar. Unwrapping it, he took a bite and chewed the candy slowly, savoring the taste. It lingered on his palate for a brief moment, sweet but fleeting, a moment's respite before he went back to work.

*   *   *

It was quiet in Dr. Ashland's office. Leslie and I sat next to each other, holding hands. Angelina was nearby, looking down at her phone, momentarily disengaged. Our daughter had landed a summer job, counselor at a local day camp for underprivileged kids, but today, for the first time in what felt like years, she expressed interest in being with us. In fact, she insisted upon it.

My second chemo infusion was last week, and yesterday I had gone in for scans. The tests would become my life's scorecard, the measurement of the tumors, the tenuous glimpse into the future. On the face of it, my body had tolerated the chemo surprisingly well. There was no hair loss and only minimal discomfort. Some fatigue and some queasiness occurred once the protective shield of the Decadron wore off. But my ability to handle the treatment was meaningless if the chemo did not successfully attack the cancer. If the tumors were shrinking, life would be extended; if they were growing, we would need a new approach.

The door opened and Dr. Ashland walked in, followed by a nurse. He shook hands with us, holding a file. And smiling. He was indeed smiling.

"How are you feeling, Ned?"

"Nervous."

"You know, he said, "when we first met you, I wanted to say what a great name you had. But my nurse didn't want me to jinx things."

"You believe in jinxes?" I asked.

"Not really," he admitted. "But I didn't want to get your hopes up. Stage four and all. We didn't know what would happen with you. Everyone responds differently to treatment."

"But how did Dad do with his treatment?" Angelina asked anxiously. "Did the triplet work? We're dying ... I mean, eager to know."

Dr. Ashland smiled more broadly. "Do you have an interest in medicine? Or oncology?"

"I do now," she said. "I read Dad's CT scans from last time. When he was first diagnosed. Dad's friend Eli explained them to me. It was actually ... pretty fascinating. I learn all this stuff in school, chemistry, math, all that. But I never have a chance to see what it all can really mean."

"It can be fascinating," Dr. Ashland said. "And rewarding sometimes, especially when I have good news to share. And this is very good news. The primary tumor in the lung has shrunk. Decreased by more than seventy percent. Remarkable."

"Wow," I said, as I quickly did the math in my head. "So it's only two centimeters now. And the tumors in the nodes and the kidney?"

The doctor chuckled. "You're sounding like a pro. But it's true, you have fantastic news. The other lesions, and we're not even sure they're tumors at this point, they could be cysts. They've shrunk by half."

"That's such great news," Leslie clapped.

"It gets better," he said. "We sent your biopsy off to Mass General for further testing. The sample came back positive for a mutation that's called the Ross One Rearrangement. Less than two percent of lung cancer patients have that."

"Ross? Is that good?" asked Angelina.

"It's like winning the lottery," he responded. "It's actually R-O-S and the number one, but pronounced Ross One. But here's what's great about it. There's a targeted treatment already developed, a pill you take twice a day. The side effects are minimal, far milder than chemo. It's in clinical trial now, and the patients on it have shown great response."

"That is ... wonderful," Leslie choked, tears spilling onto her face.

"Additionally, it's a phase three trial, which is good, they're getting close to asking for FDA approval. The timing couldn't be better."

"How so?" I asked.

"If you had been diagnosed two years ago, we wouldn't have known that this drug would work on you. If you were diagnosed two years from now, the clinical trial would be closed. Your timing is impeccable."

"Finally," I smiled.

"You were unlucky to get lung cancer. But you are very lucky to get this news."

I sat back and drank all of this in. I would be getting a new lease on life, and the death sentence I had been fearing had been given a divine reprieve. I was being granted the one thing you can never count on in life, that being more time on this Earth. I had put on as brave a face as I could muster over the past month, and it had been exhausting.

"I'll make arrangements with the doctor running the trial," Dr. Ashland continued. "And we'll get you an appointment with her, I think you'll have no trouble getting in. This is truly fantastic news. The best of both worlds. The chemo worked, it reduced your tumors. But now you can go off it. For a while at least."

"I'm so happy for you, Daddy! Happy for us!" Angelina exclaimed.

"Yes," I nodded and then held up my hands. "Can I ask a few questions?"

"I'd be surprised if you didn't," he chuckled.

"Just so I'm clear, this isn't a cure, is it?"

"No, not a cure. There is no cure for cancer. Not yet. But this is the next best thing. Cancer medicine is becoming personalized. Different drugs work for different people. In your case, we were able to isolate the genetic mutation of the tumor, and luckily we have a drug that works for patients with this specific mutation. It's been proven to extend life for years. How many, we don't exactly know. Everyone reacts differently to the drug. The goal is to keep you around long enough for the next drug in the pipeline."

"To outlive the cancer?"

"That's exactly right. We're trying to turn cancer into a chronic condition that can be treated almost indefinitely. For certain people, it's working. We have some patients who are on their third line of drugs, and they're still with us."

"I'd like to be one of those people."

"You're on your way. I'll be honest, the long-term survival rate is not high right now, but some people do make it."

"No reason why I can't be one of those people," I said.

"Someone has to be."

"Sure. And I also understand the ordeal you've been through recently. If anyone deserves some good news, it's you."

"I have one other question," I said.

"Go ahead," he smiled paternally.

"You mentioned something earlier. About my name. What did you mean when you said I had a great name? This isn't the first time I've heard that, but I didn't think it really sunk in. What does Ned mean?"

"Ah. In the cancer world, Ned is an acronym. N-E-D. It stands for No Evidence of Disease. It's what I hope to tell every cancer patient. You're not there yet, but you're on your way."

"That's ... all wonderful," I said, reveling in what was, by far, the best news I had heard in the past two months, perhaps in my whole life. There is no better gift than the gift to keep waking up each morning.

"Do you have any more questions?" Dr. Ashland asked.

"No," I said. I had no more questions. None, in fact. None at all.

THE END

About The Author

David Chill is a USA TODAY bestselling author. In addition to *Curse Of The Afflicted,* he has written eight mystery novels as part of the Burnside Series: *Post Pattern, Fade Route, Bubble Screen, Safety Valve, Corner Blitz, Nickel Package, Double Pass* and *Tampa Two.* His first novel, *Post Pattern,* was an award winner in the St. Martin's Press contest for First Private Eye Mystery Writers.

Born and raised in New York City, David Chill was educated in the public schools. After receiving his undergraduate degree from SUNY-Oswego, he moved to Los Angeles where he earned a Masters degree from the University of Southern California.

David Chill currently lives in Los Angeles with his wife and son. If you would like to contact David Chill directly, please email him at the following: davidchill3214@gmail.com

If you enjoyed Curse Of The Afflicted, then be sure to read the first novel in David Chill's Burnside series....

Post Pattern

Here is a sample chapter of this terrific book...

Post Pattern Preview

Chapter 1

The people who tried to kill Norman Freeman last night came dangerously close to succeeding. Or at least Norman thought they were trying to kill him. Despite having the passenger window of his car shot out on the Santa Monica freeway, he still wasn't entirely sure.

"They may have been after my brother," he said. "It's very confusing."

"Getting shot at often is," I answered. During my tenure on the police force, I had exchanged gunfire on two occasions. Both times I escaped without physical harm but paid an emotional price. There were the countless nights where sleep never came, and many others that were altered by petrifying nightmares. Each shooting incident took a couple of months to overcome, but I don't think I ever fully recovered. The bad dreams still slip in occasionally. Trauma can stay with you forever.

"I'm just stunned at what happened," he said, as his pretty blonde fiancée sitting next to him took his hand and squeezed it slightly. A large diamond ring glittered from her finger.

"You told me that over the phone," I reminded him, "but let me ask you something. How did you happen to select me? Burnside Investigations doesn't exactly stand out in the yellow pages."

Norman brightened for a moment. "Dick Bridges recommended you."

Dick Bridges was director of campus security at Los Angeles University, more commonly referred to as LAU, and we had known each other since I played football across town at USC. That was almost twenty years ago. Time goes by so quickly. It seemed like yesterday that I resigned from the police department; in fact it was only two years.

I nodded. "Dick and I go back a long ways. He's done well for himself."

"Mr. Bridges told me you were the best."

Laughing, I said, "Dick owes me a few favors. Has he lost any weight?"

Norman shook his head. "No. He'd make a good offensive tackle. I could have used him two years ago. I played quarterback at LAU."

I was well aware of Norman Freeman. His name or photo had appeared almost daily in the Los Angeles Times. The blond hair, blue eyes, rugged jaw, and muscular frame were right out of central casting. He wore a long sleeve oxford cloth shirt with a button down collar and pressed khakis. It was as if Frank Gifford, the all-American boy of the fifties, had magically reappeared. He made me feel old, but at forty, that was far from a herculean task.

Norman had been a second round draft pick of the Patriots, but his pro career was short-circuited by an injury during a pre-season game. When no receivers were open on one fateful play, he took off on a scramble and attempted to hurdle the safety who stood between him and the goal line. The defender upended him brutally, separating the shoulder of his throwing arm and causing a concussion when he landed on the unforgiving turf. Despite attempts at rehabilitation, the shoulder never fully recovered and headaches became a regular part of his day. And Norman Freeman's gridiron career came to a sudden halt.

"So what are you doing now?" I inquired.

Norman smiled shyly. "Working for my father. He owns a bunch of car dealerships on the Westside. I'm being groomed to take over the business."

"Nice work if you can get it," I remarked. Being a smart ass was a gift which came naturally to me. And as off-putting as it might be at times, it often got people to say things they ordinarily didn't intend to.

But Norman Freeman sat in silence for a minute, pondering the end of his left thumbnail. I noticed that it had become slightly warm in my office, and I made a mental note to contact the property manager to fix the air conditioning. Had I something more interesting to do that afternoon I would have hurried him along, but Norman was more entertaining than staring out my window. And his fiancée was certainly a sight to behold.

Her name was Ashley and she was about Norman's age, tall and slender, with golden hair that flowed freely down her back. She wore a black top, white slacks and pink and white Nikes. Despite the warm weather, she carried a white denim jacket with little silver stars sewn into the collar. She wore a face full of makeup including violet eye shadow and scarlet lipstick. When she smiled, her teeth were big and white, a gleaming Pepsodent smile if there ever was one. I tried not to linger too long on her and began to mentally review my calendar for the rest of the day. I needed to be at Mrs. Wachs' house at five o'clock, but that was a few hours away. Aside from that, the only thing I had to decide was what to have for dinner.

"Mr. Burnside, you're probably wondering why I'm here," he said.

"The thought crossed my mind."

"As I told you over the phone, somebody tried to shoot me last night. Actually it may have been Robbie they were trying to kill."

"So you mentioned. Robbie's your brother."

"Right. He played for LAU also. He was a really good wide receiver. You may have heard of him."

I nodded. "All-Conference if I recall."

"Yes."

"You were All-Conference as well, weren't you?" I inquired.

He nodded eagerly. "Three years. Robbie was my best receiver the last two. Freeman to Freeman."

"Then you graduated."

"I was a year older."

"Of course," I said.

"They changed around the offense after I left. Started using the Read Option. That was probably why Robbie didn't have a great senior year."

"So I gathered. I still follow the game."

"Sure," he commented. "I remember watching you when I was a little kid, Mr. Burnside. You played safety at USC, didn't you?"

"You've got a good memory. But why don't we get back to why you're here."

"Oh yeah," he paused. "Well it was like this. I was driving Robbie's car last night. You see, our parents had an affair up at the house. I needed to leave early and Robbie's Honda was blocking my car in the driveway. So I just borrowed his."

"Sure. I do the same thing when someone double parks in front of me."

Norman gave me a confused look but continued on. "Anyway, I'm driving on the freeway when all of a sudden someone pulls alongside and fires a gun at me. Shot the side window clean out. I was really lucky they missed, the bullet got lodged in the head rest."

"And you think they were after your brother."

"Who would want to kill me?"

I decided to answer a question with a question. "Who would want to kill Robbie?"

He thought for a moment. "I don't know."

"Did you get the plate number?"

"No," he said sadly. "I was too startled. I can't even describe the car to you."

I asked if he had gone to the police, and both Norman and Ashley responded with concurrent nods. Norman had the perplexed look of a football player facing a Cover 2 defense for the first time. Ashley responded.

"The police took a report," she said, "but they told us that without a license plate number there wasn't much they could do. They also seemed very busy."

"Business must be booming," I mused.

"Excuse me?"

I held up my hand. "Never mind," I said, and turned back to Norman. "Before I start sticking my nose into your brother's business, have you talked to him about this?"

He nodded yes. "Robbie... Robbie told me not to worry about things. Not to get involved. He'd be very angry if he found out what I'm doing here. But I'm his brother. I care about him. And I'm worried for him."

I watched Norman's face to see if it would reveal anything more than golden boy looks. He spent most of his time talking with his gaze aimed at the floor. That might have meant either he couldn't look me in the eye or that my linoleum was developing serious wax build-up. Trial judges often instruct their juries to consider a witness's body movements during testimony, but I've concluded that theory doesn't always work well in practice. People can tell the god's honest truth with a drooped head and slumped shoulders, while others are able to commit blatant perjury while looking someone dead in the eye.

"I understand."

He continued to fidget. "So will you help me?" he finally asked.

"I doubt I'll be able to find the guy who took a shot at you last night."

A pained expression filled his young face. "Can you at least find out why?"

I pondered the question while I glanced at the bare walls in my spartan office. I kept meaning to hang some pictures, but procrastination got the best of me. While I scanned my white walls, I also considered whether to order a pizza tonight or splurge and go for some steamed clams near the beach.

"I can't guarantee I'll find the answer. But I can promise you the same thing I promise every client. I'll do the very best I possibly can and I'll give you your money's worth."

Norman nodded. "Okay."

"Does anyone else know you've come to me for help?"

"Just my father. And he's completely supportive. In fact he'll pay for it."

Time to test the waters. "My usual fee is six hundred a day," I said, watching Norman's expression carefully. "Plus expenses."

Showing not the least bit of hesitation, Norman Freeman pulled himself to his feet and reached hastily into his pocket for a wad of greenbacks. He peeled off a small stack and handed them to me.

"Here's a week's retainer. Would you mind keeping receipts for the expenses? Dad would like to deduct them."

In my hand sat thirty pictures of Ben Franklin. I tried to spread them like a deck of playing cards but they barely budged. The bills were fresh and crisp and clung together as if they were bonded. They felt good in my hand. It had been a while since this much cold cash had dropped into my lap and I savored the feeling. Steamed clams, I decided. Definitely the clams.

*

Before they left, I instructed Norman to jot down a list of

Robbie's friends and acquaintances, and how I could reach them. He also mentioned that many of them would be attending his, Norman's, bachelor party the following evening. He invited me to join the festivities as well, although he warned me Robbie was going to bring some rather outgoing ladies to liven up the gathering. I told him I'd be on my best behavior.

So now I had two paying clients: Norman Freeman and the Differential Mutual Insurance Company. The Differential, as they were so fond of referring to themselves, had hired me to investigate one of their claimants, a middle-aged woman named Cindy Wachs. She lived in Carson, a smoggy, blue collar suburb about twenty-five freeway minutes from my office on Olympic Boulevard in West Los Angeles.

It was a warm day in the Southland with the mercury rising to the mid-seventies. This summer was very typical so far in the basin: warm days followed by cool evenings. As was my custom in the summer, I spurned the button-down look and wore a red knit shirt with a little tiger crouched over the heart, dark slacks and black sneakers. My hair was short and black, and parted on the right side. While I'd never be in football condition again, I still was lean and strong. I left the windows open as I navigated the San Diego freeway, the warm winds lapping at me as I drove.

Mrs. Wachs lived in a modest, working class neighborhood lined with stucco homes that featured pickup trucks parked inelegantly on the front lawn. A few of the local gentry sat on the curb and sipped refreshments contained within a surreptitious brown paper bag. A couple of ten year olds were carefully playing with matches in the middle of the street.

I pulled out my file from the Differential and examined it once again. Mrs. Wachs was about forty years old and had been involved in a rather curious car accident. While stopped at a red light, her Plymouth Fury was rammed on the passenger door by a van which had rolled mysteriously down the embankment of a driveway. Despite being on the other side of the vehicle, Mrs. Wachs complained of a stiff neck and an aching back. Her doctor happily provided an exhaustive battery of medical tests and physical therapy to the tune of forty-two thousand dollars. Mrs. Wachs herself had filed a multi-million dollar lawsuit against the Differential, the van owner's insurance company, of which two thousand dollars was for vehicle damage and most of the remainder geared towards compensation for pain and suffering. To say the least, the Differential was not pleased.

My client's person of interest had yet to arrive home, so I parked my black Nissan Pathfinder across the street and awaited her arrival. I used to own a Jeep, but after spending a few evenings tailing a wayward wife through a series of torrential winter rainstorms, I decided to invest in a vehicle with a permanent roof. Unpacking the camcorder, I played with the zoom lens and pretended I was directing a documentary about the other side of Los Angeles. I inserted a George Winston CD into the tray and used it as a soundtrack. My career imitating Ken Burns lasted ten minutes. Mrs. Wachs had arrived home.

Cindy Wachs may have been forty, but she looked every bit of fifty-five. She had a stocky build, a pug nose, brown hair combed without much attention, and an enormous brace wrapped around her neck. She parked her car in the driveway, exited it gingerly, and went to unlock the padlock on her garage door. All the while, the camcorder whirred and picked up her every movement. After opening the door, she walked back to her car and drove it into the garage, and my work day had come to an abrupt conclusion.

Driving up to Santa Monica I took Vista del Mar, the coast route, and watched the sea gulls mingle among the surfers and the hang gliders. A pair of bikini clad girls wearing baseball caps tapped a volleyball back and forth. It was June, sweet June, and the golden sunlight would linger past eight o'clock. I would have time for a leisurely dinner at The Lobster, and if the clams didn't fill me up, the crab cakes certainly would. Afterwards, I might sip on a *Mojito* and help the sun fall below the sea. Summer was here, and the climate was warm and pretty. Life seemed good right now and I was eager to take advantage of it. I knew things wouldn't stay that way. They never do.

To read the rest of Post Pattern, please purchase it at your favorite online book retailer.